T0367505

Jaga Na Kala

John Bacon

authorHOUSE®

AuthorHouse™ UK
1663 Liberty Drive
Bloomington, IN 47403 USA
www.authorhouse.co.uk
Phone: 0800 047 8203 (Domestic TFN)
        +44 1908 723714 (International)

Published by AuthorHouse 11/14/2014

ISBN: 978-1-4969-9676-3 (sc)
ISBN: 978-1-4969-9677-0 (e)

Contents

To Mum on her ninetieth birthday.

Warm thanks go to many good friends who supported and helped me complete this book, especially Rifat Nabi for the use of her kitchen table, which I used when writing the majority of this book.

Prologue

Somewhere in Central Canada 1632

The early autumn day was bright and clear. Leaves, on the trees and ground, were every colour from green and yellow through to a deep russet red. Sunlight filtered through the multi-coloured leaves, speckling the ground with small pools of flickering light.

A slight breeze touched the surface of a large lake with the gentlest of caresses just sufficient to create a shimmer of sparkling white, which for a while, destroyed the reflection of the mountains on the opposite shore. Mountains where the dark colour of the pine trees on their lower slopes contrasted with the peaks where winter's finger had already placed the white of snow.

A little way back from the southern shore, not far from the western end of the lake, stood a log cabin. The area in front of the cabin still showed signs of the cabin's construction. Unused logs lay to one side, chippings of wood, some still fresh others showing the passage of time, covered the ground in front of a woodpile. Behind the cabin lay a large meadow surrounded by trees in which there were two plots of growing crops. From slightly higher ground to the west, a small stream meandered over the flat terrain beside of the meadow, then with a rush it tumbled over sloping ground eager to make its way past the cabin to the open water of the lake.

The early autumn air was cool, yet no wisp of smoke issued from the cabin's stone chimney. A young girl barely sixteen years old, dressed in a brown skirt and dirty pinafore, sat with her back against the front wall of the cabin not far from the door. Her lack of movement, to attract the eye, made it almost impossible to see her from a distance. Her face and hands were dirty her long brown hair unkempt. She had been sitting there most of the day, her mind going over and over the events of her short life.

* * *

For the majority of her life Ruth had lived on an estate a little way from the village of Devizes in England where her mother and father were estate workers. Neither her father or mother received a great deal by way of payment for their labours, but they did have a one-room bothie in which the family lived. Even though a completely impossible dream, her father had always wished for his own land, a small plot where he could grow crops to sell in the market. When a gentleman come to the estate and spoke about a country over the great ocean, where there was land for the taking; her father wanted to go. To him it was a dream come true; he wanted the family to go to the New World. So at the tender age of fourteen Ruth set off with the rest of the family and journeyed to the New World.

The voyage on that dreadful boat from Avonmouth took its toll; of those who set off only a score arrived in the New World. Boat fever had taken the rest including her sister and mother.

In a settlement, not far from the coast, her father had cared for her. The talk was of war with the French, and the Iroquois Indians. People said that the Indians could not to be trusted, though Ruth had never had cause to fear the Huron and it was from the Huron that her father learnt about the inner land. The Huron Indians spoke of good land the other side of the mountains and swamps, an empty land, where moose and deer lived. After many days of indecision, her father finally decided it would be better for the two of them to flee to the west rather than stay in the settlement, to escape from those in the settlement who wanted war with the French. They left the settlement with a small band of Huron Indians who were also going to find a new home. These Indians guided them through the first part of their journey, and before they parted, they gave her father a piece of deerskin, with various patterns on it, telling him to show it to those they met.

Her father had been her protector and provider throughout the long journey. At times, other Indians helped them and provided shelter during the winter. Eventually having crossed the mountains, passed by a vast lake and the swamps they reached a huge grass plain with gentle rolling hills. The Indians told them to head towards the setting sun until they saw the mountains. The undulating plain seemed to be endless; eventually the mountain peaks came into sight towards the northwest. The two of them walked beside the horse and cart day after day, slowly approaching the distant mountain peaks, which could see on the horizon, but never seemed to get nearer.

Tired and weary, they reach a large lake after a journey, which had lasted the best part of a year. The lake was long but narrow and on the other side, the hills were steep and behind those hills stood the mountains. There beside the lake, her father decided they had gone far enough, and the search for a place to settle started.

It took several days walking along the southern shore of the lake looking for a suitable place to call their own. Finally, after almost reaching the far end of the lake, her father chose a large meadow surrounded by trees on three sides and the lake on the fourth. Slightly rising ground to both the east and west provided protection from the worst of the winds. Another point in its favour was a cave not far from where her father wanted to build the cabin; it would offer them protection until they had a place to call home.

The first year had been a difficult one; her father worked hard on the construction of the cabin; cutting down trees, using the horse to drag the logs to the meadow, preparing the logs and building the walls. Ruth struggled when she use the horse to plough and created two fields. She sowed the seeds and then tended the crops, which would provide their food over the coming winter.

Once her father had built the cabin, they moved some of their possessions from the cave into the cabin. The first winter was cold, much colder than those Ruth had experienced in England and with a lot more snow. During the second year beside the lake, Ruth continued to work tending the crops, while her father continued to add to the cabin.

Her father had impressed on her that the first few years would be the hardest; once they were settled they would be able to explore the neighbourhood looking for others who might have come to the area. Work during the second summer had indeed reduced a little; there had been times when the two of them could relax.

That summer her father started to explore the western end of the lake; he would ride the horse around the shore or through the woods. When, one early autumn day, he had taken the horse and told her he would return with a rabbit or two, Ruth was not particularly concerned.

Having spent the day cleaning the cabin and its surrounds, Ruth's thoughts turned to the evening meal. She prepared the turnips to go with the rabbits her father had promised to bring back and then walked down to the western headland of the small sandy cove to watch for his return.

From the small headland, Ruth could see most of the western end of the lake around to the northern shore. Looking towards the high ground to the west of the lake Ruth could just make out her father in the distance moving along the top of a small cliff set a little distance back from the shore of the western end of the lake; it would be a while before he reached home. For a while, she watched a large eagle as it hunted in the early evening's light, then saw her father start to ride the horse down the cliff. She assumed there was a path down the cliff although at that distance she could not see it. The horse stumbled and fell; Ruth watched in horror as the silent figure of her father fell, disappearing below the tops of the trees. It was a while before his distant cry reach her; even though he was a long way off Ruth heard his cry suddenly end. She stood there stunned as the sun set and the sky started to darken. Shocked and uncertain she did not know if she should immediately go to him or wait until the morning. She believed there was little chance of her father surviving the fall and it would be dark soon.

First light the follow day Ruth set out on foot to find her farther. She followed the shore of the lake to and then round the western end. She had to wade through the shallow water of the river, which fed the lake. Wet, cold and tired Ruth continued towards the base of the cliff. She discovered the horse first; its head twisted round at an unnatural angle. There were various patches of dark dried blood covering areas of its neck and body. A little further on Ruth found the body of her father. She sat holding him to her, his battered and broken body cold and unmoving. It took her the rest of the day to find and then pile rocks over his body until all there was to show where he lay at rest was a mound of rocks.

Chapter 1

The day after the dreadful day when Ruth had buried her father below a pile of rocks, she sat outside the cabin her mind repeatedly going over what she should do. She had cried until there were no more tears to cry. She was alone, and by her father's reckoning more than fifteen hundred miles away from the nearest settlement; in a strange and deserted land with wolves and bears, both of which had to be avoided. Had either found her today she would not have moved; she had lost all will to live. She felt her life was over. Only just sixteen, she did not consider the possibility of her reaching her seventeenth birthday, the following summer, a very high one.

The light breeze, which had brushed the surface of the lake a few moments ago, reached her; although its touch was gentle, it chilled her. She pulled her knees closer to her chest, rocking slightly as she stared at her boots just showing below her skirts. She brushed some mud from them as she thought of the day her father had bought them for her; it had been in Bristol just before they had gone to Avonmouth in order to board the ship.

As dusk fell, she stirred. Without any real desire, Ruth made her way into the cabin, lay on the bunk without eating and waited for night to fall. She did not sleep, her mind constantly going over and over the hopelessness of her situation.

Dawn broke; soft light entered the cabin through the window in the rear wall of the cabin. Her father had been so proud of it, a window with glass in it and in the New Land. From her position on the bunk, she studied the window as dawn turned to the full light of day.

Ruth woke for the second time beneath several layers of blankets and lay there staring up at the roof, her mind full of thoughts. She believed it would be impossible for her to walk back to the settlement on the coast, she would never be able to carry all the food needed for such a journey and she no longer had the horse or cart. Winter was also coming; she would not be able to reach the beginning of the plain before the snow started. Above all the thought of all that walking, alone and through the wilderness filled her with dread.

She looked around the cabin; it was a simple structure: logs placed one upon the other; the ends keyed into each other formed the four walls and roof. Mud, which had now hardened, filled even the smallest of gaps between the logs so the cold air of winter could not find its way into the cabin. It was a spacious cabin; in the centre of one end, to the left of the door, stood the fireplace built of stone, its chimney extending up through the roof. The furniture was basic. A bunk built from the base of the cart, supported on a wooden frame and topped by a large straw mattress stood at the opposite end to the fireplace. Her father had used the two sides of the cart to make a bench like table situated along the rear wall of the cabin and into the corner near the fireplace. Another prepared plank of wood from the cart supported by unshaped branches formed a shelf on which the cooking pots sat. A chest had been attached to the rear wall of the cabin above the table its lid now the door to a cupboard. Her father had sectioned off the area between the fireplace and the cabin's front wall to form an open topped box for firewood. The door consisted of long lengths of prepared wood joined by cross members.

Eventually Ruth got off the bed, she was chilled, the days were getting cooler, winter would not be long.

Without real resolve, Ruth put kindling in the fireplace and lit it using a flint. The small flames gave out little warmth; it would require logs placed on well burning twigs before she would gain any benefit from its heat. It was a good well-built fireplace, with several metal bars embedded in the sides from which she could hang pots over the fire. It drew well too; and had provided more than enough heat to warm the cabin the previous winter. It took a while for the fire to build up and start to warm her body. She remained crouched in front of the fire, until its heat drove her away.

Warmed by the fire she felt hungry; the lack of food during the last two days had caught up with her. She looked at the meal she had partly prepared two days ago and wondered if any of the snares had a rabbit in them. She caught sight of her hands; they were dirty, rough and had several abrasions; hands which had placed stones over her father's body. She held them out in front of her as if she no longer wanted them and looked around the cabin. The larger bowl she kept full of water was not there. She left the cabin and found the bowl, on a three-legged stand, where her father had last used it to shave. It still had the water he had used in it; she plunged her hands into the water rubbing them together in order to clean them, and then washed her face.

Hungry and knowing she should check the snares; Ruth decided to walk round them. It was normally her father's job, but now it would be up to her now, to both find and cook the meal.

Her father had laid out the snares in the wood to the west and south of the cabin. Her father's passage from one snare to the next had created a well-trodden path. Leaving the cabin, Ruth went round into the meadow. Her two fields were a short distance from the rear of the cabin and separated by a wide path. She passed between the two small fields of root vegetable, which she would need during the coming winter, then followed the path to the first snare.

The first six snares led her away from the cabin each snare was empty, although a couple of them had been tripped. The sun now stronger, as midday approached, had removed the chill of early morning; it shone through the thinning leaves of the trees. Continuing her journey round the snares the path turned to the south each one she checked and reset as her father had shown her.

After reaching the furthest snare, instead of turning back towards the cabin, she continued walking; idly kicking the red and golden leaves which covered the ground. As she walked, her mind went over the tasks she would need to do before winter settled in for good. It seemed a lot of work. She would need to dig up the turnips, cut sufficient wood to fill the woodshed at the side of the cabin and all before it became difficult to move around in the snow.

She reached a clearing in the trees; it was much the same size as three-acre field back on the estate. The grass was long with a few bushes growing here and there. Good grass, she thought, it would have done for the horse all it needed was a fence round the area. A little far from the cabin she thought, almost to the plain with its endless unbroken expanse of grass. She stood still and watched several rabbits on the far side of the clearing. The rabbits here were much larger than those in England were, and in the winter, they were almost white. Thoughts of how to catch one of the rabbits went through her mind. She had nothing she could use. One of the rabbits looked up then hopped a short distance away from her followed by the others, before they continued nibbling the grass.

She heard a noise behind her, but before she could turn, a hand came round her mouth strong arms pulled her to the ground. She struggled to get free but the Indian had her pinned to the ground covering her mouth with his hand. Ruth lay there frightened, her heart beating as if it was trying to escape from her chest. She was expecting the Indian to kill her. He said something very quietly repeating it several times, but she could not understand. His voice was soft and quite, at first she did not know what to make of this. His hold on her was firm but not rough. She relaxed a little as he slowly took his hand away from her mouth. He continued to speak, in the same quite voice as he moved away. Ruth glanced towards the Indian; he was crouching about six feet away from her his back towards her and appeared to be watching something. Ruth realised he was not paying her any attention, he was

5

more interested in the rabbits; there was nothing to stop her from trying to run for it.

Preparing for her dash by slowing easing her body off the ground, her eyes remained fixed on the Indian. If she moved when he was not looking, she believed there was a reasonable chance of getting away. Glancing round she could see a gap in the bushes to her left and slightly behind her. She looked towards the Indian; he was still more interested in the rabbits than he was of her and was about to shoot them with his bow.

Ruth judged now was the best time to run. She had only covered a few yards when the Indian shouted something at her. Ruth ran for the gap between the two bushes then weaved between the trees as she dashed blindly away from the clearing. Having run to the point of exhaustion, she stopped running and started to walk. Constantly looking around, she recovered her breath a little, as she continued to move away from the clearing.

Having worked out the direction to the cabin she headed towards it, walking fast then running for a while. She reached the far end of the meadow; running across it towards the safety of the cabin. Once inside Ruth slammed the door closed, she had managed to escape and get back home.

Relieved and feeling safe in the cabin Ruth continued to lean against the closed door while her body calmed down, then she moved to the fire putting a couple of logs on the hot glowing embers. It was not long before the fire was burning brightly. The warmth calmed her nerves; she was still alive the Indian had not killed her. She put the pot over the fire, to cook the turnips she had prepared two days ago, then lay on the bunk and waited. Sounds of the wood in the fire crackling and the water bubbling in the pot filled the air. Another sound reached her ears and it caused her nerves to react; someone had lifted the door catch.

He stood there; framed by the doorway the light behind him silhouetting his outline. Ruth was unable to see any details other than the fact he was Indian. He said something, which she did not understand. Holding up his arms, he moved into the cabin. Ruth could now see him more clearly, and believed he was the Indian who had pulled her to the ground. In each hand, he held a rabbit by the rear legs. Ruth jumped off the bunk, wondering how she was going to protect herself.

He dropped the rabbits and moved towards her 'No!' Ruth screamed as he pushed her back onto the bunk, but once he had her sitting, he turned his attention back to the two rabbits. Ruth was unsure what she should do. The Indian wore long leggings and a top, which had no sleeves. On his feet were the soft shoes Indians always seemed to wear. She had seen Indians dressed as he was before. There was only one feather in his dark hair, towards the back of his head. He was definitely not Iroquois and she didn't think he was Huron either. According to her father, one feather meant he was not important.

Having picked up a stout twig from beside the wood box, he used it to poke around in the pot, which was bubbling away on the fire. He spoke again. Ruth did not know what to do other than remain there motionless and watch him.

Having poked her turnips, he turned his attention to the two rabbits. After slit their stomachs open, he picked out certain internal bits dropping them into the pot.

He stood and looked around the cabin. 'Poola,' he said pointing at the rabbits. 'Poola,' he repeated. Ruth did not know what he wanted; he pointed at her said something but Ruth was none the wiser, then he picked up the two rabbits and left the cabin.

Having watched him leave, Ruth looked around the cabin; he had not taken his spear or bow and arrows; they were lying in front of the wood-box. Wondering what he was doing, she went to the door. The Indian was nowhere to be seen so Ruth ventured out to look around. Having reached to high bank she saw him crouched down on the shore washing the rabbits in the water of the lake.

She trod on a twig, it snapped and the sound attracted his attention; he looked round, waved, then turned back to his task. Ruth watched from a distance, he finished and stood up. The rabbits were now pink in colour; he had skinned and washed them. He walked up the sandy beach and then up the slope onto the bank Ruth was standing on. 'Ella daqua,' he said nodding towards the cabin.

Ruth felt sure she was not in any immediate danger; she had been in several Indian villages with her father during their journey to the lake, they had not harmed her. She followed him back into the cabin then stood watching as he used a bone knife with a sawing action to cut the two rabbits into pieces, dropping each piece into the pot. He tapped the pot with his knife. Turning towards her he nodded, 'Por, por.' Ruth did not understand. He tapped the pot again seemingly pleased with the dull ring it gave out, then stood and look round the cabin, 'Por,' he said nodding as he studied everything. He noticed a tin plate and picked it up; again, he tapped it with his knife. 'Por,' he said again, then made as if he was eating from the plate with his fingers. He put the plate down and immediately saw the knife Ruth used when she was cooking. This he examined in great deal testing its sharpness. Ruth became concerned but again he nodded and said 'Por' before putting it down. Ruth wondered if he had seen a knife made from metal before. He looked at the fire, 'Ah, nakpor,' he said, then seeing the box containing wood he took some and arranged the logs on the fire, so the pot would continue to boil. Ruth considered what she should do; she recalled the events in the clearing; he had knocked her to the ground, but then had done nothing. She thought her best chance of survival was to remain calm. He had cut both rabbits up and put all the pieces into the pot; it was going to make a good meal with all that meat and she could do with that.

It took a while to cook, the time passed slowly for Ruth but when he thought it was ready, he looked towards the table, 'E ap,' he said picking up the tin plate. 'Apa,' he said pointing to each of them.

'You want another one, in that,' Ruth said pointing to a box her father had fixed to the wall to act as a cupboard.

He looked at the knob then pulled it. 'Por,' he said, taking another plate from cupboard then closed and open the door several times. 'Por,' he said leaving it closed. He set both plates down in front of the fire then looked around and saw the large ladle; using it, he shared the contents of the pot out between the two plates. The over-cooked turnip had broken up and thickened to a sort of broth with pieces of rabbit in it. 'Por mesh, umta,' he said beckoning her towards the fire. Ruth did not think he would do anything he was more interested in his meal than he was in her; she moved towards the fire.

John Bacon

'Sor!' he said dropping the piece of meat he had in his fingers. Ruth picked up a spoon and passed it to him. 'Porpog,' he said taking it. Ruth took the other plate and sat on the large, upended log she used as a stool. She had not eaten for almost three days the rabbit tasted good. The Indian sat on the floor eating his meal beside the fire. He did not seem bothered about her; he watched the flames as he ate his meal. He sucked the meat off each bone then tossed the bone into the fire. Ruth placed her pieces of bone on the side of her plate. He sat there after finishing then looked at his plate for a while before getting up. 'Nak dash,' he said looking around the cabin. Ruth could not understand him; he came across and took her plate and, after tipping the bones onto the fire, put both plates back on the table. Having placed more logs on the fire, in such a way that they would burn well, he sat back down. Ruth thought she had better remove the pot or it would burn. He watched her intently. Ruth put the pot down beside the table. It would need washing; she did not know when she would be able to do that.

It was not long before the inside of the cabin became quite warm. 'Por,' he said pointing to the fire. Ruth wished she had paid more attention when her father had spoken to the Indians, not that he did it well, but at least he had managed to make them understand him, and the first group had given him a strip of hide with various patterns on it. Each time they met Indians her father showed them the piece of hide and the Indians would then talk to him. Ruth thought she should show him the strip of hide; she stood up and went to the cupboard, he watched but did nothing. She handed him the small strip of hide. He

10

looked at in then smiled at her. 'Da por, tak meecha, pi meecha, jadpog gegenta e ella pe daqua, por umta.'

Ruth was unaware of what he was saying; she believed she should try to learn the meaning of the word he used most. 'Por,' she said trying to make her voice sound as if it were a question. 'What is Por,' she added.

Waving his hands round the cabin. He pointed to the fire it was por and the plates they were also por. 'Everything can't be por,' Ruth said knowing he would not understand her. Por seemed to be important to him and pleasing him seemed the right thing to do at moment. He shrugged his shoulders. Ruth did not know what to do, speaking with him was a problem and they both knew it.

It started to become darker in the cabin; light from the dancing flames became stronger than the reducing light coming through the window. Ruth watched as he got up and went across to the bunk. He examined the blankets, and once again found them por. 'Tashka,' he said pointing at the bunk. 'Tashka,' he repeated Ruth stood not knowing what he wanted but believing she knew will enough. 'Tashka,' he said again then removed the top he was wearing. His body looked strong; Ruth watched as he took off the leggings. It left him dressed only in the loincloth most Indians seemed to wear in the summer when it was hot. 'Tashka,' he said again pointing to the bunk. He then lay on it pulling the blankets over him and leaving a space for her. Ruth did not know what to do. It was plain to her that he wanted her on the bunk and that, she thought, was not all he was wanting. She felt trapped. 'Tashka,' he kept saying indicating she should lie on the bunk. Ruth decided that it was the only thing she could do; believing he would stop her doing anything else. She went to lay down on the edge of the bunk. 'Nak, lementa, nak,' he said.

'I don't know what you want,' Ruth said aware she had failed to do what he wanted.

'Nak lementa,' he said again; Ruth froze as he reached over to her. She stared at his hand as he tried to undo the buttons on her dress. 'Nak lementa nakpor, tashka,' he said. Ruth undid the top of her dress then slipped her arms out, and took her dress off. He pointed at her under-clothes and laughed. She did not know what to make of it, he was laughing at her. He stopped laughing and for a while looked her up and down before pointing at her boots. Ruth took them off. 'Tashka,' he said still looking at her and smiling; he patted the bunk beside him. When she lay down, he put the blankets over her. 'Tashka,' he said again. Ruth laid there her body tense fearing what would happen next. It was becoming dark in the cabin, the fire which had provided what light there was had started to die down; Ruth lay there watching it slowly die, her back to him and expecting him at any moment to do something.

Ruth woke the moment he moved; it was light the morning had come and nothing bad had happened 'Por tashka,' he said getting off the bunk going to the fire. He said something Ruth did not catch as he started to kindle a fire. It was not long before it was burning. 'Ella hi, lementa,' he said pointing at her dress. Ruth got off the bunk and quickly put her dress on. He kept on saying, 'Ella hi,' until she was beside the fire getting warm. Ruth glanced at him as he crouched there beside the fire. 'Pe nak daga mesh,' he said turning his face towards her. Ruth shrugged her shoulders not understand what he had said. He shook his head as he said something else, more to himself than her, and then adjusted the wood on the fire so it burnt brightly. Ruth had never been this close to an Indian before. Dressed only in a loincloth, Ruth could see the individual muscles in his body. His physique looked strong, his facial features were pleasant, he had not harmed her and during the night, he had just slept there with her, much as her father had done. Ruth wondered about him, it seemed to her that this Indian was a good person, he had brought her the rabbits he had caught; he did not have to do that. Having warmed himself, he went and dressed; Ruth watched him.

After saying 'Pi jadpog,' which Ruth did not understand, he left the cabin taking his spear and bow with him. Ruth watched him leave then went to the door; he was heading off towards the woods to the west of the cabin. He waved as he passed between two bushes and was lost to her sight.

Ruth sat outside the cabin for most of the morning. There were numerous jobs which required her attention if she was going to be prepared for the coming winter, but she did not start them. She could not stop thinking of the Indian and the way he had acted; he was friendly and did not appear to be a threat to her. The sun was high in the sky when he returned with a rabbit, 'Nakpor jadpog ap gegenta,' he said holding it up.

'I don't know what you mean,' Ruth replied shrugging her shoulders.

'Ap gegenta, gegenta,' he repeated holding out the rabbit.

Ruth looked towards the rabbit, 'Gegenta,' she said pointing at it.

'Da,' he said smiling at her, 'gegenta,' he pointed to himself, 'Ap,' he said then pointed to her 'Ap,' then added as he pointed between the two of them, 'Ap e ap apa.'

'Two,' Ruth questioned holding up two fingers. 'Da apa,' he said pointing to Ruth's, extended fingers. He dropped the rabbit on the ground then reached out folding one of her fingers down. 'Ap' he said pointing at the remaining finger. He pointed to himself, 'Natlatan,' he said. 'Pi Natlatan,' he repeated then pointed to her, 'Pe?'

'Ruth,' she said guessing he was asking her name.

'Roof, pe Roof,' he said pointing at her, 'Pi Natlatan,' he repeated indicating himself. Ruth nodded; he seemed pleased, nodding and smiling, 'Por' he said. Then added 'Pi ella daqua Daga Kala,' he said pointing to the west. Ruth nodded; he smiled at her then picked up his spear and bow. 'Portak meecha,' he said as he left.

Ruth left it until late in the day before she cleaned the rabbit, believing he would return when it became dark. He did not and she put the rabbit in the pot to cook. That night she slept little believing, the Indian would return. The following day she became less concerned and as time passed, it became obvious to her he was not going to return.

Over the next few days, Ruth worked in the small fields gathering the root vegetable. Her father had brought plenty of sacks with them on their journey from the coast; she had used some of them the previous year to store the crops. In the field, she dug up a row leaving the large round roots on the top of the ground. Then having reached the end of the row, she retraced her steps with the sack, cleaning the dirt off the turnip before placing them in the sack. Two rows usually filled a sack; it was then hard work lugging the heavy sack to the cave. Each additional sack she put in the cave gave her a sense of achievement.

Ruth was pleased with the way her store was filling. She had planted enough for her and her father, now he was no longer there she was going to have more than enough food for the winter. She dragged another full sack into its place then stood there looking at her stash, very content with what she had achieved. The rest she would leave in the ground they could go to seed, which she would collect as her father had shown her. The beans to use as seed for the following year were already set aside from the harvest.

Next, she started to gather wood, once she had a large pile she would use the axe to cut the wood into lengths, ready to use on the fire. It was hard work and she worked day after day preparing for the winter, which was now approaching fast. Each day she needed to go further and further afield in order to gather wood. She remembered in England they cut part of a wood down in the spring; the wood dried out during the summer and the stumps would sprout. She considered doing the same the following year.

It lightly snowed a few times, but not enough to stop her collecting wood, however, Ruth knew it would soon snow hard, several days non-stop, which would leave deep snow all around the cabin.

The first real snows came a few days after she had filled the woodshed; she had even managed to gather some extra wood, which was stacked up beside the woodpile. The snow continued on and off for several days. The first few days of snow allowed her to rest after the constant work of the autumn. Ruth was content to just get her meal and lie on the bunk with a good fire burning keeping the whole cabin warm and comfortable. When she needed to venture out she would put her father's winter jacket on, it was warmer than hers and even though it was on the large size for her it kept her nice and warm. She cut the sleeves to the right length and sewed the cuffs up again.

As with the previous winter, the immediate area around the cabin seemed to escape the worst of the snow. It would be two feet or so around the cabin, not enough to stop her making her way to her store in the cave or the woodshed at the side of the cabin. Farther away, it would form drifts higher than she was, making it dangerous to venture too far away.

Other than being bored with nothing to do, Ruth was content within the cabin, it was warm and she had plenty of wood. At times when she was lying on her bunk, she would think about the Indian. There had been no signs of Indians in the area during the year her father was building the cabin; they had seen no one and thought themselves alone. Was the Indian alone as well; she pondered this possibility, but if so, where did he go?

Chapter 2

The nights became longer, the days shorter. The small stream froze and then snow covered it over as it had the previous year. Ruth melted a pot of fresh snow in order to provide herself with water. On the better days, she tried to walk round the snares without success; the depth of snow forced her back. Although the days were short, they dragged by with no one to talk to, unable to venture out Ruth had nothing to occupy her, all she could do was sit on the bunk and watch the fire. Once she had fetched wood for the fire and a supply of beans and roots, the only task she had to employ her was to maintain the fire, and cook her meal. Ruth remained on her bunk for lengthy periods thinking of her father and her past life.

The fire was only a few dimly glowing embers when Ruth woke up. With the blankets still wrapped around her, she crossed the cabin to the fireplace. Selecting a few small twigs from a separate pile beside the wood-box, she put them on the embers and blew. The embers glowed brighter; she blew numerous times before the kindling caught, and flames started to flicker. A few twigs of increasing size were placed on the fire letting it burn brightly before placing larger logs on the fire. The heat from the fire built up slowly, but as it did, Ruth started to feel warmer. It had been trouble-free to re-kindle the fire. Other days that was not the case and every so often, she would have to clean all the ashes out and start afresh.

It had been her habit to make more than she needed for her evening meal, then in the morning all she had to do was reheat what remain and she had a meal quickly without a great deal of work. She hung the pot over the fire and watched as it heated. Today had started well, and now the cabin was warmer she shed the blanket around her and thought about what she needed to do that day before the sun once again set. Her water was all right, plenty of that but the wood chest needed re-filling and she needed to fetch in some more roots and beans. She gave the pot a stir as it started to heat up, with the fire burning well it would not take long before it was ready to eat. She ate it directly from the cooking pot.

Opening the door in winter was sometimes a problem, on occasions snow piled itself up against the cabin and she would have to make a path through the snow to the woodpile and the cave. With her father's jacket on, along with her gloves, she opened the door. A small amount of snow had fallen during the night, a few inches. She ventured out, the snow crunching below her feet on every step she took. The day was dull, the sky overcast, but she didn't think it would snow. The woodpile at the end of the cabin still held a large amount of wood, all cut ready for use. She gathered some up into her arms and returned to the cabin. It would take a few trips to fill her wood box again. Ruth went back and forth from her woodpile. She ventured out towards the wood pile for what she thought would be the last time, one more good load of wood and she would have sufficient inside the cabin for a couple of days. The path through the snow between the cabin and the woodpile became well trodden, and at times was slippery. Today with a slight covering of fresh snow, it crunched under foot as she made her way back to the cabin her arms full. She reached the cabin door. Unable to open the door with her arms full of wood she backed into the cabin pushing the door open as she entered. She turned and dropped the wood.

A wolf was snarling at her, its body low to the ground, its head down with its ears back, flat against the top of its head. Ruth backed away, along the wall, towards the bunk; the wolf took half a step towards her still snarling, its eyes a fire red as they glared at Ruth. The fire behind the wolf cracked. The wolf's head snapped round looking at the fire then quickly back to Ruth; she watched as the large wolf slowly lowered its body onto the cabin floor. It had a heavy brown and grey, flecked coat with a large head and flaming eyes, which watched Ruth all the time, but it had stopped snarling at her. Ruth slowly moved away from the wolf until she reached her bunk; the wolf intently watched her every movement, but did nothing.

The standoff continued with the wolf guarding the fire; it seemed content to let her be at the other end of the cabin. The fire, however, was starting to die down and with the door jammed open by one of the logs, she had dropped; cold air was coming into the cabin. The wood she had been carrying lay scattered around the cabin's dirt floor; two pieces were close to where Ruth was standing. She moved very slowly; the wolf watched her without moving from its position not far from the fireplace. Having reached a position where she could crouch down and pick up the wood Ruth stood there for a moment or two before slowly lowering herself, her eyes fixed on the wolf. Slowly without any abrupt movement, she picked up the first piece of wood and then the second. Still moving slowly she stood and stepped back to her position beside the bunk. She had two pieces of wood and the wolf had done nothing other than watch her. From the bunk, she tossed a log towards the fire. The wolf snarled a warning at her but did nothing other than watch the log curve though the air landing at the back of the fire. The second one bounced in front of the fire ending up on the embers.

Her father had told her, wolves do not usually attack unless they feel threatened. She spoke quietly, 'I have to keep the fire going,' she said. The wolf's head tipped to one side, its ears no longer folded back against its head. She spoke again without the wolf reacting. Ruth decided she would try to reach the fire, there were several logs lying beside it ready for her to use. Slowly, without any quick or abrupt movements, Ruth started to ease herself along the rear wall of the cabin. With her back to the wall, she passed the window without the wolf reacting but now she had to leave the wall and make her way around the table. Slowly she took a step, which took her nearer the wolf. The wolf let her continue; it snarled a couple of times but its snarls were no longer as threatening as they had been, more a warning not to approach too close. Slowly without taking her eyes off the wolf, Ruth inched herself round the table until she reached the fire. Now, if she was going to do anything, she had to turn her back on the wolf. She crouched down sideways to the fire in such a way, as it was possible to keep one eye on the wolf. Slowly without any sudden movements, she placed five logs onto the fire, which by this time had died down considerable. She arranged the logs so they would burn brightly.

Ruth noticed her large pot was half-full of water; if she put it on the fire to heat; she believed it would be possible to throw the hot water at the wolf driving it from the cabin. Without any abrupt movement, she hung the pot from one of the metal bars. The fire started to produce nice bright flames, it hissed as the heat drove the sap out from the centre of a log. She backed away moving along the rear wall until she was once again beside the bunk. The wolf studied the fire without appearing bothered by it. 'The fire makes you warm,' Ruth quietly said; the wolf looked at her without snarling. 'Wolves are supposed to run away from fire, why don't you.' The wolf tipped it head to one side as it listened to her voice.

The door was still open, the fire was going to waste. Ruth considered what she should do. If she did throw hot water at the wolf, the door of the cabin had to be open. Once the wolf was out, she could then slam the door shut and keep it out. She thought that would be the best plan; it was the only plan she had. It was not until she thought the fire needed more wood and was about to return to the fire did she realise that she would had no food in the cabin; she would need to fetch some before she drove the wolf out.

Instead of going to the fire, Ruth eased her way round to the door and slowly backed out into the snow. She was becoming less frightened of the wolf; it did not seem to be doing anything other than occupying the centre of the cabin in front of the fire. Ruth went to the root store in the cave. The first thing she noticed in the half-light of the cave was her long handled axe; it was leaning against the wall of the cave. She took a few turnips then picked up the axe before setting off back to the cabin. Her mind pictured the hot water on the fire; she went through the actions she would carry out. Throw the hot water at the wolf, and then swing the axe at it until it ran away. As she came round the corner of the shack, she saw the wolf standing a short distance from the front of the cabin. Ruth judged how far she was from the door of the cabin and compared it to the distance the wolf was from the door. Slowly she inched her way nearer the door then, when she judged it right, she made a dash for the door, kicked the log away from it and slammed it shut, her back against it in order to stop the wolf from forcing its way into the cabin. She dropped the axe and made sure the catch was on before going to the fire. She knelt in front of it. She was cold and shaking from her narrow escape. Slowly the warmth of the fire relaxed her and calmed her nerves.

As dusk came, Ruth lay on the bunk, the fire was burning nicely and the cabin was warm. The wolf had left the cabin of its own accord; which pleased her, but she decided to keep the axe in the cabin from now on. Ruth felt safe inside her cabin; she told herself to be more careful when going outside. She glanced at the fire; it was burning slowly; and would keep in most of the night. She pilled all the blankets over her and went to sleep.

Ruth was woken by a scratching sound; her worst fears were founded the wolf had returned. She lay there unable to sleep frighten by the fact the wolf was outside and trying to get in. As time passed she became less frighten and more annoyed; it would not stop its incessant scratching at the bottom of the door.

Ruth woke as dawn broke she looked out of the window in the rear wall on her way to the fire a light fall of snow had occurred during the night but nothing much. She brought the fire back into life and crouched in front of it until she felt warm enough to leave the cabin. When she opened the door, she took a step back the wolf had curled up in the doorway its fur covered in snow. It looked up at her without snarling then slowly got up. Ruth backed away from it. The wolf stood and shook the snow from its body then slowly walked into the cabin. Ruth froze as the wolf passed her, but it did nothing other than sniff her skirt as it made its way towards the fire. Ruth had to go out to see to her needs, when she returned the wolf was lying in front of the fire, it looked up at her as she entered. Then put its head down on the cabin floor as it watched the flames of the fire dance. Ruth let the door swing closed.

That day the wolf lay sleeping by the fire; Ruth gave it a wide birth but it seemed to accept that she had to move around the cabin, and keep the fire burning. All day she talked to it telling the wolf what she was doing. It watched her as she made her meal and even more intently while she ate it. 'Do you want some?' Ruth asked which caused it to prick its ears up and tilt its head. Ruth put the plate on the floor and pushed it as far as possible towards the wolf. It was ravenous and ate all of it then licked the plate completely clean. It arched its back, and then stretched each of the rear legs. Ruth watched as the wolf looked round the cabin before making its way to the door pawing at the bottom of it. 'You want to go now do you?' Ruth said as she carefully made her way to the door. As soon as she opened the cabin's door, the wolf left, running away from the cabin. Ruth closed the door and put the catch on.

Again, the sounds of the wolf pawing at the bottom of the door woke her. She lay there a while before giving in. The wolf entered the cabin and made for what was left of the fire.

Ruth woke in the morning to see the wolf watching her in the new light of the day. 'It's cold,' Ruth said getting up and making for the fire the wolf watched as she got it going again then settled down quite content to be warmed by the heat from the fire. That day Ruth felt less concerned about the presence of the wolf, it had stopped snarling at her.

As the days passed, Ruth became used to the wolf being there it would occasionally snarl at her if she move too near it but it did little other than lie beside the fire. The first time she touched it she was kneeling in front of the fire about to get it ready to cook her meal when the wolf came to her pushing its head under her arm resting its head rested on her legs. Ruth slowly moved her hand away from its large jaws. 'You are a good wolf really, you just want to get warm don't you,' she said as she put her hand on its head. It let her stroke it. 'My mother use to tell us stories of the big bad wolf, but are not are you, you are a good wolf. Let me stroke you, I will not hurt you.' The wolf did not move as she gentle stroked it. The wolf's fur was harsh, but under the top, course fur was a thick soft under coat. The wolf remained completely still while she stroked it, Ruth wondered if it had gone to sleep using her legs as a pillow. 'I should give you a name, I don't know what though, how about Zak that sounds a good name for a wolf, do you like that.' The wolf remained completely still, 'I will call you Zak I like that name.' Ruth needed to move she gently lifted the wolf's head and placed it on the floor. Zak did not move as she got up.

Later just before it became dark Zak stood and watched her eat as he had done each day. Ruth ate what she needed and then put the plate on the floor that was his cue; he would eat all she had left, licking the plate clean, then he would want go out. Zak was still licking the plate; Ruth had the door open for him. 'Come on Zak time to go out.' The wolf looked round; as it passed her, Ruth stroked its back, and then watched as Zak ran off towards the lake. She closed the door and got ready for the night. Zak returned pushing his way into the cabin. Now the wolf was in Ruth put the catch on and went to her bunk.

'Zak!' Ruth exclaimed as he jumped onto the bunk and settled down beside her. Ruth put some of the blanket over him. 'Go to sleep Zak; it will be a long night; you be a good wolf.'

The days passed slowly, although less so than before. Ruth had Zak; often he grabbed a piece of wood in his large jaws, snarling and tugging like mad, as the two of them fought over the length of wood. Whenever Ruth lay on the bunk, Zak would lie down beside her. Ruth was lying on the bunk it was passed midday Zak was beside her and she was stroking him. 'I have to make our meal Zak; winter will soon be over then I will be busy. It is boring having to stay in the cabin all the time; isn't it?' Zak suddenly moved his head came up. 'What is wrong?' Zak jumped over her as he dived towards the door, the catch was on and he could not get out. Ruth opened the door. As soon as it was a faction open, Zak forced his way out and ran snarling as he did. Ruth thought she saw a dark shape move amongst the bushes towards the lake. She watched Zak disappear in that direction still snarling at something. It was not long before Ruth watched him run back towards the cabin. 'What was it Zak?' Ruth asked as he reached her, her hand automatically going out to touch him. He yapped at her. 'Good boy, you are a good wolf Zak.'

Most of the snow had gone although it was still very cold. Ruth thought she might take a walk round the snares she could reset them; she would like a bit of meat with her evening meal again turnip was all right to keep her alive but it was very bland and she had long ago run out of salt. Zak came with her bounding along in front of her then coming back to find out what she was doing. 'Zak no, they will smell you and not get caught,' she said pushing him away. She was making her way to the next snare when Zak stopped dead in his tracks his body low to the ground. She followed his line of sight and saw the small deer scratching the snow away from the ground below a tree.

Slowly she lowered herself and watched as Zak lifted one leg, moving deliberately as he stalked the deer. Suddenly Zak charged; the deer was startled; it froze with fear. It was only a split second but sufficient for Zak to have the advantage. By the time, the deer moved, Zak was too near for the deer to escape. The small deer had no defences against the speed and huge jaws of Zak; within moments, Zak had the deer. Then with a power, Ruth had not seen before Zak picked the deer up by the throat and shook it. Snow flew up as blood splattered out in all direction spotting the white snow. Then Zak was standing over his kill the snow stained red around the dead body. 'You got it Zak!' Ruth said as she approached him. He snarled at her not letting her get near the deer. After several attempts, Ruth gave in and let Zak eat his meal.

She took more roots from her store it was getting low if winter continued much longer she would have to reduce the amount she ate; feeding Zak had used the extra she had gathered in the autumn. There was still a lot in the frozen ground but it would be a while before she could dig them up.

Zak returned as she was eating her meal. It would have been so much nicer had it a little meat in it. Despite Zak's insistence that she feed him, Ruth ate all her meal well aware that Zak could find his own. Ruth stopped feeding Zak; he started to go out more, and she cut back on the amount she ate, winter showed no signs of going, more snow had fallen and it appeared as if spring was moving even further away.

Zak had gone out around mid-day Ruth worked around the cabin then started to get her small meal ready. The beans had all been used she had only turnip left she cut it up and put it in the water. She heard Zak snarling outside, a grumbling sort of snarl, she went to the door to see what was wrong. Zak was dragging a deer towards the cabin the trail of blood in the snow showed the route he had taken. With her appearance at the door he stopped and looked towards her then redoubled his efforts putting his whole body into the task of pulling the deer towards the cabin door. Ruth left the cabin moving towards him expecting him to snarl at her when she was too close. He did not snarl, instead he dropped the leg he had been using to pull the dead animal and looked up at her. 'You want it pulled to the cabin,' Ruth said. Carefully she reached out towards the deer. Zak did not snarl. Ruth picked up the two rear legs of the deer then started to pull it towards the cabin. Zak immediately grabbed the deer and tugged at it.

The deer was thin and half-starved but it was meat, Zak was standing over it looking up at her. Ruth took her knife from the table and started work on the deer. Zak watched intently and as soon as Ruth cut the stomach open, he went for the innards, which he ate ferociously. Ruth put a lot of meat with her turnip. The rest of the meat she carried to the cave hanging the leg joints high out of Zak's reach then returned to the cabin to finish cooking her meal. She ate all of it; its taste was wonderful the meat was so good. She knelt in front of the fire and cooked small pieces of meat over the fire. Zak had his fill and was now sleeping in the warmth of the fire. That night Ruth went to bed without the pangs of hunger. The deer lasted them five days; it gave Ruth strength.

Zak brought back a large white rabbit then a huge bird the likes of which Ruth had not seen before. She cooked it over the fire it smelt good as it cook; not only to Ruth but also Zak who wanted to eat it before it was fully cooked; Ruth had to keep pulling him back. They ate it together the meat was good and Zak would crunch up any bones she gave him as well as a good helping of meat she had given him. It felt good as Ruth knelt beside the fire its light dancing around the cabin, she was warm, well fed and Zak was sleeping his head in her lap as she stroked him. 'You are a very good wolf Zak you bring me back food. You are a good wolf,' she quietly said as she continued to stroke him. Spring, she thought, could not be far off now, and then she would need to care for her fields. Ruth thought about the work she would have to do in spring, in her mind, she was planning to sow the fields; she was going to stay there without actually deciding to do so but when she thought about it, the journey back to the settlement on the coast was not really a practical proposition.

Chapter 3

Spring came almost overnight; it was a miserable day it rained most of it; Ruth stayed in the cabin, so did Zak. The rain continued during the night. In the morning, the sun shone and there was no longer any snow; the rain had washed it all away. What had been a snow and ice path between the cabin and both the woodpile and root store was now a waterlogged, muddy path. Zak bounded away as Ruth went out to explore her surroundings spring had come, the snow and the cold had gone; where there used to be white, there was now green. She skipped and danced around the area in front of the cabin Zak yacking at her as he rushed around. Her fields look good; the soil would soon be soft enough to gather more turnips. That had to be the first task. She watched Zak jump into the air in a futile attempt to catch a small bird. Having been in the cabin for so long Ruth wanted to walk round the snares. It would get her out and away from the cabin for a while. Her mood was light, as she happily went from one snare to the next. Zak was bounding around the place, sniffing the ground then rushing off after whatever he had smelt.

For all his rushing around, he did not find anything, but who cared the snow had gone.

During the following day, Ruth tended her fields. She harvested additional turnips so that she had one or two small turnips for each day until the harvest. The rest, she left to go to seed. It was hard work without the horse to turn the soil but she enjoyed the work after the long days of winter shut up in the cabin. Zak was always around. Although she had no hold over him; he would only go away from the cabin for a while often returning with a small deer or a rabbit, he caught another one of the large birds and this time it was much fatter, and could not be eaten in one meal. Ruth shared her food with Zak and he returned it tenfold.

Her fields started to grow the days became warmer and warmer, Ruth replaced all the wood she had used during the winter, filling her woodshed. She dragged the bathtub out of the cave into the cabin and boiled as much water as she could. It was good to sit in the warm water and wash. Ruth washed her clothes thinking she should do that more often, and take better care of herself. She laid her clothes over the bushes not far from the cabin to dry. With a clean body and clean clothes Ruth felt good, life was not as bad as she thought, she wasn't even alone she had Zak and he was a good friend, never far from her and would come the moment she called out his name.

Flowers blossomed, Ruth picked some and took them into the cabin, which was now neat and tidy and she had washed all her blankets. Zak followed her. 'They look nice don't they,' she said looking for somewhere to put them. With nowhere obvious to put the flowers, she placed them on the small ledge of the window. 'It is nice now isn't it

Zak, come on we will go for a walk see if the snares have any rabbits in them.'

Zak followed her then ran off; he knew the route round the snares Ruth followed him. She heard him yap several times. One of the snares, she thought, must have a rabbit in it; she quickened her pace. Zak was standing by the dead rabbit, caught in the snare. 'Good boy Zak,' Ruth said as she took the rabbit from the snare then reset it. She went to pick up the rabbit but Zak beat her to it. He looked up at her with the rabbit hanging from his jaws. Ruth started towards the next snare. They were not halfway there when Zak went down. Ruth instinctively dropped down she couldn't see what Zak had spotted but she recognised his posture and knew she had to remain still and let him deal with whatever it was. Ruth watched as Zak stepped over the dead rabbit, he had been carrying, his eyes fixed on whatever it was.

As spring turned into summer, Ruth and Zak became a good hunting team, and Zak was not always the one who saw the rabbit or small deer first. Ruth's higher line of sight gave her some advantage, when she spotted something she would crouch down and Zak would react. Then she would guide Zak towards the kill.

The hot days of summer arrived Ruth sat by the lake as the sun beat down on her there was not a cloud in the sky, she was hot and the water of the lake looked inviting. She hesitated looking around, 'What am I looking for Zak I am miles from anywhere.' She patted him on his head then undressed and slipped into the water. It felt wonderfully cool. Zak yap behind her, Ruth turned to look for him. 'Oh Zak you came for a swim as well.' It was not long before Zak made for the shallow water and stood watching her as Ruth enjoyed the pleasure of the water. She lay in the grass to dry off before she dressed again feeling much better for her swim.

During the hot days of summer Ruth fell into a routine, she would be out early in the morning, before the sun became hot, working in her two fields. Then as midday arrived, she would stop and go to the lakeside in order to lie in the sun and swim in the lake during the afternoon. Evenings were long and were her time for hunting, and preparing her meal.

It was a particularly hot day; by the time Ruth made her way out of the water, Zak had wondered off somewhere. She headed for the patch of grass on which she normally sat when she heard a noise off to her right, a twig breaking and too large for it to be Zak. Two Indians were standing there.

They started to run towards her. Ruth looked towards them then the lake. 'Zak!' she screamed out, at the top of her voice, as she ran for the safety of the water. Ruth called out for the wolf several times before she reached the water and started swimming away from the shore. She turned her head to check on the position of the Indians to witness the arrival of Zak on the high bank above the small sandy bay. He jumped off the bank running towards one of the Indians who was making his way over the rocks. Zak jumped at him knocking him off his feet. Ruth heard the Indian's scream suddenly cut short, and then she saw the one swimming towards her. Zak was running across the rocks towards the small headland on the eastern side of the bay; Ruth made for it. Zak jumped into the water and swam towards her.

Feeling that Zak offered protection, Ruth swam in his direction. She reached him; Zak passed her heading for the Indian who was now not far away. His snarls coming from deep within him contained all the venom he could muster. Zak's snarls when she had first met him were nothing more than a friendly hello compared to his threats towards the Indian with his lips curled back to show his large teeth. The Indian turned and started to swim back towards the shore, with Zak following him. Ruth swam behind Zak feeling safe he would not let the Indians harm her. The Indian reached the beach and started to run. It was a while before Zak reached dry land, but once out of the water he was now much faster than the Indian was. Ruth ran out of the water towards Zak who had trapped the Indian against a large bush and was preparing for an attack, his body low to the ground, his eyes fixed on those of the Indians. 'No boy; Zak don't bite him!' she cried out as she reached the wolf. 'Come on Zak be a good boy he is not going to hurt you,' Ruth said stroking the top of Zak's head. Zak continued to let the Indian know he was not wanted.

Binojar had never felt fear as much as now; it welled up from the very centre of his body until his whole body was trembling. The wolf had come at her command and now had him trapped. Something flashed in the sunlight. She moved towards the wolf without any fear as she commanded it. Her naked body moved gracefully, almost effortlessly, her white skin sparkling in the sun. Natlatan had been wrong when he spoke of a woman, this was no ordinary woman, she was a spirit and it had to be the spirit of the wolf her long hair hanging down like the tail of a wolf. No one other than the spirit of the wolf could stand and stroke the head of a large, vicious, snarling wolf without any concern, and she had spoken to it in a strange tongue. He saw the wolf look up at her, it said something to her and she replied now it was snarling at him again. Natlatan was dead; killed by the wolf at her command and now he was going to die. Desperately he looked around he could see her arm coming up, pointing him out to the wolf; the sunlight glistened off her outstretched arm as she commanded the wolf. He turned and ran, his body trembling in fear, a knot in his stomach tightened when he missed his footing and almost tripped. He managed to stagger and regain his balance; he heard the spirit of the wolf command. Even greater fear swelled up from within him as he ran and ran his heart almost busting.

Ruth did not recognise the Indian as one who came from any tribe she had seen before he was dressed in just a loincloth, and she thought he had two feathers on his head. He was definitely afraid of Zak. 'It's ok Zak, be a good boy,' Ruth said looking down at him.

He looked up at her grumbling as he did. 'It is all right Zak, be good.' Once again, Zak let the Indian know he was not wanted. She looked at the Indian raising her arm palm uppermost towards him hoping he would recognise it as a friendly gesture. He looked very frightened his eyes were looking everywhere at the same time. She saw him start to run, immediately Zak ran after him; the Indian nearly fell over. 'Zak! Back boy back,' she cried out and went after Zak. Zak stopped, and she held him round the neck. 'Be a good boy, let him run away.' Zak yapped at her, 'Good boy,' Ruth said then ran away from him. The chasing game he liked a lot.

'Oh Zak your claws are sharp when I have no clothes on,' Ruth complained as Zak knocked her to the ground. 'Zak, you are a good wolf, you chased him off.' Ruth had only just spoken when there was a grown from the rocks. Zak was off straight away. 'No Zak, don't hurt him,' Ruth called out as she scrambled to her feet.

The Indian's arm was bleeding badly from several wounds where Zak had bitten him and he must have knocked his head on the rocks as he had quite a bad wound on his forehead. He was moving but completely unaware of his surroundings. Ruth went to dress, before running back to where the Indian was lying, still moaning quietly, with Zak standing guard over him. She helped him up and led him towards the cabin. He could only just walk and had to lean heavily on her. She bathed his wounds, he looked familiar she felt sure he was the one who had found her last year. Zak positioned himself between her and the Indian whenever she moved away to get fresh water, or a strip of cloth to bind his wound. Slowly he became more aware of where he was. He became frightened of Zak, Ruth was sure he was the one she had met before, but he did not seem to recognise her and he was getting more and more frightened. She opened the door to the cabin. It did not take him long to leave and run away.

The following day Ruth found where the two of them had left their spears and bows; she picked them up and took them to the cabin. That evening she studied the bow and arrows, paying attention to how they were made. The points of one of the spears and several arrows had been burnt in a fire in order to make a hard and sharp point. It was the other spear and two of the arrows she paid most attention to, they had a bone point attached to the shaft with a very sharp edge. Ruth could see these were better than the others were.

The next day she tried to shoot an arrow, it missed the target by a long way landing well to the left. She tried again but the arrow again went off to the left by much the same distance. Ruth tried several times but every time the arrow went, crooked. Then she tried aiming the arrow to the right of what she wanted to hit. It was better but she still could not hit what she was aiming at.

Five days after the incident with the Indians, the heat of the day had passed; the evening was going to be pleasant now the power of the sun had reduced. Zak was besides her looking out over the lake as they sat on the high bank. He turned and gave a grumble and turned his head towards the west. Ruth looked in the same direction she could not see anything. 'It's ok Zak there is nothing there.' Zak continued to grumble. Ruth became uneasy and stood up; as she did, three Indians emerged from between two bushes at the edge of the wood. They saw her at the same time and put their weapons down before moving towards her.

Zak was at Ruth's side and letting them know he was not going to let them come too close to her. Ruth was nervous; there were three of them this time. She recognised the one Zak had bitten he still had the dressing on his arm and she felt sure one of the others was the one who had run away. The third Indian seemed more important he had four feathers on his head. Ruth saw this Indian say something to the one Zak had bitten; the one she thought had brought her the rabbits the previous autumn. Ruth watched as he took a couple of steps towards Ruth and then place a red coloured blanket on the ground before he took a couple steps back and once again was standing beside the other two.

Ruth wondered what the blanket was for as she approached it. Zak was there first sniffing it. Ruth crouched down; the blanket appeared as if it contained something. She folded back the top; there were several small pebbles, a strip of hide with markings on it, a bone knife and a string of beads. She wondered what it all meant. Zak let her know one of the Indians was approaching her. She stood up. 'Zak be a good boy, don't snarl too much.'

The Indian with four feathers was standing in front of her. He was older than the other two, though not by much; dressed in leggings and a top, rather than a loincloth he looked important. 'Portag meecha,' he said with a small nod of his head and a friendly look on his face. Ruth had no idea what he had said. Zak snarled at him, but Ruth did not think there was any reason to fear the Indian.

'Be good Zak,' Ruth said as she reached out towards him.

'You talk with wolf,' the Indian said with a strange heavy accent.

Taken aback by his use of English, Ruth looked at him. 'You speak English,' she exclaimed.

'Not good talk, winter with man; me learn talk, he die,' the Indian said.

Ruth was relieved she could at least understand him, it would have been impossible had he not understood English. 'That was good,' she responded, then added, 'not that he died, I mean that you learnt to talk.'

'Por.'

He had used that word that everything seemed to be. 'What does that mean?' Ruth asked.

'Good por, por good,' the Indian responded

'Ah!' Ruth exclaimed as she relaxed a little more. The tension of the situation was rapidly abating. It all made sense. 'Now I understand what he was saying,' Ruth replied pointing at the Indian, she knew.

'Not know what say,' the Indian responded glancing towards the other two before he once again looked directly at Ruth.

'It's all right; what is this?' Ruth asked pointing at the red blanket.

'You say Natlatan life good; wolf not kill and eat him, you take show how strong word is.'

'Zak will not kill him. Zak is good,' Ruth said, then thought and added with a smile on her face, 'Zak por,'

He beamed a huge smile at her. 'Por tak,' he said nodding at her. Ruth smiled back pleased she had used his language and that it had pleased him. 'Wolf called Zak,' he asked.

'That's his name.'

'I talk good with you. You say Natlatan good man, take from blanket, show words are strong.'

'I don't know what though; I will take a pebble is that all right?' Ruth asked crouching down to take a pebble. Looking up to see what his reaction would be.

'Not say much,' he responded shaking his head, 'say Natlatan not good.'

'I don't know; the blanket looks warm; could I have that?' Ruth asked more to herself than him as she felt the thickness of it.

'Blanket; you take blanket!' The surprise in the Indians response told Ruth the blanket was not one of the things she should take. She guessed the bone knife was important to the Indian and did not want to take that. She was wondering what next to suggest when he smiled and almost laughed. 'Blanket, you take blanket,' he repeated with a broad grin on his face.

Ruth felt she should at least explain why she had said the blanket. It was the most practical thing. 'Well it would keep me warm,' she said.

His grin turned into a warm smile 'Da, por say much,' he said almost laughing. He seemed very happy with the suggestion. 'Good take,' he chuckled to himself. 'Por you take blanket, say much.'

'That is all right then?'

'Da, say much good, por suta,' he said with the broadest of grins on his face. Ruth could not help but smiling. 'You take blanket,' the Indian said.

'All right then,' Ruth crouched down again and started to take the items off the blanket. She put them on the ground, but as the Indian picked them up, she passed him the last two items before taking the blanket and standing up.

'Por suta meecha, portag meecha,' the Indian said.

'Portag, I don't know what that is,' Ruth said.

'Good-bye e hello.'

'Both!' Ruth exclaimed hardly believing one word would have two meanings.

'Da, you learn talk. Go now, Portag meecha, say good-bye friend.'

'Yes, Portag meecha,' Ruth responded. With that, the Indian returned to the other two, who had been standing there watching, and spoke to them, laughing as he did. Then they headed off to where their weapons were and picked them up. Ruth watched them leave; pleased the meeting had passed without any trouble in fact it had been friendly with the older Indian laughing.

The one Ruth recognized turned towards her and gave a half wave before he was lost to her sight as all three disappeared into the woods. When Ruth took the blanket to the cabin she found it was not as large as she thought it would be, it would certainly not go over her; round her shoulders was the best it would do. She folded it up and put it on the floor under the bunk. It had been strange the way the Indian, with four feathers, had thought it highly amusing she would select the blanket. Zak had a sniff of the small blanket then forgot about it. After a few days, during which Ruth felt a little unsure, she returned to her normal routine. The summer weather was good, and some days were very hot.

Over the days of summer, she got better at shooting the bow, but was not yet able to hit what she wanted to, and she had lost three of the seven arrows, which were with the bows. Throwing a spear was easier, she was much better at it, a spear did not need her to aim off; she just had to throw it. Ruth took the best spear with her when she went hunting with Zak; not that she needed to but she felt better if she was carrying it.

Ruth's crops were growing well, and needed little attention. Ruth decided to tidy up the area in front of the cabin; she made herself a new swish broom and cleared away all the wood chips. Then she moved the larger logs until all that remained was one large one on which she could sit and look at the lake and mountains.

That evening she ate her meal outside in the cool of the evening pleased it looked much better around the cabin. Zak came as sat beside her. 'It's nice now, isn't it,' she said as she stroked him.

Ruth had run out of beans the previous winter so this year she had planted all the seeds she had. They had grown well and provided her with a huge crop. It took her two days of constant work to gather them and then shell them all. She ended up with three sacks two more than she had the previous year, and she had a good stock to use for next year's seed.

The autumn arrived and the work of preparing for winter started in earnest, she had again filled the sacks with turnips and had a pile of them in the corner of the root cellar. There were at least four hundred of them, more than enough for her over the winter and the following year, and there were more in the field. Ruth looked at them all; she had almost run out of food during the previous winter but had over compensated for it this year.

She was ready for winter before it started to become cold. She dug the two fields so that the frost and ice would till the ground for her. As it became colder, she hunted a lot with Zak until she had a supply of meat as well as vegetables.

Winter came but it was not as harsh as the previous one; there were many days, during the winter, when the two of them could go out hunting. Ruth and Zak ate well that winter. Coming back from one of her hunting trips Zak was walking beside her when he started to grumble. Ruth watched him as he sniffed the ground along the path. Ruth emerged from the wood and started out across the meadow towards the cabin. Zak ran towards the cabin snarling as he did. Ruth ran, as best she could, through the snow after him, he was acting strangely. Ruth wondered what was upsetting him the only thing she could think of was an Indian had come back.

Ruth could hear Zak snarling at something inside the cabin. She reached the door and went in. Zak had the Indian pinned into the corner of the cabin. 'Back boy, it's all right Zak,' she said believing she recognised the Indian even though he had wrapped a large number of furs round himself.

'Nak umta pi!' the Indian called out.

Ruth dragged Zak away. To her relief he came away although he was still grumbling and occasionally snarling at the Indian. 'Natlatan are you Natlatan.'

'Da, pi Natlatan, pi meecha.'

'Come away Zak.'

Ruth looked at the fire, it was burning brightly; the Indian had obviously tended to it. He had a good fire going and it was nice and warm in the cabin. Zak had calmed down a bit. 'Portag Meecha,' Ruth said, believing she should greet him as a friend.

'Da pi meecha, kala nak umta, pi meecha. Ella daqua e jad pe.'

'I don't understand. Kala what is kala.'

'Kala,' the Indian said pointing at Zak, 'kala nak umta pi.'

'You have added a bit there. Nak, I think is no; umta what is umta?'

'Umta, mesh, umta,' the Indian said making out as if he was eating.

'Zak will not eat you,' Ruth said pointing at Zak, 'nak umta,' she wondered what the word for you was, she did not know it she thought she would use his name, 'Natlatan.'

It was a struggle talking to the Indian; Ruth pointed at various things in the cabin, some of which he did not know what they were and could not say the Indian word. 'She pointed to the fire. 'Alsor,' he went to it, watched by Zak. Ruth watched as he pointed all round it. 'Alsor, e,' he pointed to a single flame almost putting his finger in it. 'Neta, apar neta, alsor.'

'Lots of flames is a fire. Por,' Ruth said becoming very interested in the way they were getting on. 'Neta, neta, neta,' she said pointing at various points around the fire that were flaming. Then she swept her hand over all the fire 'Alsor.'

'Da, por, porpog.'

It had taken most of the afternoon to learn a few Indian words and it would soon become dark. The Indian was showing no signs of leaving. Zak had long ago stopped grumbling at the Indian. Ruth felt comfortable talking to him trying to learn the Indian language. She thought she would try to ask a question to find out when he was going to leave. 'Pe ella,' she started to say then did not know how to continue.

'Pi ella aptag, ella daqua Daga Kala aptag.'

'I don't know what you said,' she responded as she pointed at him. 'Ella.'

'Da, aptag.'

'Aptag, what is aptag.'

Natlatan tried hard to get Ruth to understand what aptag was without being able to do so. It became quite amusing as each attempt failed. Ruth became concerned it would soon be dark and she needed to make her meal.

Maybe, she thought, he needed a meal. He had come to see her; maybe he was a long way from where he lived. Ruth tried this thought out. 'Pe umta.'

'Da, porpog.'

Ruth smiled, she had understood him to say yes, well done or thank-you. The snares she had walked around were empty. Ruth had not been surprised at that; she had some meat hanging in the cave, which would do for making a meal. 'Pe ella e pi,' Ruth said pointing at him and then herself.

'Da,' he said as he followed her out of the cabin. Ruth went to the cave, she saw a couple of deer legs, which had frozen stiff with the cold. Natlatan looked around the cave. 'Por!' he said still looking around the cave with its sacks of roots lent against the sides of the small cave. 'Por apar mesh, apar.' He looked in each of the sacks; Ruth did not understand what he said when he opened one of the sacks containing beans. 'Beans,' Ruth said believing he may have asked her what they were. 'Take some we will have some with this leg of deer, they will make the stew nice and thick.'

'Ah! Por, apar e apar mesh. Reela,' he said pointing at the frozen meat Ruth had taken down from the cave roof. 'Por, mesh'

'Da,' Ruth said, not that she fully understood what he had said but it sounded ok. She put several handfuls of beans in her pinafore, and then headed back to the cabin. Natlatan followed her carrying two turnips and the leg of deer.

He watched intently as she made the meal intrigued with the beans. Ruth put plenty in and only a little water, it made a good, thick stew. Natlatan wanted to eat it before it was fully cooked; Ruth tried to tell him to wait. When Ruth thought it was ready, she put some on each plate and passed it to him along with a spoon. He tasted it. 'Ah! Por mesh, por,' he said patting his tummy, 'Porpog.' To Ruth he seemed very pleased with the meal. He was certainly enjoying it would definitely eat it all. Ruth gave Zak some of the stew he would eat it without question; then she started on hers. It was good and filling, it would be better if it had a little salt in it, but salt was something she had learnt to do without.

It was dark by the time the two of them finished the meal, the cabin only lit by the light of the fire. 'Porpog, pe pog por mesh,' Natlatan said as he put his plate down. Ruth felt comfortable in his company she no longer feared him, and had understood that he had thanked her for the meal. However, it was dark outside now and she did not think he would leave until the following day.

It was difficult for Ruth to get him to understand he had to sleep on the floor. He wanted to sleep on the bunk and would not or could not understand why she wanted him to sleep on the floor. Eventually he got the idea. Zak jumped up on the bunk when Ruth lay down. The mild spell continued the following day. Natlatan left around midday leaving Ruth alone in the cabin again.

Ruth was content in her cabin. There was another cold spell with more snow, but it did not last long. When spring came, she was keen to get her crops in and was already looking forward to the lazy days of summer. Life here was not as bad as she had originally thought; she could live here. When lying on her bunk in the evening she wondered if any others were making their way inland, she could picture them crossing the mountains helped by the Indians, did any stay in the large Indian camp on the other side of the mountains during the winter, ready to cross the mountains in the spring. Zak disappeared for a few days; she was not worried he had done so last year in spring and he came back; she had no reason to believe he would not return this year.

Chapter 4

Ruth worked hard in her two fields, she dug up another sack full of turnip and made sure those she left were going to provide her with the seeds she would need for next year's crop. That done she prepared the soil for this year's crop and by the time, she stopped for the day her fields were ready to sow. That evening she lay on the bunk for a while before making her meal pleased with the day's work. She had a nice fat rabbit for her meal, which was not normal for this time of year; they were usually a bit on the thin size after winter. She had not been lying there, looking up at the logs, which formed the roof, for long before she heard Zak scratching at the door. She got off the bunk. 'You are back then Zak, where do…' she stopped speaking as she opened the door to find five or six young wolves there, they snarled at her only to be reprimanded by Zak who chased them into the cabin. An older female her body low on the ground followed, unsure of where Zak was leading them. Not long after the arrival of Zak and his family, Ruth was surrounded by the young wolves all wanting to be stroked and petted. 'Ouch! You little bugger, you have sharp teeth, I am stroking you now don't be so fussy.' Ruth made a lot of food that evening with all the scraps of meat she had. They all eat it up then found somewhere in the cabin to curl up and go to sleep.

She woke in the morning to find six wolves watching her. Zak was in his normal position lying beside her on the bunk. Ruth got up going over to the door and opening it. 'Out, all of you out,' she told the wolves, 'come on; go and run around outside for a while.' It took her a while but the young wolves were eventually outside and starting to explore the area immediately around the cabin.

Later that day Ruth went hunting with Zak the older female came but was unsure to start with but by following Zak's example she soon learnt. It was a good hunt; they returned to the cabin with four rabbits. The young wolves had all stayed around the cabin but as she approached, they came bounding up to her, yakking as they did very interested in the rabbits.

With needing to find food for the cubs, Ruth spent a lot of time hunting with Zak and the female wolf she had named Sheiba. The cubs grew quickly and started to come hunting, they soon learnt what to do; hunting was second nature to them and by late spring early summer, Ruth hunted with a pack of wolves all of whom knew what to do and when to do it. It took only a little effort on Ruth's part to teach the wolves to stay where she told them and lie low. Ruth would then circle round the deer, which would invariable run straight into the centre of the pack. It meant Ruth, with the aid of the pack, could overcome larger animals. The first time they found a moose, it became quite a chase, but with seven wolves, the outcome was always going to be that they would have plenty of meat for a good few days. Ruth hung the meat up high in the root cellar cave. It kept the meat well away from the wolves, although they ate most of it as whole moose was far too much for her needs, and the wolves were only too happy to lie around in the sun rather than hunting for their evening meal ate most of it.

Ruth's fields were doing well; the relaxed days of summer had arrived. Sitting on the upper bank looking over the lake at the mountains in the distance Ruth noticed smoke slowly rising from a position past the western end of the lake. Having waded across it when she had gone to find her father's body Ruth knew the position of the river. The smoke appeared to be coming from somewhere upstream, maybe as much as a mile from the end of the lake. Having had some contact with Indians Ruth guessed it must be them and they were by the river. She was not concerned they were well away from her. Natlatan had come to the cabin several times; he had never harmed her, and last year when several had arrived, they had not been hostile towards her. Over the next few days Ruth checked on the smoke it was not always there, but on still days or days with only a slight breeze it could, if she looked carefully, be seen.

The thought of going to see the Indians crossed her mind several times, each time she noticed the smoke she thought about them, if the Indians were a mile or so upstream from the end of the lake, it would not take her long to walk there. She decided she would go and see what their camp was like; if she went early in the morning, she could easily get there and back in a day.

Ruth ate her breakfast surrounded by wolves, all of whom wanted to lick her plate the moment she put it down. 'What are you all looking at as if I didn't know? What do you want Mary, there is a nice bit of meat here.' A young female wolf put her nose a little nearer; Ruth picked the piece of meat off her plate and held it so she could take it. One of the others pawed at her for its bit of her breakfast. 'Now be good and you all get a bit.' She gave the one that pawed her a bit then Zak thought that was the signal to finish off her breakfast. She held the plate as they all tried to get at it. 'That is it you can't eat the plate as well. Come on let me up. Shift yourselves,' Ruth said as she got to her feet. 'Jake, get down there is nothing there,' she complained to the young wolf who always wanted to be involved with whatever she was doing.

Ruth waded across the small stream, not far from the cabin, and headed west. As far as the wolves were concerned, they were going hunting, when they caught a rabbit and Ruth was not interested in it they ate it squabbling between themselves. Having eaten the rabbit, they were content enough to follow her. Ruth continued, winding her way through the wood. Several times, she had to backtrack and wondered if she should not have gone along the shore of the lake to start with. After she had gone about a mile, the number of bushes blocking her way, decreased and it became easier to walk in a straight line. Zak walked at her side with the young ones running around interested in everything. Ruth continued to head west for a while then when she thought she had passed the end of the lake turned and moved north towards a particular mountain she could see whenever there was a space in the trees. The wood thinned out on the slopes of a long hillside.

As she approached the top of the hill, Ruth could see down the length of the lake off to her right. She was level with the southern shore of the lake. It allowed her to get her bearings. The top of the hill was almost flat which meant she could not yet see what was on the other side, but she guessed it would be the river, which flowed into the lake. There were no signs of any smoke, but the mountain was right in front of her. She continued walking towards it, wondering what she needed to do in order to find the Indians.

The wolves became excited long before Ruth reached the crest of the hill and a position from which she could look down into the valley. The river, which fed into the western end of the lake, did indeed flow through the valley. The Indian village stood in a large U-bend of the river with what looked like a line of stakes closing the area off. To her left and upstream from the village were fields with crops growing in them, quite a large area Ruth thought. It was completely different to what she had expected; these Indians did not have large, round, pointed tents as the others she had seen during the journey to the lake with her father; these Indians had huts.

She could see the Indians moving around the village, there were children as well. It all appear quite normal people were working and children playing. Ruth started to made her way down the hill towards the village, not knowing what she would do when she got there she would have to do whatever was necessary, but she didn't think they would harm her they hadn't when they had come to see her. She remembered the strip of hide the other Indians has given her father and cursed herself for not brining it with her.

Ruth and her pack of wolves were halfway down the hill when some of the Indians noticed her; it sent the village into a panic. She heard people calling out and then they ran around trying to find a hiding place it was not long before she could no longer see anyone.

Ruth stopped and studied the village; three Indians were running along the bank of the river. She guessed they had come from the fields and were heading for the village. She stood and watched as they reached the village and disappeared into one of the huts. She saw another Indian run from one hut to another. Ruth believed they were preparing to defend the village and for a while did not know if she should continue down the hill. She decided to carry on, at least to the line of stakes. As she walked down the hill, she would occasionally see an Indian moving quickly from one place to another

It did not take her long to reach the gap in the centre of the outer line of stakes. The wolves were around her and had starting to examine the closely spaced stakes which extended well above her head and close enough together to stop even a wolf from squeezing between them. She peered through a gap between two stakes. The huts appeared larger than they had from the top of the hill. She heard someone call out but could not understand. 'Portag!' she shouted between the two stakes. She shouted it out several times before she saw someone coming towards her.

The Indian had almost reached the other side of the line of stakes before Ruth recognised him; he was the one who could speak a little English. 'Portag Meecha,' she said not shouting it out this time.

'Portag Jaga na Kala,'

He had said portag, Ruth understood that but he had added something else, which she could not understand, but believed it had something to do with the wolves. Kala was wolf she was sure of that. 'Portag,' Ruth replied then having run out of words she knew, she spoke slowly in English. 'I came to see you.'

'Da apar kala.'

'What?' Ruth responded knowing he had said something about the wolves and trying to remember what apar was, she had heard it before, but had forgotten what it meant.

'Many wolves,' he said as he reached the other side of the line of stakes and indicating the wolves most of whom were now just sitting waiting for something to happen. Jake wanted to know about the person on the other side of the stake; he was trying to stick his head between two stakes.

'They are all right that is Zak, Sheba, this is Jake he always gets into trouble. He will not hurt you; he only wants to smell you.'

'I come talk with you.'

'All right,' Ruth replied then stood there watching him as he headed towards end of the line of stakes. Ruth waited for him to go round the far end of the centre line of stakes and then towards her. 'Portag meecha,' Ruth said as he reached her.

'Portag,' he responded backing away from two of the wolves, which had gone up to him

'That is Jake; he is only going to smell you.'

'Nak umta pi.'

'They won't eat you. See Jake smelt you and now has gone to find out about that stake. Not eat anyone.'

'Por kala.'

'Kala is wolf.'

'Da, Jaga na Kala,' he said pointing at her.

'What is that?'

'Jaga na Kala, mother of wolves,' he repeated pointing at her. 'Meechamegan, Friend of Bear,' he added pointing to himself.

'Oh, Jaga na Kala,' Ruth repeated. They had given her one of their names she rather liked it 'Jaga na Kala,' it sounded quite pleasant to her. 'Meecha is friend.'

'Da,' Friend of Bear responded.

'I am learning.'

'Da you learn talk.'

Ruth felt more relaxed, at least she was now talking to one of the Indians and he did not seem upset. 'I came to see you,' she said hoping he would understand.

'Porpog, ella,' he said beckoning her to follow him and taking a half step back along the line of stakes. Ruth wondered about the wolves, it might have been better had she not brought them with her. 'Can wolves come?'

He looked at the wolves; they were now just sitting or standing waiting for something to happen. He looked from one to another for a while. Sheba stuck her nose out towards him then turned away. 'Da,' he said after a while, and again beckoned her to follow him.

Ruth started to walk with him as he led her along the path between two rows of stakes. The wolves seemed to know they had to behave they followed Ruth walking quietly behind her with Zak at her side. There was only a small space at the end where the path turned round the centre line of stakes and back towards the centre. Ruth walked with Friend of Bear; Zak walked beside her with the rest of the pack following them. It did not take them long to reach the centre. The gap in the inner line of stakes was longer than the gap in the outer row. 'Daqua na Daga Kala. Home of Wolf Tribe,' Friend of Bear said as he stopped walking, sweeping his hand around until he had covered the entire area.

'Daqua is home?' Ruth asked checking on what she had learnt from Natlatan.

'Da.'

Ruth looked round to get her bearings then pointed towards her cabin. 'Daqua na Jaga na Kala,' she said a little uncertainly. He beamed a huge simile at her 'Da, da, you learn good. Por.'

Another Indian appeared, from the area of the huts, and was now approaching the two of them. He was older than Friend of Bear and had a heavily decorated top on. He looked important to Ruth; the way he was dressed and walked would suggest that. 'Who is this?' Ruth asked, believing she should know before the Indian reach them.

'Paga na Daga Kala, Chief of Wolf Tribe,' Friend of Bear told her.

The two of them waited for the chief to reach them. Ruth checked the wolves were behaving themselves. Pleased the wolves were sitting Ruth turned her attention towards the chief who was now not more than ten feet away.

'Portag Jaga na Kala, meecha na Daga Kala,' the chief said as he arrived. Ruth had worked out what he had said; he had greeted her and said she was a friend. She was about to respond when Friend of Bear translated for her, 'Chief say, hello Jaga na Kala friend of wolf tribe.'

Ruth put together in her mind what she should say. 'Portag paga Daga Kala, meecha.'

'Por,' the chief said smiling 'Por tak. Pi paga na Daga Kala,' he added looking at the wolves around Ruth. Ruth studied his face, guessing he was a little older than her father had been.

'Chief say you talk good; he chief not brave of Daga Kala.'

'Oh, did I get it wrong.'

'Chief say you talk good.'

Ruth saw the chief look at the wolves 'Apar kala,' the chief said, addressing Friend of Bear.

'Da, kala por,' Meechamegan replied.

The chief continued to pay attention to the wolves; they were not doing a great deal other than looking at whoever spoke. 'Por, por Meechamegan, peapar por kala.'

'Da kala meecha, jad Zak yarween, kala nakella Jaga na Kala.'

'Pe jad.'

'Pi jad Zak daqua na Jaga na Kala.'

Ruth could do nothing other than look between the two Indians as they spoke. A couple of words she understood and knew they were talking about Zak and her cabin.

'Peapar por,' the chief said.

Fried of Bear looked at Ruth, 'Chief say wolves are good me tell him that Zak stays with you.'

'Tell the chief I came to see you, like you came to see me,'

'Jaga na Kala ella daqua na Daga Kala, tak Jaga na Kala meecha e kala meecha e jad daqua na Daga Kala.'

'Daga Kala tak meecha na Jaga na Kala.'

'Chief say we are friends with each other.'

'Good por,' Ruth said smiling at the chief.

'Por,' the chief said nodding at Ruth. Ruth was pleased it appeared as if the Indians were going to accepted her.

The chief was smiling and so was Friend of Bear. The Chief then turned towards the village. 'Jaga na Kala Meecha! Kala meecha! Ella! Ella! Meecha!' he called out.

As the others started to emerge Ruth realised the chief had shouted out telling the tribe she was a friend. It was not long before the Indians, greeted her with 'Portag Jaga na Kala meecha.' Their numbers grew until she was, surrounded by them.

The wolves became interested in the sudden activity Jake went to have a sniff of a small child then licked its face. The child reacted Jake immediately went down and yakked, wanting to play he yakked again at the child then another child came to find out what was happening Jake wanted to know about them, satisfied they smelt all right he ran round then went down other wolves wanted to know what was going on. Sheba greeted one of the Indians then walked off having smelt them to check on someone else.

'Jad! Kala meecha, por!' Friend of Bear pointed out to the chief.

'Da, pi jad,' the chief responded smiling and nodding at both Friend of Bear and Ruth. 'Kala meecha,' he added. Ruth was pleased; it all seemed to be going well. The wolves were behaving and the Indians appeared to be pleased to see her and the wolves.

'They are good wolves,' Ruth told Friend of Bear.

More from the tribe greeted her with a 'Portag Jaga na Kala,' some added their names. Natlatan greeted her with a smile on his face and even spoke to Zak. Ruth's pleasure in the occasion increased, she relaxed completely they had accepted her and everyone seemed pleased to see her. Those who had come to greet Ruth started to drift away back into the village, no longer were they hiding; the village had come back to life.

'Chief say me talk with Jaga na Kala show home of Daga Kala.'

'Yes, da, that is yes.'

'Da, yes, nak no.'

'I thought so.'

'Come me show.'

Friend of Bear showed Ruth round the village; Zak remained with her, while the rest of the wolves were exploring the village for themselves. Where people regularly walked, the grass had been worn away forming a network of paths around the village. Walking around the area the huts occupied reduced the distance Ruth could see. At times, she could only see five or six huts and nothing else. Each hut had skins hanging over the entrance; most were tied back so that the entrance was open. Ruth noticed all the entrances appeared to be on the same side of the hut. She asked Friend of Bear why this was so. 'Wind apar wind from there.' Ruth nodded it made sense to have to door on the other side to the prevailing wind.

The huts were not lined up as houses in towns were. The paths round the huts formed a maze without any obvious route from one area in the village to another. Having made their way through the area occupied by the huts, Ruth and Friend of Bear reached the back of the village near the river. There was a large circle of stones in front of a huge, elongated hut. The stones, which formed the circle, were flat and disk like. In the centre of the stone circle, a burnt area showed where a large fire had been. Friend of Bear sat down on a small grass bank only a few

feet from the edge of the stone circle. Ruth did likewise.
'Jad,' he said pointing to three children who were playing
with Jake. He was having a great time trying to get a stick
from them. 'Kala meecha por pog.'

'Pog,' Ruth said in a questioning way having heard a
word that she did not understand.

'Do, work, play; pog many things.'

'I understand.'

Ruth sat there watching the children with Jake; one
ran off. Ruth knew running away from Jake was not a
wise thing to do. She was on her feet going towards the
child Jake had knocked to the ground expecting it to be
hurt. The child crawled out from under Jake laughing
and shouting to the others. A young boy ran away from
Jake and moments later Jake had him pinned to the
ground. Then Jake was after one of the others. Ruth sat
back down. Other children arrived and they went into a
huddle, Ruth watched, as one of the older boys took them
all to a burnt area at the centre of the stone circle. She
could not hear what he was saying but from his actions,
Ruth thought the idea was to run from the centre of the
circle to the outside; she guessed they had to reach the
edge without Jake knocking them over. When they all
ran away from him Jake was not sure which one to chase.
He picked one, and then having flattened them he was
off for another one. The children ended up on the edge
of the circle dancing up and down while Jake ran round.
Then the children headed back to the burnt area lead by
the older boy. Rules were changed and another mad dash
for the edge of the circle started Jake rushed around; he
managed to stop three of them that time. Other children

arrived wanting to play; Jake was out numbered but then Mary arrived and evened it up a little.

Before long, all five young wolves were in the circle flattening any child who attempted to move towards the edge of the circle. It became more difficult for the children to win. Disturbed by all the noise, Friend of Bear sat up and started to pay attention to the game, which was now in full swing. A boy almost made it to the edge. He stood still the moment he saw Mary coming towards him, she smelt him then ran off; he moved and Jake who had come up behind him had him pined to the ground only a matter of a few feet from the stones. 'Porpog Kala! Nak Daqua!' Friend of Bear said jumping to his feet, 'Nak Daqua!' he repeated as the boy got up dejected then he pointed at someone else who had been stopped. Friend of Bear was off round the stone circle to pronounce his decision it was a nak daqua again. Ruth sat amazed as the game continued she wondered how the wolves knew it was only those running for the edge that were to be stopped and not those walking back to the centre to start again. Friend of Bear was in his element as the one that pronounced on a child's fate. Other members of the tribe arrived to find out what all the yelling and screaming was about; they started shouting advice to the children and cheering them with whoopees when they made the edge of the circle. The game came to a natural end with exhausted children and panting wolves sitting in the centre of the circle. Friend of Bear returned to where Ruth was sitting with Zak. He had a huge smile on his face, 'Por pog, kala por.'

Someone fetched some water, for both the children and the wolves. Having had a drink Jake came across to Ruth and lay down, panting, his tongue hanging out the side of his mouth. 'You liked that did you?' Ruth asked as she stroked him. Ruth thought it was time she should set off back to her cabin. She believed she knew enough to attempt to use the Indian's language. 'Pi,' she said pointing to herself, 'Pi ella daqua na Jaga na Kala.'

'Nakella, e umta.'

'Stay here and eat,' Ruth said believing she had understood what Friend of Bear had said.

'Da, Daga Kala umta tala jehi,' Friend of Bear said pointing to the sun and then moving lower towards the western horizon.

'You eat when the sun is there is that right,' Ruth responded guessing what Friend of Bear had said having understood his actions more than what he said.

'Da you learn good.'

For a while, Ruth sat with Friend of Bear as he taught her a few new words. Ruth liked the way her visit to the Indians was going, they had treated her as a friend, even the wolves were acceptable, particularly by the children and now Friend of Bear was teaching her to use their language.

When it came time to eat Friend of Bear stood up, Ruth followed him to the area occupied by the huts then round the maze of paths to his lodge. 'Nakella, he said as he ducked into the lodge. Ruth understood; nakella literally translated to, not go, which in the context Friend of Bear had used it, became stay here. She did not have to wait long within a few moments Friend of Bear emerged with two wooden bowls. Then he directed her back to the circle and the large hut, which seemed to be attracting everyone's attention.

Ruth wondered if the second bowl was for her, but he gave it to one of the women in the large hut. There was a bit of a fuss while they found what looked like a new bowl and a strangely shaped wooden spoon. With her new bowl, Ruth waited in the line for a portion of stew. It looked and smelt good, and it had a lot of meat in it. Having received a portion of the stew, Friend of Bear then led Ruth to one of the stones on the edge the circle. 'Pi daqua,' he said pointing at the stone as he sat down; Ruth sat beside him. He had used the word daqua, which Ruth understood as home, but it would appear that it like many other words could have a wider meaning. When the children were playing with the wolves, it was daqua when they made it to the edge of the circle. In this case, Friend of Bear was using daqua to indicate his place in the circle, which by now was filling up; people were sitting round it having their meal.

Ruth noticed the one called Natlatan who had visited her on several occasions, and the one that had run away. The smell of food attracted the wolves' attention. Ruth saw a wolf take some food from a child who had not intended it for the wolf. Ruth thought she should control them. She stood up 'Jake! Come here!' Ruth shouted at the wolf. The chief shouted something. Ruth thought trouble was about to occur. 'Sit chief say feed wolves,' Friend of Bear said. Ruth sat back down as several women brought bowls of food for the wolves, they knew straight away it was for them and waited for it to be put on the ground. Everyone settled back down, the wolves were given and extra portion; it satisfied them. The woman who Friend of Bear had given the bowl to came and sat with them; Friend of Bear introduced her as Porjadseeni, which meant clear water. 'Porjadseeni suma pi, Take me.'

'She is your squaw.'

'Da, she take me.'

Towards the end of the meal, a child held out something towards the nearest wolf. The wolf took it and licked the child's fingers. Then every child wanted to feed a wolf something. Ruth put her bowl down for Zak, 'You have not had any have you,' turning to Friend of Bear, she said, 'Zak nak umta.'

'Pi ella,' Friend of Bear went to the large hut, where the pot of stew was. He came back with a full bowl and put it down in front of Zak, who immediately started to eat it.'

'Por Zak umta por.'

'Stroke him he likes that.'

'Me do.'

'Stroke him he will let you.'

Zak was too interested in his meal to bother about who was stroking him.

It slowly started to become dark in the long twilight period; people started to drifted away from the circle. Ruth felt a little uneasy; she believed Friend of Bear had said she could stay in his lodge. She relaxed a little when Friend of Bear and Clear Water took her to their lodge, and indicated Ruth should enter.

Not knowing what to expect Ruth entered the lodge, it was dark inside. Very little light came in via the open door. Ruth paid attention to the way Porjadseeni lit a small wick by using the light fluffy seed head from a thistle. She placed the seed head on a piece of bark and then using a small bow with the string twisted round a short length of wood, and another piece of bark; she spun it at great speed until the heat caused the seed head to burst into flames. It took her less than a minute to light the lamp. It was still dim in the hut but in the limited light, Ruth could look around the lodge. It was circular and at least twelve or more feet across. A vertical wall came up to about her shoulders then arched towards the centre of the hut to a height of ten feet, certainly higher then she could reach. It was very spacious. Around the walls of the hut were spears, bows and arrows. In another part of the hut were what Ruth took to be clothes, made of hide. The most noticeable item was the fur, spread out on the floor. At first, Ruth thought it was one fur but on closer examination saw it was two and more than likely from a bear, they were large enough to be so.

Now there was light from the small lamp Friend of Bear released the skins over the entrance; with the entrance closed, the area inside the hut became an intimate space lit by the small flame of the lamp. Zak pushed himself under the skins over the opening; he sniffed around the wall until he came to the ashes of a fire, which had long ago gone out. He plonked himself down; satisfied he had found somewhere, which would do him for the night.

'Tashka, piapar tashka, sheep,' Friend of Bear was saying indicating the furs as he spoke.

'Sheep; what have sheep…'

'Tashka, sheep.'

'Sheep! Nak sheep, sleep, nak sheep, sheep is an animal.'

'Sheep not tashka.'

'No, sleep.'

'Sheep, shleep, not know different.'

'Tashka.'

'Da piapar tashka.'

Ruth was a little uncertain about taking her dress off and getting between the furs. The first night when

Natlatan had been in her cabin, he has slept on the bunk and nothing had happened. She slipped her dress off and exactly like the time with Natlatan; her underclothes were a cause of amusement. Ruth lay down between the furs with Friend of Bear still laughing at her. When Clear Water extinguished the lamp it became pitch black, unlike her cabin which normal had a small amount of light coming through the window particularly if there was a moon. The two large pelts had been placed together with the fur sides innermost; it made a warm and snug place to sleep.

By the time she woke in the morning, there was a fire burning, the small amount of smoke from it went up the hut wall as it curved towards the top and then out at the top of the hut. The entrance to the hut was open letting daylight into the hut. 'Daga mesh, piapar umta,' Friend of Bear said as Ruth sat up. Believing she should get up and put her dress back on; she did so. It was not long before Porjadseeni handed Ruth the bowl she had used the previous evening. It had a sort of porridge in it with a golden yellow substance on the top of it. The yellow substance was sweet and added to the flavour of the porridge. Friend of Bear explained that each lodge made their own meal in the morning; he called daga mesh or family food.

Having learnt the previous day that those who went hunting took all they managed to find to the tribe hut where the squaws used it to make in the evening meal. Ruth believing she should do something to help; her wolves could hunt as well as any Indian. That day Ruth sent the wolves away to find rabbits and bring them back. She watched as her family of wolves, led by Sheiba, ran off negotiating the path round the lines of stakes. 'Kala ella!' Friend of Bear said pointing to the wolves as they ran up the hill as a single pack. 'I told them to get some rabbits.'

'Kala jadpog, gegenta,' Friend of Bear said with a surprised look on his face.

'I don't understand.'

'Jadpog, look for, when look for mesh.'

'Hunt.'

'Da, da jadpog hunt; me not know word, now know jadpog hunt.'

During the couple of hours, the wolves were away Ruth walked along the river towards the large area where the Indians were growing crops. It looked very much like the oats she knew on the farm, which would explain the porridge Clear Water had made that morning. It was growing well, and would provide the Indians with a good crop.

It surprised the whole tribe when the wolves managed to find and bring back three rabbits and a small dear. The chief came to see the dead animals the wolves had caught. 'Por,' he said 'Por.'

'Tell chief they are for the meal.'

'You say have gegenta e reela make mesh.'

'You said everyone gives to the tribe lodge to make mesh,'

'Make food from gegenta e reela.'

'Yes, da.'

'Por, say much, kala jadpog.'

'Tell the chief.'

'Da me say.' Meechamegan turned towards the chief, 'Jaga na Kala tak kala jadpog gegenta e reela mesh na Daga Kala.'

The chief looked first at Ruth then at Zak and the other wolves who were there, before looking towards Meechamegan, 'Daga Kala tak nat por, nat por, pi tak kala nat por. Meechamegan tak Jaga na Kala nat por meecha na Daga Kala.'

Ruth looked to Friend of Bear for a translation of what the chief had said. 'Chief say it big good, kala big good, say we big friends with kala e Jaga na Kala, big friends. Chief say much you very big friend of tribe.'

Ruth was delighted the wolves had done well and now the tribe completely accepted them; there were smiles all round as two Indians took the dead animals to the tribe lodge. 'Big good,' Friend of Bear said, 'Nat por, make Daga Kala strong, kala jadpog.'

When Ruth went with Friend of Bear to the large hut that evening, she took a better look around. There were three large fires in the hut, over which the squaws cooked the evening meal. Porjadseeni seemed to be the one who was organising everything in the large hut. Ruth noticed what, at first glance, appeared to be a large rock. 'Salt, you have salt! Um, what is that there?' She asked Friend of Bear, pointing at it.

Friend of Bear looked to where Ruth was pointing. 'Cash, you have cash not know your word.'

'Can I taste it?'

'Ah, no nakpor, in mesh por.'

'Da I know, I haven't any where do you get it from?'

'Pe nak cash.'

'No, it makes food better.'

'Da,'

Ruth spent another night with the Indians sleeping in Friend of Bear's lodge. The following day Friend of Bear took her to the tribe lodge and to the large slab of salt. Ruth tasted it checking it was what she thought.

'Por.'

'Da.'

'You have; me get you cash.'

'Where do you get it from?'

'Not know how to say. Apa tag, ne ojar, hole in ground apar cash.'

Friend of Bear had trouble cutting a piece of salt from the large slab; he succeeded and gave it to Ruth. Ruth was delighted with the salt, 'Porpog,' she said as he handed it to her.

'Por, you learn good.'

Ruth said her good-byes and midmorning started back to her cabin. She waved from the top of the hill as she made her way back to her cabin. The time with the Indians had gone well; they had been very friendly towards her accepting her and her wolves. She felt good as she made her way back to her cabin. The few words of the Indian language she knew made all the difference.

Chapter 5

Back in her cabin Ruth soon caught up with the work, which required her attention, summer was not over by a long way; life was good. Ruth felt she had friends, no longer was she alone. She was happy to be in the cabin, to swim in the lake; life was in many ways easier here than on the farm in England. Where in England could she have a family of wolves as her protectors and visit a tribe of Indians, let alone hunt for small deer or rabbits with a pack of wolves. She even had some salt and that made her meals even better. She put the precious salt in her cupboard in order to protect it, and even a small amount in her meals made such a lot of difference.

Ruth had been back in her cabin for fifteen days, she was lying dozing in the sun when she was disturbed; Zak had started to grumble. She turned her head in the direction he was looking and saw several from the tribe emerge from the trees running towards her. Ruth stood unconcerned, waiting for them to reach her. 'Portag Jaga na Kala nat meecha na Daga Kala,' the one who had reached her first said as he stopped running. He was out of breath as were the other two who were with him.

'Portag meecha,' Ruth replied then recognising one of them she added, 'Portag Natlatan.'

'Portag Jaga na Kala meecha na Natlatan.'

'Jaga na Kala,' the first one to arrive said. 'Paga na Daga Kala tak porella hi daqua na Daga Kala,' he spoke slowly giving her every opportunity to understand him. Ruth thought carefully about what he had said, she thought she understood. 'Paga tak Jaga na Kala ella,' Natlatan added.

'The chief...' Ruth started to say then stopped herself none of them would understand her she had to use their language she spoke slowly, 'Paga na Daga Kala,' Ruth said remembering to add the na so they would know it was the chief and not a brave she was talking about, 'tak ella daqua na Daga Kala.'

'Da!' Natlatan immediate responded. 'Da paga tak porella Jaga na Kala e kala.'

Ruth understood she was wanted with her wolves. 'E kala,' she said in order to make sure she had understood correctly

'Da, porella.'

Ruth was pleased she had managed to use their language; she had understood they wanted her to come to the village with her wolves. She was not too sure what good go meant. She turned it over in her mind for a while, deciding it was probable a good journey. Was the chief wished her a good journey. She wondered why they all looked out of breath she guessed they had run all the way. In her mind changed good go, to, quickly. She gave them a drink before she set off back to the village with them.

The wolves bounded along with them excited with what was going on. The Indians took a far more direct route to the village than the one Ruth had used, it was a lot easier as well as being quicker. It did not take long before they reached the top of the hill overlooking the village.

Her arrival in the village with the wolves caused a great deal of excitement. It was not long before the chief came up to her. 'Jaga na Kala tak,' he said as he led her towards the circle. Friend of Bear came running towards them as they approached the back of the village and the circle of stones, 'Portag Jaga na Kala, pe tak.'

Ruth thought she knew what he had said but it did not make any sense, 'Say what?' Ruth asked.

'Nakpor,' Friend of Bear said shaking his head as he spoke. 'Binojar tod.'

'I don't understand.'

'Dead, Binojar dead.'

'Dead!' Ruth exclaimed; surprised one of the Indians she knew was dead. He was young, strong and fit. Ruth could not understand; if he was dead what was it she had to say.

'Da, killed with white man knife,' Friend of Bear added.

'What!' Ruth felt shocked, and did not know what to say. The Indians were all starting to sit around the circle, Ruth had not seen them do so before they only sat in the circle for the meal it was nowhere near time for the evening meal and they were all talking and highly excited. For a brief moment, Ruth became frightened, were they for some reason, blaming her for the death of Binojar. Friend of Bear has said it was with a white man's knife and she was the only one who had a knife like that. 'You say who did it.'

'It wasn't me.'

'Da, peapar tak nak Jaga na Kala. apa e ap hish paga, you say which one.'

'Hish paga what does that mean.'

'White man.'

'Apa e ap, that is three.'

'Lots of words for apar, me not know them. Apa e ap.' Friend of Bear said holding up three fingers.'

'Da,' Ruth responded as she watched the circle filled she looked around and saw Natlatan then looked across to where his friend sat. There was a squaw with a small child sitting there, one look at the Indian woman was sufficient to tell Ruth. 'Binojar sat there' Ruth asked Friend of Bear pointing so others would not notice.

'Da, nakpor,' Friend of Bear told Ruth to sit down beside the chief. The circle settled down with an air of expectancy. The chief spoke to a group who were standing slightly to his left. They left the circle, Ruth sat there wondering what was happening something was about to, that was easy to see. It did not take long; six Indians dragged three dirty trappers, bound and tied, into the circle and made to kneel in front of the chief. 'One kill Binojar Jaga na Kala say who,' Friend of Bear said.

'I don't know.'

'Talk with white-man; say who kill Binojar.'

Ruth was still disturbed with the news that Binojar was dead. 'Did one of you kill an Indian?' She asked them. Even as she asked the question, Ruth did not think it was the best approach she could have taken.

'Get us out of here,' one of them responded, 'you're a decent god fearing woman you can't let them kill us,' he added.

'I have to say who killed Binojar, did one of you.'

'None of us did it, we're just trappers. Tell them it was someone else.'

Ruth knew she was not going to get anywhere; she turned to Friend of Bear. 'Why kill Binojar?'

'Not say, not know words; can show.' Ruth shugged her shoulders. 'Show me,' Friend of Bear said.

After a conversation with the chief, Friend of Bear took Ruth around the back of the tribe lodge away from the circle and out of sight of the three trappers; another Indian and a squaw came with them.

'Paga e squaw,' Friend of Bear said pointing at them

'Da,' Ruth responded fully aware of what he meant.

'Jad,' Friend of Bear said pointing to his eyes with two fingers. He went to kiss the squaw the other brave stopped him, the squaw ran away and Friend of Bear stabbed at him until he fell to the ground. 'Binojar tod,' Friend of Bear said pointing at the brave on the ground.

'He stopped you kissing the squaw.'

'Da, not know words, Binojar tod,' he said again pointing to the Indian on the ground.

'I think I know.'

'Nak,' Friend of Bear made a kissing shape to his lips then a far more sexual jester.

'Squaw nak tak da.'

'Da, da, nak tak da, you learn good.'

'Yes, I know what happened,' Ruth said more to herself than anyone else.

'Binojar tod, squaw jad apa e ap hish papa pogtod. Not know which one, Jaga na Kala tak.'

'Da,' Ruth responded, 'da,' she repeated nodding as she spoke now that she fully understood what had happened.

Ruth returned to the position beside the chief. She sat down and looked at the three trappers. They were dirty and all three looked as if they could kill someone without being too bothered about it. 'Now I know what happened,' Ruth said. 'Who tried to rape Binojar's squaw.'

'Not us, and anyway they are the only women around here,' the one who had done all the talking so far said.

'No one is leaving here until I find out,' Ruth said more confident of her position now she knew what had happened and well aware the Indians would not harm her. She was there because she could talk to them better than Friend of Bear.

'None of us had any Indian woman.'

'You are the only ones round here other than the Indians and he was stabbed with a knife, the Indians don't have that sort of knife,' Ruth said guessing most of it but believing she was not far wrong.

'It wasn't us; they can't say it was they were not there.'

'How do you know that?'

'Because I do,' he replied.

Ruth was sure the one doing the talking was the one who had indeed kill Benojar. She thought about the first time she had met Binojar, on that occasion Zak had him pinned against a bush. How could she tell for sure; Ruth did not want to point to one of them if she was not certain. She did not know what the Indians would do, but she felt there was a strong possibility he would die. Zak pushed his nose towards them. 'Back Zak' Ruth said then thought about the other wolves. She would use them to frighten them into telling her; it seemed like a good idea.

She looked at all three trappers, 'Wolves can smell death on someone they will know who it was without me needing to ask a single question. Two of you have nothing to fear, but the wolves will know who killed Binojar.' Then turning to Zak, she stroked his chest. 'Call Zak, call the others; call Zak.'

Zak gave a long howl his head back as he called the others. They arrived within a few moments and immediately wanted to know about the three trappers. Two were frightened but the one Ruth thought was guilty was terrified and the wolves knew it. They were all threatening him their heads low and ears flat back against their heads as they snarled at him. Ruth glanced towards the chief who was staring wide-eyed at the wolves. She looked at Friend of Bear and quickly round the rest of the tribe; there were all watching the wolves hardly believing what they were seeing. Ruth did not need to tell the Indians they had all seen the way the wolves had acted. 'Kala tak!' the chief cried out.

'Back all of you,' Ruth said half standing in order to move the wolves away from the trappers. 'Come on.' Jake was still intent on an attack. 'Jake come on back boy,' Ruth said pulling the wolf away from the trapper who she could see was now trembling with fear his eyes fixed on Jake. By the time she sat down again, the Indians, who were standing behind the three men, were dragging the other two trappers away.

Ruth watched as two strong braves stood behind the trapper. The chief said something she did not understand.

Then Friend of Bear translated talking to the trapper. 'Chief say, you guard spirit of Binojar tell him when to see Great Spirit.'

Ruth saw the Indian knife in the hand of one of the braves. The other held the trapper she looked away when she realised they were going to cut his throat. The trapper's scream turned into a gargling noise, cut short when the windpipe was severed.

When she looked back, Ruth was almost sick. They had cut his head off; it was now on a red blanket another Indian in the skin of a wolf was standing behind it and two were carrying the trapper's body away from the circle towards a large fire some distance from the circle. The chief stood and picked up the blanket with the head on. Walking beside the one in the wolf skin the chief slowly made his way to the bank of the river. Binojar's squaw got up from where she was sitting and followed them carrying a small child. Friend of Bear helped Ruth up and the two of them followed with the rest of the tribe. Several of the stakes beside the river had been removed; it allowed the procession to leave the village. They continued a short way down stream towards the lake before they reached an area, which even to Ruth looked as if it was a burial ground. This was confirmed when the chief went to a freshly made mound of earth and placed the head at one end of it. There was a lot of chanting from the one in the wolf's skin then both he and the chief covered the head. The rest of the tribe watched in complete silence. When it was over, they all slowly returned to the village.

People started to talk to each other again. Ruth felt ill she wanted to find somewhere to sit and recover. Friend of Bear took her to his lodge; they sat down on the small grass verge around his lodge beside the entrance leaning against the side of his lodge.

For the rest of that day, and with a lot of difficulty, Friend of Bear explained to her about the Great Spirit. He told her that everyone had a time to go and meet the Great Spirit but if their life was cut short they would not know when, and their spirit would wander forever unless it had a guard to protect it and tell it when to go to meet the Great Spirit. He explained that all animals had a spirit; if you hunted and killed them properly, they too would meet the Great Spirit. It all seemed to make sense to Ruth as Friend of Bear explained it. He explained how the Great Spirit looked over all the other spirits from each animal and each person, and how it provided for each. The rabbit which became a meal was pleased because it was their time to meet the Great Spirit, but if you tried to kill the wrong rabbit you would miss and it would run away because it was not its time yet, you had to look for the right rabbit. If you just killed a rabbit, or any other animal, for the sake of it that was very bad because it was not the rabbit's time to meet the Great Spirit.

By the time they went for the evening meal Ruth believed she knew a lot more about how the Indians saw the world around them. It all made a lot of sense to Ruth. That evening when they ate together, she looked on Indians differently. Several came with a bowls of food for the young wolves but before putting the bowls on the ground for them, the Indian in the wolf's skin talked to the wolves they all sat there watching him but with more than half an eye on the food. Then the Indians ceremonially fed the wolves that had shown them which trapper had killed Binojar.

After the meal, Binojar's squaw went to the chief with her child taking the stone, which had marked her position in the circle with her. The chief took the stone from her and put it on a pile of flat stones behind and a little to the left of him. Then he said something to the tribe. Natlatan and another brave stood up. Ruth heard the squaw say something the only bit Ruth understood was when she heard the Indian woman mention Natlatan. He went to the chief and after a conversation between the three of them; Natlatan took the woman and child back to where he sat in the circle.

'Por,' Meechamegan said, 'Now Natlatan squaw.'

'What happened?'

'Natlatan stand, she say Da. He good paga.'

That night in Meechamegan lodge, he and Porjadseeni explained to Ruth that a woman had to have a man. Only a brave had a position in the tribe's circle and a woman had to choose one if their man was killed. 'What am I then I am not your squaw but I sit with you.'

'Da pe binjaga, pi paga na Jaga na Kala.'

'Father!'

'Da, pe pi binjaga.'

'Daughter.'

'No know word.'

The following day Ruth felt she should return to her cabin there was work to do; Friend of Bear stopped her leaving telling her to wait for the chief to come and speak to her. The chief came later that morning, some distance behind him were the other two trappers their hands and arms still bound, but they now had their legs free; they were guarded by three Indian braves all of whom were carrying spears. 'Portag Jaga na Kala,' the chief said then added a lot that Ruth did not understand. She turned to Friend of Bear. 'Chief say what to do with them. No know all words to say what chief said.'

'Jaga na Kala suma…' Ruth didn't know how to continue, but the chief's expression had already turned from a smile to a look of horror. She turned to Friend of Bear; he was trying not to laugh. There was a brief moment during which Ruth looked between the two Indians. The expression of the chief's face changed, then the chief burst out laughing and so did Friend of Bear. 'Suma!' he said pointing at Ruth.

'What is funny about that, suma is take. I will take them away and say stay at end of lake.'

'Nak suma, nak.'

'You said suma is take.'

'Nak suma take like.' He made a sexual move.

'Ah! Nak! I don't know tell the chief for me.'

'Suta,' Friend of Bear said empasising the T.

Ruth smiled, 'Pi suta,' she said, then added, 'tak nakella,' before she ran out of words that she knew, so in English continued to speak, 'end of the lake, I don't know what that is.'

'Por, tak nakella yar seeni'

'Stay after water,' Ruth said as she worked out what Friend of Bear had said.

'Da,' he responded.

'That is not the same as I would say.'

'Not know what you say.'

'I will tell them to stay away from here.'

'Da,' Friend of Bear said smiling at her.

'Suma,' the chief said with a board smile on his face. Ruth smiled; she had made a mistake with the Indian language; all three of them ending up laughing and joking.

'Natlatan ella e Jaga na Kala, poota Jaga na Kala,' the chief said.

'Da,' Friend of Bear said.

Ruth took it that Natlatan was there to make sure nothing happened to her. Ruth did not think the trappers would attempt anything, if they did, there would be seven very angry wolves around them. She said good-bye to the chief and Meechamegan then led the two trappers out of the village her wolves around her and Natlatan just behind with several spears and a bow.

'You gone Indian; laughing with them when they have killed one of our kind.'

'You killed one of them and you tried to rape one of the women.

'What is that one behind doing? Cut us free we can't fight like this.'

'Later and should you even think of attacking Natlatan or myself you will have to deal with the wolves first. If you ever harm one of my wolves, I will feed you to the rest of them. Now if you don't mind I would rather not talk to you.'

'Cut us free.'

'No, now move,' Ruth ordered then looked towards Zak, who was standing beside her. 'Zak, move him!' She called out pointing to the two trappers.

'All right, call the wolf off we're moving.'

Ruth felt confident she had seven wolves and Natlatan; the two trappers were no match for her. Taking a wide route, away from the cabin so the trappers would not learn the whereabouts of the cabin Ruth kept moving south until she reached the plain. Ruth stopped and spoke to the two trappers. 'Follow the tree line along there until you get to the far end of the lake, don't come up this end again or I will set the wolves on you. Turn round. They did and Ruth cut the bindings holding their arms. 'Now go,' she said as the two trappers freed themselves from the vines that bound them.

'We can't walk all night.'

'Go or I will have a couple of wolves show you just how fast you can run.'

'You're all mouth.'

'Sheba! Jake! See them off!' she shouted at the two wolves pointing towards the two trappers. The two trappers were already running away with the wolves chasing them by the time Natlatan came up to her.

'Peapa porella,' he said pointing at the two fleeing trappers.

'They will not be back,' Ruth said knowing that Natlatan would not understand. 'Ella pi daqua,' she added.

'Da,' he replied then started to walk along the tree line for a while before turning in towards the cabin. Ruth had not realised the clearing in which she had first met Natlatan was so near the edge of the wood. They reached the path along which her snares were set. The wolves started to fan out. It was not long before Ruth heard a snarl off to her right. Two wolves dashed across the small path, not far from where two of them were walking. 'Jadpog,' Natlatan said.

'Da,' Ruth replied as she turned off the path towards where the wolves had killed a deer. Natlatan carried it as they continued their journey towards the cabin. They arrived there around midday and sat on the log with Natlatan teaching her new words and trying to talk about the Great Spirit. When evening came, Ruth started to prepare a meal. She went to the cave for some beans knowing he liked them while he lit the fire. Soon Ruth had good pieces of deer cooking in the pot. She opened the cupboard and took a small amount of salt.

'Por, cash por mesh.'

'Pi tak salt,' Ruth said.

'Salt,' Natlatan repeated.

Once their meal was underway, Ruth gave one of the deer legs to Zak then tossed the rest of the deer out of the cabin. Her family of wolves set upon it. Natlatan kept the fire burning nicely while their meal cooked.

When it came to the time to sleep Ruth was unsure what was expected. Having spent time in the village she could now understand why Natlatan had objected to sleep on the floor. Ruth believed she should act in her cabin as she would in the village; Natlatan would expect her to. 'Tashka,' Ruth said pointing to the bunk. Natlatan nodded and started to get ready. Ruth took her dress off then lay on the bunk, Zak jumped up and she had to move over so that Natlatan had enough space to lie down. She need not have worried Natlatan slept on the bunk with her just as Friend of Bear and Porjadseeni had in their lodge.

The following day he looked at the bow Ruth had, recognising it as his. Ruth told him to take it; he refused to and spent the morning showing her how to shoot it, and teaching her how to throw a spear. Ruth enjoyed the day with him. Sheba and Jake returned early evening coming to where Ruth was sitting on the log looking out over the lake. She petted the two wolves, telling them they were good wolves as she stroked them. That night Ruth did not hesitate to lie on the bunk with Natlatan, she knew she was completely safe and took pleasure in the fact she could act correctly as Indians saw it.

The following day Natlatan left in order to return to the tribe. Ruth returned to her normal life, the lazy days of summer ended and the busy time of year arrived, during which there were always more tasks to do than would be imagined possible. By the time the snows came, she was ready, and the cabin became her only space. The cabin, the trips to the woodpile and the cave, which acted as her store, were the limit of her world. The hunting in autumn had been good, not only did she have roots and beans stored away she also had meat, which had frozen hard in the bitterly cold weather. Friend of Bear had told her they did the same to meat and it was still good meat in the spring. Ruth also had the wolves and although most days she could not venture out there were times when it was possible, and she was getting better at hunting with the wolves.

Chapter 6

When spring came, all the female wolves gave birth. Ruth's cabin was full of wolves. The cubs grew very quickly; she found it difficult to walk across the cabin without treading on a paw or tripping over one of them. Deciding there was not enough space in the cabin Ruth looked around for a new home for them. She moved things around in the root cellar and opened up the rest of the small cave. It could hold most of her wolves she thought.

Ruth then started to kick them out of the cabin whenever they tried to get in. Zak soon caught on and kept them all out. Ruth made sure they found new homes. The largest group were in the root cellar the other, smaller group, set up home in small cave which Ruth couldn't get into but the wolves seemed quite happy in there they would all come out when she went there with some food for them.

She was working in her field when a large bear came into the clearing. It was black or dark brown in colour, its massive body rocking from side to side as it walked. Ruth called for Zak; he arrived and howled, before long wolves were arriving in their tens all intent of seeing off the bear. Confronted by a large pack of wolves, the large bear decided this was not the place to be and ran off chased by a number of wolves.

Ruth turned back towards her field to find herself surrounded by wolves some of whom she had never seen before she tried to count them without being able to do so; they milled around her. She reached out and stroked one she had never seen before, it did not complain as she patted it on the head. 'Hello, where did you come from? You are not one of mine are you,' she said as stroked another unknown wolf. Zak walked beside her. 'Look Zak look at them all.'

By midday, only her family of wolves remain. Over the next few days, Ruth finished her work, thinking she would visit the Indians. Her fields looked good and the crops were starting to grow; small seedlings were poking their leaves above the surface of the ground, they would continue to grow without her aid. The following day Ruth set off for the Indian village followed by her wolves. The chief welcomed her and with difficulty managed to tell her that Friend of Bear was on the northern shore of the lake hunting bear.

That afternoon Porjadseeni gave Ruth an Indian dress. She was still amused at the amount of underclothes Ruth wore they all had to come off. In return, Ruth received a soft skin loincloth, which had much less hanging down the front than the men's loincloth. Then she put on a tan coloured dress made of deerskin. It had long sleeves with fine strips of hide hanging from the seam where the arm joined the body. It took on more shape when she put a belt round her waist. Then Porjadseeni showed Ruth how to put two feathers into her hair. The shoes she gave Ruth did not look suitable, they were soft much like slippers not strong as her boots were. It felt strange when walking she could feel everything under her feet and was very conscious of the ground beneath her.

Ruth became embarrassed when they left the lodge, her legs from just below the knees were bare and she felt sure everyone was looking at her. She was also very conscious of the two feathers on the right of her head. She met nothing but smiles whenever she met anyone they all seem very pleased to see her dressed as she was. When Friend of Bear returned with three other braves, Ruth went with Clear Water to look at the two bear skins they had. Friend of Bear took one look at her smiled and pronounced his opinion. 'Por Jaga na Kala por.'

Ruth watched as several squaws stretched the bear skins out over a large frame and then started to scrape the underside and wash off any blood on the fur side.

By now, Ruth was used to being in the village, she felt comfortable walking around it by herself or going into the large tribe lodge in order to find out how the squaws prepared the meal. She learnt a lot by just watching the Indians working.

When it came to the time to go to sleep Ruth was not so sure; if she took the dress off all she would be left with was the loincloth. It was with considerable concern that she took the feathers out of her hair and removed the dress to get under the furs that night. She need not have worried, and as she went to sleep, Ruth started to feel part of Friend of Bear's family.

The Indians gave her some of their oats. The winter had not been harsh and the previous year they had a good crop. She went home to her cabin loaded down with items she had received from the Indians, including some more salt.

When she woke the following day for a brief moment, she considered dressing in her normal clothing then decided she would put the indian dress back on and even put the two feathers in her hair. As she did, she wondered why she had two feathers; it made her more important than those with only one.

It still felt strange to Ruth with the slipper shoes on, but her boots would not last forever, she had already removed the last of the padding and if her feet grew anymore, her boots would not fit her. It took a while; however, as time passed Ruth became used to the soft Indian shoes. She started to move lightly over the ground, feeling for the ground below her feet. Summer came; Natlatan arrived early one morning and made her use the bow and arrow again. After practicing for some time the two of them went hunting. Ruth started to judge the flight of a bird; not that she managed to hit them. After shooting at birds, rabbits were much easier, and throwing a spear at a deer just behind the front legs would kill it. She still had the good spear with a shaped and sharpened bone point.

Ruth still preferred to use the method of hunting she had worked out with the wolves; in the afternoon, she took Natlatan hunting her way. A mile or so to the west of her cabin they found a moose grazing in a small clearing. Moose were something the Indians did not often tackle Ruth set the trap of wolves and then skirted the moose with Natlatan. With Zak at her side she ran towards the moose; she almost reached the animal before it became aware of her. Ruth was still well up with the moose when the other wolves started to leap at it. The moose, concerned about the wolves paid less attention to where Ruth was; it slowed and turned slightly. When another wolf joined in the chase Ruth found herself running beside the moose with the wolves snapping at it. Holding on tightly onto her spear, she jumped and grabbed the moose round the neck. The moose staggered, more wolves joined in repeatedly attacking as Ruth clung to the animal's neck. Ruth felt the moose stumble as it tried to free itself from her hold. The moose stumbled again and this time its front legs buckled under it, throwing Ruth forward; she scrambled back and flung herself over the moose as her spear penetrating the flank of the animal. The wolves were all around it; there was no escape for the moose.

The moose was dead, her spear in its side and its throat torn out by the wolves. Natlatan arrived on the scene; he was delighted with their hunt. 'Por! Latan jadpog latan!' Ruth got off the ground and brushed the dirt from the Indian dress. 'Oh, I'm puffed,' she panted, resting a hand on Natlatan she spoke in his language, 'Latan tod, kala jadpog.'

'Da pi jad! Jaga na Kala e kala jadpog, nat por jadpog.'

They were a long way from the cabin nearer the village than the cabin. 'Ella daqua Daga Kala, e tod latan,' Ruth suggested.

'Da,' Natlatan responded nodding his head as he spoke, very pleased they had a moose to take with them.

Ruth would have dragged the moose, Natlatan did not; he cut two stout poles and bound the moose to them. It was a lot easier to drag the moose towards the village using the two poles, although it was still hard work. Several from the village came running out to meet them and helped drag it down the last hill. The chief came to look at the moose. 'Por, por jadpog.'

'Jaga na Kala e kala jadpog,' Natlatan told the chief. Ruth stood trying to follow what Natlatan was telling the chief. She guessed he was explaining how they had caught the moose. The chief listened nodding. 'Por umta,' he said, 'Natmesh.' To Ruth the chief's last statement sounded like an order rather than saying, they had a lot of food. She was more certain of that when several who were standing around looking at the moose left quickly going to the large woodpile. They were soon building a large fire in the centre of the circle. The squaws took the moose to the tribe lodge.

'Natmesh,' Natlatan said, pointing to the fire, which was now burning in the centre of the circle. It did not take long to prepare the moose with a stout pole though it. Several carried it over to the fire in the centre of the circle, which was by now a mass of glowing embers, and placed over it. Ruth and Natlatan watched for a while as the moose was slowly turned. 'Por, natmesh.'

When it came time to sit in the circle and eat everyone became excited. When Friend of Bear waved her over to him, Ruth went to where she sat in the circle. 'Por natmesh.'

'Natmesh, big eat, what does that mean.'

'Feast, we have feast.'

'Ah,' Ruth responded as she took her bowl from him. It was quite a feast and the Indians did not forget the wolves, they ate well. Zak lay down between Ruth and Friend of Bear he had a large bone with a lot of meat on it, grumbling away to himself as he enjoyed it.

That summer saw Ruth visit the Indians several times she would go to the village for a day or two. Often the Indians visited her; when they arrived, all work stopped. Ruth would spend the day swimming in the lake with them. Wolves were a common sight around the village and Ruth's cabin; no one paid a great deal of attention to them. Given free range, a wolf would wander around or sit in the sun watching what was going on around it. Should, for any reason, a wolf need food it was fed.

Natlatan continued to teach Ruth how to shoot a bow and throw a light spear. He also showed her how to select a branch and make a spear. He cut down a small tree not far from the cabin, telling her that it would grow good spears. Ruth knew from an area of coppiced wood on the farm in England that the growth in two or three years would make good light spears. Using a thicker branch Natlatan showed her how to make a heavy spear, shape and then sharpen a bone point and bind it to the stave. 'Por latan jadpog,' he said when they had finished. Ruth could see that by using the larger and heavier spear to stab a moose it would certainly bring a moose down. It took a lot more effort to throw the heavy spear, but the light one would not be as effective when thrown at a moose. Natlatan explain that the heavy spear was for hunting moose and bear.

One day when several Indians came to see her, they ended up showing Ruth how to build a lodge. First, they cut a large number of branches from the trees then stripped most of the smaller branches off to form a number of fans. Two of them used a length of vine the height of a man to scratch a circle in the dirt; having marked the edge of the hut large, the fan shaped branches were knocked into the ground. Once she had seen what they were doing, Ruth helped weave smaller fan shape branches into the framework using the other small branches, which had been cut off the fans. Until it formed a framework of twigs the width of a hand. With the framework completed, the Indians used mud on both the inside and outside filling the spaces between the open structure of twigs until the lodge was a strong structure with a hole at the top to let the smoke out. Additional branches supported the roof while it dried. They told her the supports had to stay there until the mud had dried and that it would take several days. In addition to the hut they made a large shallow bowl, which once the roof had dried and become hard, would cover the hole in the centre leaving a space between it and the roof for the smoke to escape. Ruth left it alone and the next time the Indians visited her they arrived with several old furs to cover the entrance. It made a good home, and hunting parties used the lodge overnight if they were nearby.

A few Indians continued to visit her during the autumn as Ruth prepared for winter. She was always pleased to see them. The days became extremely short, yet still no snow had fallen, though it was cold. Eventually the snows came and turned everywhere white.

Winter that year was very short; spring came early and with the spring, the work started again. Ruth worked in her fields preparing and then planting her normal crops of beans and turnip. After sowing her normal crops, she started to create a new field into which she intended to sow the oats she had obtained from the Indians. Her two fields were the same size; she decided to make the new field the same length but only half the width to start with.

It was hard work creating a new field; after two days Ruth still had at least another days work before she could think of sowing the seeds. She was busy the following day when several Indians arrived. 'Portag!' they called out. Ruth turned over the sod before responding. 'Apar pog,' one of them said.

'Da, apa e apa tag pog.'

'Piapar pog, ap tag pog.' With that, they all set about clearing an area the same size as Ruth original fields. She showed them how to use the hoe and rake in order to break the large lumps up and create a tilled field. Everyone worked hard and the field was ready to sow that evening. 'Por,' Ruth said standing back to look at a very nice field, which was ready to seed. She now had three fields extending into the meadow behind the cabin, and would be able to sow all the seeds she had been given. 'Da porpog peapar porpog. Nakella pi pog mesh e piapar umta,' Ruth said believing she should at least feed them as they had worked hard most of the day.

'Da porpog peapar tashka daqua,' one of them said pointing at the single lodge.

'Da.'

Ruth went and made a meal while they lit a fire in the lodge. They all sat outside the cabin to eat the meal. Ruth sowed the oats seeds the following morning. The Indians swished long bunches of twigs over the area she had cast the seeds covering them slightly. It did not take long to finish sowing the field. With the work finished, Ruth returned to the village with them. The children were pleased to see her wolves as they could play with them. They were soon chasing Jake all round the village and the more they chased him, the better Jake liked it.

While Ruth was in the Indian village, she learnt how to make the soft shoes; unlike her boots, they were easy to make and if they wore out you simply made another pair. Ruth soon found out she needed four or five new pairs a year. She also learnt how to prepare and then cut skins to make a loincloth or a dress. Ruth was sitting by Meechamegan's lodge trying to make herself a better pair of shoes than her first attempt at it. She had marked a skin using her feet as a template and had managed to cut the two soles out. Meechamegan arrived as she was stitching the side of one shoe up. 'Paga na Daga Kala tak Jaga na Kala ella pi daqua,' he said coming to where she was sitting.

'The chief said come to his home,' Ruth responded as she got up.

'Da you learn good.'

Ruth accompanied Meechamegan to the chief's lodge; inside it was different to Meechamegan's. The large chief's headdress of feathers was hanging on the wall of the lodge and there were many decorative spears leaning against the wall beside the headdress. The furs on the floor covered most of the ground except for an area around the fire. He invited her to sit down with him by the small fire, which was burning with almost no smoke. Meechamegan sat with her ready to translate when necessary. The chief produced four large knives, Ruth guessed they come from the trappers; he spoke to Friend of Bear for a while.

'Chief say what made of.'

Ruth did not quite know what to say, 'Metal,'

'Not know,'

'I know you don't, you can't make it and I don't know how it's made.' Ruth thought about the blacksmith back on the estate; it would be impossible to explain how metal was worked to the Indians.

Meechamegan spoke to the chief for a while then turned to Ruth. 'Chief say you have.'

'Da,' Ruth said taking her knife from the sheath on her belt. She passed it to the chief for him to look at.

'Por,' the chief responded taking the knife and examining it. They talked for some time about what to do with the trappers' knives. Ruth suggested they use them in the tribe lodge so that those who needed to cut the most had them, as it would be better than the bone knives. The chief would not hear of the squaws having them. In the end, he took the largest one. Meechamegan had another and then the two best hunters. Ruth spent time showing the four of them how to sharpen their knives on a stone. It was not a great deal different to the way they shaped and sharpened their bone knives. That summer Ruth learnt a lot; she was more able to use their language and being able to speak to the Indians using their language, made it easier for them to explain things to her.

Back in her cabin, Ruth worked in the fields until they were all right. She was dragging one of the unused logs towards the stream which ran past the cabin with the intention of making a bridge over it so she would not have to wade through the stream every time she went in that direction. Meechamegan and another brave appeared; they could not understand what she wanted to do with the log. Never the less they helped her. The brave walked across the log balancing as he did. 'Nakpor,' he said, shaking his head.

'Apa e apa ella,' Ruth responded. The two of them followed her back to where the other logs were and the three of them dragged the next one and placed it beside the first. 'Da, pi jad, por, e ap,' Meechamegan said as soon as he understood. After dragging the five logs to the stream and making sure, they were all at the same level. Ruth started to take medium stones from the stream putting them between the logs filling the space between each log with stones large enough not to fall between the gaps between the logs. The two Indians soon understood and followed her example. It did not take that long to have a smooth surface of stones over the length of the bridge. Meechamegan stood back and admired their work. 'Por, nak poola, Por,' he said going back and forth across the bridge.

There was a good crop of beans; towards the end of summer, Ruth harvested them first, then it was the turn to gather in her oats. This meant she had to work out a method of threshing them and then had to search for two suitable stones, which she could use to crush the oats. The summer ended, and with that, the hard work of autumn started. Ruth was now stronger, she thought about this while cutting the wood and comparing her present ability with the first time, she had chopped the wood for the winter.

She was fully prepared when winter arrived and turned her wilderness white. That winter she spent a lot of time making clothes from the skins she had saved; it kept her occupied during the winter. She wrapped warm leggings, made of rabbit skins, around her legs. She carefully stitched a layer of fur into what was her father's jacket until she had the perfect coat.

'Hello Zak,' Ruth said as the wolf came into the cabin, pushing the door open with his nose. 'It's cold out there isn't it?' She added as Zak settled down in front of the fire.

The winter was neither good nor bad; it was long enough to have Ruth waiting impatiently for spring to come. She had plenty of food and it lasted well. Now she had salt, her meals were not so bland. On very cold days, she let the other wolves come into the cabin to get warm, but in general, they seemed happy enough in the cave, though they had managed to jump up and get some of the meat.

Another year started the sun had warmth in it again; Meechamegan came with Porjadseeni while Ruth was still hard at work. 'Paga tak ella hi Jaga na Kala piapa pog e Jaga na Kala.'

'The chief said help me.'

'Da, pe ap e nat pog, piapar por pog.'

'Da, porpog.'

The work was much easier with the three of them. Ruth continued to work with Friend of Bear while Clear Water went to make their meal. The three of them completed the work of spring in far less time than it usually took Ruth.

When Meechamegan and Porjadseeni had first arrived, Ruth noticed that Porjadseeni had with her several small, bucket-like, containers made of wood; at the time, she had wondered why she had them. Having now finished the work in the fields the two of them took Ruth into the woods telling her to bring her largest cooking pot. Having selected a particular tree Meechamegan used a stone axe to cut a V-shaped gash in the tree. It started to bleed sap almost immediately. Porjadseeni used several leaves in order to guide the sap into one of the small buckets she had. 'Por, make daga mesh por. You learn good,' Meechamegan said. By the time they had tapped the fifth tree, the first small bucket was ready to empty into her cooking pot. By the time the three of them returned to the cabin, Ruth's pot was half-full. The sap they had collected then had to be boiled over a fire; it reduced the amount in the pot by about half. Pleased she had some syrup Ruth looked for one of her jars in order to store it.

Later that day after their meal, Ruth was sitting beside Meechamegan. 'Pe nak paga, pe paga tod?' He asked.

Ruth looked down at the ground, 'Da,' she responded thinking of the way her father had died.

'Pi jad pe paga.'

'You saw my farther!'

'Da, apar yar ween.'

Ruth had to think what that meant, 'Many summers ago,' she said.

'Da.'

'Pe paga jad Natelena, tak Natelena poota Jaga na Kala. Natelena tak Elena na Kala, poota Jaga na Kala. Elena na Kala por poota Jaga na Kala.'

Ruth had not understood all Meechamegan had said, but she did understand one bit. 'Pi paga jad Natelena,' she said supprised that he should think that.

'Da.'

For a while, Ruth sat in silence thinking about her father and what she knew about the Great Spirit. He had not been killed by anyone, it was an accident, he died at the right time; it was his time to see the Great Spirit. It was some time before Friend of Bear spoke and when he did, it was in a quiet voice. 'Paga na Daga Kala tak, pi tak e Jaga na Kala, tak Meechamegan paga na Jaga na Kala.'

'You are my father!'

'Nak, pi tak pe paga.'

Ruth did not understand, he had said he wasn't her father then said he was. It took her a while to work it out; he was asking to be her father; her stepfather. She liked the idea a great deal. 'You will be my father,'

'Da you say por?'

'Da,' Ruth responded.

Meechamegan smiled at her. 'Por, pe e pi tak Paga na Daga Kala.'

Ruth returned to the Indian village with the two of them. That first evening after the meal, Meechamegan took Ruth to the chief. The chief stood up as the two of them approached smiling at Ruth as they stood in front of him. Ruth liked the chief he was a man who had a lot of wisdom and led the tribe in a quiet way. 'Paga na Daga Kala pi tak Jaga na Kala binjaga na Meechamegan,' Friend of Bear said. The chief nodded in his direction then looked at Ruth. 'Jaga na Kala tak,' he said.

Ruth had to think fast Friend of Bear had told the chief that she was his daughter; she believed that she should say something along the same lines. 'Pi tak Meechamegan pi paga.'

The chief beamed a huge smile on his face. 'Por, tak por,' he said, speaking to Ruth. Then in a much louder voice, the chief spoke to the rest of the tribe, 'Daga Kala, Jaga na Kala binjaga na Meechamegan!'

'Portag Jaga na Kala, binjaga na Meechamegan,' those sitting around the circle responded.

'Say hello to tribe,' Friend of Bear quietly said. 'Turn to see them,' he added as he turned to face the rest of the tribe. Ruth did the same turning her back on the chief. 'Portag Daga Kala,' she said as clearly as she could.

'Por,' Meechamegan quietly said. 'Ella piapa daqua,' he added as he led her back to their place in the circle. 'You now family; it right now,' Friend of Bear said as they sat back down.

'Portag Jaga na Kala,' Porjadseeni said.

'Portag, it's nice to be part of your family, tell her what I said.'

'Da.' Ruth listened as Friend of Bear explained to Clearwater.

Ruth felt completely accepted by the Indians, she was part of an Indian family she had a position in the tribe and the village felt like a second home to her. She helped around the village, doing whatever she could; most of all she liked going hunting particularly when they let her take her wolves. One of the Indians who had three feathers in his hair came to their lodge early one morning. Meechamegan and Ruth went with him to see the chief and spirit man. Ruth did not understand a lot of the conversation, and Meechamegan translated little of it, however, the meeting with the chief and spirit man finished with smiles and nodding of heads. 'Por, nat por chief e spirit man say it right you hunt with wolves. Great Spirit say it right to hunt like you.'

One morning Natlatan came to Meechamegan's lodge. They spoke for a while then Meechamegan came to where Ruth was sitting making a new dress. 'Piapa ella ojar, pog cash, pe ella.'

'Cash, ah da pi ella.'

'Por aptag piapar ella ojar.'

The following day the three of them set off early in the morning. Natlatan carried two long poles, while Meechamegan and Ruth had a fur each. They set off heading north towards the mountains. By midmorning they were in the mountains walking north all day the peaks of the mountains towering above them. It was hard going, Natlatan kept up a good pace. The sun was starting to set by the time they reached a large cave. 'Por, piapar hi,' Natlatan said as the three of them walked into the wide entrance.

Ruth sat down; she was pleased to be off her feet for a while. Zak came and lay beside her. 'Are your paws sore, we have walk miles?' Ruth said as she stroked him. Natlatan gathered some wood and soon had a fire burning. Evening was coming and there was a chill in the mountain air. They had a meal and sorted out the two furs. Ruth was pleased to get between the furs and close her eyes.

'Nak tashka,' Natlatan said shaking her in the morning.

That day they went deeper into the cave, they needed touches made of brush twigs with fat wrapped round the twigs in order to light the way. It was difficult to make rapid progress in the dim light given off by the torches. They reached the salt in a huge cavern. The wall of salt showed signs of previous working. Ruth watched as the two of them started to cut a slab; it was going to be hard work cutting it out with their knives. Ruth took her knife out, 'Nak, pi pog,' she said moving the two of them away from where they were working. In the dim light of the torch, she could just make out where the two of them had marked the line they intended to cut a slab of salt. With all the effort she could muster, Ruth stabbed her knife into the soft rock. She repeated it several times the knife penetrating to the hilt as she drove it into the salt. After several stabs at the large area of salt, the rock split. 'Por, porpog,' Natlatan called out, kicking the sizable block of salt, which was almost free, with his heal. On the third or fourth kick, it broke loose. 'Por,' Meechamegan said as the two of them started to wrestle the block of salt out of its resting position. Then they had to drag it back to the opening of the cave.

On the second trip into the cave, Ruth gave Natlatan her knife. He attacked the wall of rock salt with gusto. It was not long before he had another slab ready for them to carry up to the caves entrance. They managed three trips deep into the cave during the day. Each time they returned with large slab of salt. Natlatan lashed all three slabs onto the two long poles, and the following day they set of back to the village. It took two days to get back to the village. The chief was pleased to see the amount they had. Meechamegan explained that they needed the knives they had taken from the trappers when they went for salt. The chief agreed telling them again that they had done well.

Ruth had been in the village for almost a full moon when she thought she should return to her cabin and find out what needed doing. Meechamegan told her they would visit her when they had a rest day. Ruth left the Indian village the following day with another small block of salt.

Back in her cabin, Ruth soon finished all the jobs, which required her attention, her crops were growing nicely. The summer was just starting and all the signs would suggest it was going to be a long and hot one. It was already getting very warm in the middle of the day. Although the water in the lake was still on the cold side, Ruth would swim in the lake then lie in the sun until her loincloth was dry letting the warmth of sun dry her body.

Summer arrived; the days were hot, the sun shone in a perfectly blue sky. Ruth had worked in the fields that morning. It was far too hot to go hunting in the middle of the day, and later this evening she believed there would be more chance of finding something in the cool of early evening. The swim had been good, the water refreshing after the mornings work. Ruth lay down in the grass in order to dry. It was wonderfully warm the grass below her felt good, she felt at one with everything around her. She was part of the wilderness, her wolves were part of that wilderness; everything was as it should be. Friend of Bear was right when he spoke of the Great Spirit, someone had to make everything and this was unlike anywhere in England. Life on the farm was never like this. Everything here was right, there was no squire in his large house, there was just people living and working. Ruth looked up into a perfectly blue sky. Everything around her was good and as it should be. She lay there thinking of the deer resting in the shade of a tree, the rabbit sitting under a bush, the wolves lying in the sun. All of them, like her, enjoying their lives, until it came their time to meet and talk to the Great Spirit.

Chapter 7

Zak came to her; he bent his head down, smelt her then stepped over her. 'Hello Zak lie down it is too hot to rush around. Have a sleep in the sun.'

He grumbled; Ruth did not like the way he sounded. 'What's wrong?' She asked sitting up her hands reaching for him. Zak grumbled again. Ruth looked around. Another wolf near her did not look happy as it sniffed the air, then it grumbled and Zak howled. Her family of wolves came down to where Ruth was from the direction of the cabin. Zak continued to howl, his loud call echoing off the mountains on the opposite side of the lake.

Another wolf arrived shaking himself as he joined those already there as they started to mass round Ruth. It was not long before wolves surrounded Ruth, she became concerned they could obviously sense danger but she could not see any cause for their concern.

Ruth crouched down amongst the wolves looking around the area, she could not see anything certainly nothing, which would give the wolves cause to act in the way they were. Several wolves had started to move towards the eastern end of the small bay. It could be a bear, she thought, remembering the last time in the fields. It was definitely something coming from the east. The wolves remain unsure of what it was but they were all uneasy and waiting for whatever it was to arrive. All eyes remain turned towards the east; it seemed to Ruth as if time had stood still. She was not frightened but she wished she knew what was upsetting all the wolves. As time passed, Ruth became more concerned. Thoughts that it could be the trappers crossed her mind; if it were then the wolves would protect her. Even if there were more than the two trappers, she had sent away, the wolves would be able to protect her. Several of the wolves were now making their way towards the far end of the small bay.

Ruth watched as one of the wolves reached the headland jump up onto the rock at the very point of the headland. It yapped; others there joined it. The additional yapping and snarling from the eastern headland sent most of the remaining wolves in that direction. There was a high degree of excitement amongst them. Ruth remained with Zak and a few of her family. She crouched down, as low as she could so whatever it was would not see her standing there. By the reaction of the wolves, Ruth knew whatever it was had at last reached them. Because it had taken a while, it had allowed more wolves to answer Zak's call.

Ruth saw a large log drift into view about twenty yards out from the headland. For a brief moment, she wondered why the wolves were upset about a log. Then her mind questioned why it was moving up the lake and not down. While she was thinking about this, she saw a man sitting in the rear and realised it was a crude canoe made from a large tree and given very little shape. The man in it was paddling slowly as he watched the wolves on the headland who were now snarling at him. The man noticed the cabin; and with difficulty started to turn the canoe towards the small sandy bay. Ruth left her family of wolves running down the bank, and across the small sandy beach, into the water. She started to swim towards the man in the canoe.

'Don't land here! She cried out 'Don't land here! The wolves will attack you.'

The man stopped paddling sitting in the canoe watching her as she swam up to it. Ruth reached out holding onto the front of the large canoe. From a distance the canoe look makeshift, close up it looked no better, no one had tried to shape it or even take the bark off. 'Don't land here they could kill you. Go across the lake don't land anywhere between here and all the way round to over there on the other side, the wolves will track you; and there are a load more at the end of the lake. Don't land there.'

Ruth noticed the man was looking past her she turned to see Zak coming to her. Letting go of the log Ruth swam towards Zak. 'Zak, go back to the shore,' she said, turning him. He was well out of his depth and could not have swum much further. Having made sure Zak was back in shallow water; Ruth swam back to the man in the canoe. 'Why have you come here?' She asked once she reached canoe again.

'Because you were here,' he replied.

Ruth did not like the fact he knew about her; he could only have known if he was with the trappers. 'If you know

I am here you are a fool coming; you must know about the wolves as well.'

'They didn't say there were so many,' the man responded looking towards the shore and the wolves.

'Who didn't?' Ruth demanded to know.

'Couple of trappers,' the man replied.

'Them!' She exclaimed, 'I told them to stay away from this end of the lake; so why are you here?'

'They were killed by a bear, nowhere else to go.'

Ruth did not want anyone in her wilderness; it was hers and the Indians. She did not want anyone else there who would spoil the way she lived. 'Why didn't you stay there?' she demanded to know.

'Alone.'

'I am!'

'You have hundreds of wolves,' the man said pointing at the wolves now lined up along the shore. Looking towards the shore Ruth saw Zak standing in the shallow water of the small sandy bay watching with Jake and the rest of her family behind him. Further back there were a large number of other wolves all watching her, their heads down. Even to Ruth who was used to having wolves around her they looked impressive she was certainly safe in her wilderness with a pack that size to protect her, but it was nowhere near a hundred wolves. She looked back towards the man. He looked younger than the two trappers had, not more than a couple of years older than she was. 'I brought all I could with me, if you need anything you can have it,' he said, his attention now on Ruth.

'I don't need anything, I have everything I need.'

'I came up this end to find somewhere round here; I will not be too near you.'

'I don't know. I don't suppose you can go far in this today; unless you go over the other side of the lake.'

'It has taken me three days to come up here from the other end. I had to stay close to the shore. Didn't like to go too far out; this leaks, didn't want to chance it in deep water.'

The canoe did not look as if it were able to go across the lake. Ruth was of two minds; the man did not seem to be a threat to her. She had the wolves, her pack would accept the man if he was with her and did not attack her. One man in a badly made canoe would not cause her any trouble. She wondered if he was alone, this could be a trap. The others could have sent him first and then when she was not expecting it attack her. 'Are you alone, are there others with you?'

'There's just me, I'm not going to bother you.'

Ruth thought he was telling the truth. Her family of wolves would look after her. 'You better stay the night I suppose.'

'Thank you, I will not bother you.'

'So you said, follow me and don't do anything to upsets my wolves.'

'I won't; I have never seen so many all in one place.'

'Don't be frightened of them they will not hurt you if you are with me. Now follow me,' Ruth ordered.

Ruth reached the shore and walked out of the water. She turned, 'Come ashore here it is sandy here and shallow.'

'Do you want to dress first?' The trapper asked.

Ruth, for the first time, became aware she only had the loincloth on. 'Oh yes, you look away,' she said feeling uneasy, he was not part of her wilderness, he was an outsider and would not understand the ways of the wilderness as the Indians did. Ruth rapidly made her way through the pack of wolves, up the bank to where her clothes were. She quickly slipped on her dress, wrapping her belt round her waist and checking on the position of her knife. Finally, she picked up her two feathers and put them in her hair as she made her way back to the sandy beach. He was standing in the shallow water holding the crude, log canoe about ten yards from the shore his back to her, looking out over the lake. Ruth put her hand out towards Zak as she reached his side. 'You can turn round now,' she told the man.

'Oh right.' He said, turning round. He stood there, his mouth open staring at her. For a moment or two, Ruth wondered what was going on; he had not moved he was just standing there staring at her. It took a while for Ruth realised he had not expected to see her dressed in Indian clothes. 'This is how I normally dress,' she said by way of explanation, 'pull the canoe up here.' He went to say something but stopped himself before he started. Zak nuzzled her hand; she reached out a hand without looking and stroked his head; still unsure what was going on. Ruth watched the man's eyes look to her left then right. Ruth looked around her. The wolves were all there, she was standing with Zak at the front of a large pack of wolves. Ruth looked back towards the man.

'You're Indian,' he said the surprise in his voice very noticeable.

'No,' Ruth responded, 'but I have some of their clothes.'

He was still standing there staring at her. Ruth looked around at the wolves. 'They will not harm you if you don't attack me,' she told him

'That is the last thing I am going to do. Why have you got feathers in your hair, if you are not Indian?'

Ruth did not like all the questions, the feathers showed her position in the tribe but she was not going to tell him that. He had no reason to know Meechamegan was her Indian father. 'Because I have, I like them. Pull the canoe out here.'

Ruth watched as the man pulled the canoe towards the shore. She moved back a little to give him the space to pull the canoe out of the water pulling it a little way up the small beach, until it stuck in the sand, its weight holding it down so that it could not be moved further up the beach. Sheba moved towards him, he turned and saw her. 'That is Sheba,' Ruth told him as the wolf stuck her nose out towards him. He started to move back. 'Don't!' Ruth called out as he continued to move away from Sheba. 'Stand still and let her smell you. The other one is Zak just let him smell you.' Ruth watched, as the two wolves nervously smelt the man then backed away from him. 'Come here Zak,' Ruth said calling the wolf to her. Then she looked at the man, he was frightened and did not look comfortable with all the wolves watching him.

'Move slowly, don't run away from them or they will chase you. Get some things out of the canoe and follow me; you can put it outside the cabin for the time being.'

Ruth went and stood on the bank where she could watch him. The man made several trips between the canoe and the cabin. He seemed to have brought a lot with him; he had snares and all manner of trapping equipment. The wolves lost interest in the man; and what he was doing; some of them started to disperse.

Ruth was standing on the upper bank waiting for him to reach her. He had an armful of items he had taken out of the canoe. Zak yapped and ran off to meet a group of Indians. The Indians paid no attention to him or the other wolves in the area they ran past them heading for Ruth. They were all carrying several spears as well as bows and arrows. 'Daga Kala ella, paga tak daqua na Jaga na Kala porella, e poota,' Friend of Bear said as they arrived. They all saw the man on the shore below the bank and prepared to throw a spear at him. 'Nak meecha! Meecha nak pogtod!' Ruth shouted.

'Tak Jaga na Kala e Natlatan pogtod.'

'Nak!' Ruth called out as she went to Natlatan and stood in front of him. He looked very strong in just a loincloth and she knew he would kill anyone if she needed him to. 'Nak,' she quietly said placing her hand on his spear arm. 'Nak pogtod,' she said as she gently stroked his arm.

'Natlatan por meecha na Jaga na Kala.'

'Da, nat meecha,' Ruth quietly said.

'Da,' Natlatan said lowering his arm.

'Paga tak poota Jaga na Kala,' Friend of Bear said.

Ruth turned towards him. They had come to protect her, they must have heard Zak call the other wolves and they had come straight away. 'Por tak,' Ruth responded believing that she should praise the chief for asking them to come to her aid.

'Hish paga meecha?' he asked.

'Da, Pi tak paga nakella ap tag.'

'Ap tag.'

'Ap apa,' Ruth said shrugging her shoulders as she spoke.

'Paga meecha?' Friend of Bear asked again.

Ruth look towards the trapper, she no longer felt threatened by his arrival. He did not look as if he knew a lot about the wilderness and he was certainly very frightened with the appearance of the Indians. 'Da,' she responded to Friend of Bear's question.

'Por, Daga Kala ella daqua, tak hish paga meecha.'

'Da; porpog, porpog.'

'Da,' Meechamegan said then looking down at Zak, he added. 'Zak, poota Jaga na Kala, por poota.' He turned his attention back to Ruth. 'Portag Jaga na Kala, Portag.'

'Portag Meechamegan paga na Jaga na Kala, peapar porpog.'

Friend of Bear smiled, 'Pe, por binjaga.' He turned to the others and told them they would return to the village. Ruth briefly spoke to Natlatan then watched them leave, waving as they entered the wood.

Ruth stroked Zak as she turned back towards the man who was still standing below the bank. 'You can come up here now, you are quite safe.'

'The wolves did not seem to bother them. I thought they were going to kill us.'

'Not us, they were sent here to kill you not me. I have more than wolves protecting me here. The wolves know they are friends and some are in their village as well as here. See those are going with them,' Ruth said as several wolves made their way towards the point the braves from the tribe had left.

'It explains why you are dressed like an Indian.'

Ruth felt strong; the young trapper was no match for her. 'It's better, I blend in more. You wouldn't see me coming in a wood, I would be on you before you even knew I was there with a ring of wolves around you.'

'I believe you; that was impressive you can speak their language.'

'They are my neighbours. Come on up the bank the wolves will not bother you; walk around as you normally would.'

'I will not stay long.'

'I told the Indians that you would be here a day or two.'

'Right that is fair, I will find somewhere round here.'

The man had emptied the canoe; most of the wolves had gone; only her family were now paying close attention to what the trapper was doing. Zak remained close to Ruth all the time and kept an eye on the trapper. Ruth thought it was getting near the time when she should be thinking about a meal. She had planned to hunt late afternoon earlier that day. Ruth felt uneasy leaving him around the cabin while she was away; she did not trust him and definitely did not want him in her cabin without her being there as well. 'I have no meat for the meal tonight so I have to go hunting,' she told the man.

'I will come,' he immediately said. Ruth thought he was just as unsure of the wolves as she was of him. Probably more so as she did not see him as a threat, he could not harm her if he tried, her family would be on him immediately. It was going to be difficult hunting with him around, but at least if he was with her he would not be alone around the cabin. 'As long as you don't get in my way,' Ruth responded as she turned towards the cabin door.

Ruth came out of the cabin with a light spear in her hand. All her spears now had two tail feathers from a tencha, the large bird she hunted, tied to the back of them as well as good bone points. The spear that she had selected had a long bone point shaped like a knife with two sharp edges and point. 'We will go this way,' Ruth said turning to the east and starting to move towards the woods. She led the trapper though the woods towards the place where Ruth knew she would find a few deer. One small deer would be all she needed. As she made her way towards the area, Ruth was aware of the noise he made while walking. Very aware of the ground beneath her feet Ruth moved lightly though the wood while he clumped along in heavy boots.

Ruth soon found the signs of a deer where it had taken the bark off a young sapling. Moving carefully now, she started to look around. She went down, as did Zak. She waved the man down, and then quietly said 'Stay here. Stay here and stay quiet; Zak stay,' she ordered before skirting round the deer until it was between her and Zak. She approached slowly at first then once she had got nearer Ruth started running towards the deer her feet light over the forest floor she was twenty yards away from the deer when it became aware of her. The deer ran towards where Zak was lying. Ruth was about to throw her spear at the fleeing deer when Zak stood up. Ruth judged the deer would turn to the right. As her foot came down her body twisted the arm holding the spear started its forward movement. As her body turned the spear arm flashed forward propelling the spear towards an empty space. The deer jumped high to its right. The spear, traveling at speed, its flight true, hit the deer slightly behind the front legs. The long knife like point penetrated deep into the body of the deer until it reached its heart.

By the time it fell to the ground the deer was dead. Ruth walked up to the deer and pulled her spear out of it then picked it up; aware it would be talking to the Great Spirit. Silently she thanked the Great Spirit for sending her the deer. 'You can stand up now! I have it.'

'How did you get there?'

'Went round it; didn't you see Zak stand up?'

'He just stood up and snarled; that was all.'

'That is what he was there to do. There are also three wolves to your right not more than ten yards away from you. Jake!' The wolf stood up and came towards her. Ruth could see in the man's face that he was uneasy; he looked around for the other wolves as Ruth walked up to him. 'There and there,' Ruth said as she pointed towards the two wolves. Ruth felt confident the trapper was no threat to her, she was perfectly safe, he would not cause her any problems; he was not at home in the wilderness. He reached out towards her. 'May I carry that for you?'

'Thank you,' Ruth replied passing the deer to him. At least he was polite Ruth thought. It did not take long to walk back to the cabin.

'Can you light a fire?' Ruth asked as she let him into the cabin. 'My bow is there and fire stick is there with the two pieces of bark.'

'I have a tinder box.'

'Don't you know how to do it without a tinder box?'

'Um,' the young trapper hesitated.

'Can you clean the deer then?'

'I can do that.'

'Well you do that; give the insides to any wolf that is around. I will get the fire going.'

'May I watch how you do it?'

'If you want, I haven't got a tinder box,' Ruth said as she reached for her small fire bow. 'I used to have one, but used up all the flints. Now I do it this way.' It did not take her long to spin the fire stick between the two pieces of bark using a small bow. The dry grass burst into flame. She placed it in the centre of the pile of twigs. 'Is that how the Indians do it?' The man asked.

'It's easy and you can get everything you need from around you; you don't have to carry a tinderbox around with you.' Ruth started to get the fire burning; the man left the cabin with the deer. By the time he returned with the cleaned deer, Ruth had decided she would roast the deer over the fire.

'This is good,' the man said as they ate slices of deer meat with turnip and beans.

'Everything eats well in the summer,' Ruth replied.

'You seem to and you are good with a spear. You have a bow there and arrows.'

'I don't have a musket, wouldn't be a lot of use out here you would run out of powder and shot then what do you do.'

'I had a little the others used it killing beaver.'

'I have some beavers; if you follow the stream up through the wood you will see them there and the big pond they have made. You don't kill beaver they are not here for us to eat or provide clothes; wolves can eat them but not us. We are given rabbits, deer, and moose, tencha, it's a big fat, funny looking bird, they don't fly much, that is what we have to eat and big fish but not small ones, and we have to grow food as well.'

'Where did you learn that?'

'Friend of Bear told me all about the Great Spirit, the Great Spirit provides for all of us, the deer I killed was pleased I did because it went to see the Great Spirit.'

'Didn't you learn about God?' The man asked.

'When I was on the estate in England, but he is not like the Great Spirit. You don't pray to the Great Spirit, the spirit man asks the Great Spirit to provide things and at other times when he talks to the Great Spirit. I don't have to, if the Great Spirit is pleased with me he will guide me and make me throw the spear in the right place and he will put the deer there.'

'But God is the one and only God.'

'That is in England not here; it is the Great Spirit here.'

'But God is everywhere.'

'No, the Great Spirit is here. That is why there is all the fighting in the settlement; the people there don't know it's the Great Spirit here not God. God he is in England and France and other places like that, but not here. Ask Friend of Bear he will tell you about the Great Spirit. It is right you can see, and I know it is.'

'How can you see and know.'

'It is easy, I didn't know about the Great Spirit when I first came here, and it was hard to find food, and my father fell off the cliff and was killed, and bad things happened to me, and I was all alone and it was a bad winter. Then Zak came, the Great Spirit sent him to show me what to do and protected me and give me food. I didn't know wolves gave you food but they do if the Great Spirit sends them to you. The spirit of the wolf is a good spirit it is a hunter. The Indian tribe is the wolf tribe the wolf is their spirit and I am Jaga na Kala. I have pleased the spirit of the wolf, which is why they come to me. The wolves know that Zak was sent to me by the Great Spirit.'

'Jaga what.'

'Jaga na Kala. You should talk to Friend of Bear. He tells me about it, he may be the next spirit man, he knows about the spirits and the Great Spirit you can tell he does. He knows what is right and wrong, what the Great Spirit has sent us to kill for food and clothes. That is what a spirit man has to know isn't it.'

'You are very interesting to talk to; they told me there was a mad girl who had gone Indian.'

'Oh them, they tried to rape a squaw and when Binojar stop them they killed him. Well those two didn't the other one did, he is now guarding Binojar's spirit so it knows when to go and meet the Great Spirit.'

'What; he fell out a tree; you attacked him with your wolves.'

'No he didn't! He had his head cut off for murder,' Ruth explained, 'Ask anyone I'll show you if you come to the village.'

'They said you killed him with your wolves.'

'No, my wolves found out who killed Binojar that is all they did, they smelt death on him, they didn't even bite him, Jake wanted to, but didn't.'

'You seem surprised I didn't know that.'

'I shouldn't be I suppose they wouldn't tell the truth because of what they did. I told them to stay at the end of the lake.'

'Well they will not be leaving it now, they attacked a bear and it killed both of them.'

'The Great Spirit does not forget; he sent the bear to them. That is why the bear didn't harm you; it had been told not to.'

'I don't think so. It just ran off.'

'It knew, I know it did, bears know, they don't come here not any more there are no bears here you have to go to the north shore that is where they live now.'

'They used to be here then.'

'They have gone away because I am here this my land well not mind but it is where I am.'

'You said your father was killed.'

'The horse slipped off a cliff and he fell, it would have been his time, he met the Great Spirit he had been a good man the Great Spirit would have welcomed him. I didn't know at the time but Friend of Bear told me and now I am pleased for him I now know it was his time; he would have seen the Great Spirit and spoken to him.'

'It is starting to get dark.'

'I better show you where you can sleep. There may be some wolves in it but don't worry about them they are my family of wolves. You don't have to be frightened of them.'

Ruth led him round to the lodge in her meadow, 'It looks sturdy,' he said when they reached the lodge.

'It needs more skins over the entrance, but it is ok when the wind is not blowing lots,' Ruth said as she pulled those hanging over the entrance to one side. 'If you make a fire don't have it big. The smoke will go out the hole up there. Make it in the same place. I thought some would be in here. That is Jake, Sheba, that one is Paul, that one Mary.'

'These have names.'

'They are my family,' Ruth replied as she noticed one that was not. 'That one's not, I don't know that one; it's here because it hasn't anywhere to be at the moment.'

'Will it be all right if it is a wild one?'

'Yes, hello, you look a bit thin, you need feeding up is that why you are here? All right don't worry, I will give you food and make you strong again. Move over a bit though. Get off the fur for me.'

'Are you sure you don't know that one.'

'Never seen it before in my life, it has come here to get food, it is quite thin; for the summer it is really thin, oh it has a hurt paw that is why. All right, it will get better, you will be all right.' Then turning to move those that were part of her family, she added, 'Come on you lot move, get off. They like lying on the fur given the chance.'

'They are like dogs with you.'

'There you are you can sleep there ok.'

'Thank you.'

Ruth was making something to eat when the man called out from outside the cabin. 'Come in!' Ruth called back. He came into the cabin and looked around. Sheba followed him in. 'This one seems to follow me.'

'That is Sheba she is the important female round here.'

'She cleared my space again when I had to go out; got them all off the fur again. I thought I would look around today.'

'What is your name I don't know?'

'Bill, Bill Thatcher.'

'Are you a thatcher?' Ruth asked, as she stirred the porridge she had made with oats

'No, far from it; I was going to be a priest.'

'Oh,' Ruth responded, she had not expected him to say that. She looked at him again and saw a different person. 'I told you about the Great Spirit!'

'It was very enlightening.'

'But you know about God.'

'I thought I did, and I said I was going to be a priest not I am a priest. There are things I couldn't accept; I came to the New World believing I would find God here.'

'Ah and he is not here is he, you would have known that at the settlement you were in.'

'You could be so right there,'

'There is lots of fighting isn't there, that is why me and my father came here; the Indians showed us the way.'

'It is almost all out war, you don't know how peaceful it is here.'

'Of course I do, it's because we live properly here. The Great Spirit is pleased with us. He will make hard winters come to test us but he will provide for us if we are strong.'

'You could be right there; you could be right Jaga na Kala.'

'Ah, you remembered my Indian name.'

'It suits you, what does it mean? Their names have meaning don't they.'

'Mother of wolves, jaga is mother and kala is wolf.'

'I can see why the Indians would call you that.'

'My Indian father is called Meechamegan, it means Friend of Bear. I am Jaga na Kala binjaga na Meechamegan, Mother of Wolves daughter of Friend of Bear. He sort of adopted me and had to tell the chief I was part of his family. He was the one I spoke to most when they came, the one with four feathers in his hair. He is quite important in the tribe. I only have two feathers. Natlatan, a friend, he only has one.'

'You seem very settled here.'

'I am, this is my home and I like it here.' Ruth turned her attention back to the cooking pot it was almost ready to eat. When it was, she spooned it out of the pot onto two plates, passing one to Bill. 'Eat then I have to work.'

'Thank you, I will find somewhere to set myself up.'

'There's some good places about five miles east of here along the lake,' Ruth told him, believing that if he found somewhere that sort of distance from her he would not be too much bother.

Ruth worked that morning, Bill had gone to look around the area while she worked but had returned when she wanted him to be away so she could swim in the lake. Ruth was hot and sticky; it was well past midday. 'If you walk down there and just follow the path you will see where I have some snares to catch rabbits. You could have a look for me if you want,' she suggested hoping he would and she would be able to have a swim. To her relief he agreed.

As soon as Bill had left, Ruth wasted no time and was soon in the cool water of the lake. The water was wonderful, but she was unable to lie in the sun for a prolonged period; it would not take Bill long to walk round the snares. She had dressed again and felt much better for her quick swim by the time he reappeared. 'Most I found were not set or had been tripped,' he told her. Ruth was not surprised, she had not used them for a while preferring to hunt correctly, as the spirit man had told her with a spear, a bow or her family of wolves.

Several times, as Ruth prepared the meal, she became aware of Bill watching every movement she made. She was unsure of what to make of it. The following day

Bill offered to help her in the fields. As she worked Ruth glanced across to where he was working, he had certainly done it before; the rows he had tended looked good, free of all weeds, and he had pulled some of the small turnips up where they were too near the others. Bill might not know about the wilderness but he certainly knew how to tend crops. 'You have done that good,' Ruth told him when she took a short rest.

'Lots of practice, used to do this in the monastery.'

'You lived in a monastery did you?'

'Ever since I was five or six years old; grew up tending the fields and learning from the monks. I thought it was going to be my life.'

'So why did you come to the New Lands?'

'I would rather not say, let's say I found it difficult to accept what I saw. It wasn't what I thought should happen. You have done well here with these fields; it must have been hard work to do all this by yourself.'

'My father helped this year; Indian father.'

'You have more than enough here to last you a year.'

'I like to have extra food, nearly ran out the first year.'

Ruth continued to work on her area of the field, spurred on by the way Bill was doing his area. They finished the whole field that morning. Ruth was pleased with the amount of work they had done. She would not have been able to do as much without Bill's help. She took the tools back to the cave; it was too hot to carry on now the sun was high in the sky.

'You want me to take a walk?' Bill asked as they finished the work for the day.

'What.'

'I'll take a walk then you can bathe.'

'Oh, um thank you, yes, thank you.'

Ruth closed her eyes, the sun felt good on her skin and the swim had refreshed her. This was her time of rest; the fields were now fine and would not require attention for a while. If Bill were not there, she would have gone to visit the village. She wondered how long it would be before he found somewhere to be and let her get back to normal. He would need to build himself somewhere before the winter came. Ruth felt Zak laid his head on her tummy; she put a hand out to stroke him. 'Have a little rest Zak,' she quietly said.

'Portag,' someone said waking Ruth, it sounded like Natlatan. 'Portag Natlatan,' Ruth responded without opening her eyes, believing only a handful of people could have walked up to her without causing Zak to even lift his head.

'Tashka.'

'Da; por tala sor,' Ruth said sitting up. She was not concerned with Natlatan's presence, but thought she better put her dress on. He sat down beside her, 'Hish paga ella?' he asked

'Nak, jadpog.'

'Jadpog!' Natlatan replied somewhat surprised at Ruth's response to his question.

Ruth laughed, 'Da, nak por jadpog.'

'Hish paga nak daqua.'

'Nak, pe jadpog daqua.'

Bill returned while Ruth was still talking to Natlatan, Zak warned them of his approach before he emerged from the wood. At least he had two rabbits with him, which would save Ruth going hunting later that day. 'Natlatan has come to visit me,' Ruth said as he approached feeling she should explain the presence of the Indian.

'I've got a couple of these rabbits, they were in the snares.'

'That's good; there are three of us to feed today.' Turning to look at Natlatan Ruth added 'pe nakella, pe umta e pi.'

'Da, porpog, pi umta e pe e hish paga.'

'Por, yes, there are three of us. This is Natlatan.'

'What do I say?'

'Portag meecha na Bill, that is hello friend of Bill. It says hello but also tells him your name. When you meet someone, you always say that. They will say the same and then you both know who you are talking to.' Ruth felt good as she helped Bill introduce himself to Natlatan.

After the meal, Ruth became uncomfortable; Natlatan was showing no signs of leaving and it was becoming obvious he was expecting to stay. Eventually Bill left for the lodge in the meadow. Ruth wondered what he thought, it was not difficult to work out Natlatan was going to stay in the cabin with her.

Ruth was practicing shooting a bow with Natlatan when Bill came round into the meadow just as Natlatan had pointed out a tencha, which had flapped into the far end of the meadow. It was too far away to shoot at. Zak had also seen it, and had lowered his body as he moved away from Ruth. Ruth waved Bill down, for a moment or two she thought he was going to carry on then he saw the reason why and ducked down.

Ruth and Natlatan slowly moved towards the large bird, when they were within range they both fired an arrow at the same time; both hit the large bird but failed to kill it. It started to run flapping its wings as it did. Ruth started out after it but Zak streaked past her heading straight for the bird. She stopped; Zak would catch it there was little chance of him not doing so. By the time, Natlatan and Ruth reached it Zak was standing over the kill. 'Good boy Zak, it's a nice fat one isn't it,' she said as she stroked him. 'It's ok Bill! We have it!'

Not long after midday Natlatan left to return to the village. Ruth had mixed feelings she wanted him to stay but she did not want him there while Bill was. That evening she roasted the large bird on a spit over the fire. It smelt good.

It rained the following day Ruth spend most of it in the cabin as the fields got a good watering. It was dull and over cast the next day but towards the evening the clouds thinned and there was a glorious sunset which turned the clouds all shades of red, gold's, oranges and pinks. 'It will be a good day tomorrow,' Bill said looking to the west as the sky started to darken.

They were both sitting outside the cabin mid-morning when a group from the village arrived. 'Look, we have visitors,' Ruth said as the group made their way towards the cabin.

'Are you sure they are visitors they have a load of weapons.'

'They are a hunting party, probably come here to see how I am and if I know where the deer are,' Ruth said watching them as they approached; she saw one of the Indians carrying two long, study poles.

'And do you.'

'I think so, I can tell them, but one of them has two poles, they don't need them for deer. Nor do they need heavy spears.'

'Portag Jaga na Kala!' one of them called out.

'Portag! Ella daqua na Jaga na Kala,' Ruth responded watching them as they came across to her.

'Portag Jaga na Kala nat meecha na Daga Kala. Piapar jadpog latan, Jaga na Kala tak ella latan.'

'Latan!' Ruth replied surprised, but it would explain why they had so many heavy spears and the two poles; they did not usually have so many when they went hunting.

'Paga na Daga Kala tak jadpog latan.'

'What is going on?' Bill asked.

'The chief wants them to find a moose. There must be something going on if they want a moose.'

'And do you know where they are?'

'Not too sure, there will always be some on the plain though. Sheba! They will know. Here they come; there is Jake he always wants to know what is going on.'

'Pi jadpog latan e pe.'

'Da, porpog,' the Indian that Ruth had spoken to immediately replied.

Ruth fetched a couple of spears from the cabin; she was ready for the hunt. 'Come on Bill we are going to hunt moose.'

Ruth had not been to the area she headed towards for some time and she had often seen moose there. Even before she reached, the area she was heading for Ruth saw a cow moose some distance off through the wood. 'Down Bill,' she quietly said waving him down.

'Why,

'There's one over there quiet now, you just stay here.'

'Jaga na Kala,' one of the Indians quietly said.

'Ap nakella e nakpog, e ap ella e nakpog, e apa ella e nakpog,' Ruth said pointing to various positions she wanted the Indians to take up.

'Da,' he quietly responded.

'Pi e kala ella. Latan porella hi pe.'

'Da,' he said nodding as he did as Ruth had asked.

'Stay here Bill I will send a moose to them. Just stay here,' Ruth whispered; then was off skirting round the moose.

A cow was much easier to kill; it was the large male bull with its antlers, which Ruth avoided at some times of the year. They were also a lot larger and stronger than the cow moose. It took her a while to skirt the moose as Ruth approached it she could see it was a decent animal, there would be a lot of meat on it. She started to run towards the moose; Zak joined her.

'Thank you,' Bill said as Ruth passed him his plate that evening.

'The Indians will be eating moose this evening, cooked in the middle of the circle and they will dance round the fire and all sorts. It is quite good, they will all be happy tonight.'

'I still don't believe what I saw today.'

'I can only do that with my family of wolves, the others don't know what to do. I pull the moose down and then stab it with my spear; they tear out the throat. That was a good cow, she was nice and fat.'

'You almost jumped on its back and then grabbed round the neck and just pulled it down while the wolves attacked. Do you ever hunt one for yourself?'

'I only hunt them in the autumn, and store the meat for the winter; it would not keep in the summer unless there were a lot of wolves to feed. If you have five days meat you don't need to hunt you have enough it doesn't matter if you see lots of rabbits you just remember where they are. They know and will not run away so much. Haven't you seen that, when you are hunting they run away a lot, when you have a lot of meat and don't need to hunt they know and don't run away so much.'

'Do you mind if I ask how they know.'

'The Great Spirit tells them.'

'I thought you were going to say that. I will admit there are times animals don't run away as much.'

'They know, that's why,' Ruth said.

'The Great Spirit doesn't talk to you.'

'No, but he guides me he makes me throw the spear to the left or right because he knows the deer or rabbit is going to go that way. If I am good and don't do wrong he will continue to guide my arm when I throw the spear. I thank him for sending the deer, but that is all.'

'Yes I see, I understand.'

'God doesn't do that sort of thing; you have to pray to him in a church. God doesn't do much; he just sits in heaven. There are no churches here so you can't pray to him. Here it is the Great Spirit and you have to find out what you can do first. The spirit man tells you that, what animals you can kill, how and when. You must not kill other animals; that is not right. You mustn't kill beavers I told you that, they are not for killing for any reason. The Great Spirit will not like that and if you do it a lot he will be angry with you and send a bear or a puma to kill you.

Then you will have to tell the Great Spirit why you did it when he said you couldn't.'

The following day Ruth was clearing the ground in front of the cabin trying to create a flat area where she hoped grass would grow when Bill came round from the meadow 'There is a moose eating your crops.'

'Did you tell it to go away?' Ruth asked as she went to look. The moose was there eating her beans. Running towards the moose, she shouted 'Shoo you can't eat that, shoo, shoo!' The moose ran off towards the plain. Ruth turned and started to return to where Bill was standing. 'It has gone it ate some of the beans,' she told Bill.

He shook his head pointing past her, 'It's not gone,' he said

Ruth looked around; the moose was back eating the beans. 'No!' She shouted at it. A wolf ran past her. 'Ah here is Jake he will chase it away.' She watched as Jake rushed up to the moose who stood for a while defying the wolf. When Jake nipped its leg a couple of time the moose decided it would leave and ran off chased by Jake.

'That is a naughty moose, she knows I will not kill her, so she comes and eats my beans.'

'It did seem quite determined to eat them.'

Ruth was sitting with Bill in the cabin. They had eaten their meal and were talking. He asked if the tribe treated her as a squaw. 'No! I'm not a squaw! I'm a binjaga a girl.'

'What's the difference then?'

'A lot; I haven't got a brave; I stay with my father. Father isn't the same as we have. You can change your father for a start. They are not the same as we are in England. A binjaga lives in her father's lodge. She can't lie with someone not until she has taken them; it is sort of like getting married.'

'Change fathers,' Bill questioned.

'Yea, but you have to go and talk to the chief to do that. I went to the chief with Friend of Bear he said I was his binjaga and the tribe greeted me. That is why I am Jaga na Kala binjaga na Meechamegan.'

'Oh, I thought that you and Natlatan were...'

'No, he only sleeps here; he mustn't do anything else because I am a binjaga; that would be very wrong the Great Spirit would not be pleased. It's different if I was a squaw. You wouldn't understand because it's different here. It's not the same as in England and places like that.'

'You seem to know what to do.'

'I live in the village some of the time. I was there lots last year, and Friend of Bear tells me so does his squaw. She told me all this sort of things like that but she can't speak English and it is difficult because I don't know lots of words yet.'

'You seem to get by alright.'

'I know enough to talk a bit. It is difficult sometimes when Friend of Bear is talking about the Great Spirit. He draws on the ground and all sorts.'

Chapter 8

Bill had been there for over twenty days when Meechamegan came to the cabin. He told Ruth the Bear Tribe had come to visit them and they had eaten the moose together. 'Paga tak ella Jaga na Kala daqua, tak Jaga na Kala e kala ella aptag hi Daga Kala daqua.' As he spoke, he put his red blanket on the ground between them. 'Suta,' he said with a broad grin on his face as he emphasised the T.

She recalled the time when she had suma and suta mixed up, both meant take but in a completely different way. She knew the purpose of the blanket Friend of Bear had placed in front of her, and the meaning of each item.

Ruth thought she had better ensure she understood what Meechamegan had said 'Pi ella Daga Kala daqua?' She said not wishing to use English.

'Da Daga Kala e Daga Megan tak aptag. Piapar Daga Kala.'

'Pi e kala,'

'Da.'

Having satisfied herself she understood what Friend of Bear was asking, Ruth looked at the items in the blanket and picked up the knife. 'Por suta, pi tak Paga na Daga Kala,' Meechamegan said smiling at her.

'Aptag.'

'Da, Daga Kala e Daga Megan ap.'

Ruth thought he was trying to tell her they were to join the bear tribe or the bear tribe was going to join them.

'Hish paga por meecha, Hish paga suma pe,' Meechamegan said with a knowing sort of look on his face.

'Nak!'

'Hish paga e pe ella na Daga Kala daqua aptag e nakella apa, apar tag.'

Ruth was becoming embarrassed with the way the conversation was going, now he wanted her to bring Bill with her to the village the following day and stay there for a while. She was glad when Meechamegan picked up his blanket and prepared to leave.

'What was all that about?' Bill asked after Friend of Bear had left in order to return to the tribe.

'We have to go to the village tomorrow, it must be important something to do with the Bear Tribe, I think the two tribes are going to join together.'

'What was that with the blanket, you have one in the cabin?'

'It is a sort of way of saying how much you promise to do something.'

'Oh.'

'I picked up the knife so I either have to be there or be dead.'

'What! They will kill you if you don't go.'

'No, I will already be dead; I died before I could get there.'

Ruth sat on a log looking out over the lake having eaten her meal. It was a pleasant evening the mountains looked good. With dusk well and truly underway, the low sun highlighted the mountain peaks without reaching the lower slopes the other side of the lake. Ruth recalled the conversation with Friend of Bear as she looked towards Bill. She liked him he was not the person she had first imagined. He turned his head towards her and smiled. 'It's a nice evening,' Ruth said.

'Yea,' Bill responded looking away. 'Your Indian friend hasn't come recently, not the one that came today the other one.'

Ruth wondered what Bill thought of Natlatan and what he was to her. 'He is with his squaw I would think.'

'He is married then?'

'Not like you know; some braves never get married in the way you think about it, but they still have a squaw. It's difficult to explain. When Binojar was killed, she chose him; Natlatan stood up without being told to, so he must like her. I would think they were good friends before,' Ruth explained.

Bill remained quiet for a while looking at the mountain peaks, then in a quiet voice he said, 'I would in other circumstances ask to call on you.'

'You can't do that here,' Ruth responded immediately slightly embarrassed with what he had said. He was handsome and she was always pleased when he returned to the cabin after having been away for a while.

'No but I would like to, I enjoy our talks a great deal, and you are a wonderful person, especially here; you bring beauty to the wilderness. A beauty which would be sadly lacking should you leave.' Ruth did not know what to say her mind struggled to find a reply. 'Were circumstances different?' Bill continued. 'Would you consider me as a possible husband? I mean, after we were correctly introduced and we had got to know each other. We can't here anyway so...' He stopped talking leaving whatever it was unsaid. Ruth look at him not knowing how to act or what to say. 'I'm sorry I have spoken out of place.'

'No,' Ruth responded. 'No, I just didn't expect you to say all that. I do like you; I like to know you are here. I don't know; this is my cabin.'

'And always will be,' Bill immediately responded.

'Not if I was your wife, it would become yours.'

'I don't think like that, we are not in England, we can't get married here for a start, can we; so it will always be your cabin.'

'No, yes, um no, you are confusing me.'

'I have wanted you as my wife from the first moment I saw you. I have an image of you standing in those clothes with the two feathers in your hair Zak beside you and a huge pack of wolves behind you.' Bill looked away staring at the ground but not seeing it. 'I know I just stared at you. I should not have but it was the most stunning thing I have ever seen. You have no idea what sort of impression it made on me. Then we start to talk and I find that you are not just beautiful, you have an alert mind one, which can accept spiritual matters, beyond that of mine. You have your god, the Great Spirit, and you live a life according to his word. I couldn't do that, I left when more was required of me. I am not worthy of you. I can't reach out as you have...' Ruth listened as Bill continued. He had never spoken like this before, Ruth wondered if he had tried to but not found the right moment before. He was an honest man, he had worked hard and well in the fields during the time, he had been with her.

'You will have to give me time to know you,' Ruth said some time after he had finished talking. 'I like you and no one has ever spoken to me like that before.'

'I will love you no matter what, whether I am here or somewhere else. No other woman could be compared to you and found to be your equal.' Ruth looked down not knowing what to say. What Bill had said would change everything. The way she lived would be different. She glanced in his direction. He was a good-looking man; he worked hard in the fields. She had become used to having him around. 'Should I ask your Indian father for you?' he asked.

'I don't know; he asked about you,' Ruth said then thought about life in the village. 'We have to be in the village tomorrow; they will not accept I was too tired to go to the village because we talked all night.'

'I will leave you then and allow you to sleep.'

'Thank you, for saying all you did. You need to talk to Friend of Bear he will know what the correct thing to do is.'

The following morning Ruth felt uncomfortable when Bill came to the cabin. She could not relax with him around her. Some of that unease had left her by the time Ruth called the wolves; then with Bill, she headed off towards the Indian village along what was now a well-defined path between her cabin and the village. The wolves knew where they were going and for most of the time led the way.

'Nearly there Bill,' Ruth said as they reached the top of the hill to the south of the village.

'They are not far are they what a couple of miles.'

'Before you came I use to visit them a lot during the summer. I go hunting with them sometimes.'

'They are not going to be too pleased with all these wolves.'

'They will be ok.' Ruth stopped walking and looked down into the valley, 'See there we are.'

'Huts, this lot don't have wigwams. They are like the shelter behind your cabin.'

'What is a wigwam?' Ruth asked.

'The tents the Indians live in,' Bill explained.

'Is that what they are called, I've seen them; round pointed tents. These have huts you stay in the one in my meadow. The big one is called the tribe lodge.'

'I thought the thing in the field was where you stayed while your father built the cabin.'

'No, it belongs to them; they use it when a hunting party is out my way late in the day. And my father used it when he came to help me get the spring work done.'

'It looks busy down there.'

'We will have to go and find out what this is all about,' Ruth said as she started down the hill. They were only just half way down the hill when Jake ran off towards the village. 'Jake! Oh well, away he goes, he likes it in the village the children play with him.'

'They play with a full grown wolf!'

'Get out the circle game, you will see.'

Ruth watched Jake as he ran round the lines of stakes and disappeared amongst the huts. Not long after Jake had vanished, there were a few whoopees from the village and several waved towards her. Ruth waved back. 'They know we are here now.'

'So it seems, they seem pleased, calling out and waving. This is quite something; I've always been a bit apprehensive as far as Indians are concerned.'

'You don't have to worry about these.'

'I see, and one would appear to be coming out to meet us.'

'That is Natlatan, Big moose. You have met him before.'

'My competitor for your hand,' Bill said.

'No he's not; you don't really have a competitor.'

To Ruth Natlatan's greeting felt more than friendly. She was glad Bill could not understand her conversation with Natlatan. After what had been said between her and Bill, Ruth started to wonder if Natlatan was in competition with Bill.

'Come on Bill we are here now,' as Ruth reached the inner entrance to the village. 'Portag,' Ruth called out as she greeted those they passed.

'This is not what I expected; they all seem very pleased to see you and your wolves and you seem to know where you are going.'

'We are going to my home here,' Ruth continued towards Meechamegan's lodge. He came out of it as she approached. He had extra decorations on his top and five feathers on his head. 'You look different.'

'Da, me tak Daga Megan, then chief talk, make all one.'

'Where are they?'

'Daga Megan.'

'Da,' Ruth responded.

'Nakella, ella tala jehi,' he responded pointing straight up. 'Meecha Bill nak pi lodge.'

'Nak pe lodge.'

'Nak, not right; me find paga meecha e Bill.'

Bill was standing looking around as the two of them spoke, he look a little bemused. Ruth thought she should explain a bit to him. 'You can't stay here in Friend of Bear's lodge; he is going to look for a friend for you so you can stay in their lodge. You have to sometimes guess what words mean.'

'You are doing fine, chatting away.'

'The other lot are coming midday and then the chiefs will talk.'

'What do we do until then?'

'Just be here I would think.'

'Paga na Daga Kala tak Jaga na Kala.'

Ruth looked at Bill, 'My father said the chief wants to talk to me.'

Friend of Bear took her to see the chief Bill waited outside the chief lodge while Ruth went in to speak to the chief. The chief's lodge was much the same as she had seen before. He had several items in his lodge, which were not in others. His spears were more decorative than others were and hanging on the wall of the hut was his large headdress, which she had seen him wear on several occasions. Ruth sat down opposite the chief, 'Portak Paga na Daga Kala,' she said.

The chief explained that he wanted her to sit beside him in the circle as she had on the occasion when the three trappers were in front of him. This time he wanted her to call the wolves, and send them to hunt. Ruth nodded and told the chief she would do that for him. She left the lodge with Friend of Bear.

'Everything all right,' Bill asked.

'I know now what I am supposed to do; he wants me to call the wolves and send them hunting.'

'You are going to be sitting there for a while then.'

'We could be there most of the afternoon.'

Friend of Bear took Ruth and Bill back to his lodge, Clear Water was there. 'Porjadseeni make you right.'

'What,'

'You not right, have to be right. I talk with Bill, Porjadseeni make you right.'

Ruth left Bill with Friend of Bear and went into the lodge with Clear Water. Ruth sat there beside the small fire while Clear Water tied and greased Ruth's hair then put several more feathers in it. Ruth checked to see how many she now had; it was four; and that made her important in the tribe. Ruth guessed she would have them for just the day to make her look more important to the Indians of the Bear Tribe. Clear Water was putting a little water into a brightly coloured mixture and stirring it with a small stick. Clear Water dipped her finger into the colour and then put it on Ruth's arm; she put blue and yellow lines on Ruth's arms and legs, ending up with some on her face. 'Da, por,' Clear Water said when she had finished.

Ruth found Bill sitting on the grass outside the lodge. He looked up at her, 'What the hell has happened to you?' He asked as soon as he saw Ruth.

'I have to be like this.'

'Por,' Meechamegan said, 'you right now, strong with Elena na Kala, Jaga na Kala por.'

Ruth sat with Bill just outside the circle on the small bank generally watching what was going on. The sun reached its zenith and shortly after that, a large group of Indians appeared on the hill and started to come down it towards the village. 'Bill look they are here, look there's lots of them.' Ruth stood up so she could see the Bear Tribe as they came down the hill with all their possessions. Leading them was an older Indian with a large headdress on. 'Oh look their chief with a big head dress on.'

'Things are happening now,' Bill said as he stood up and watched.

Friend of Bear left the village and went to meet them. Ruth watched her chief who now had on his headdress with lots feathers. He went to the entrance of the village and waited there with the spirit man. After a while, Friend of Bear led the other chief into the village to meet the Wolf tribe's chief. For a while, several huts blocked Ruth's view of what was going on. All the tribe seemed to be gathering round the circle. 'Here they come,' Bill said pointing towards the two chiefs who were now coming towards the circle followed by the rest of the Bear Tribe. Friend of Bear was running towards the two of them. 'Jaga na Kala sit with chief, Zak come with you.'

'Da, you stay here Bill,' Ruth said as she headed off towards the position in the circle beside the chief.

'I will.'

Ruth left Bill on the bank at the back of the circle with the women and children and let Friend of Bear lead her across the circle to an unmarked position to the right of where the chief sat. She noticed two large flat stones and assumed both chiefs would sit there. She did as Meechamegan ask and sat down. All the braves were now starting to sit down in their position round the circle. Braves from the other tribe came and the spirit man showed them where to sit none of the positions were marked with a flat stone. When all the braves from the two tribes were sitting, the two chiefs arrived.

They both sat down with her chief next to Ruth. He turned towards her and in a loud voice so that the others could hear he said. 'Jaga na Kala, tak kala ella.'

'Da,' Ruth said then turned to Zak, 'Call boy.' He gave out a long loud howl. Her wolves came almost immediately, then a few of the braves who were sitting on the side of the circle where they could see the hill started pointing, Ruth could only just see the hill so only managed to catch glimpses of the wolves running towards the village.

When there were about twenty wolves around her, Ruth stood up, 'Rabbits get rabbits, off you go, Jake find Rabbit!' she called out. Jake knew what was required and ran off; he stopped, and then started to run again as soon as the other wolves showed signs of following him. It was not long before the wolves were running up the hill as a large single pack. Ruth sat down again beside Zak who had not joined the pack.

Time seemed to pass very slowly; everyone was waiting for the wolves to return. Ruth started to worry; they might not be able to find anything. People started to talk amongst themselves as they waited. Ruth sat there willing the wolves to find something. After a long time, one of the Indians from Ruth's tribe pointed towards the hill. 'Kala!' he shouted. Everyone started to become very excited. A small group of wolves were coming back, running down the hill towards the village. Ruth sat there wondering if they had found anything.

Jake and another wolf found their way into the centre of the circle and came towards Ruth. They both dropped a rabbit in front of Ruth, Jake yakked at her and Ruth stroked him. 'Good boy,' then she stroked the other wolf, 'you are a good wolf as well,' she said.

Then four wolves arrived one of them had a small deer in its jaws. Ruth sat there very pleased. One of the squaws standing on the bank called out 'apar kala!' pointing towards the hill. Ruth looked but could not see anything; however, a few moments later a wolf dropped another rabbit in front of her. Before long, Ruth had five rabbits and a small deer in front of her. The braves of her tribe were highly excited with the results. The wolves were now wandering around as a pack inside the circle. Ruth got up and walked into the centre of the pack. She stroked a few of them 'Good wolves, you are all good wolves.' Zak yapped a few times and then sort of snarled. The other wolves started to leave. Ruth gathered up the six dead animals turning over in her mind what she should say to the chief. 'Apa e apa e ap gegenta e ap reela, kala jadpog, mesh na Daga Kala,' she said putting the rabbits and deer down in front of the chief.

'Porpog, kala por jadpog.'

'Porpog Paga na Daga Kala,' Ruth responded then sat down in her place pleased her chief had shown the Daga Kala to be strong with the spirit of the wolf. The circle was still excited but starting to calm down. Ruth guessed the Indian in the bearskin was their spirit man. She watched as the two spirit men placed two small decorative blankets in front of the two chief. She could see the blanket in front of her chief held a small clay bear; he picked it up. The other chief took whatever was in the other blanket; Ruth guessed it was a wolf. Then the other chief gave the clay wolf to Ruth's chief. Who put both back onto the blanket in front of him. The wolf tribe's spirit man folded the blanket over and then took it away.

Ruth could not understand what they said, both chiefs spoke to those sitting in the circle and watching from the bank. Then the Wolf Tribe spirit man brought one of the bear tribe braves to her chief. They spoke for a while and her chief gave the brave a flat stone, which he took back and placed, on the edge of the circle; this was repeated for each brave until they all had a place in the circle marked with a stone. The two chiefs then walked across the circle to an empty place, which was already marked with a stone. The bear chief sat down and the chief of the wolf tribe returned to his position. 'Porpog Jaga na Kala, Porpog,' he said as he sat down, then he turned his attention to those sitting in the circle. 'Daga Kala natmesh, e apa tag nak pog.'

Everyone seemed pleased, those in the circle were now starting to stand up and talk to each other. Friend of Bear helped Ruth to her feet. She stretched her legs glad it was over and she could move around again. Ruth made her way to where Bill was standing on the small bank outside the circle. 'That was quite something to watch,' Bill said as Ruth went up to him.

'I was part of it; the chief was very pleased the wolves found five rabbits.'

'I was watching the braves, those from this tribe were pleased and smiling but the others were completely stunned, they did not expect that.'

'The chief wanted to say they are strong with Elena na Kala, the spirit of the wolf.'

'Oh he did that all right or rather you did. I know they bring the odd rabbit back to the cabin but to see them bring it back to you and not eat it. It must be important for them to have you here. You should have seen the difference between those who belong to this tribe and the others. It was Jake wasn't it that brought the first one back. He came past one to get into the circle; the Indian didn't know what to do. He sat there staring at Jake with a rabbit in his jaws, that one there talking to your friend.'

'Natlatan,' Ruth said seeing him speaking to a brave from the Bear Tribe.

'Yea,'

'Porpog Jaga na Kala, Porpog,' Meechamegan said as he came up to Ruth and Bill.

'The wolves found some.'

'Por say much to be strong with Elena na Kala.'

'It's like I was saying.'

'You strong you make Daga Kala strong, we now all Daga Kala; we ap. You come talk with spirit man.'

Bill remained by the circle while Friend of Bear took Ruth to the lodge of the spirit man. He had several wolf skins in his lodge and many other strange looking items. Ruth could not take her eyes off the skull of a wolf attached to the end of on a short, carved, wooden stick. The spirit man talk to her for a while about Elena na Kala and the Great Spirit, most she already knew from Friend of Bear. The spirit man seemed very pleased she knew most of what he had said. Friend of Bear translated or drew in the dirt whenever he did not know what words to use.

'Jaga na Kala fron e Elena na Kala e Natelena.'

'Elenapaga said you strong with spirit of wolf and Great Spirit.'

'Da, I understood,' Ruth told Meechamegan.

'Jaga na Kala tak por,' Friend of Bear told the spirit man

'Da, porpog Jaga na Kala porpog. Por tak pe por tak Jaga na Kala.'

'You are back again,' Bill said when Ruth reached him.

'What have you been doing?'

'Just sitting watching, I can see a lot from the top of this bank, what happened with the spirit man?'

'He wanted to tell me about the Great Spirit I knew most of it, but it was a good talk to him, he has all sorts of things in his lodge.'

'Here comes that Friend of Bear one again.'

'Looks like it; I wonder what I have to do now.'

'Natlatan tak hish paga meecha e ella daqua,' Friend of Bear said when he reached Ruth.

'It's you he wants now,' Ruth said looking in Bill's direction.

'Natlatan say he friend, you stay in his lodge,' Friend of Bear told Bill.

'That is where you are going to stay, you know him so it will be all right.' Ruth explained.

'I don't know what is expected of me.'

'You sit in his place with his squaw when it's time to eat. Don't worry about sleeping, just take off your outer clothes and get between the furs. Natlatan is a good brave he will look after you.'

'Me take Bill, say what to do.'

'Yes, go with Friend of Bear Bill; he will make sure you are looked after.'

Ruth did not see much of Bill for the rest of the day; she sat on the bank watching as they prepared a large fire in the middle of the circle and started to cook a moose over it. Several of the squaws from the bear tribe went to the tribe lodge. They introduced themselves and the squaws talked for a while before they all started working again. A group of children came to the circle with three of her wolves, but as the circle had a large fire in the middle of it they were unable play their favourite game with the wolves.

When it came time to sit in the circle Ruth went first to Meechamegan's lodge and found her bowl, she was about to leave when Meechamegan arrived, she handed him the other two bowls. 'Porpog; umta por natmesh tag.'

'Pi jad latan.'

'Da, por latan por mesh,' Meechamegan said as they left the lodge. Ruth sat down beside his stone in the circle. 'Bill with Natlatan he learn good me talk to him.'

'Bill por paga.'

'Da,' Meechamegan said nodding his head. 'Por paga pe jad ap mesh apar Daga Kala.'

'You keep saying things different, he see one mesh all...ap is first as well.'

'Da ap,' he said holding up one finger, 'ap mesh.'

'Da.'

'You learn good.'

'I am learning lots, when do I take this blue and yellow off.'

'Aptag, dagasham.'

'Dagasham.'

'Da,' he said pointing at the yellow and blue lines on Ruth's arm.

'That is dagasham.'

'Da; tribe paint, nak war paint e spirit paint. You not have spirit paint Elenapaga have that.'

That evening the spirit man, with several of the items Ruth had seen in his lodge and with lots of yellow, blue and red paint on him, talked to the Great Spirit. The braves danced round the fire for a while led by the spirit man. They got a rhythm going after a while with them all dancing in step. They all seemed to be happy and there was a lot of talking amongst them. Then the spirit man said the moose was ready to eat. Four braves lifted it off the two supports holding it over the fire and moved it to another two so people could get some meat. Meechamegan took Ruth to where the squaws had placed a lot of fruit; she put some in her bowl taking her lead from him then went to the moose. She cut several strips of meat from it and put them in her bowl. She went back and sat down. 'Zak nak mesh, me get.' Meechamegan returned with a large bone with a lot of meat on it. Zak did not need to be told it was his. 'Zak like.'

'He will like that all right.'

'Por Kala.'

Ruth saw someone feeding Jake; he sat down beside them with his meal. 'Bill mesh kala.'

'That is Sheba she stays with him.'

'Por; he por paga.'

It was dark, the area around the circle lit by the flames of the fire, when Ruth noticed Bill stand up. He came across the circle towards her with a red blanket in his hands. She wondered who had given it to him, as he put it down in front of her. She waited for him to ask her something. He lifted back the top of the blanket. 'Jaga na Kala, pi mesh Jaga na Kala, umta,' Bill said rather hesitantly. Ruth looked towards Meechamegan; he was smiling at her then back to the blanket and the small biscuit that it contained. 'Umta,' Meechamegan prompted her. Ruth took the small oatmeal biscuit from the blanket and ate it. The tribe whooped and cheered.

Shortly after that, the circle broke up, everyone heading for his or her lodge. 'You nak squaw you binjaga man has to ask show he can feed you, show paga he can feed you,' Meechamegan explained as Ruth entered his lodge.

'An oatmeal biscuit,' Ruth queried.

'Da it say I feed you.'

'Then what?' she asked.

'You take man. Bill not paga Daga Kala, still have daqua e lodge spirit man and chief say that is good. You binjaga na Daga Kala.'

The following day Bill did not seem to be around a great deal. She eventually found him. He looked a little sheepish. 'Friend of Bear said, take it to you.'

'I guessed that.'

'If you think that…' Bill started to say

Ruth cut him off. 'No, I like you and well you said before…'

'I wanted to ask again as an Indian would.'

'You know what the answer will be.'

'You have made me a very happy man. I will look after you. Well here I am not too sure who will be looking after who. It may be you making sure I am all right.'

'You will learn and then be strong. You know how to look after fields all right.'

'I can do that, without being told how and I know about herbs and can make potions.'

'Do you, you didn't tell me that.'

'No reason to, you are healthy.'

That evening after the meal, Bill again placed a blanket in front of her. Ruth ate the small biscuit, smiling at him as she did. He smiled back then returned to his position beside Natlatan.

The following afternoon Clear Water took Ruth to their lodge. Several other squaws were there. A new dress was lying on the furs one with a lot of work in it. Ruth had to take her dress off. The squaws there painted her body. Ruth became excited with all the fuss; she was getting married. She wondered what would happen, everything she had learnt would suggest that it would be in the circle when they sat down for the meal. Porjadseeni and the other squaws were making sure Ruth was ready in time. They did her hair and finally Ruth put the soft dress on. It looked good. The other squaws left the lodge leaving Ruth with Porjadseeni 'Nakella lodge.'

'Da,' Ruth replied, not sure, why they had to stay in the lodge.

Porjadseeni stopped Meechamegan entering the lodge when he came for his bowl; she passed the bowls out to him. Ruth sat on the furs with Porjadseeni wondering what was about to happen. She was going to get married, she was well aware of that; she wondered what Bill was doing; it was past the time to sit in the circle and have a meal.

Ruth heard shouting in the distance it sounded as if it was coming from the circle; it sounded quite heated; there was definitely an argument going on between several people. Not long after that, the spirit man came into the lodge. 'Jaga na Kala ella e pi.'

'Ella e Elenapaga,' Porjadseeni said. Ruth stood up, left the lodge and followed the spirit man to the circle. She saw Bill; he had dressed in Indian clothes, and had a spear in his hands. It looked as if he was threatening Friend of Bear. He looked good standing there as he waited for Ruth to reach her place; behind him stood Natlatan and his squaw. Sitting in his position in the circle was Meechamegan; he indicated Ruth should sit down.

Ruth sat down. Bill immediately gave his spear to Natlatan taking from him the small red blanket of a brave. He put the blanket down in front of her. 'Jaga na Kala binjaga na Meechamegan, suma pi.'

Someone must have told him what to say, he did look good to Ruth standing there dressed in new Indian clothes. She folded back the top of the blanket there was a small clay figure of a man in it. A little on the nervous side, she reached forward and picked it up. 'Ella e pi, Jaga na Kala, tak Paga na Daga Kala pe suma pi,' Bill said reaching out a hand towards her. Ruth let him help her up; he had done well to learn the correct words, when he had told her to tell the chief that she had taken him. The two of them walked towards the chief who was standing smiling as he waited for the two of them to reach him. Meechamegan and Natlatan walked beside her while Porjadseeni and Natlatan's squaw were on Bill's side. They all stood in front of the chief.

'Natkala suta mesh hi Jaga na Kala e Jaga na Kala umta mesh?' the chief asked Bill

'Da pi suta mesh...' Bill hesitated as he thought of what he should say, then added, 'hi Jaga na Kala.'

'Jaga na Kala, pe umta mesh na Natkala.'

Ruth liked the name Bill had chosen Big wolf was a good name for him to have, 'Da,' Ruth replied. The chief then asked her if she had taken the man. 'Da,' she replied holding out the small clay image.

The chief asked Meechamegan if he had seen Bill give her food. Then Natlatan's squaw gave Bill a bone knife which he then handed to Meechamegan. Friend of Bear made a fuss about examining the knife before he said it was good.

'Portag Jaga na Kala squaw na Natkala,' the chief said in a loud voice. 'Portag Jaga na Kala squaw na Natkala,' the tribe responded.

Ruth had greeted by the tribe before when she had become part of Meechameega's family. She turned round smiling at Bill as the both greeted the tribe. 'Portag Daga Kala,' she said in a firm voice. Then Porjadseeni led her to a large flat stone in the centre of the circle. 'We have to sit here,' Bill said.

'Right in the middle,' Ruth responded as Bill helped her to sit down then sat beside her. 'You look good like that.'

'You look nice dressed in those clothes, better than your others; you look nice and strong like that. What was that with the knife?'

'I had to give Friend of Bear a present; actually it's his knife.'

Ruth chuckled, as she watched several squaws were carrying a fur towards where they were sitting. They spread it out on the ground in front of the two of them. Porjadseeni and the other squaw made a great deal of fuss as they examined it before they said it was good and rolled it up before placing it beside Ruth. Then several braves brought another fur. This time Meechamegan and Natlatan examined it before saying it was good. Ruth did not understand a lot of what the spirit man said but got the general message that he was asking the Great Spirit to bring the two of them a good life.

Ruth and Bill had their meal brought to them. After Ruth and Bill had finished their meal, Porjadseeni smashed the bowl Ruth had used; it was a symbolic ending to her relationship with the family. Natlatan's squaw gave her a new one. Bill's bowl was also broken; he received a new one from Porjadseeni.

The four who had sat in the circle with them left for their position in the circle. 'I have to take you back to your place in the circle,' Bill said as he helped Ruth up. When the two of them reached Meechamegan's place he refused to have her there pushing her away. The spirit man came to them with a stone in his hands. 'Pi nak daqua,' Bill told the spirit man. 'Ella pi,' the spirit man responded then led Bill and Ruth to a gap in the circle he placed the stone there. 'Daqua na Natkala,' he said pointing at the stone.

'Porpog,' Bill responded before he helped Ruth sit down. 'We have our own place now.'

'What happens now is that it, we left the new bowls in the middle.' Even as Ruth spoke, she saw Natlatan and Meechamegan going towards the centre of the circle. Meechamegan picked up one of the furs then both of them came towards where Ruth was sitting with Bill. They wanted her to go with them.

They took Ruth to a lodge she had not been to before. 'Natkala lodge,' Meechamegan said as he lifted the skins over the entrance. Ruth went in. The lodge was empty Natlatan spread the fur out on the ground. Then the two of them wanted the clothes she was wearing. They left the lodge leaving her there lying naked on the fur. A short while later Ruth heard the skins being lifted. Porjadseeni came in with the other fur in her arms, which she placed over Ruth. Then Ruth had to translate for Bill and tell him that Clear Water wanted his clothes.

Bill quickly got under the fur. They were by themselves. 'That's it, but we have to go to Friend of Bears lodge in the morning but only when his squaw comes and gets us.'

'I hope she comes with my clothes.'

'You looked really beautiful with all that paint on you.'

'I'm painted all over.'

'I saw.'

'I'm your squaw now.'

'I will love you all I can.'

'I know you will.'

Bill reached a hand out towards Ruth, she felt him touch her and put her arms round him so they could kiss.

The following morning Porjadseeni arrived with both their clothes. She told them to come to her lodge then left them. 'Oh Ruth you are so wonderful,' Bill said holding her tightly to him.

'I don't think they will want to wait long for us to get dressed.'

'You are nice and warm.'

The two of them joined Meechamegan and Porjadseeni for the normal morning family meal. It was not to save Ruth from cooking it was to say they were friends again. Apparently Bill had to demand Ruth be brought to the circle and threatened to kill Meechamegan.

Three days later, they returned to the cabin. Ruth liked having Bill on the bunk with her. They had brought the furs back to the cabin and replaced the blankets with them. It was far more comfortable to sleep between the two furs.

A few days later a large group of Indians including the chief visited them, the weather was hot and Ruth enjoyed the days of leisure. 'You should make more lodges in the meadow then you would not have to go all the way back.'

'I tell chief what you say.' Ruth listened as Friend of Bear explained to the chief. The chief was nodding and said da several times, as he listened. 'Chief say da, we look now see where.'

'If you want,' Ruth said standing. Bill Ruth, the chief and Friend of Bear went round the cabin into the meadow. The fields met with the approval of the chief he took a good look at the growing crops. It did not take long to find a suitable location away from the fields and close to the lodge, which was already there. The chief agreed to build another four lodges, then when people had several days of rest they could come here and stay in the lodges. 'It looks as if it is all sorted out,' Bill said when Ruth explained it to him.

'They can stay here the same as we can in the village, that will be good, and hunters can still stay here over night if they have to.'

'It's a good idea.'

Several Indians came and stayed in the one lodge which was already in the meadow while they worked on building the four additional lodges. Ruth took the wolves hunting and in the evenings provided those building the lodges with a meal, letting them take what they wanted for their family meal in the morning. They ate the main meal sitting outside the cabin. Although there were no home stones, the Indians still sat in the same positions in the circle. When the work was finished, the five lodges looked good. One of the Indians returned to the village in order to find out if there were any old sleeping furs, to cover the entrances. Several returned with a lot of old firs, which did the job well. The wolves thought the lodges were for them and soon went to inspect them. 'Kala jad,' one of the Indians said.

'Da, tashka ne lodge,' Ruth replied.

When they visited the Indians, it was now obvious that Porjadseeni was soon going to have her baby. Twenty or so days later Friend of Bear came to the cabin with a huge smile on his face. 'Me binpaja.' Ruth gave him a huge hug. 'I don't know words to say, porpog.'

'Has she had the child?' Bill asked.

'A boy,' Ruth responded.

'Well done,' Friend of Bear was not going to let Bill off without a big hug. He didn't stay long before setting off back to the village.

'He came all this way just to tell us.'

'He is really pleased isn't he,' Bill responded.

The easy days of summer ended the visits from and to the Indians stopped as the work of preparing for winter arrived. Their crops were gathered and stacked in the cave. Bill took charge of chopping wood while Ruth hunted with the wolves. With two of them working, they completed the tasks well before the first snows arrived.

Chapter 9

The winter started like most then more snow fell than usual and it became bitterly cold. At times, it was almost impossible to venture out of the cabin and several mornings, snow piled itself up to the very top of the door and Bill had to dig his way out of the cabin and then dig his way into the woodshed. Ruth had never known it snow so much; hunting became impossible, venturing any sort of distance from the cabin was impossible. At one point, the meadow was below four foot of snow. The wolves found it hard coming at times to the cabin in order to get warm. Ruth let her family of wolves in and fed them. Food was not going to be a problem Ruth had made sure of that and they had more than enough to see them through to the next harvest. Not only was there more snow and the temperature colder than other winters it was also longer, spring refused to come even though the length of the day had increased considerable.

Bill had the fire burning brightly before Ruth emerged from the furs. Wrapped in a blanket she huddled in front of the fire 'It is still very cold,' she said as she pulled the blanket around her.

'It is the hardest winter I have ever known,' Bill replied.

Ruth put a hand out and stroked Zak. 'It's worse than the first one when Zak came to me. We should be planting the fields by now; the days are getting quite long.'

'It was raining when I looked out.'

'That might be good, it rained a lot that first year then all of a sudden winter was over,' Ruth responded. They still had some oats and Bill had already put some on the fire to cook. Ruth took over giving it a stir. 'It's cold Zak; you like that fire don't you,' she said stroking Zak again. That day Ruth and Bill looked out from the cabin as the rain started to wash away the snow and ice. It did not manage it in a single day, the weather was miserable for several days, but it became considerable warmer. Spring was coming; the winter was at last over.

Everywhere was wet; the stream was a torrent as it drained the waterlogged land. Bill suggested they leave it a few days before they started working in the fields. Ruth agreed, the fields in places had water lying on them and doing anything would only turn them to mud. What she could do though was to take the wolves hunting.

Ruth returned empty handed, even with the wolves, she had not been able to find anything. It did not really matter as they still had some meat in the cave they would need to use it before it went bad.

Three days later most of the water had gone, so the two of them started in the field which was least water logged. Ruth and Bill worked hard getting their fields ready for the seeds.

'We should go and see the Indians see how they are.' Ruth said as she looked at the second field of turnip containing those they were going to leave to seed.

'A couple of days and we should be able to.'

The immediate jobs of spring were all finished, the seeds were in and the weather was starting to get warmer. They decided to take a day or two off and visit the Indians. Ruth stood on the bridge and watched the water in the stream as it rushed down the slight hill. There was still a lot of water draining from the land. Then she called to Jake, who was rooting around under a bush, before setting off after Bill.

The trees were coming into leaf, grass was growing and early spring flowers were in bloom. The wilderness was coming back to life and apart from it being wet underfoot Ruth enjoyed the walk to the Indian village.

The village had found it hard to survive the winter; Ruth went to find Friend of Bear eager to see the baby, which had been born last year. 'Nakpor, pap tod,' Meechamegan said when Ruth greeted him.

Ruth felt sad, he had been so pleased the previous summer to have baby a boy. 'I don't know the words to say,' Ruth said.

'Apar tod, cold kill them, it was their time.'

'Piapar jad Natelena.'

'Da,' Meechamegan replied, but Ruth could see he was almost crying, she put her arms round him and held him for a while. He was very upset and telling her had brought it back to his mind. Porjadseeni was much the same. They sat for a while in silence before the four of them started talking of the good times until it was time to eat.

They went to the tribe lodge for the evening meal; it was not much of a meal in both content and quantity. The following day Big Bear the son of the chief of what had been the Bear Tribe came to Ruth. 'Pe jadpog e piapar?'

'Da, pi e kala jadpog.'

'Porpog Jaga na Kala.'

'Nak flata,' Ruth said wishing she had brought at least one of her spears with her.

'Pi apar,' Natmegan replied as he handed her one.

Ruth quickly examined it, it was a good spear, well balanced, with a very useful looking bone point.

'I think I will walk back and get a couple of axes I can cut wood with them better than the ones they have. I can help that way. Do you think we could spare a sack of turnip? It will help them a little. We are not short of food, more than the two of us need before we reach harvest again.'

'We will have a load of fruit in the summer as well. We could spare a few and there are plenty in the ground which we were going to let go to seed we don't need that much seed do we. Maybe some of them could be taken as well; we don't need to keep all of them.'

'I will have a look, and talk to Friend of Bear,' Bill said.

'Bring back my spear with the long knife like point will you.'

'I know the one you mean.'

With a borrowed spear, Ruth went with the hunting party they returned late afternoon with hardly anything to show. A couple of rabbits were all they had been able to find even with the wolves to help them. Ruth entered the tribe lodge with Zak beside her. 'Porpog Jaga na Kala, porpog, apar mesh,' the chief said as he came up to her. Ruth shook her head two thin rabbits were not good. She was about to disagree with the chief when Bill joined them. 'We had ten sacks so I got them to bring three from the cave and dug an additional one up. It will do us for a few days here.'

'Good,' Ruth said as she realised why the chief had said porpog and apar mesh. She turned to face the chief, 'Daga Kala umta mesh,' she added

'Porpog, Natkala tak apa e ap Daga Kala mesh.'

Although the meal that evening contained little meat, it was better for the turnips and more filling. There was certainly a lot more of it.

The following day Ruth went hunting again, this time with her spear. The deer they found was so thin it was barely alive. 'Nak pogtod, nakpor,' Ruth said as she looked towards the small deer.

'Da, nakpor, nakpor jadpog,' Big Bear responded.

Early the following day, Ruth set off once again with the hunting party to the north of the village. Much as the other two days, they found little. Ruth and the rest were making their way back to the village. They had been hunting for the whole day and had just three thin rabbits nowhere near enough to feed the tribe. It was going to be turnip again with the three rabbits in it just to add a little flavour but certainly no nourishment. Ruth saw Jake and Zak go down. She instinctively did the same then slowly moved so she could see what they had. Five moose were in a small clearing not more than fifty yards from her busily eating the newly grown grass. They were far from the fittest animals she had ever seen, but one of them would turn the day into a good hunt. Ruth looked around to find the others had also ducked down and saw the lake below and to her left. Ruth realised they were on the top of the cliff her father had fallen from.

Pointing to the positions she wanted them to take up Ruth had the Indians lie in wait just as she did with her wolves. Then Ruth started to skirt round the moose, pleased it was her family of wolves with her, they would know what she was going to do. She left them in ones as she went round the moose and closed the route to the west. She left Zak then went a few yards further behind the moose. The moose were by now were starting to get her scent. Seeing the moose starting to move Ruth became concerned they would all flee and get away. She started to run at the group of moose. Zak sprang up and started towards the five moose.

The moose already skittish saw the danger and started to flee away from Ruth and the single wolf. In turn, her family joined in the chase; it stopped the moose moving to the west. The moose became a tighter group as they moved north towards the Indians lying in wait. With additional wolves coming at them from the west, the moose moved ever nearer the cliff's edge. Ruth running, with Zak not far from her, saw the Indians stand up and start to throw spears at the moose. She believed that at least one moose would be killed and that would be enough. The moose, now running at full speed, saw this additional danger and took the only turning open to them. At full flight they turned east, none of them could stop in time. Ruth heard them bellowing as they went over the edge of the cliff.

Her first thought was that the moose had escaped, however, by the time; she reached the edge of the cliff the wolves were finding paths down to where the moose lay.

The cliff at that point was not high and one of the moose was trying to get up. Spears showered down onto it.

Silence fell for a brief moment then the Indians gave out wild ecstatic whoopees as they realised just how much they had. It was not difficult to get down the cliff. Ruth cut open the stomachs of a couple of the moose so that the wolves could feed. The tribe were not the only ones who had not eaten well for some time.

'Porella daqua, apar ella,' Big Bear called out as he pointed to one of the other Indians. 'Da pi ella daqua!' The Indians shouted back to Big Bear and was off heading for the village in order to get help. Those who remained got the moose ready to drag back, lashing each of them onto two long poles. Help arrived by the time they had three ready to go, those who arrived took them. Ruth remained with the hunting party and helped drag the remaining two back.

'Ruth, Ruth!' Bill said coming to her as soon as she entered the tribe lodge.

'We found something today,' she said smiling back at him.

Two large fires in the centre of the lodge had joints of meat cooking over them; the smaller fire had a large pot of turnips cooking over it. It was a hive of activity everyone seemed busy.

'How did you ever get five of them?' Bill asked.

'Made them fall off the cliff. I chased them off the edge with my wolves,' Ruth replied as she saw the chief notice her.

The chief was full of smiles as he came towards her. 'Porpog Jaga na Kala, Porpog,' the chief said as he reached the place where she and Bill were standing in the tribe lodge. 'Paga tak Jaga na Kala jadpog apa e apa e ap latan Jaga na Kala e kala,' he added with a broad smile on his face.

'Por mesh piapar umta.'

'Da. Por porpog Jaga na Kala porpog. Natkala porpog apar yep.'

'He thanked you for all the wood you cut.'

'Is that what he said, I guessed he was pleased with the moose.'

'They must have told him it was me who made them fall off the cliff.'

They all sat down to a good meal that evening, people were talking and seemed to Ruth to be a great deal happier than the two previous evenings. Her family of wolves sat amongst them accepting any bones that came their way. When they had finished the Spirit Man came to Ruth and asked her to come to the chief. Much of what he said to the chief Ruth could not understand though she knew he was talking about the hunt and that she had given them the turnips. 'Jaga na Kala, Daga Kala tak nat Porpog,' the chief said as he handed her another large feather. It was a good feather. 'E ap,' the chief said as he pointed to those already in her hair. Then having seen someone else receive a feather the previous year, she did the same and turned to face the rest of the tribe. 'Porpog Daga Kala,' they all replied then the spirit man led her back to where she was sitting with Bill.

As she made her way back to where Bill was she passed Big Bear, he looked at her nodding his head. 'Por, porpog,' he said.

'Porpog NatMegan,' Ruth responded.

'It's nice and warm in here,' Ruth said as she sat down on the firs in their lodge.

'I think Porjadseeni lit the fire while I was chopping wood for them.'

'That was nice of her, Oh Bill, I am tired but at least I am well fed tonight.'

'You are a remarkable woman Ruth, I don't know anyone who could take half-starved Indians and come back with five moose. You now have five feathers, that is important isn't it. You seem to be quite a senior member of this tribe now.'

'I have the same number as Meechamegan now. He is important.'

'The spirit man and he seem to be the ones that organise everything round here.'

'I think Big Bear is the hunting chief.'

'Probably,' Bill responded. 'You are very beautiful when your hair is done with the feathers. You have that necklace as well.'

'It is just beads.'

Chapter 10

The Indians had started to recover after the hardest winter Ruth had known in all the time she had been in the cabin. Bill helped the Indians sow an extra area of oats while Ruth went hunting. Their main hunting area was to the north and on both banks of the river to the west of the village. Slowly life in the village returned to normal. Ruth and Bill left them returning to the cabin in order to tend their fields and sow the beans which did not need as long to grow as the turnips did. The two of them worked hard, the fields looked good, the crops were growing well. It would not be long before summer arrived and with it would be the hot lazy days when they could all swim in the lake and enjoy life before the winter returned.

Ruth returned to the cabin with a small deer and a rabbit. She cut one of the rear legs from the deer for them then tossed the rest out of the cabin for her family of wolves. Zak had the rabbit for himself.

'It's a lot warmer these days,' Bill said as he tended the fire, which was cooking their meal

'Won't be long now before they come here for summer days,' Ruth explained.

'We have done all our work; do you want to go over to the village?'

'Not yet, we were there a long time in the early spring.'

'You will get no argument from me.'

With the hard work done, Ruth and Bill started to take life easier. The weather was starting to show the promise of the coming heat of summer. Ruth once again turned her attention to the area around the cabin. She tidied the woodpile; Bill came to help her repair the roof that was supposed to keep most of the rain and snow away from the wood. It never had and Ruth had given up trying to make it do so. It looked a lot better when they had finished and that pleased Ruth.

Ruth woke up, the sun had already risen and summer had almost arrived. She lay there for a while before she got off the bunk and went to the door to find out what sort of day they could expect. Something did not feel right, she could hear noises coming from the direction of the Indian village and she could hear wolves calling. She moved a little distance from the cabin trying to make sense of the distant noise. Zak and Sheba came up to her so did Bill dressed only in a loincloth. 'What is going on?'

'I don't know,' Ruth replied, 'We better go and find out.'

'Right,' Bill responded.

'I think I will take the bow and spears with me, I don't like the sound of that.'

The two of them returned to the cabin to dress. Ruth was ready first she went to the door. Zak was just outside; he drove her back into the cabin. Ruth could not understand why he was snarling at her. 'Right that is me ready let's go and find out what is going on,' Bill said as he reached her; he went to leave, but was immediately stopped by the two wolves. 'What has got into them?' He asked looking towards Ruth.

'I don't know; Zak would not let me out.'

'I don't like this Ruth,' as Bill spoke Zak gave out a long and loud howl. 'I don't like this one little bit, something is going on.'

'It's all right Zak,' Ruth said as she went to leave the cabin again. Both Zak and Sheba drove her back into the cabin. 'Bill.'

'There are others coming now look,' Bill said pointing at several other wolves that had arrived in the space at the front of the cabin.

'Zak will not let us out; he wants us to stay here.'

'I think we had better prepare for whatever it is.'

'Whatever it is it is in the village, and there are wolves there I heard them. What is...?' A scream coming from not far from the cabin filled the air and stopped Ruth from speaking. The wolves in the front of the cabin left running towards the path, which led to the Indian village. 'Come in Ruth that was not far from here,' Bill said going to the window in the rear wall. 'Can't see anything out here,' he added after looking out over the meadow. Ruth thought that maybe a large band of trappers, were attacking the village, but it would have to be a large group and so far, she had not heard musket fire.

Ruth put and arrow on the string of her bow ready to shoot it. 'I am going to open the door so that I can see where to shoot.'

'Be careful,' Bill said picking up the axe, which he had recently put a longer handle on.

'I will be.'

'There's still nothing…' another scream and the sounds of snarling wolves cut short Bill's comment. It came from the path to the village, whomever it was if they remained on the path, they would reach the cabin.

'The wolves are attacking people! Who though!' Bill called out still looking out of the window into the meadow.

'I don't know it can't be the Indians they pay no attention to them. There are wolves in the village I heard them howl.'

'That is another one,' Bill said as they heard a scream which came to an abruptly end.

Ruth saw a young Indian woman run into the clearing in front of the cabin. 'One of the Indians!' she cried out as she ran towards the woman. 'Iroquois apar Iroquois!' The young woman, Ruth thought her name was White Flower, said as Ruth reached her. 'Daqua porella Daqua,' Ruth shouted as she started back to the cabin. The woman almost fell into the cabin. 'Apar Iroquois!' she called out again. More screams came from along the path. 'Iroquois, what are they doing here?' Ruth asked.

'I don't know but they are very warlike,' Bill responded.

'Look after her Bill she has a bad cut on her arm. I need the two spears as well.'

'Don't try to fight them Ruth they will kill you.'

'I am not going to but if they come here I will have to.'

The screams of the Iroquois as the wolves attacked them were still to be heard not that far from the cabin. Ruth took up a position beside the door her bow prepared and two spears stuck in the ground beside her ready so she only had to put her hand out to get them. Several other women reached the cabin; some were badly hurt one had a lot of blood coming from a head wound. Bill looked after them; Ruth believed it was right, he knew about things like that. Porjadseeni came out of the bushes and ran towards the cabin. 'Iroquois.'

'Da, apar.'

'Da, daqua apar tod.'

'Meechamegan.'

'Tod, pi nak jad; apar tod,'

'Meechamegan nak tod,' Ruth said, 'Meechamegan nak tod, por paga,' Ruth said trying to assure her that Friend of Bear was not dead. Ruth continued to stand guard in front of the cabin. Her bow was ready and she was prepared to shoot at anyone she did not know or recognise as being from the wolf tribe. She could still hear the wolves attacking the Iroquois but not as frequent now after the initial onslaught the wolves must have undertaken. Ruth was surprised just how relaxed she felt standing there holding her bow with an arrow ready to fire.

Ruth started to venture further from the door. An Indian with an axe in his hand ran into the area in front of the cabin having followed the path; several wolves were chasing him. Ruth fired the arrow too quickly and missed him, but the wolves where onto him. He tried to defend himself but with four wolves attacking at the same time, he was unable to do so. He screamed as one of the wolves jumped at him. As he fell back, the wolf's jaws closed around his throat and bit down hard. The other three continued to attack until the Indian lay still blood pouring out of his neck, it wasn't long before he died and the blood stopped flowing. The wolves backed away.

'The wolves have just killed one,' Ruth called out without turning round.

'I saw,' Bill said, as he put his hand on her shoulder.

Ruth took another arrow before she approached the dead Indian; he definitely wasn't from the Wolf Tribe. She bent down and picked up the axe, it had a stone head, much the same as those the wolf tribe had but this one had a couple of medium sized feathers tied to the shank.

It had been quiet for a while; wolves were again massing in front of the cabin. Zak was no longer forcing Ruth back into the cabin. 'Ella daqua Daga Kala, porella,' Porjadseeni said coming up to Ruth, 'Porella.'

'Da,' Ruth said deciding immediately what Porjadseeni had asked for was the best course of action now that there appeared to be no reason for staying close to the cabin. She ran back to the cabin. 'Bill I am going to the village. I will take some wolves with me.'

'Be careful.'

'I will, you come later when you have done with them. Some will come with me. Porjadseeni will; she wants to go.'

'All right, don't take all the wolves.'

'Some will stay with you and you have Sheba she will not leave you.'

Ruth took several of the women who were not hurt with her and set off towards the village. Zak walked beside her, his body covered in blood from the fight with the Iroquois; several other wolves joined the possession. Ruth saw Jake amongst the pack in front of the group. The wolves were walking purposefully, their heads lowered, constantly looking around checking each side as the moved through the wood along the well-developed path to the Indian village. They had just crossed the bridge when they came across the first body of an Iroquois; it was laying just off the path its throat torn out. As they passed through the area in which the wolves had fought, the Iroquois Ruth believed she saw around ten bodies. She also saw two dead wolves, killed in the fight. It did not take Ruth long to walk and run the two miles to the Indian village, they saw the smoke long before they reached the top of the small hill to the south.

From the top of the hill, they looked down on a sight of complete devastation; smoke billowed from the tribe lodge as well as several of the other lodges. Bodies were lying around the village and in one area; a battle was still going on. Ruth ran down the hillside heading for a gap in the line of stakes. The rest followed her. The line of stakes, which kept out wild animals, had been no obstacle to the Iroquois, they had destroyed several sections and one section was burning fiercely. Ruth entered the village though a gap in the line of stakes her wolves around her as she started through the village towards the area in which the fighting was still going on. She saw Friend of Bear he was stumbling around blind then he fell over crashing into a partly burning lodge. Porjadseeni ran in his direction.

Ruth continued towards the fighting they needed help. She ran past the chief, he had a spear though his chest, one of those, which were normally in the ground behind his position in the circle.

As Ruth approached the area of the village, where the battle was going on, she slowed a little as she readied her bow. Then with her bow ready, she continued to run towards those still fighting the Iroquois. 'Jaga na Kala ella,' one of those defending the village called out as she approached them. The other five braves called out as she arrived. A spear narrowly missed her, as she stood there looking towards the Iroquois, she drew the arrow back. This time she didn't panic, she aimed where she knew the one who had thrown the spear would move to. The arrow met the moving Iroquois. Ruth wasted no time the second arrow was already on its way when the Iroquois went to duck down, it hit him in the throat. Ruth's third arrow, with a good bone, arrowhead on it, found it true target slight left of centre of the Iroquois chest. 'Pog,' someone called out as the hapless Iroquois collapsed to the ground. All five threw a spear towards the group of Iroquois. Ruth fired arrows into them until she had run out; then discarding her bow, she tested the weight of the spear in her right hand. It was her second best light spear.

Now Ruth judged, she needed the wolves to attack. 'Go Zak!' Jake had only been waiting to hear her cry out he was off and going straight for the group of Iroquois leading a pack of seven or eight wolves. Ruth was running beside Big Bear. 'Elena na Kala!' he screamed out at the top of his voice. Spears passed over the wolves' heads as Ruth and the five braves started to press home the attack.

Ruth reached the first of the Iroquois stabbing him with her best and last remaining spear. It was a fight where stabbing spears and wolves fought against axes being wield or thrown at them. Ruth was in the thick of it with Zak close by, her reactions working faster than they had ever done before. She ducked as an Iroquois swung and axe at her then jabbed at him with her spear, she was low, the Iroquois grasped and tried to swing his axe at her. Ruth thrust her spear into him again, this time higher up into his chest. It was like having a knife on the end of a long pole. He coughed; blood came out of his mouth. Ruth pulled her spear out of his chest then plunged it back pushing him backwards with the spear. He fell; she turned quickly ready to fend off another attack on her. The Iroquois threw his axe at her Ruth moved quickly to her right as the axe brushed against her arm. Then with her spear she attacked, the Iroquois died as Ruth stabbed him in the chest. She had to use the back end of the spear in order to dispatch the one who came up behind her. She pulled it out of the one she had killed and thrust backwards into the stomach of the other, a wolf jumped at the throat of the Iroquois as Ruth tried to pull her spear out of him. The Indian fell back jerking the spear out of Ruth's hands. She went to get her spear back, when another Iroquois swung at her. She managed to duck down low, he missed her but she did not have a spear or anything she could use. She saw an axe on the ground not far from her. She managed to block the next blow from the Iroquois but was on her knees with him coming at her for the third time. Ruth's hand closed round the axe 'No!' she screamed at the Iroquois as she swung up under his attempt to hit her, the axe in her hand hit him on the chest then glancing up under his chin. He stumbled forward. Ruth stood up and brought the axe down on the back of his neck. Turning quickly ready to fend off the next attack, she swung the axe knocking the spear right out of Natlatan's hands. 'Meecha!' he screamed at her. Ruth moved quickly grabbing a spear and throwing it to him then picked up one for her to use. The Iroquois who tried to attack the two of them stood no chance of success and when Zak jumped at his throat, Ruth turned her attention elsewhere. Quickly she looked around for an Iroquois; there were none left. The six of them stood with a small pack of wolves; around them were dead and dying Iroquois. Ten maybe twenty yards away was a fleeing Indian Ruth took a short run in his direction and launched her spear high into the sky, Jake set off after it. Ruth watched as the spear started to arch down. She saw the Iroquois look back towards her, but he failed to notice the spear high in the sky and looking back caused him to trip and fall; the spear descended, pinning his body to the ground.

'Pog,' Natlatan cried out jumping into the air with both hands above his head. Jake reached the Indian and tore his throat out. Ruth looked around she felt vulnerable without a spear; she picked up one then looked for her spear. She found it and threw the other one away. Her best spear looked to be all right, she tested its weight and balance. 'Iroquois! Ap,' one of the braves called out pointing in the direction he has seen the Iroquois.

The group of them set off in the direction of the sighted Iroquois. Zak reached him first and was dealing with the Indian when they arrived. Ruth and another wolf joined Zak and finished the task. More blood spurted out over Ruth as she stabbed the Iroquois through the chest with a spear.

'Por pe pogtod,' Big Bear said.

'Da,' Ruth responded pulling her spear out of the dead Iroquois, 'apar Iroquois tod.'

The battle was over; smoke billowed around the village from all the different lodges that were burning. Ruth thought they should all get together in one place. She did not think it was completely safe yet. 'Jad squaw e binpaja, tak ella krath,' Ruth told Natlatan

'Da peapar ella krath,' Big Bear ordered.

The band broke up to search the village for any who were hiding. Zak found the hiding place of a squaw and three small children, Ruth told them to make their way to the circle. Ruth picked up a heavy spear in order to knock down the furs over the entrance of a burning lodge to ensure no one was inside; it was empty. Ruth coughed stepping back to avoid the dense smoke. She continued to look in each lodge in turn.

Through the smoke Ruth saw Friend of Bear leaning against a lodge, not far from where she was, with Porjadseeni looking after him, she headed towards them. As she approached Zak snarled; the Iroquois, axe in hand, came round a lodge fully set to attack Porjadseeni. Ruth already warned by Zak was prepared; she took two steps and hurled the spear with all the force she could muster. The spear, its flight true, passed over the head of Porjadseeni, who was still unaware of the danger. It found its target in the centre of the Iroquois' chest, the force behind the spear drove half the spear though his body; the Iroquois gasped, staring at the spear in his chest, his arms flew out, the axe in his hand sailed through the air, bouncing off the lodge against which Friend of Bear was leaning. The Iroquois died without knowing where the spear had come from and without making a sound. His momentum carried his body towards Porjadseeni who had yet to realise what had happened. Porjadseeni screamed as the Iroquois collapsed over her. Ruth was there in moments, dragging the body away from her. Ruth used her foot to hold the body down so that she could recover her spear. There was a cracking sound as the spear came loose. It had blood over most of its length. Ruth looked at the broken point. It had been a good spear, but it would now need a new point. She would need a moose shin bond for that. 'Jaga na Kala,' Porjadseeni called out looking at Ruth with an expression of horror on her face.

'Iroquois tod, pi por,' Ruth said.

'Jaga na Kala pogtod Iroquois,' Meechamegan said looking at her.

'Da'

'Nak ap,' Meechamegan said pointing to the Iroquois Ruth had just killed. 'Pogtod apar,' he added pointing at her clothes. Ruth saw him looking her dress up and down.

Ruth stopped and looked at herself; splashes of blood covered her dress. 'Da, I don't know enough words. Pi apar pogtod. People are going to the circle, you can't stay here you will have to come to my meadow.'

'Da Friend of Bear say; not hurt bad, strong head not bad hurt.'

'That's good, Paga tod.'

'Nakpor e Elenapaga.'

'I don't know I have not seen him. Natlatan is alive he was fighting with me.'

'Natlatan fron pe nak tod.'

With Porjadseeni and Ruth's help Meechamegan got to his feet, he was a little unsure on them and needed help to walk to the circle. When they arrived, Ruth believed there must be others around who had not yet reached the circle. However, it soon became apparent the small group were all who remained of the tribe. Standing looking at the burning tribe lodge was Big Bear, son of the chief of the Bear tribe. Smoke billowed around from all the burning lodges. Ruth went to Big Bear, 'Portag Natmegan.'

'Nak portag Jaga na Kala nak por, apar e apar tod.'

'Da, nak por.'

'Natlatan tak ella daqua Jaga na Kala.'

'Da, apa e apa e ap lodge e cabin.'

'Da, pi paga tod.'

'I'm sorry,' Ruth said in English as she put her hand on Natmeegan's arm.

'Paga na Daga Kala e Elenapaga.'

'Apar tod.'

'Da apar e apar.' Big Bear stopped talking and point past Ruth. 'Jad! Natkala ella.'

Ruth turned to where he was pointing to see Bill with four squaws coming into the village; flanked by four wolves with Sheba leading them, 'Pi ella tak Natkala'

Ruth left Big Bear and the other braves and went to the circle where Bill and the other squaws had arrived. 'Ruth! What happened to you?' He exclaimed as soon as he saw her.

'I'm in a bit of a mess the fighting was not over when we got here, had to do my bit.'

'The state of you and your arm, you are hurt.'

'No,' Ruth said but then saw her upper arm, Bill had pointing to; there was a gash, which was still bleeding a bit but in the main had stopped, the dried blood having run down her arm. 'Oh I don't know how that happened,'

'We have some clean cloth strips. Let me do something, what do you mean you don't know how it happened you have been hit with axe by the looks of it.'

'Maybe I don't know,' she said touching her arm near the wound. 'Ouch! That hurts.' Ruth let Bill bandage her upper left arm. While he was doing so, Ruth watched Big Bear and Friend of Bear along with the other braves move a little away from the circle. She was pleased that

Friend of Bear seemed to be all right though he did have a nasty looking gash on the side of his head. Once Bill had finished with Ruth's arm, he turned his attention to the others. Ruth could see those needing help were being looked after, as she did not know how to help she went to find out what Big Bear wanted to do.

'Jaga na Kala, por jad Natkala grashan peon drancalota.'

'Um, sorry what was that?'

'Big Bear say that we saw Big Wolf making arm better.'

'I have blood all over me,' Ruth complained as she looked down at her dress.

'Jad lementa na binpaja na Jaga na Kala.'

'Da' two of the braves said before leaving the group to go and look in the nearby lodges. 'Big Bear say go and look for better clothes for you.'

'I need them, are you going to come to my lodges in the meadow.'

'Da, you say come, it best place, much work first.' As Friend of Bear spoke, the tribe lodge collapsed into a heap of burning wood. 'Not good Jaga na Kala not good,' He added as the wind blew smoke and hot embers over them. 'Ella!'

Ruth and Friend of Bear ran away going in the same direction as Big Bear. 'You can't live here.'

'We come to Jaga na Kala daqua.'

'We will need cooking pots I only have small ones.'

'Da, and furs to sleep in, much, we take.'

The two braves soon returned with leggings and a top. 'Better for you; Big Bear say you good brave,' Friend of Bear said.

Ruth did not have much of a say about it, they stood round her, took her bloodstained dress off then put the top and leggings on her dressing her in the clothes of a brave. Her loincloth was smaller and lighter than those the braves wore, and did not have the right sort of waistband to take the leggings. Several of them went looking for a better one. It did not take them long to return with one which was suitable. Now they could attach the leggings correctly. Ruth looked down to see how they were doing that. She ended up with a pair of trousers on. Ruth straightened the front flap down with her hands. 'You now paga, look better,' Friend of Bear said.

With clean clothes on Ruth now worked with the braves looking for long poles much the same as they used to drag heavy animals back to the village. There were plenty around the village. They collected them up and then tied a short cross member at one end. Over this frame was stretched a fur so that a person could lie on it and be pulled along. Once Ruth could see what was needed she got on with the task. Ruth checked with those in the circle to find out how many they needed. She returned, 'e ap.'

'Por, e apa,' Meechamegan ordered.

'Why are you dressed like that?' Bill asked when Ruth went to the circle to tell them the caribous were ready.

'They found me these; my dress was covered in blood.'

'I saw, it looks good on you.'

'We have made the stretchers, and we have an extra one for things we need. There was only one large pot which was not broken and they are looking for furs now.'

'We have seen to most now, one of the braves will not survive the journey to the cabin I can't stop the bleeding.'

Ruth went to the badly injured brave; a large gash in his stomach caused by a large spear was bleeding badly. She crouched down beside him. 'Hishojar,'

'Jaga na Kala,' he quietly said.

'Nak tak,' Ruth said taking his hand and holding it aware he was dying and it would not be long.

'Pi jad Natelena.'

'Da,' Ruth responded, but immediately a doubt came into her mind. It was not his time; White Mountain would not see the Great Spirit. 'Da pe jad Natelena,' she said as reassuringly as she could.

'Por,' he quietly said as he closed his eyes. Ruth felt his hand tighten around hers for a while then his hand relaxed and fell away.

Ruth had tears in her eyes as she stood up. 'Are you all right?' Bill asked.

'He has died.'

'I'm sorry; I couldn't help him.'

'It's not your fault, you did what you could.'

By mid-afternoon most of the fires had burnt out, however, smoke still bellowed round the village from the smouldering remains of what were once lodges. Ruth helped place the injured onto the stretchers and then those who were able prepared to drag them up the hill towards the cabin. It was a difficult two miles to cover; fortunately the path between the Indian village and Ruth's cabin was a well-defined track, and the bridge she had built with Friend of Bear made it possible to cross the stream with the stretchers. Eventually they all reached the meadow behind the cabin.

Ruth watched, from a distance, as Friend of Bear argued with Big Bear for a while then took charge, putting people into the lodges so that there were both fit and injured in each lodge. Big Bear left. Ruth decided that whatever it was she should not become involved in the squabble between them.

Friend of Bear was definitely in charge of matters sorting out who was in each lodge and he did not tolerate any objections. He also spread the children out so they would have someone to care for them. Friend of Bear, Porjadseeni and two children were to be in the cabin.

'There is not that much space,' Bill said.

'There's enough, two lots of furs on the floor, the children can be under one lot.'

'I suppose that will have to do. We will have to build more lodges.'

'We all need something to eat,' Ruth said thinking about more immediate things they needed.

'Now that I can arrange; I will light a fire outside,' Bill said, eager to get on with a job he could do.

'We have plenty of food in the cave not much meat though.'

'I can get it done. Porjadseeni will work with me, get a couple more.'

'We need more furs as well.'

'Tell Friend of Bear, he seems to have taken over after an argument with Big Bear.'

'He's gone off in a huff and we really could do with him right now,' Ruth said thinking about all the jobs which needed to be done right now.

Ruth found Friend of Bear in the meadow, he was organising a small group of squaws. 'Bill is making mesh.'

'Por,' then turning to the squaws he said. 'Ella Natkala, pog mesh,' he ordered.

'Da,' the squaws responded without any questions; they immediately set off towards the cabin.

'Pog pi?'

'Nak, pi e pe jad piapar por.'

'Look to see if all good.'

'Da,'

Ruth did as Friend of Bear asked. Several lodges needed firewood; those in the lodge were looking after the injured so Ruth went to the woodpile for them fetching back wood so they could light a fire in the lodge. While she was engaged in this task, Big Bear reappeared and started to help her. She was busy with the jobs that needed doing for a while. When Ruth looked around for Zak, she could not find him and started to wonder where he had gone. The last time she had seen him was when she had gone to Meechamegan in the village, but she could not remember seeing him on the way back to the meadow. 'Where is Zak?' She asked Bill as he checked the cooking pot.

'I don't know; I don't know where Sheba is either.'

'Jake is not here where have they gone.'

'I don't know. He will be around somewhere.'

'He needs a wash they all do; both Zak and Jake are covered in blood.'

'The meal is nearly ready.'

'Thank you, I am going to find Friend of Bear see what else is to be done.'

When Ruth went round into the meadow in order to find Friend of Bear she saw him talking to Big Bear. The two of them were all smiles again, having sorted out whatever the caused the argument was. She reached the two of them. 'Jaga na Kala, por paga,' Big Bear said as she approached.

'Natmegan tak Jaga na Kala pogtod apar Iroquois,'

'I sort of had to. Do we have to bury the dead if so when?'

'Aptag,' Meechamegan said in answer to Ruth's question on when to bury the dead. 'Put all in mound, no guard to look over their spirits, that bad, very bad, not good, people not like to know there no guard.'

'Why can't the Iroquois guard there are a lots of them?' Ruth asked.

'Not know, must know you are guard. All dead no one to tell guard spirit.'

'Is Big Bear the chief now, he has most feathers.'

'Nak, Big Bear not chief; I chief for two day. Brave say I am chief, then squaw choose. Natlatan he good. Not matter how many feathers brave has.'

'You will be the spirit man.'

'Da, pi Elenapaga.'

Ruth returned to the front of the cabin. She sat on a log just outside the cabin where she had often sat and talked to Bill while the sun set. It gave a view out over the lake and the mountains. Today however she watched Bill and the two squaws who had come to help get the meal ready. Someone had moved the body of the Iroquois who had been killed by the wolves just short of the path. A squaw and a young boy arrived with a large stone. They placed it on the ground; others started to do the same. Friend of Bear became involved he wanted stones for those who were not here, stones were found and placed in a circle, it was not large, but for every lodge the village had there was a stone in the correct position.

The meal ready, food was taken to the wounded that were unable to come to the circle before anyone else ate. Then the rest sat in the circle with their meal. 'Jaga na Kala sit there on log. I sit here with you.' Ruth sat back down on the log; Bill was sitting in the circle with the rest in the same place as their home stone would have been.

'Are you now the spirit man?' Ruth asked Friend of Bear.

'Da, I talk to Great Spirit, it hard to say.'

'I know.'

After the meal Ruth through Friend of Bear told them, the cave had plenty of oats for their family meals in the morning and that they should take what they needed and make a meal for all those in each lodge. Bill came across to where Ruth was talking to Friend of Bear. 'He's not come back,' Ruth told Bill assuming he would know she was talking about Zak.

'He will,' Bill replied putting his arms round her shoulder.

Ruth held him closely to her; it had been a day she did not want to repeat. 'I wonder where he went; it was all over. He was there when I went to Friend of Bear. He warned me of the Iroquois, so I know he was there then, but that's the last time I can remember seeing him. In fact he wasn't there when I help Friend of Bear walk to the circle.'

Ruth went into the cabin with Bill, Friend of Bear, Porjadseeni, and two children were in the cabin spreading furs on the floor. Ruth help the two children, they were still frightened.

By the time everything was ready Ruth discovered they had an extra person; White Flower had been working taking furs to each lodge when Friend of Bear had made the rough and ready allocation of lodges. 'White Flower with you,' Friend of Bear told Bill in such a way that Bill knew there could be no discussion about the matter.

In the morning, Ruth woke before dawn she quietly made her way out of the cabin and down to the shore of the lake. A couple of wolves came to find out who was walking around at that time of day neither were Zak. Ruth sat on the bank and watched as the sun rose over the eastern end of the lake, then lay back as the warmth of the sun started to reach her.

Bill woke Ruth. 'I came out to be by myself,' she said looking up at him.

'I woke up to find it was White Flower and not you.' Ruth smiled at the thought of him waking up and finding White Flower with him. 'Yea, I thought you would find that amusing. It looks as if it is going to be a nice day.'

'We have to bury them today; at least it will then be done. They will not see the Great Spirit they have no one to guard their spirits until it is their time. It's very sad.'

'Is that what's bothering you?' Bill said sitting down next to her.

'They will be lost and not know when to go to the Great Spirit. I told Hishojar he would see the Great Spirit, but I knew he wouldn't,' Ruth said her face showing the stress and pain she felt for those who had died in the battle.

'Come on my love. I know you're very upset,' Bill said putting his arm round her.

'I am sorry. I would hate that to happen to me. They have done what the Great Spirit wanted it is not right they should not see him.'

'I don't know what to say I am sure the Great Spirit will give you strength.'

'They seem to think that I am now a brave.'

'From what Friend of Bear told me you most certainly are. You fought like mad so I am told, battling with the braves. I am sure it is not quite right but apparently he said that Big Bear told him you threw a spear up into the air and it came down and killed an Iroquois who was running away.'

'He tripped up and fell over; I would have missed if he had carried on running.'

'So you did.'

'It was luck; anyway Jake would have caught him.'

'For someone that left the settlement on the coast because of the fighting you seem to have done more than a little here.'

'I had to and the Great Spirit guided me I know he did,' Ruth said then sat quietly with Bill with her own thoughts.

Chapter 11

Porjadseeni had prepared the morning meal by the time Ruth and Bill returned to the cabin. While they ate the meal, Ruth sat, on her log stool, and discussed with Friend of Bear what they needed to do that day. He told her, they would place the dead in a shallow grave, and would burn the Iroquois so their spirits had no home and would forever be lost. It was work only braves could do and though their numbers were small, Friend of Bear would not hear of the squaws helping. On the other hand, he expected Ruth to do this work. 'You brave, not squaw you have blanket and kill many in battle you strong, not even know hurt, still fight very strong. You strong Iroquois not kill, too strong for Iroquois.'

'Do you want Bill to help?'

'He not brave of tribe, when he gets blanket then he brave of tribe.'

One of the wounded braves came with them; although he was not badly hurt he was going to find it hard work. The seven of them set out with three stretchers. The dead Iroquois not far from the cabin were piled onto the stretchers it was too much for the wounded brave to pull Ruth helped pull one with Big Bear. It was hard work and they had to go back for the rest.

They lit a large fire and started to throw the Iroquois bodies onto it. The wounded brave said he would take on this task with one of the other braves.

Ruth joined the other four and started to dig the shallow grave they made it as wide as a person was tall and about twenty yards long. The work was heavy they all rested in the heat of the day going to the river to cool off. Ruth was pleased to get away from the stench of burning flesh for a while.

When they return to work, they paired off in order to fetch the bodies on a stretcher Ruth was with big Bear. He wanted the bodies of the wolves place in the grave. Friend of Bear came across to make the decision. He stated they had died in the same battle fighting on the same side that made them braves of the tribe. They placed the dead wolves together at one end of the grave.

Where they could they placed families together so their spirits would be close and before they started to put the mound of earth over them they searched a large area around the village to ensure they had everyone.

After placing the mound of earth over those who had died, they all took another rest before starting to collect up as many weapons as they could find. Bows, arrows, spears both light and heavy were all piled onto one of the stretchers. Then they went around the village gathering anything, which might be of use. Ruth was pleased to see some of the Iroquois had metal knives they would come in handy. The two who had been dealing with the dead Iroquois had a collection of knives.

With all three stretchers loaded, they set of back to the cabin. It had been a long and hard day for Ruth, difficult not only because of the hard physical work it was also emotionally draining. They dragged two loaded stretchers into the meadow. Ruth left Friend of Bear and Big Bear there sorting it out and went to the cabin. Once in the cabin she lay on the bunk. It was almost time to eat.

'Hard work,' Bill said in an inquiring voice.

'It's done; lot of talk about not having any guards though.'

'In time that will heal,' Bill said as he tried to reassure her.

'No it won't; they will never meet the Great Spirit they will not know when because they will not have someone to tell them. Friends will miss someone when they die and we are sad they are gone, but we also know they have met the Great Spirit, because it was their time to and that is good to know. But if they are killed and the guard can't be found then not only do you miss them you know that they will never meet the Great Spirit.'

'My God meets everyone no matter how they die. I am sure my God will ask the Great Spirit to look for the spirits of those that died.'

'Does God know the Great Spirit?'

'I am sure he does.'

'Will God guard them and tell them when to meet the Great Spirit?'

'I am sure he will. I have seen how they have lived a good life without sin and like the Great Spirit says; that is what God asks of you.'

'Maybe he will guard them then.'

The meal that evening was eaten in almost complete silence, people sat there with their own thoughts. Ruth looked at them; they had won the battle, but they were a beaten tribe, and tomorrow they would have to choose a new chief. Ruth looked at Big Bear; he was definitely strong and had proved himself in the battle. The chief had been an older man; from what she knew, he had been a good chief.

The snarl of a wolf interrupted Ruth's thoughts; it came from the woods to the east. It was followed by someone calling out Ruth did not understand it but was aware it was the Indian language she had heard. Ruth had not been the only one to hear it. Big Bear was already getting up; Ruth was off the log glanced in his direction then towards where they had left all the weapons. Natlatan ran there at Big bears nod. Ruth stood in the centre of the circle waiting for Natlatan to throw her a spear; he threw several Ruth selected two. By the time, the wolf snarled for the second time four of them were already between the circle and the edge of the woods, and Natlatan with the injured brave were carrying bows and arrows across to them along with more spears.

Ruth could feel her heart beating faster and harder as they waited. Her nerves tightened, she saw a figure, its back half towards her as if they were walking backwards. She saw the wolf's head, only momentarily, but then she only needed a glimpse of that head. 'Zak' she cried out running towards the figure and the wolf.

Ruth almost ran into the two Iroquois she came to an abrupt halt her spear ready to jab at them. One of them move but Sheba and Jake knocked him to the ground, Ruth pushed the other Iroquois with a decorated top and a lot of feathers in his hair back with her spear Zak snarling at her side. By the time Big Bear and the others arrive, she had the Iroquois back against a tree with the tip of her spear on his throat. The other Iroquois was trying to get up but Jake would not let him.

'Pogtod Iroquois,' Natlatan called out.

'Nak,' Ruth shouted, 'Poota!'

There was a pause, and then Friend of Bear said, 'Da, da, nak pogtod.'

They did not need the wolves help, three onto each Iroquois was always going to be in their favour. 'Is it ok,' Bill asked as he came into the area of the woods.

'Ella Daqua, nak squaw.'

'Keep them away Bill, go back to the circle and keep them away from here, we can do this. Go back and tell them it is all right if you can; say por several times it means good, and nakella that is stay.'

'Right then por and nakella it is.'

The two Iroquois were stripped naked. Big Bear and the others pulled lengths of vines off the trees; then used them to bind the Iroquois until all they could do was move from the knees down. Additional vines were then wrapped round the neck of each prisoner and held by two braves. Ruth did not have hold of a vine. 'Sit in circle Jaga na Kala. Porella,' Friend of Bear ordered.

Ruth did as she had been told and was back sitting on the log before the braves dragged the two prisoners out of the woods. The squaws all of whom were still sitting in the circle started to jeer and shout at them. The braves dragged the two Iroquois into the centre of the circle, stones were tossed at them; dirt was thrown in their faces. Ruth could now see why there were several loops around their necks; it allowed the braves to hold them up so they could not collapse onto the ground. Although they were immediately, the target of all manner of abuse nothing was to such a degree that would kill them. Ruth was aware everyone knew the two Iroquois must live until they were told to guard the spirits of the tribe.

When Friend of Bear thought it had gone on long enough, he ordered the squaws back. The circle settled. Friend of Bear spoke quietly to Big Bear then sat down to the right of Ruth. Ruth watched as the naked Indians were dragged from the centre of the circle to a position just in front of her. 'Jaga na Kaka! Elena na Kala! Apa Iroquois nakmeecha, nakmeecha! Iroquois pogtod apar e apar Daga Kala e pogtod apar e apar kala!' Big Bear spoke so that all could hear his voice almost loud enough to be heard the other side of the lake. He stood there tall and proud, towering above the two Iroquois. Ruth sat stroking Zak and watching the eyes of the two Iroquois. Big Bear had called her the spirit of the wolf neither of the two Iroquois could believe she was stroking Zak while he snarled at them. She sat up right as tall as she could, with Zak beside her, Bill not far away with Sheba, and Jake lying down in front of her grumbling to himself; she knew they were frightened of her. Big Bear had stopped speaking, Ruth knew it was not the right place to tell them to guard; it had to be the last thing they heard, it had to be in the other circle. 'Aptag Jaga na Kala tak ne daqua na Daga Kala.'

'Da Jaga na Kala, Elena na Kala,' Big Bear said and with that, he and the other braves lashed the two Iroquois to a tree. Two braves armed with spears stood guard over them. Those in the circle went to their lodges. Ruth stroked Zak and talked to him for a while then went to the cabin. Big Bear and Friend of Bear were there talking to each other. They stopped when Ruth entered the cabin.

'Big Bear say you Elena na Kala and say guard spirit, more powerful if spirit tell you to guard.'

'They were very frightened of me.'

'You had Zak he is cross with them. Call many to circle show that you are Elena na Kala.'

'Does Big Bear want me to do that?'

'I tell him.'

Ruth listened as Friend of Bear explained.

'Da, Da! Por Elena na Kala tak kala, kala ella. Por aptag'

'He say yes.'

'I know what he said.' Ruth sat down on the bunk; she was tired.

'Did I get that right you have been elevated from mother to spirit?' Bill asked sitting beside her.

'That is what they want me to be tomorrow.'

'They were not that pleased to see them, the women I mean, throwing stones and all sorts at them.'

'They will not hurt them enough to kill them though.'

'I was aware of that; that happens tomorrow; doesn't it. Will Big Bear or Friend of Bear put the heads on the mound?'

'No, if I say guard I have to show them where, and Friend of Bear has to be the spirit man, I have seen this done before. He has to talk to the Great Spirit tomorrow. I hope the Great Spirit is pleased with us.'

'Can you do that?'

'I have to, it will make the tribe strong again, we have to be strong we are so small now.'

'You sleep now I can see you are very tired.'

'I am.'

Ruth moved over a bit when White flower got onto the bunk. There was not a lot of space with three of them trying to sleep on the bunk; it would have to be sorted out, but right now sleep was what she wanted to do.

Big Bear and three braves were not there in the morning, nor were the two Iroquois. Those that were there ate an early family meal. Ruth had to be painted and this time it included red. 'You Spirit of Wolf,' Friend of Bear said.

All the tribe returned to the old stone circle, those that could not walk were dragged there on stretchers so they could see the guards being placed and hear the words of the spirit man when he spoke to the Great Spirit. Ruth saw two braves standing outside one of the few remaining lodges not far from the circle. They had brought the Iroquois there earlier. Those with Ruth sat in the circle Ruth sat down where the chief use to sit. The spaces in the circle acted as a reminder of just how many of the tribe had died in the battle for the village. Meechamegan with the wolf skin of the spirit man over him, sat down beside Ruth. When everything was ready, Big Bear brought the two Iroquois in front of Ruth again. One look at Ruth and one of the Indians was trying everything he could to stop them dragging him in front of her. Big Bear once again addressed her as Elena na Kala and told her the two of them had killed many braves from the tribe and many of her wolves.

'Kala ella,'

'Da,' Big Bear said. 'Tak Elena na Kala, tak apar kala ella!'

'Call boy call Zak,' Ruth said stroking Zak's chest. He gave out a long howl. Ruth watched the eyes of the two Iroquois they were already frightened of her. Ruth could reason that were she the spirit of wolves she would speak in another language, one the wolf would understand. She wondered if the Iroquois understood English thinking it was unlikely. Zak had called at her command, the brave's whole body was trembling and the arrival of the first wolf did not help him. It was not long before wolves massed around Ruth, there was no doubt in her mind the two Iroquois would do as she said, and guard the spirits of those who had died in the battle. She looked directly at the brave who by now was almost paralysed with fear.

'Tak poota Elena na Kala!' Big Bear called out. Ruth did not think he needed to impress the two Iroquois any further; they were both frightened, the brave very much so.

Ruth thought she should deal with the brave first. She looked straight into his eyes. 'Paga Iroquois Elena na Kala tak, Paga Iroquois tod apar e apar Daga Kala e apar e apar Kala. Pe nakpor Elena na Kala tak poota paga Daga Kala e kala.' The effect of not only telling him that he must guard those in the tribe but also her wolves, petrified the Iroquois brave; he lost all ability to control his body. Ruth looked up at Big Bear he held in his hand one of the knives that had been taken from the trappers. She did not turn away this time; first, he cut the throat then the muscles down each side of the neck. It was quick, and surprised Ruth just how easily a head came off. Big bear placed it on one of the two blankets. Without warning, or someone telling them, the wolves attacked the now lifeless body tearing it to shreds in moments. Those holding the Iroquois made him watch as the wolves tore the limbs off the dead brave. With parts of the body now scattered around the area the wolves were waiting for the second one. Ruth looked directly into the eyes of the war chief. 'Paga pan pog na Iroquois, Elena na Kala tak, por poota paga Daga Kala. E poota Elena na Kala, kala.' Ruth believed she had said what she needed to. His eyes told her everything they showed nothing but fear. 'Elena na Kala tak poota,' Ruth added as she looked up towards Big Bear who was standing behind the now terrified war chief who could see the ring of wolves waiting for him.

It was difficult for Ruth to carry the Iroquois war chief's head. The spirit man walked beside her with the other. Ruth placed the head at the end of the mound looking inward. The spirit man passed her the other head, which she placed at the other end also looking inward so it could see those it must guard. She stood and listened to the spirit man as he spoke at some length to the Great Spirit. Some phrases she could understand others were not yet within her ability to translate. Then she and the spirit-man covered the heads with soil. The tribe watched the whole ceremony in complete silence. Then the braves led the tribe back to the cabin with its five lodges in the meadow behind it.

The moose, which kept on eating the beans, was there, spears flew through the air each finding its target. The moose would not be eating any more beans.

The place became busy. The area in front of the cabin was not big enough to hold a circle large enough to have a fire in the centre of it. Ruth and Friend of Bear selected an area of the meadow and stones placed in the correct position. Friend of Bear was busy organising it; using a length of vine to ensure that each stone was the same distance from the centre. The circle completed to his satisfaction the braves lit a large fire in the centre.

While the women prepared the moose, Ruth went down to the lake the water looked good she slipped the leggings and top off then walked into the water. It was fresh and cooling and Ruth enjoyed the moments of peace as she washed the spirit paint from her body. She saw Bill coming down the upper bank; she swam towards the shore. 'Does the water feel good?' he asked.

'I like swimming; I can't remember a time I didn't swim in the river. I needed to wash the paint off as well.'

'It feels completely different here now, everyone seems better.'

'The dead have a guard now, that is why they are please and the Great Spirit sent us a moose we didn't even have to look for it; he gave it to us, all we had to do was throw a few spears at it. The Great Spirit must be very pleased with what Friend of Bear said to have sent us a moose like that. Friend of Bear will be a good spirit man the tribe will get strong with him as spirit man, you watch.'

'And are you going to eat the biscuit when he offers it tonight.'

'I can't be chief. Big Bear will be a good chief; I know he will.'

'A lot want you.'

'A woman can't be chief.'

'Apparently it has happened before where a woman has shown she is a good brave. Well that is what Friend of Bear said.'

'A white one.'

198

'That may not have happened before, but what does that matter, you are the best we have Ruth, the things I have seen you do. You took eight half-starved Indians hunting and returned with five moose five! You fought like a wild banshee for all I hear killing Iroquois left right and centre. You throw a spear up into the sky and it comes down onto one that ran away. Your wolves brought back the two who guard the dead and you placed them there as Elena na Kala; what more do you think you need to do to prove you are the best we have.'

'A lot happened all of a sudden.'

'Put your top on and the leggings. Start being the chief you are.'

They were a little late sitting down in the new circle the moose was cooking nicely and smelt good. Friend of Bear told her she must sit with Bill in their place in the circle. He laid the chief headdress and top in the place normally occupied by the chief along with a spear, which had several feathers tied to it. It was then time to eat. Each came to take some then sat eating. Everyone was talking and for the first time the injured had all been able to come to the circle. As they finished the atmosphere became excited people were waiting for the Sprit man. Friend of Bear who had sat beside the empty chief's position, with the pelt of a wolf over him stood, and the circle fell silent. He told them he had selected three possible braves and he would ask each now if they wanted to be chief. He then carried the tribe blanket round the circle and placed it in front of Big Bear, who took the small biscuit and ate it.

The second person he placed the blanket in front of was Natlatan. He looked at the biscuit for a while, then picked it up and threw it away. That led to a lot a hushed

199

chatter around the circle as all eyes turned towards Ruth. The Sprit man placed the blanket in front of her. There was a single small oatmeal biscuit on it. She looked up to see four eyes looking down at her, the wolf's head over the spirit man. She picked the biscuit up, hesitated for a moment then ate it. The effect around the circle was immediate.

'You talk to tribe tell them why you best chief; I say words for you.'

'Tell them that… Ruth stopped to think a little then started again 'Tell them today the Great Spirit is pleased with us, we have done well and he very pleased. Tell them I said you are a very good spirit man you spoke to the Great Spirit today and he must be very pleased with what you said as he sent us this moose without the need for us to hunt it first. Tell them if I am chief I will keep us strong with the Great Spirit and if I could talk to the Great Spirit, I would not ask for good hunting. I would ask him to let us live here in peace, live a good life, as he wants us to, and for all the time I am chief there will never be any reason why we will need to fight. I would ask we never have any battles while I am chief; I want that more than lots of animals to hunt.'

Ruth listened as Friend of Bear told the tribe what she had said. Even the little she knew of their language she understood most of what he said and he had told them what she had said. 'I have said words for you. Good words strong.'

Ruth listened to Big Bear talk about what he would do. Then the spirit man stood in the centre of the circle beside the fire and asked the squaws to move to the brave of their choice. All except the squaw of Big Bear came and sat around Ruth. She saw Big Bear speak to his squaw; she got up and came to those who were sitting in front of Ruth. Big Bear nodded in Ruth's direction. 'Apar e apar,' the spirit man said looking at Ruth, and then turned to look at Big Bear.

'Nak ap,' Big Bear shouted out throwing his arms up and looking around him. He saw a young girl sitting not far from him. He jumped up and fetched her. 'Ap,' he said to the great amusement of everyone.

'You now come with me,' Friend of Bear said. Ruth got up and went with Friend of Bear. He took her to one of the lodges. Big Bear arrived with the headdress and top of the chief. 'Piapa pog Jaga na Kala,' Big Bear said as the two of them started to dress Ruth as the chief. Dressed as the chief for the first time Friend of Bear held the skins so that Ruth could leave the lodge. 'You greet tribe say portag Daga Kala, me say when you not know.'

The two of them led her to the position occupied by the chief. 'Portag Daga Kala,' Ruth said once Big Bear had reached his position in the circle opposite her; the second most important position in the circle.

'Portag Jaga na Kala Paga na Daga Kala!' the whole tribe, who were now all back in the right positions in the circle, responded.

With Friend of Bear prompting her, Ruth went to each home stone and greeted the brave. 'Portag Natlatan.'

'Portag Paga na Daga Kala.'

Ruth having gone to each daqua then sat down in her place with Zak beside her. Meechamegan then as the Elenapaga spoke to the Great Spirit thanking him for sending them a chief. Ruth sat and listened. He returned and placed the tribe blanket in front of her again. 'Suta

Jaga na Kala Paga na Daga Kala,' Friend of Bear said. Ruth lifted the top of her blanket back, then reached out and picked up the knife without any hesitation. She held it up so that all could see. 'Por suta, por you say much.' Then the Spirit man led the rest of the braves in a dance round the fire again before he sat down beside Ruth. 'Tell tribe no work next day.'

'Can we do that?'

'Nak, but still say.'

'Ap tag nak pog.'

'Por.'

In the cabin, Big Bear spoke for a long time to Friend of Bear. 'Jaga na Kala, Big Bear say much, he say he know you not Elena na Kala but you very strong with Elena na Kala and the Great Spirit. He said we have best chief and he said you make tribe strong bring Daga Kala much good.'

'I must learn lots, I don't know how to be chief. Big Bear should have been chief.'

'I know what you say I say to Big Bear.'

Ruth listened to what the two of them were saying. 'Big Bear say you know what Great Spirit wants, he not know that,' Friend of Bear told Ruth.

'But you can tell him just as you told me.'

'You strong with Great Spirit, I not tell you all and you know without me telling you; Great Spirit show you more than I say.

Big Bear left for his lodge, Ruth took the large headdress off and looked for somewhere to put it where it would be safe. 'Give it to me,' Bill said, 'It can hang there if you want.'

'Da, porpog Bill that will be fine.'

It had been another busy day, Ruth was pleased to get between the furs and relax. 'This bunk is too small,' Bill complained as the three of them tried to find room enough to sleep.

Ruth laid between the furs the following day and watched White Flower make the family food. Friend of Bear returned to the cabin, 'Por, pe nak tashka, nat pog apa e ap yartag.'

'Pi nak pog ap tag,' Ruth said telling Friend of Bear she would only take one rest day.

'Natmegan e apa paga jadpog.'

'Por.'

Ruth got out from between the furs when White Flower had the porridge ready. Having eaten, Ruth wandered out of the cabin to find out what the day was like. Ruth went round each of the lodges to make sure everyone was all right. She sat and spoke to Fast Deer one of the injured braves, for a while before making her way to the bay. Bill was there sitting on the top of the bank. Ruth sat down beside him. 'You heard what Friend of Bear and Big Bear said, but I don't know if I am the right person,' Ruth said.

'You are Ruth there is no mistake about that. I left the church because I didn't see many living up to the word of God. I came here searching for something I don't know what, I told myself I was searching for God. What I found was a beautiful young woman, not much more than a girl. She was alone in the wilderness surrounded by wolves and Indians; by all accounts, she should be dead, killed by the wolves or the Indians. If not that, she should have starved to death, but she hadn't; she grew food, she had made friends with the wolves and the Indians. You have embraced the wilderness, the wolves, the Indians, but more importantly, you embraced the Great Spirit, as I have never seen anyone embrace God. You have a stronger faith in the Great Spirit than I have in God. Others also see this, Friend of Bear, Big Bear, Tall Mountain, Big Moose all the rest of the tribe, they can all see this strong faith in you and they believe this is what they needed in their chief. They know the Great Spirit has guided you and especially in the last few days. That is why you are the chief and why you are the best person to guide all of us. I have no doubts you will make one of the best chiefs there has been.'

Ruth sat and thought about what Bill had said. 'I think I will swim out to the rock and be by myself for a bit, I need to get use to the idea and think about what I should do for the best, I don't really know.'

'You do that, I am sure the Great Spirit will show you the way.'

Bill sat on the top of the bank, he watched Ruth swim out to the rock and disappear round the other side of it. He sat there in thought, she had a difficult job but he was sure she would be able to do it and do it well. 'Jaga na Kala nak jad,' someone said disturbing his thoughts. He look up it was Friend of Bear.

'Sorry Friend of Bear nak jad.'

'No see.'

'Ah, Jaga na Kala ella...' then not knowing the word for rock he pointed at it, 'that rock,' he added in English.

'Por, she talk with Great Spirit come back strong.'

'Da.'

'Jaga na Kala por jaga e por paga.'

'Good woman and good man.'

'Da, not long you talk good.'

'Nak apar tag pi tak por.'

'Da, da porpog.'

'I am learning more than that Friend of Bear I have all my life looked for someone like Jaga na Kala we are all fortunate she is here, I don't believe any of us would be able to survive without her.'

'Not know all words you talk of Jaga na Kala say much I think.'

'Da.'

'Natelena tak Zak, Jaga na Kala ella; Zak por kala e poota Jaga na Kala.'

'There was not much that I understood.'

'Say great spirit tell Zak go to Jaga na Kala he good wolf.'

'Da, he is a good wolf.'

'He guard Jaga na Kala, he Elena na Kala.'

The sun had moved a long way before Bill saw Ruth swimming back to the bay. He waited for her to put her top and leggings on before he spoke 'You're back,' Bill said as Ruth sat down next to him.

'Had a long think to myself,' Ruth said.

'Good, I have discovered who they think Elena na kala is; it's Zak.'

'Zak!'

'Friend of Bear was talking to me; he said Zak was Elena na Kala.'

'He could be, yes, that would explain a lot. Now I'm beginning to understand things.'

'You think he is.'

'I do now, yes. He is definitely Elena na kala, it explains everything.'

Ruth went to find Big Bear and Friend of Bear then sat in the cabin with them talking about what needed doing. They needed more lodges so each brave would have a lodge for himself. They needed to tend the fields and hunt for meat. Ruth asked how Bill could become a brave; Friend of Bear told she only had to give him the blanket of a brave. The discussion took a long time but in the end, Ruth had a clear idea of what she needed to do.

Bill came into the cabin not long after the others had left it, 'Big talk,' he said speaking as the Indians would but using English words.

'Nat tak da, tak, tak e tak but I know what is required. There was a feeling that you would be better working in the fields.'

'After my attempts at hunting Indian style that is not unexpected, I am happy doing that, you tell me what you want grown and I will get it done for you.'

'You are good at it, I know that. What we do need to do is go and find out what the Indians fields are like.'

'I will walk over there tomorrow and have a look, I could even go today.'

There was little time to relax. The lodges were built Ruth had two extra ones built so that wolves had somewhere to stay. Once each brave had a lodge, new families became the priority; Ruth had a precession of squaws coming to her with a stone; most of the time at least one of the braves stood up. The same applied to the children. White Flower remained in the cabin with Ruth and Bill. 'Take the bunk out will you Bill, then we can sort the furs out properly.'

'Is White Flower going to stay here with us?'

'I would start getting used to it if I were you. Looks like you have two squaws. But I think she better come to me with a stone, you will have to stand up for her.'

'I can't have two…'

'Why are you so special then, everyone else has to look after at least two squaws?'

'But I want you…I've just had to lie there recently it seems like ages.'

'You have to keep both of us happy.'

'You can't mean that.'

'I'm an Indian chief, you told me to start acting like one, now you act like a brave would, and look after two squaws. You will like White Flower she is nice and I like her.'

That evening White Flower came to Ruth with a stone. Bill was the only one to stand up. White Flower beamed a huge smile at him as he came and stood beside her in front of Ruth. 'Thank you Bill, we will be fine I know we will.'

'I'm a brave of this tribe.'

Chapter 12

With only eight braves, the work was hard and seemed never ending. Ruth thought it was about time they all had a couple of days off; at the meal that evening once everyone had eaten she spoke to the tribe. 'Apar e apar tag Daga Kala pog porpog; apa tag nak pog.'

'You not say right, know what you mean,' Friend of Bear said, 'You say work many, many days and then two not work.'

'We have worked.'

'Porpog apar e apar tag, nak pog apa tag.'

'It's the wrong way round.'

'Da,'

'Daga Kala porpog apar e apar tag, nak pog apa tag.'

'All pleased now.'

The following morning Ruth thought it was about time she repaired her favouit spear. She had long ago kept a shin bone from a moose that was in the cabin. She went and fetched it laying it down on a large flat stone she used to sharpen her knives. She also had a large round rock there. Having smashed the bone she looked to pieces over, one was just right about eight inches long, straight with a point and a slightly curved cross section. By rubbing the bone over her large flat stone she soon had the basic shape she wanted. It was hard work she wanted a rest.

Ruth lay in the sun enjoying its warmth, the summer was going to be a good one and this was the first time they had been able to enjoy it. 'Are you asleep?' Bill asked

'No, just lying here. I don't have to do anything and that is really good. Started to make a point for my good spear.'

'I saw that when I went to sharpen my knife. There is talk that you will go on the bear hunt.'

'What bear hunt?'

'Some of them are going to ask you if they can go and hunt bear, get a few more furs.'

'They can if they want.'

'Are you going?'

'No, bears are big and have a nasty habit of killing you. A male chief may want to show he is brave by hunting bear, but I'm not going to.'

'I thought you might, it's the sort of thing you do.'

'You are trying to get rid of me so that you can cuddle White Flower and have her all to yourself.'

'Ruth!'

'Sorry, you are good with both of us now you have got the idea.'

'I don't have a lot of choice; you two keep on fighting me.'

Later that afternoon Friend of Bear along with Big Bear came to Ruth to ask if they could go bear hunting. 'Who else is going,' Ruth asked.

'Natlatan, you come learn how to kill bear.'

'Me!'

'Da learn about bear, you good, learn much.'

'Um…'

'Pe e Natmegan por, pogtod ap megan.'

That night Ruth woke and lay there thinking of the following day. She would be all right she told herself, she could throw a spear as well as anyone else. An accurately thrown spear she reasoned would kill a bear and Friend of Bear had told her she would be with Big Bear so there would be his spear as well.

The following day Ruth looked over the heavy spears she had and selected two good ones, each with a good bone point. Big Bear arrived and checked both spears. 'Por nat flata. Por megan flata, he said indicating one of the spears with a long bone point. The main difference between a light and heavy spear was the size of the shaft. Heavy spears were not designed to be thrown a great distance.

Meechamegan and Natlatan arrived ready to go, the four of them left to walk round to the north shore. Zak was with her. 'Nak, Zak, Zak nakella.'

Ruth led Zak back to the cabin, 'you stay there look after Bill,' she said then left and soon caught up with the other three. By midday, they were on the Northern shore. Meechamegan and Natlatan were going to go further along the shore to a place Natlatan knew. They parted and Natmegan led Ruth a little way along the lake before he thought they had found a good position.

The rest of the afternoon was spent building a platform in one of the trees by the time they finished it was firm. Big Bear put the two furs on it along with the heavy spears they had brought. Some distance from the tree, he lit a fire in order to cook the meat they had with them. There was more than enough to give them a good meal. Then he started to tell her how they killed a bear.

Ruth's idea of a bear hunt changed rapidly. Big Bear was telling her that in the morning if a bear came they would drop out of the tree onto its back with the heavy spears. Ruth climbed up into the tree up to the platform she had built with Big Bear while he placed a dead rabbit directly below the platform.

Big Bear woke Ruth before it became light the following morning. She went to put her top on; he stopped her dressing leaving her with just the loincloth on. Ruth was a little on the cold side and for a while sat there with one of the furs round her. She heard a noise at the same time as Big Bear. He held a finger to his mouth. Ruth nodded, shed the fur and took the heavy spear he passed to her. It was the one with a long bone point. She tested each edge, it was certainly sharp so was the point.

Big Bear wanted her to crouch on the edge of the platform with him. In signs, he went over what he wanted her to do. Ruth crouched there her heart beating fast.

In the dim light of dawn, Ruth saw the bear come into sight. It smelt the air attracted by the scent of the dead rabbit as it slowly padded towards the tree in which the two of them were crouching. Ruth could feel her body trembling; this was not something she wanted to do. The bear's body rocked from side to side as it plodded along. Big Bear was indicating on her back where she should spear the bear and how the two of them should drop onto the back of the bear.

The bear was almost under the tree, to Ruth it looked huge its wide back covered in dark fur hid the power of the animal. Big Bear prepared to drop; he looked at Ruth and nodded. Before Ruth could respond, he had dropped down onto the bear's back his spear in the back of the beast. Ruth looked down; Big Bear had landed across the bear's shoulders facing backwards. It would require Ruth spear in the right place in order to kill the bear. She looked only at the spot her spear should hit as her body fell from the tree.

The bear's body was warm; her spear penetrated its back, a few inches from Big Bear's, the bone point cutting deep into the body of the bear. Ruth griped the bear with her legs as it struggled, working her spear deeper into the bear's body towards its heart. She was barely aware of Big Bear as he did much the same as she was. The bear tipped first one way then the other. Ruth held on to her spear and gripped the bear with her legs. The bear slumped forward, and then its back legs collapsed. Shortly after that Ruth realised the bear was no longer moving.

Ruth slid off the dead bear intending to walk away, but her body would not let her. She had to sit down her legs would not work. She lay on the ground gasping for air, it was difficult to breathe and every time she tried to get up, she found her body was trembling so much she could not stand up. She lay back and tried to relax.

Ruth's body was still trembling with excitement ever nerve was on edge. The two of them had skinned the bear and now Big Bear was leading her down to the lake, Ruth looked at the blood on her. 'Nakpog, pi poola Jaga na Kala,' Big Bear said as he led her into the water of the lake. Once standing in thigh-deep water Big Bear started to cup water in his hands pouring it over her head and then her shoulders. Ruth stood there in a partial trance as he washed her body. 'Nakpog.'

'Da.'

'Jadpog por megan.'

'Da.'

'Pi poola Jaga na Kala, Jaga na Kala tak Natelena, nakpog.'

Ruth did not stop him taking her loincloth off she stood there naked as he continued to wash her. Then once Big Bear had washed all the blood from the bear off her, he stood behind her. 'Jad tala,' he said turning her to face the sun. 'Tak, Natelena pi Jaga na Kala tak...' Ruth prompted by Big Bear repeated the words thanking the Great Spirit for sending the bear to her and telling the Great Spirit that the bear had been a good bear and would be pleased to meet the Great Spirit.

'Tak Natelena, pi ella.' With that Big Bear left her standing in the water and looking at the sun. Ruth wondered what she should say to the Great Spirit would he understand English. God did and God knew French. Ruth looked straight into the sun; it was bright.

She did not know how long she stood there looking at the sun, with its shimmering sphere; she could see Zak's head surrounded by the light of the sun. For a while, she stared at Zak's head, he was a good wolf, a wolf above all wolves. Ruth thanked Zak for everything he had done for her. She felt sure she heard him yak in the peculiar way he did. Her eyes were watering with looking at the sun she turned her head away. She couldn't' see a thing; she staggered and almost fell over and would have had Natmegan not caught her. It took a while for her eyes to adjust and she could once again see. Natmegan helped her make her way out of the water. 'Por Jaga na Kala megan paga, pe tak Natelena,' Big Bear asked as she reached the shore.

'Da,' Ruth responded

'Jad pe Elena?' Big Bear asked.

'Jad Zak.'

'Da,' he said nodding, 'da, pe jad, Elena na Kala,' he said as he handed her back her loincloth, 'Por.'

Ruth felt different as she walked back to where the skin of the bear lay on the ground. Her body was no longer trembling with excitement; she was calm. She did not fully understand everything that had happened. Natmegan had washed her but it had been more than that he had prepared her so she could speak to the Great Spirit. She knew the Great Spirit had heard her, even though she was unsure of what she had said. Her body felt different, it was the same as it always had been, yet at the same time it was different. Big Bear took sufficient meat from the bear for a single meal then left the rest for the other animals.

Ruth and Natmegan made their way up the mountain a little further before they came to an old platform in a tree. Ruth pointed it out as soon as she saw it. 'Da, ella daqua aptag,' Big Bear said.

'Da,' Ruth said pleased they would not have to build a platform as they had the previous day. They climbed up into the tree and for the rest of the day sat a talked. Before it became dark, they climbed down and cooked the meat they had. The bear's flesh had a strong taste. They finished their meal then climbed the tree. That night Ruth relived the experience gripping the bear with her legs; it was a wild fight until both were satisfied and lay quietly.

The following day they met Friend of Bear and Big moose, they had a fur with them. 'Por,' Ruth said nodding when they laid it out. Then it was Ruth's turn to show the fur her and Big Bear had obtained. The other two nodded saying it was good. With the furs rolled up the four of them headed back round the end of the lake to their home.

No one said who had killed the bears; four of them had gone out to hunt bear four had come back with two furs. Those that came to see the two furs nodded then left saying they were good furs. Bill came and looked at the two furs, spread out on the ground in front of the cabin. 'My God Ruth they are huge.'

'They look larger than the bear was.'

'How did you kill it?'

'The way the Great Spirit wants us to,' she said as she held him tightly to her.

'Was it very exciting?'

'I thought Natmegan was the bear last night and I was fighting it.'

'It's all right, you don't have to explain.'

'But...'

'It's all right Ruth, I understand. You are the chief of an Indian tribe you must act in the way expected of you and so must I if I am going to be your paga.'

'You are the right man for me Bill, you really are. It's not wrong Bill, it's right. I know it is and I have seen Elena na Kala, I saw him in the sun. It was Zak; I spoke to the Great Spirit after I had killed the bear. Big Bear washed me so I could talk to the Great Spirit.'

'It sounds as if it was very important.'

'It was; I felt different afterwards.'

'You would have, I can understand that. You had seen a spirit; you couldn't be the same after that.'

The tribe set about the work after their rest with more vigour. Ruth came out of the cabin to see what she could do; she went to help those building the tribe lodge. They were building it in a similar way to a lodge except on a larger scale and as it increased in height, it was necessary to build ladders in order to reach the higher level. It took almost the rest of the summer to build the tribe lodge, but it was a good lodge by the time they finished.

Ruth turned her mind towards the coming winter. She would like to give the tribe a couple of days to relax before the work of autumn began. She called Big Bear and Friend of Bear to the cabin.

'Natmegan e apar jadpog,' Ruth said

'Da Jaga na Kala,'

'Pi jadpog e kala. Meechamegan pog daqua na Daga Kala.'

'Da.'

They then spent some time discussing the tasks, which would prepare the tribe for the coming winter. If everyone worked hard, the tribe would have everything it needed before the winter arrived.

The hunting party led by Big Bear left before Ruth they were going to the east an area in into which they had not been for a while. Ruth decided to check on the area to the west. She had a good day and returned with three deer, the others had also returned from a very successful days hunting. 'Por,' that evening they decided that before winter approached that they would hunt and fill the cave with meat. Ruth let the tribe have two days' rest.

Bill was already talking about harvesting the crops the Indians had planted and it looked as if there was going to be a good crop from Ruth's fields. As winter approached so, the amount of work increased.

'We have ten or so days at least.'

'I know but I want to know we have enough food, as long as we have food we will be alright.'

'I will make sure the wood pile is as high as the mountains over the other side of the lake.'

'We need a lot of that as well, we should think about coppicing an area.'

'Ruth, what I was thinking, is that…well you know the clearing west and then towards the plain.'

'What of it, it's good grass there, I once thought of putting the horse in that…'

'Exactly, well what about moose in there,' Bill suggested.

'They will get out they can jump.'

'So have a high fence.'

'That would be good we would have…can't do it this year.'

'I know, but for next winter.'

'Jaga na Kala,' someone called out.

'That sounds like Friend of Bear. I will have to go and find out what he wants.'

Ruth left Bill and went to where Friend of Bear was talking to Big Bear. Big Bear had two Indians with him whom Ruth had not seen before. 'Apa paga ella, tak nak mesh, nak umta apar tag,' Big Bear said.

One of the Indians went down on his knees. 'Porjad meecha na Hishglish. Jaga na Kala, Elena na Kala, suma

Piapa. Piapa nak mesh, e nak lodge. Tak nakella Elena na Kala, tak nakella.' The two looked as if they had been walking for a long time. The other was now also kneeling in front of her. 'Elena na Kala tak nakella.' They look exhausted and the one who had spoken was pleading to stay.

'Nakella e Daga Kala,' Ruth said. Telling them they could stay, but would have to build a lodge for themselves, as the tribe was busy getting ready for winter. Friend of Bear told them they could sleep in the tribe lodge until they had built their lodge and that Jaga na Kala would decide after winter if they could remain.

'Porpog Jaga na Kala. Porpog, piapa por jadpog.'

'We have two more braves,' Ruth told Bill as she returned to the cabin.

'They didn't look that strong from what I saw.'

'I guess they have been wandering around for some time. Must have heard about us here or just happened to find us. I said they could stay at least over the winter. One said they were good at hunting but if they are; why were they not able to find food?'

'I don't know; he was on his knees begging at one point.'

'Bit embarrassing to have him do that, and calling me Elena na Kala; maybe he was talking to Zak he was there with me.'

'I have been looking at the food we have and it is more than enough for all of us.'

'Good, that is important,'

'The problem I have is storing it all.'

'I think we will build a store next year that will be good, and keep it full so we never run out of food, we can keep skins and other items in it as well.'

The winter came with its cold winds and snow. The tribe lodge proved to be a good one with three fires going it would remain warm. Most of the tribe spent the day in the tribe lodge there talking and just waiting for spring. Winter was also the time to turn the skins into clothes. Ruth spent a lot of the time sitting in the cabin working on new clothes for Bill as well as her. The tribe had plenty of food in the various stores; they got through the winter well.

The work of spring started. A large area was cleared Bill took charge of that and the sowing of the seeds. Big Bear selected those he wanted to hunt and generally took over that area, leaving Friend of Bear to maintain the village. It worked well with Ruth only needing to suggest a few things she thought needed doing.

Ruth took Friend of Bear to the meadow west of the village and looked around it with him. He nodded and agreed it could be fenced in. Summer arrived, unlike the previous year; there were many occasions when they could all relax in the sun. Ruth was lying in the sun when Big Bear came to her, 'Megan jadpog,' he said. The blood rushed through Ruth's body at the mere thought of dropping out of a tree onto a bear 'Da,' she immediately responded. 'Da, aptag.'

The following day Ruth and Big Bear set off for the northern shore of the lake and the area where the bears lived. They had killed one bear and were making their way further to the east planning to attract another bear the following day so they could return with two furs. Ruth froze in her tracks; Big Bear had also heard it. Without speaking or making any sound, the two of them were up into one of the large trees. Ruth saw a brave and a squaw coming along the shore. 'Paga e squaw,' she whispered to Big Bear.

'Piapa tak e paga,'

'Da.'

Ruth let Big Bear approach the two of them, following him as if she were his squaw. 'Portak, meecha na Natmegan,' Natmegan said as he approached them

'Portak, meecha na Hishojar.'

'Peapa ella?'

'Daga Kala, tak nakella suma Daga Kala.'

Ruth listened to the conversation between Big Bear and White Mountain. His squaw's name was Blue Water, and she was studying Ruth a lot. Although she had an ordinary top on with no indication she was the chief, Ruth had on the clothes of a brave rather than a squaw, and far too many feathers in her hair to be a normal squaw. Big Bear told them that there were hunting bear. Which made the squaw look again at Ruth? By this time, Big Bear was pointing out where the tribe's home was and telling White Mountain how to get there. The two of them continue their journey saying they would go to the home of the wolf tribe and ask to stay.

'Por paga,' Natmegan said as soon as the other two had left them.

'Da, squaw nat jad pi.'

'Pe paga lementa, pi nak tak pe Jaga na Kala.'

'Apara paga Hishojar,' Ruth said thinking that White Mountain was a popular name.

'Da, apa e ap,' Big Bear replied.

The two of them set off again to the platform they were going towards. That night the wolf and the bear came together until each was content with each other. She was no longer the chief, in their relationship it was definitely Big Bear who led. In the early morning, they moved as one dropping from the tree onto the back of a large bear, their spears finding the target.

It was a hot day, which made it hard work carrying a fur each, Worn out Ruth dropped the fur on the ground as soon as they reached the cabin. Bill was sitting on the log watching for them. As they arrived, he got up and came to Ruth. 'It looks as if you have been successful let me help you. A brave with his squaw turned up while you were away.'

'We met them, he is another Hishojar and his squaw is Pallarseeni.'

'Friend of Bear said they could stay and ask you when you returned. We could do with a few more like him I would think. There is other news, White Flower is with child.'

'Oh wonderful, that is good news, has she spoken with Friend of Bear.'

'She went to him; he said it will be a daughter.'

'That's good.'

'You are not though.'

'I know I think there's something wrong with me. I lie with you at the right time and everything like that.'

'We must try harder.'

After the rest days, Ruth went to look at the meadow near the edge of the wood. The high fence was being built between the trees which flanked the area it was half as high again as a man was tall. Ruth decided it required a few more to work on it to make sure they completed it before the winter came. They worked in the height of the summer. When it was finished, Ruth gave the tribe three days of relaxation. They were all pleased with the three days of rest.

'I think I might go bear hunting again.'

'I get the feeling Big Bear would stand were I not here.'

'You are not upset are you?'

'No,'

'Do you want to come?'

'No, I haven't the courage to hunt bear. I know that, I am a man for the fields. That is between you and Big Bear he knows a part of you that I will never get to know. If we ever have to defend the village, you will stand with him and protect all of us. I know the tender and loving side of you, he knows the brave and bold Jaga na Kala Paga na Daga Kala.'

Ruth went on a two-day bear hunt with Big Bear. Bill was right; she would be with Big Bear in any fight. It was an enjoyable time with him; they returned to the village with two more furs. Meechamegan took Ruth to one side while the others were looking at the furs, 'Por jadpog,' he said.

'Da,' Ruth responded.

'Jadpog latan, pe ap ween Paga na Daga Kala, natumta.'

When Ruth asked Big Bear to hunt a moose he knew straight away why, 'Da piapar jadpog. Por natumta, pe por Paga,' he responded.

During the feast, the spirit man gave Ruth a spear, it's yellow and blue shaft decorated with feathers. It would not have been that useful to hunt with; the spear was placed in the ground behind her position in the circle. Everyone enjoyed the feast and Ruth gave the tribe an extra day of rest, which pleased the tribe even more.

Late summer White Eagle returned to say there were many moose not far from the edge of the trees. Ruth went to have a look and decided it was time to try to get some in the enclosure.

She explained how she believed they could drive the moose into the neck of the enclosure and that everyone, including the squaws, would take part in the round up of the moose. The following day the tribe gathered the braves, squaws and the older children. The moose were still there. Ruth with the help of Big Bear used the tribe and all the wolves she could find to surround a large number of moose out on the plain. Then they started to herd the moose towards the funnel, which led to the enclosure. At first, it seemed to go very well. They had about twenty moose moving towards the trees and the open neck of the funnel, which led to the enclosure. Whether it was because they became over confident or the moose saw danger near the woods Ruth could not tell. The tribe's organisation started to break down becoming completely disorganised by the time they chased the moose into the clearing. About half the moose escaped, but they ended up with eleven moose in the enclosure. Despite the disorganisation at the end, it was a great success with eleven moose in the closure. The whole tribe was pleased as they gathered on the edge of the meadow and watched the moose run around the meadow.

'What do you think Bill?'

'They look all right in there. That was fun at the end.'

'It was a bit wasn't it? But we have these in there, that's a lot of food there walking around.'

'Eleven is good.'

'I'm happy with that,' Ruth said looking into the enclosure at the moose in the meadow.

Ruth had grass cut early autumn and stored so that they could feed the moose during the winter. Bill took on the building of a haystack. Ruth was inwardly please, it gave the tribe a safe supply of meat over the winter.

By the time winter came, they were prepared for it the cave was bulging with supplies and the eleven moose had settled down in their enclosure. Bill would toss hay into the enclosure each day. The moose soon learnt food would be there and started to come to the place waiting for their hay. There were still five moose in the enclosure when spring arrived, one bull and four cows. Bill thought they would breed and they should only round up cows when they had the chance to.

Big Bear was right, others did come and over the years, the tribe grew. They were still only a small tribe but getting stronger every year. Having the enclosure there with moose in it gave them the edge. Never before had the Indians had animals to look after, Ruth and Bill had just enough knowledge between them to manage the moose herd. The following year the tribe once again rounded up a small group of moose and drove them into the field. As Bill had thought, the moose did breed in the enclosure. The young being used to contact with people would come for food and had no fear of them. Even the adult moose began to accept those from the tribe walking around in their field as long as the bull was left alone. He would always chase anything that came into his area of the meadow.

The following year the tribe built a large lodge to store food, not as large as the tribe lodge, but it did provide a good place to store food, skins and other items. Friend of Bear became involved with it and had a group go out searching for straight lengths of wood. The lengths of wood cut to size and bound together made low shelves to hold the sacks off the floor. It made the job of storing the crops much easier. The roundup that year was even better and by the time winter came the store was full of crops, twenty moose were in the enclosure and two large haystacks in a fenced off area. Ruth was pleased, no matter how hard the winter was there was no possibility of running out of food. Everyone would eat well over the winter. This security of food supply pleased those in the tribe; no longer would a hard winter weaken them.

Life settled down, the tribe had everything it needed. Ruth would at least twice a year go to the Northern shore with Big Bear to hunt bear. She always enjoyed her time with him. Friend of Bear and Natlatan also hunted bear. With eight or ten new furs, a year Ruth set aside an area in the store for them and other prepared skins. Friend of Bear organised additional shelving.

From other Indians in the area who came to the village Ruth learnt that settlers were coming into the area. She worried about this and became alarmed when they learnt a settlement was being built at the far end of the lake. Bill calmed her down and suggested they make a claim for their land. It became a major job that summer. Most became involved placing stakes with the yellow and blue tribe colours on around the boundary of the tribes land. Ruth planned an extended bear hunt and boundary-marking trip. Ruth, with Big Bear and Friend of Bear with Natlatan set off to complete the task of marking their land on the northern shore of the lake. It took them almost a moon to complete it. Ruth was pleased to return to the village but they had marked out the western and northern shore. They had completed the task and Bill had done the writing for the claim. Ruth felt more secure as winter arrived, winter might be hard one but during winter, others would not be able to come into their land.

Chapter 13

Summer had not yet arrived although it would not be long before it did. The tribe now had thirty-four braves the circle looked good to Ruth on the first occasion they ate in the circle that year. The moose from the enclosure had a lot of meat on it. Even in the height of summer, it was not common to find such a well-fed moose. Ruth liked the atmosphere around the circle; people were enjoying themselves, talking, laughing and joking. More importantly, the tribe was eating well. Of all the things she insisted on it was that they had food to spare at all times. Bill provided well with his fields and the moose enclosure meant hunting was not critical during the winter or early spring. Ruth looked around the circle; her braves were strong, her tribe was strong. The spring feast lasted a long time after sunset and well into the night.

Ten days later Ruth did not feel quite so comfortable. The sound of a howling of a distant wolf reached the village, and then one nearer them howled. Ruth wondered what was going on the wolves knew something was happening. Friend of Bear came to her wanting to know what was happening, the whole tribe started to become tense. The wolves had provided a warning but what the warning was about Ruth did not know. She sent out several braves to find out. Mid-afternoon, Natlatan returned, he came running into the village, with the news there were men sitting on large animals coming towards the village. Ruth became alarmed. 'Calm down,' Bill told Ruth

'But there are solders and they are coming here.'

'Five or six riders, I will go and meet them tomorrow, I would think they know we are here. We know of the settlement at the other end of the lake, known about it for a couple of years now. If it is them I can give them the claim, I expect one of them will be leading this group; just stay calm.'

Ruth looked at her clothes; she did not look like any woman those coming would expect to see. 'I am not going to meet them like this, not the first time, I don't want them knowing who I am. I have to be what they expect to find here.'

'I will tell them you are my wife, that you are Mrs William Ruth Thatcher.'

Ruth felt uncomfortable in the European clothes they were a little small for her and restricted her movements, but she had managed to alter them enough to put them on. She wondered how she ever worked in them. Bill had left early morning with Sheiba and three other wolves. Ruth watched though the window in the back of the cabin her hand going several times to the side of her head where she should have five feathers it felt wrong without them. It was well after noon before she saw them arrive in the meadow; Bill was walking beside the one in the lead talking to him. The man on the horse looked important to

Ruth. Several of the Indians stopped whatever they were doing and stood watching Bill show the five of them to an area in the meadow the tribe did not use. It was well away from the lodges grouped around the tribe lodge with the circle in front of it. The riders dismounted, Bill continued to talk the smartly dressed one and from where Ruth was in the cabin, it looked as if Bill gave the young gentleman something. Ruth left the cabin when she saw Bill walking with the man towards the cabin. Ruth sat on the log wondering who they were and what they wanted. Bill brought the well-dressed young gentleman round the corner of the cabin disturbing her thoughts; Ruth stood up. Before Bill could make any introduction, the young gentleman approached her and spoke first. 'Mrs Thatcher I am pleased to meet you, I am captain John Upton I represent His Majesty in the inner lands. You have a fine cabin there.'

'I am pleased to meet you sir,' Ruth replied. He was young for his position a lot younger than the men in the settlement on the coast who had decided what was to be done.

The young man continued, 'I like to get to meet those who live around here thought it was time we came to see your husband and yourself.'

'Thank you Sir.'

'Your husband has given me your claim; there shouldn't be any trouble with that.'

'Oh good we like it here.'

'So your husband was saying, not so sure you should have the Indians quite so near and on what will soon be your land.'

'They are all right, very peaceful,' Bill said joining the conversation, 'As I explained they don't bother us and they do provide us with some protection.'

'That's different to the stories brought to me. This lot packed off an Iroquois war party, killed the lot of them. They may look peaceful but what I hear is that the chief is not one for taking prisoners. We only have a small garrison at the settlement, though I would not like that known by the Indians; have to put a bit of a show on.'

'I understand,'

'Going to meet the chief this evening; have to powwow with him I suppose. Your husband is going to introduce me to the spirit man.'

'I am sure the chief will be pleased to talk to you,'

'This one is said to have mystical powers...' With every word, the captain spoke Ruth felt stronger. Bill was smiling at her; he joined in the conversation with the captain when it came round to clothing. 'I need decent clothes,' Bill said. Ruth was pleased that Bill was playing along making it seem to the captain that they were man and wife in the wilderness and in need of things.

'You only have to come to the settlement we have a store,' the captain explained.

'We don't have any money to buy things with,' Bill explained.

'I am sure skins or some other items could be traded.'

'We can get money for something like that then, Ruth is in desperate need of clothes.'

'I can see and I know there are suitable clothes for both men and women in the store. Bring something to trade and I am sure arrangements can be made.'

'Thank you sir,' Ruth said

Bill took the captain back to his men and returned to the cabin with a big smile on his face. 'Was that all right for you?'

'He thought we were normal people, he didn't know. The trade bit was interesting though. We could get tools and that sort of thing.'

'True very true, yes I could take a few things there sell them get axes and the likes.'

'Knives, we really need more knives, we only have eight for the whole tribe. And they are getting worn down.'

Ruth left it late that day before she went to the circle. She watched from the cabin as the circle began to fill. When she judged it time, Ruth put her large headdress on and left the cabin fully dressed as the chief of the wolf tribe. The rest of the tribe were already there. So was the spirit man, he was standing a little way off along with the Captain and his men. The captain may be putting on a show but now was her time to impress and the tribe looked strong to her sitting there, each brave with his family around him. Ruth sat in her place with the eleven spears behind her. A wolf sat down beside her. Ruth glanced towards the spirit man. She saw him speak to the captain and then set out towards her.

With the large head dress on it hid her hair, the captain had not recognised her; Ruth sat there and watched as he reached her. 'You sit in front of chief; you talk to chief, chief called Jaga na Kala,' Meechamegan said.

'I have heard that; what does it mean, do you understand that?' the captain asked speaking to the spirit man.

'It means mother of wolves, captain though in the past I have been called Elena na Kala, spirit of the wolf,' Ruth said.

'What!' The captain exclaimed as he finally recognised Ruth.

'Please sit down Captain.'

'You; you can't be!' the captain exclaimed.

'An Indian seeing me dressed as I am now would not question it, particularly as I have my wolf companion here with me.'

'You are the chief of these Indians?'

'Indeed I am. Please sit down. We can then talk about Indian matters rather than clothes. As you see I am not really in need of them.'

The Captain sat down and for a brief moment studied Ruth. 'What happened to the war like chief I've been told about?'

'The previous chief was killed by the Iroquois, I was then chosen to lead the wolf tribe and have done so for eleven summers, as these spears behind me would have told you if you had counted them. For those eleven summers we have lived here in peace.'

'But you are an English woman.'

'I was an English girl, I left England when I was fourteen, with my father and mother and ended up here. I am now Jaga na Kala Paga na Daga Kala. I have had difficult times but I also have had many pleasurable moments.'

'Who is everyone here, why is your husband sitting over there with an Indian woman and a couple of children?'

'She is White Flower and is also Bill's wife.'

'What, he can't have two wives that's illegal.'

'Not here it isn't,' Ruth responded.

'It most certainly is.'

'Captain, you are mistaken here on this land my word is the law. Bill, as far as your law is concerned, is not married I took him in an Indian ceremony. White Flower chose him after the battle with the Iroquois. The children are from White Flower.'

'So you are the chief because you have a pet wolf is that it.'

'Oh no. Call boy, call,' the wolf howled.

'So you can make him howl.'

'Be patient Captain, I will introduce you to my family. Here comes one. Do not fear them they will not harm you.'

'It's a wolf.'

'He is Jake, and if it be known he is my favourite.' Ruth continued to talk to the captain, as more and more wolves arrived. 'Meet my family Captain, my wolves helped defended the tribe against the Iroquois. This is the Wolf Tribe captain and we are very strong with Elena na Kala. It was the wolves who told us you were coming and Bill brought you here surrounded by them.'

'There were no wolves when I met Bill.'

'You are not supposed to see them Captain.' Ruth looked towards Friend of Bear who then placed Ruth's blanket between the two of them. 'What is this for?' the captain asked.

'Captain you have been given a claim for this land by an Englishman. You have told me you will record it, and pointed out there will be no trouble doing so. In this blanket are several items, you select one and take it, by doing so you will show the tribe and me the strength of your word. Please lift back the top of the blanket and take something.'

The captain turned back the top of the blankets and studied the items for a moment or two. 'I assume they have meaning,' he said looking towards Ruth.

'Indeed Captain. Take a pebble and you can break your word for almost no reason, take the beads and you should have a reason why you have not recorded the claim. If you take the strips of hide I would expect a very good reason why our claim has not been recorded.'

'And the knife,' the captain questioned, 'you haven't told me what the knife signifies.'

'There is no acceptable excuse.'

'What none!'

'None, you died before it was possible for you to keep your word.'

'What if I don't go along with this, there is no reason why I should take anything.'

Ruth was aware he was correct; he did not have to. 'That is true,' she said giving her a little extra time to think of a reply. 'You will leave tomorrow; we will provide you with any food you need for your journey back to the settlement.' Ruth believed what she had said would let him know he would not be harmed should he refuse to take anything. She continued, 'There would be no reason why you should wish to return, whatever you said would not be believed and I would have to assume you were here for a reason I would not like. The symbols on the two strips of hide would suggest it would be an unwise course of action for you to take.' Despite having to think fast Ruth was pleased with what she had said, she believed she had said enough for him to take something from the blanket. She doubted if he would have the courage to take the knife.

'I have walked straight into a trap haven't I?'

Ruth had not expected him to think that. It was not her intention. 'I have set no trap; I would not like to you think that. All you are doing is showing me the strength of your words. You have already said you will record the claim; all I ask is that you show me and the tribe of us how strong your word is.'

The captain looked her straight in the eyes, Ruth sat there, inwardly she was concerned and at the same time, she was excited. This was a challenge but not one, which required weapons; this fight required words and a strong belief in what she said. She look back into his eyes and saw him look down towards the blanket. 'I don't think I want to test you. I will pick the strips of hide.'

Ruth's mind was ecstatic, she had won he was going to take from the blanket. It was difficult for her to remain calm on the outside. 'You do have to take them so the tribe can see,' Ruth said. 'Return them to me when you have done what your words say. They will act as a reminder to you of your word to me.' She felt confident now the captain was reaching out for the strips of cloth, he would not know she had added a little to the small ceremony. Those that could see saw the captain pick up the two strips of hide. It caused a buzz to go round the circle.

'What's going on?'

Ruth relaxed, it was over; she no longer needed to put on an act. 'Don't worry captain, por suta means good take. The tribe is pleased to see your word is strong. It also means our conversation is over and we can start to eat which is important don't you think. Come with me Captain we can get our meal, my braves will invite each of your men to sit with them as guests so they may also eat with us.' Ruth stood up and waited for the captain to do the same then led him into the tribe lodge Porjadseeni handed Ruth her bowl and wooden spoon and then a new one to the captain. 'Come Captain I believe you will enjoy this meal.' Ruth led him to the tribe lodge where the meal was being kept hot over a gentle fire. With their meals, Ruth led him back to the circle. 'Sit beside me now. It will show the tribe you are important.'

'Thank you,'

'Please eat there is no need to wait for all to return.'

The captain sampled his meal; he took a small tentative taste to start with then a larger amount. 'This is a fine stew,' he said.

'I am glad you like it, deer and fruit it is a summer meal and one which is enjoyed by all. Not all Indians live as savages, captain.'

'So I am learning.'

'When the meal is over it is what we call family time people will move around the circle and talk to others. Then we will sleep for the night. Your men are quite safe here, do not be concerned about the wolves moving around at night they will not harm you.'

'There's a lot of them.'

'There have on occasions been more, and many wolves gave their lives in the defence of this tribe. We owe the wolves our thanks, they don't harm us and if a wolf is in need of food then we provide it. This one here stays at my side most of the time. He is the second to do so.'

Ruth sat talking to the captain while they ate the meal. She checked her braves had taken the captain's men to the lodge. All four of them were sitting in the circle eating the meal they had been given. Ruth was pleased the visit of the captain from the settlement had gone well. He would leave tomorrow believing the Indians were friends.

Ruth went to the door of the cabin, the following morning, in response to a knock; it was the first time anyone had knocked on the door. Even before she opened the door, Ruth believed it was the captain. It was, 'Captain, do come in,' Ruth said moving back so that he could enter.

'Thank you. I came to tell you...' He stopped talking and stared at Ruth.

'Is something wrong Captain?'

'Um, no sorry, I didn't expect to see you like that.'

'This is how I normally dress captain.'

'It is most becoming.'

'Please come in and sit down, Sit on those furs.'

'Thank you. I didn't quite know what to expect, I didn't expect to find the cabin empty.'

'It's not Captain, we have the furs, when you sit on the floor to eat, a table and chair is not much use and furs are better than a bunk with blankets.'

'I see you have weapons in here.'

'Of course they are for hunting, please sit down we have some oats, which we eat as a family meal in the morning.' Turning to look at one of the girls Ruth said, 'Pallarleptan mela mesh na Captain.'

'Da.'

'Your children?' the captain asked.

'They are not mine, for some reason I can't have children, these are White Flower's, but I love them and they are part of my family and children of the Wolf Tribe.'

'Captain pe mesh hi umta.'

'She said here is your food to eat.'

'What is that on it?'

'Sap from a tree it is sweet and very pleasant to taste. Try it I think you will like it.'

The captain did, he nodded having tasted some, 'Yes that is quite sweet and a distinctive flavour.'

'I am glad you like it.'

'You surprised me last night, and again this morning.'

'I realise that. You may have heard stories of me, and you may fear me but you have no reason to. You have stated your words are strong; I hope your actions live up to them. That is all I want from you. Bill and I want this land to be ours, and if it is ours the tribe can remain here on their land free from any settlers.'

'I see what you are wanting. I am glad to hear you are not thinking of any sort of action against the settlement, I am certainly not thinking of attacking you.'

'I wish to protect our land, settlers would not understand the Great Spirit has given us this land to live on and live here the way he wants us to. I have no desire for your land; you may live there as you wish. It is our land that I wish to protect.'

'I will record your claim.'

'That is all I ask, if Bill is the rightful owner of this land according to your law then I feel we are safe.'

'It will take a while it has to go back to the authorities on the coast. It will take best part of a year.'

'As long as it is done that is all I want. I am interested in what you said yesterday though, the possibility of trading with you. We usually have extra furs, deer, sometimes bear and moose. We make clothes such as these that I am wearing from deer skin and we have a lot of that already prepared.'

'And what would you want in return?'

'Tools, knives, axes, saws; the saw I have is worn out. A new saw would be most useful, also tools for the fields, hoes and such as well as spades. Bill could bring the skins to the store in order to trade them for tools.'

'I am sure that would be acceptable.'

'Good, that is good, I am glad we have been able to speak of this.'

'It's been useful to pay you a visit, I will come back as soon as I have you land recorded and bring you the recorded claim and the deeds.

'Thank you.'

Early summer Bill along with one of the braves set off with a large number of skins. It would take three days to walk to the settlement and the same back. Bill believed it would take at least a day to do the trading. He returned on the eighth day with five knives a large saw and two axes. 'They were quite pleased to get them.'

'What is it like in the settlement?'

'There are two lines of shacks and other buildings. There's an outpost of sorts at the far end, but it is not much more than a stable with two shacks and a wall round it.'

'Did you see the captain?'

'Spoke to him and a couple of others, they were not too bothered about Quick Water.'

'You must be tired after all that walking; you should rest a couple of days.'

'I will for one at least, everything all right.'

'No problems here, crops look good, the moose are also fine. The calves are coming along well.'

'Good.'

Ruth called Big Bear to the cabin; once he was there, she discussed with him who should have the knives or where they should be put. He liked them a lot and took one to replace his, three were placed in the tribe lodge the last one going to Natlatan.

Chapter 14

It was approaching late afternoon; the four of them, the Captain and his lady along with two militiamen rode along the edge of the wood. They had left the settlement early that morning. 'We will stop in a while my dear,' the captain said turning in the saddle towards his lady.

'I'm all right John.'

'Never the less we will camp along there somewhere; we are more than half way there.' Then turning to one of the men behind him he added. 'We will camp up ahead for the night.'

They reached a flat area of grass, protected on three sides by trees. The captain drew his horse up and looked around. 'This will do us,' he said, as he got off his horse.

The others did the same looking around the area. 'I'll tether the horses captain.'

'Do that Barns,' the captain responded as he helped the lady off her horse. 'Are you all right Rachel?'

'I'm fine, glad to walk a bit, but I am all right.'

The two militiamen started to sort thing out, the horses were tethered, wood was gathered and a fire lit.

They were about to heat the beans they had with them when the woman screamed. A wolf had come out from between the trees. 'John! Do something there is wolf there!'

The captain looked in the direction his lady was pointing to was to see a wolf with a small deer in its jaws. 'Don't shoot it!' the Captain cried out to one of his men as they reached for a musket.

'I can get it with the first shot.'

'No!' The captain shouted as he nervously approached the wolf. 'Look at the horses man; they are not skittish are they,' he added as he walked towards the wolf. The wolf stood there waiting for the man to reach it then dropped the deer in order to smell his hand. 'Has she sent you?' The captain asked, speaking to the wolf. Three others appeared; one of the additional wolves also had a deer in its jaws. 'So Barns you would have hit all four would you.'

'John! Do something you are surrounded by them!'

'There is nothing to worry about.' The captain reached out towards the one they had first seen and stroked the top of its head. 'Quite friendly see I can stroke it.'

'Strangest thing I have ever seen,' the man the captain had called Barns responded, staring at the captain as he stood stroking the wolf.

'You will see more than this Barns. She sent them to us.'

'There's witchcraft here captain we had better get back to the settlement.'

Slowly the captain moved towards the deer the first wolf had dropped; the wolf stood there watching him as he pick the deer up. 'They have brought us supper as well,' he said holding up one of the deer. 'She sent them Rachel; she sent them.'

'John it just a small tribe with a woman as chief.'

'But a woman the likes of which I have never met before.'

The woman straightened her dress backing away from a wolf as it approached her.

'Don't be frightened of it Rachel, it will not bite you. Look.' The captain said as he reached out and ran his hand down the wolf's back.

'I will put more wood on the fire that will get rid of them.' The other man said being careful not to approach to close to the wolf that had now smelt the dress of the woman and having done so had moved away.

'They will warm themselves beside it if I am not wrong.' The snarl of a wolf caused the captain to turn. 'Leave that one alone Barns that must be theirs, this one is ours.'

'This is not natural.'

That evening the captain, his lady and the two men sat round a fire cooking the deer while the four wolves having eaten theirs sat with them. 'Made friends with that one Barns?' the captain asked looking at the wolf lying beside one of his militiamen

'This ain't natural; it lets me touch it without even moving. It's gone to bloody sleep I think.'

'They will lead us to the camp tomorrow.'

'Weird if you ask me.'

'Wait till you see score of them around you.'

That night the four wolves stood guard over the four visitors as they slept and the following day they walked beside the horses as they made their way to the village.

Bill and Ruth were standing with Friend of Bear in the entrance to the tribe lodge. The squaws working in the tribe lodge were preparing a moose, while others were gathering fruit. Bill pointed towards the riders coming into the far end of the meadow. 'They are here; I better go and meet them,' Bill said as he started to move those that had arrived.

'I do hope we are not deceived, it will be difficult to explain the moose feast if we have not got our land. I will go to the cabin I want to meet them there first.'

'I am sure we will have. I will bring the captain to you.'

Ruth went to the cabin then watched through the window as Bill met the four riders. She saw him talk to the captain and a well-dressed woman with him. When Bill started to bring the captain and the woman towards the cabin Ruth turned away from the window and went outside ready to meet them. It was a nice day she thought looking up to the sky.

It was not long before she saw the three of them come round the corner of the cabin. 'Captain welcome and you bring your lady wife with you this time,' Ruth said as she approached them. 'Please come and sit down,' she added indicating the log outside the cabin.

'I hope that I don't exceed my welcome I brought Rachel so she could see an Indian village.'

'That is perfectly all right,' then turning to the young woman she added. 'Welcome to our home, I should say Portag meecha, it means welcome friend. I hope you will enjoy your time here.'

'I am pleased to meet you, you speak English.'

Before Ruth could answer the captain spoke, 'I have with me the deeds to your land and your strips of hide,' he said holding out a document with a red ribbon round it. Ruth recognised her strips of hide with the symbols of her position on them.

'Thank you captain your actions live up to your words,' Ruth said taking them from him. Pleasure was her only emotion she had in her hands the security of the tribe's land.

'Your land is as your claim shows and covers all this land round the western end of the lake and the northern shore. It is a large area but of little use to others,' the captain explained.

'It is our home; I am so pleased to have this. Please sit with me I often sit on this log and look out over the lake.'

'It sure is beautiful.'

Pleased their land was safe Ruth relaxed all her problems were over. She smiled at the woman as she sat down on other log so she faced Ruth and the captain. 'So the preacher finally arrived,' Ruth said now the serious business was out of the way.

'Oh no,' the Captain responded, 'we are still not married; I don't think we ever will be.'

'You should lay a blanket in front of them and force them to take the knife,' Ruth responded light-heartedly.

'If only I could. Rachel this is the chief of this tribe, her name is Jaga na kala. It means mother of wolves.'

'There is one there, it's just lying there.'

'Is that the same one?' the captain asked pointing at a wolf lying asleep in the sun.

'Nan, yes he doesn't do a lot other than sleep, too well fed I think.'

'We had four come to meet us, brought us a deer for supper.'

'I hope they behaved.'

'The men didn't know what to make of it.'

'We are strong with Elena na Kala the whole tribe are, we are a very fortunate tribe to have such a good spirit. The Great Spirit has always looked after us and sent us everything we need even in our hardest times, and he sent you here so the land is ours by your laws as well as his, he chose well in you as you have given me this. I can't read it but Bill can; he will tell me what it says and I will tell the tribe. Our preparations for your arrival have not been wasted time.'

'The captain has two men with him this time,' Bill said, 'I should ask two braves to accept them as guests.'

'Maybe Friend of Bear would accept the captain as a guest he will be able to speak with him.'

'I will ask.'

'The captain's lady can be our guest.'

'Da, pi ella,' Bill said as he left. Ruth continued to talk to the Captain and his lady.

'What was all that about being guests?' The captain asked.

'Well if you are to find out about how we live you should experience it closer. Rachel can if she wants stay in the cabin with our family. I have suggested that Friend of Bear should have you as a guest. As you know, he can speak a little English. Your men will also be guests of a brave, it will be better than sleeping in the open. And you will learn about the way we live here.'

'I did not tell the settlement much about your tribe just that you were peaceful.'

'That is all you needed to tell them. How is the settlement?' Ruth asked.

'We have built most of it now, enough for our needs, supplies are a bit haphazard. Bill saw a bit of it when he was there last year, they were very good skins he brought with him. You can certainly bring us more like that.'

'That is good to hear. It is a long walk there and back. It took him eight days but we are pleased with the tools he brought back. The saw has been particularly useful.'

'Well there is more of that sort of thing just bring the pelts treated or not.'

'I will send some more.'

'This Friend of Bear that I am to be a guest of is the spirit man isn't he?'

'He a good spirit man he speaks well to the Great Spirit he will this evening to thank him for sending you to us. We have a feast tonight a moose with a bowl of fruit. Most of the squaws are out gathering the fruit now, we already have the moose that was given to us yesterday.'

'If it is anything like the stew last time it will be good I told Rachel about deer and fruit stew.'

'We are very lucky here, we have been given a lot of fruit around here,' Ruth explained. She continued to talk to the two of them until Bill returned to tell her everything had been arranged and that Friend of Bear would like to have the captain as a guest. 'I have already sorted out the other two I left them trying to talk to them.'

'Good,'

'I will take you to Friend of Bear Captain.'

'Yes thank you.' The captain left with Bill, leaving Ruth to show Rachel into the cabin. 'This is my home,' Ruth said as they entered the cabin.

'Where do you sleep?'

'There where the furs are.'

'Oh.'

'I was going to have a swim in the lake today it is hot would you like to bathe.'

'I would like to but...'

'Don't worry, no one will come here today, that is what I asked Bill to tell everyone, I didn't like to tell the captain why.'

'Oh, so we will not be disturbed,' Ruth assured Rachel that the small bay was quite private; she took Rachel out and down to the sandy beach. Ruth thought Rachel would take advantage of a chance to wash she was hot after having reached the camp. Rachel slipped her dress off as Ruth undressed and went in to the water. 'That's better.'

'You just undressed, you have nothing on.'

'I have this on and will not have to lie in the sun while my underclothes dry as you will. No one can see you here. Can you swim out to the rock there?'

'I think so.'

'Come on then.'

Ruth swam slowly in order to allow Rachel to set her own pace. Rachel made it to the rock; Ruth helped her out of the water onto the flat area of rock. 'I like sitting here; it is very quiet and peaceful.'

Rachel went onto tiptoes looking to the East, 'I thought I might see the settlement from here.'

'We are too low,' come and sit down and rest a while.'

'This is quite private here isn't it.'

'Very, I sit here and think a lot. You are not married then.'

'I don't think I ever will be properly, we wrote it down in the book but I wanted to be married properly.'

Ruth thought that if she could not get married their way then there was nothing stopping Ruth from marrying them. 'You want to marry then.'

'I want some sort of blessing it's important, I don't suppose you would agree living here as you do.'

'No, I fully agree with you, I married Bill in a very important ceremony. Let me say for now that if John offers you a biscuit in a blanket you should eat it.'

'What, you make biscuits.'

'Oatmeal ones not quite the same as my mother use to make but they are a sort of biscuit.'

Ruth sat for a long time with Rachel before they swam back. It did not take long for Rachel's underwear to dry in the sun, she dressed and the two of them went to the cabin. They had only been there a while when Bill came in. 'Everything is coming along fine.'

'I have just seen out the window, the moose is being cooked.'

'Big feast this evening Rachel.'

'What for,'

'Getting our deeds,' Bill replied then looked at Ruth, 'I have read them love and it is what we asked for.'

'Wonderful, we can really celebrate it this evening then. Ah, Rachel, you sit with Bill at the mealtime that is our family's place.'

'Don't you sit with him?'

'No I am the chief so I sit in that place with the spirit man. After the meal is over I often go and sit there but not to start with.'

Ruth left Rachel talking to Bill and went to find Friend of Bear. She needed to organise John now she had primed Rachel. 'John!' she called out, seeing him sitting outside the lodge of the spirit man.

'What happens this evening, they are roasting that moose over a big fire.'

'We will eat it, you will see a lot this evening, sit with Porjadseeni and her children you will be looked after.'

'I was told to take a blanket to Rachel with a bit of oatmeal in it.'

'Oh who did that then? Never mind we are all thinking the same.'

'Apparently Bill has something to do with it.'

'I should have asked him before rushing off. If you want to get married, that is the first step. You must show Rachel and just as importantly Bill that you can bring food to her, and she must show you she will accept it. Bill is by the way is her father, not really but he is here.'

'Because Rachel is staying in your cabin,' John said.

'That's right. Do what Friend of Bear tells you.'

Ruth went to the circle dressed in all the trappings of the chief that evening. The tribe greeted her with a great deal of whoopees; she sat down next to the spirit man. 'Daga Kala, Captain John porpog.' She held up the deeds in her hand. 'King na England tak Daga Kala canada. Captain John e Rachel nat meecha na Daga Kala. Captain John Daga Kala tak nat porpog.'

After the fuss died down the spirit man, went to the centre of the circle and thanked the Great Spirit for sending them the captain. Thanked the Great Spirit for telling the king to give him the land for the wolf tribe and he thanked the Great Spirit for the moose and asked him to speak to the moose when they met. Then the braves danced round the moose Friend of Bear took a small piece tasted it and declared it ready to eat.

It was a good feast, the moose had a lot of meat on it and it tasted good. The tribe was happy, Ruth sat in her place watching them enjoy the time pleased they were all safe. It was almost dark when she watched John set off towards Bill and Rachel with a blanket; he placed in front of Rachel. When she took and ate the biscuit the tribe whoopeed much to the embarrassment of both John and Rachel.

It was well after dark before people started to leave the circle; Ruth went back to the cabin. She had checked the furs were all laid out neatly and had gone outside when Bill brought Rachel back to the cabin, 'I am going to see Natlatan, Hishpawa and binjaga are there now I'll not be long.'

'I will sit and talk to Rachel.'

'It's the middle of the night,' Rachel said as she sat on the log

'It has been a good day and a good feast, and a very large moon up there this evening.'

'Everyone seemed very happy and enjoyed it all.'

'We have our land it is safe from the settlers that is important to all of us.'

'I can see that; am I getting married Indian style. What happens are we married just because I ate the biscuit?'

'Not yet, John has only brought you food once, he must show you that he can do it several times, twice actually then John will bring you himself, and you take your man if you want to.'

'How?' Rachel asked.

'You will see you will know when the time is right. I don't think you should be married in those clothes though.'

'They are all I have here.'

'I can find you something more suitable for around here tomorrow.'

'How did you become the chief?'

'The squaws chose me.'

'But why, what did you do to make them choose you.'

'It will turn you more than white if I told you that, I am not the lady you are.'

'I am not squeamish; this country has taught me that.'

'I beat the Iroquois, killed several of them myself in the battle, it was over there in the old village.'

'Oh, so you fight good do you.'

'I have thrown a spear into the heart of a man; it is not something I like to think of these days.'

Bill did not take long he returned with the rest of the family Ruth and Rachel followed them into the cabin. 'Porella tashka,' White Flower told the two children as she got their furs ready. 'Porella,' she said to chivvy them on; once they were under the furs, Ruth started to undress.

'Where do I sleep?' Rachel asked.

'Here with us, take your dress off and lie down. Bill is over there so don't worry; you are part of this family at the moment. John will be doing much the same in Friend of Bear's lodge. At the moment you are our daughter.'

Ruth woke Rachel in the morning when the family food was ready. She got up saying the furs were more comfortable than they looked. They had the meal then Bill took the children away with him saying he would keep them away for a while.

'I can't wear that!' Rachel complained when Ruth produced an Indian dress.

'Yes you can.'

'It doesn't even cover my legs!'

'Come on, you can't get married in those clothes not here you can't.'

With a lot of complaining from Rachel Ruth got Rachel into the Indian dress, all that she needed now was a feather. Rachel complained again. 'It is just a feather; you need it in your hair. Only one, then you will look good.'

'I am not going out there like this. I have almost nothing on.'

'You are like everyone else.'

'I am not an Indian. Why can't I have something like you have that is better than a short dress thing it's nothing more than a sack?'

'How many have you killed in battle?'

'None.'

'Well when you do, and after I have given you the blanket of a brave then you can dress like this. Until then you dress as you are; you look good in it John will like you I am sure of it.'

'He is not dressing up like an Indian.'

'You could be wrong there. Bill is coming.'

'He can't see me like this!'

'He will not see anything strange with it.'

Bill called out before he came into the cabin. He looked at Rachel 'Very nice. John is complaining but mine fit him well. You look nice in that Rachel it fits you well.'

'I can't be seen like this.'

'Why not, you look fine to me.'

'Time you went and saw John.'

'No! Not like this!'

'He will like you, come on outside and walk around.'

Reluctantly Rachel left the cabin in her Indian dress. Ruth took her round to the village area and saw John immediately. 'Here you are, and there he is and he is waving at you.'

Rachel made her way over to where John was. 'Don't say anything she made me wear this.'

'You look wonderful in it, you really do.'

'You are only saying that.'

'You do, you look really good, more beautiful than I have ever seen you look before. I don't think I look quite so good in this.'

'It's all right you look quite strong in them.'

'It feels strange, but I tell you what I learnt a lot about her from Friend of Bear. She is a lot more than the chief here, the things she has done.'

'She fought the Iroquois she told me that.'

'She did a lot more than that, and there was a wolf called Zak I was shown where it's buried, it has seven spears in the ground around the grave.'

'She has a load behind her where she sits.'

'One for each summer she has been chief, there will be another one in a month's time; mid-summer, Friend of Bear told me all about it; been talking to him a lot; mainly about her. We have not heard all the stories about her, all the Indians round her know about her though, even those that are moons away according to Friend of Bear. I don't know how far a moon is I guess it is the distance you can walk in a month.'

'What did she do then?'

'After the bad winter the Indians were all but starving; she took her wolves hunting and chased five moose off the cliffs just her and seven wolves. This Zak wolf was one of them; he was the spirit of wolves and protected her. When the Iroquois attacked the old village, they killed most of the tribe and dragged the women off. Her wolves rescued the women and then she came to the village leading her wolves and charged straight at the Iroquois. Attacking them with a spear, she stabbed them with it. Then she threw a spear into the air and the Great Spirit guided it down onto an Iroquois who was running away from this battle. And another thing, there was a murder a bunch of trappers that were here, anyway she talked to this Zak wolf and he called others and the wolves found out which of the trappers had killed the brave.'

'She is white isn't she?'

'Was, she and Bill are Indian now. Look around here, look! There! A wolf just walking through the village and no one is paying any attention to it! Think what would happen if that occurred in the settlement there would be complete panic. Now you tell me this lot are not in direct contact with this spirit of wolves. Look! Look at it now it has just lain down and is watching that child. It's completely at home here. Look Rachel! Look! The child has just sat with the wolf! I have never seen anything like it!'

'It is different here; you can feel it a bit.'

'I tell you these lot and not just Indians, this is somewhere special, and she is the reason why, Jaga na Kala means mother of wolves, last time I was here she called a score of them to her. Look at that now, that Indian has just walked right past where a wolf and a young child are sitting in the grass and he didn't even notice them; or if he did, he didn't see anything dangerous about it. And what about those the other night they brought us food.'

'Here comes Barns.'

'Hello captain.'

'You look hot.'

'It is, just finished fixing the enclosure for them been working for them seems right to me. They have a load of moose in a field with a high fence round it. You look good in that you both do, you get married today.'

'Tomorrow.'

'Right.'

'Where are the horses?'

'In the enclosure they have for the moose; there's good grass there, they are ok can't get out and there's a small stream in the field.'

'I tell you Rachel this is more than a bunch of Indians, these are special.'

The following day Ruth took Rachel to the cabin around mid-afternoon; three other squaws were there to help prepare Rachel so that she could take her man.

'I'm not taking that off as well.'

'Yes you are, stop complaining you have to be right you can't get married if you are not right. It's only yellow and blue paint. You can rub it off tomorrow or go for a swim that will get rid of it.'

Ruth decorated Rachel's body until she thought it looked right. It was then time to dress her in her new dress. White Flower did her hair and Rachel was ready. 'Now we wait.'

'What for?' Rachel asked.

'For John to demand Bill lets you come to the circle. We have to sit here and just wait.'

Sounds of an argument reached the cabin. 'What is going on?' Rachel asked

'An argument between John and Bill, John is threatening to kill Bill right now unless you are allowed to come to the circle. The bigger the argument the better it is; the spirit man will break it up don't worry it is all show.'

Meechamegan came into the cabin. 'You come with me.'

'This is it Rachel you are about to get married. Big Bear is acting chief; he will marry you. I can't because you are my daughter right now.'

The ceremony went well. Ruth went into the new lodge, and covered Rachel with the fur she was carrying. 'There you are.'

'Now what?'

'Undress John I need all your clothes, you get under the fur and you stay there until I come back in the morning.'

'I will go along with that,'

The following morning White Flower took John and Rachel's clothes to them and invited them to the first family meal. Rachel was the first to arrive. 'I'm here!'

'Come on in.'

'Is that it, it must be I am married now.'

'You seem pleased about it.'

'Oh yes. I didn't know what to think when Bill took all my clothes away and made me lie on that fur. Then you covered me with another one and took all John's clothes. Those new furs are sensuous aren't they? Put something extra into John all right.'

'So your wedding night was enjoyable was it?'

'No complaints there. It was fantastic, I'm glad you didn't tell me too much of what was going to happen; it made it really exciting. Thank you. John will be here soon he can't get dressed as quickly as I can in this.'

'And you complained like mad when you first put it on.'

'I wasn't used to it then.'

'Thank you Jaga na Kala,' John said as he came into the cabin.

'You wanted to marry you are now in the eyes of this tribe.'

'Thank you, I know Rachel is pleased.'

'I am; I feel married even though it was the Indian way of doing it.'

'There are not many around this morning.'

'Everyone is very busy today they are hoping I will let them have two or three days off to enjoy themselves.'

'You decide that do you.'

'In summer I like to have as many days as possible where we can relax and enjoy ourselves, autumn will bring a lot of work.'

'Getting ready for winter,' John suggested.

'Yes.'

'How did Bill end up with two wives?'

'It is difficult to explain. Life here is not the same as in England; a woman has to have a man here.'

'Most men have two some three.'

'We don't have many old women, two, but they still have to have a man.'

'What if they don't want a man?' Rachel asked.

'You don't elect to not eat, they have to have somewhere to sit in the circle, when you were here with us you were Bill's daughter and sat with him. Now you are John's squaw, if John is killed, you have to come to me and I will ask which braves will have you and you choose from those who stand up. If none stand up I look round the tribe and pick several for you to choose from.'

'What if I don't like him?'

'You find one you like and will have you. You do that before your man dies so you know someone will stand up when the chief asks.'

'Oh.'

'It is not the same as in England, you can only sit in the circle by yourself for two days and then you have to take the stone to the chief. I ask if you want to stay in the tribe. If you say yes you have to have a man.'

'I think I will stick to John.'

When it was time for the tribe to sit down for the evening meal Ruth thought that it would be correct to have at least two days' rest, the tribe had done most of the work. The meal was fruit and deer stew John and Rachel were in the lodge getting theirs when Ruth entered. 'It's the one you like John.'

'I saw, I'm glad it is the meal for this evening I have been telling Rachel about it.'

'She will know what it is like soon.'

The meal was over but before Ruth could tell the tribe they had two days without work there was a matter to attend to. Ruth stood as Friend of Bear set off towards where John sat. She waited while he returned with John. 'Stand in front of chief,' Friend of Bear said.

'John, do you know why the spirit man has brought you to me.'

'No I am not too sure.'

'John, you can become a brave of this tribe in many ways. You may have fought in battle, you may have learnt how to live, hunt, or reached a particular age. More importantly, it is a way of making someone feel part of the tribe, making him feel accepted as part of the tribe, even though he may not be here all the time. It is a way by which the tribe can tell someone they are welcome at any time. Once a brave becomes a member of this tribe a young man would be expected to learn to hunt, that is not so in your case, however there is one thing, which is expected of all braves in this tribe. It is something I have asked them all and I now ask you the same question. In becoming a brave of the wolf tribe you have a responsibility towards all members of the tribe are you prepared to help anyone if they need your assistance?'

'Yes Jaga na Kala I am, I truly am.'

'Then this is where you tell me your name.'

'I'm called Hishpaga, quite often.'

'That is just white man, it would be better to have a stronger name.'

'The spirit man is Friend of Bear could I be Friend of Wolf.'

'Meechakala,'

'That sounds all right.'

'Then that is your new name when you are here.'

'I would be honoured if I could be Meechakala.'

'Portag Meechakala paga Daga Kala,' Ruth said so that the rest of the tribe could hear.

'Portag Jaga na Kala paga na Daga Kala.'

'You said that correctly well done.'

Then in a louder voice so the rest could hear Ruth told the tribe the name John had chosen. 'Portag Meechakala,' the tribe responded.

'Turn and greet them.'

John turned and faced the tribe before saying, 'Portag Daga Kala.'

As Ruth started to speak, the Captain turned and faced her again. 'You are now a brave of this tribe, you know what the blanket should have in it,' Ruth said handing him the small red blanket of a brave.

'Thank you,' John replied taking the blanket from Ruth. 'I feel very honoured. I have not earned this position as you did, but I will live up to the responsibilities of a brave from this tribe.'

'I am sure you will.'

'Thank you, thank you, I am deeply moved by this.'

'Go back to your position in the tribe and sit there, later others will come and talk to you, they will in the main say porpog it means good work, well done all sorts of things like that.'

'I understand.'

'Daga Kala, piapar ap daga Captain John, Meechakala. Daga Kala apar tag porpog, pi tak porpog e tak apa tag nak pog.' Several whoopees and a lot of talking met Ruth's announcement. She left her the position of the chief and went to her family stone. 'That pleased everyone,' Bill said as she sat down.

'They were expecting it a couple of days ago but we had work to do; now we can rest for a while.'

'Apa tag.'

'Da.'

'I am going to say well done to John.'

'Others are I see.'

'I think it was a good thing to do, I will not be long.'

Not long after Bill had gone to John's home, stone Rachel came across to Ruth, 'Can I sit here with you?' she asked.

'Of course you can, people can visit others that is what this time is for.'

'John has Meechamegan translating for him as well as Bill, a lot have come to talk to him and want to help him find the things for his blanket. John wants it to be correct.'

'That is nice,'

'He is really proud you think he should be made a brave of this tribe.'

'Tomorrow you can both lie in the sun and just forget about work.'

'Um Ah,' a voice that was not Indian said. Ruth sat up 'Hello, what is it, you are Barns aren't you?'

'Yes, um can we swim here?'

'Oh course you can, the braves are out there jumping off the rock, you can swim out there and join in if you want to. You can get onto it round the other side there is a flat bit there.'

'Thank you Jaga na Kala.'

Rachel came and sat beside Ruth. 'Everyone is here today.'

'Not quite everyone but almost, it's a rest day we can relax and just enjoy the sun.'

'Even the wolves are paddling in the water with the children.'

'They like it just as we do.'

'One came in the hut.'

'Did you chase it out?'

'It sort of left by itself.'

'That will be one that stays in the village. Your lodge was home for a few. That water looks too good to just sit and look at it. Let's have a swim.'

'I don't know if I want to.'

'No one will see the slightest thing wrong. Come on I am going to have a swim.'

Rachel a little unsure took her Indian dress off and followed Ruth into the water. She swam around for a while then swam up to Ruth 'Oh, yes you are right, this is good.'

'I sometimes think back to when I lived on a farm in England. It was nothing like this, even in summer we worked all the time.'

Ruth and Rachel left the water and lay down in the warm grass. 'As you said this is not like England is it. It's not even like the settlement can't see everyone just lying around on the shore of the lake, particularly like this.'

'Have a doze for a while.'

'This really is the good days of summer, isn't it?'

The two of them had only just lain back when the captain arrived. 'Hello John darling it is really nice here.'

'Getting to like it are you.'

'I went for a swim while you were jumping off the rock.'

'It's a long way up when you are on the top of it. It was good though.'

'Well lie in the sun for a while it's nice and warm.'

'You look relaxed.'

'I wouldn't like those in the settlement to know what I am doing right now.'

'No, that would be unwise. Life is much simpler here; everyone here is just here to have a good day. This is wonderful Jaga na Kala. This is how you should live; no one trying to do someone down.'

'We get a bit of that, why can't I have two feathers, he has more than he should. We have our problems just the same.

'Ah! What's that?'

'Be careful of him, hello Jake old boy, come and lie down it's far too hot for you to run around.'

'Oh he is old looking.'

'He is, aren't you baby, you will soon talk to the Great Spirit. That's it you lie down there and have a rest.' Having stroked Jake Ruth looked towards Rachel and John. 'I have known him all his life; he was one of Zak's cubs. He's thirteen now nearly fourteen. When he was young, he was a very good wolf, very brave. He is the last one of my first family.' Ruth looked back towards Jake running her hand over his back, 'You are very precious aren't you baby.'

'You can see he loves you.' Rachel said.

'This is what amazes me with your wolves, the trust they have in you, in everyone here.'

'We don't harm them, they don't harm us; it's that simple. Now I am just going to lie here and have a little doze in the sun.'

John, Rachel and his two men remained in the village for another ten days before they prepared to return to the settlement. Ruth went to see them off. 'Ruth all of us, the two men as well, have enjoyed being here, the days have gone so quickly. Thank you and thank all those in the tribe not only for making us feel so welcome, but for everything.'

'You can return whenever you wish to.'

'Maybe next year you might come to the settlement.'

'I can't say at present but I might.'

'Good-bye Nan, you be a good wolf now; look after Jaga na Kala.'

'Good-bye John, Good-bye Rachel. Good-bye you two.'

'Good-bye Jaga na Kala. I will be back.'

'Portag meechakala meecha na Daga Kala.'

'Portag Jaga na Kala meecha na Meechakala, see I know what to say.'

Chapter 15

Summer was good that year, people were doing jobs, which made life better; there were many occasions when Ruth could afford to let the tribe rest. On the day they rounded up more moose, everyone had great fun. Ruth made it a special day with a feast in the evening and a day of rest following it.

The harvest that year was good so much so they once again had a problem of where to store it all. When winter came, it was by some winters an easy one though there was a lot of snow.

Although winter was not extreme, it did hang on for a long time. It did not stop those who went hunting but Bill could not start on this year's crops. Most of the snow had gone but the ground was still frozen. Ruth was walking around the village thinking of where the best place for an additional store would be when much to her surprise John rode into the village at the gallop his horse struggling and sweating. 'John what have you done to this horse. Look at it, it is half starved and almost exhausted.'

'I have to talk to you,' he responded as he dismounted.

'After you have looked after this horse, look at the state of it,' Ruth said patting the animal's neck.

'It's the best one we have.'

'It has to drink and eat.'

John wanted to tell her of his problem but Ruth would not have him do so until they had looked after the horse. Once that was done, she took him to the tribe lodge. John was still very agitated. 'Now calm down John!' Ruth said as then entered the tribe lodge. 'I would already know if there was any danger near here.'

'There's not.'

'So whatever it is can wait until you have eaten.'

'It's been a hard winter.'

Ruth did not think that was right, it had been long, maybe, but could not be described as hard. She let John's comment pass. 'We survived quite well, didn't run low on food, we had a good autumn plenty of meat in the store before the winter came. In addition, we have the moose in the enclosure. Now come and get warm. You are very early this year.'

'Some of your lot came to the settlement they are there now.'

'No, everyone is here; no one went to the settlement.'

'No, not from here from somewhere else, I don't know I can't understand them, I only know a few Indian words.'

'Calm down, now tell me, some Indians have come to the settlement.'

'Yes.'

'How many?'

'There are five men about twice that number of women some old looking and four children.'

'A small band.'

'I had to give them some food.'

'Obviously they were in need.'

'They are a bit pathetic not like your tribe. I talked to one of them, or I think I did. He seemed to understand.'

'What did you tell him?'

'I said nakella that is stay here isn't it.'

'Yes, stand still or stay here, don't go, what else did you say?'

'I said Meechakala ella e Jaga na Kala ella. I don't think he really understood what I was trying to tell him. I wanted to tell him that I was going to fetch you.'

'Did he know your name was Meechakala?'

'Um, maybe not,' John said a little hesitantly.

'Then it would not have made a lot of sense to him you said Friend of Wolf go and Jaga na Kala go, but who Friend of Wolf is he will not know, he may know who Jaga na Kala is.'

'I think he did; what should I have said?'

'Nakella ne pe daqua, stay in your home. Then if you had met him and said portag meecha na Meechakala he would know you are Meechakala. You should have said "Pi ella Daga Kala daqua e tak Jaga na Kala ella ne pe daqua, I will go to the home of the wolf tribe and ask Jaga na Kala to come to your home. It's, say Jaga na Kala come in your home really but we say to.'

'Ah, yes I see, I didn't know. Will you come they are your people well Indian I mean like your tribe.'

'It may be possible, tell me about the one you spoke to.'

'He has a bit much like you do with symbols on it.'

'Can you scratch in the dirt what they looked like?'

'I think so. There were a lot of wavy lines with an arrow sort of thing like that.'

'Quick Water; that will be his name,' Ruth said.

'Oh right, then he had the same as you this sort of face thing.'

'Oh did he, right then he is a chief. What was this bit like?'

'It was a bird.'

'One or many?' Ruth asked.

'One,'

'Eagle. So you want me to come and talk to the Quick Water Chief of the Eagle Tribe do you?'

'I knew you would understand a lot more than I could. I want you to tell them to go away or bring them here. I can't keep on feeding them the settlers are already complaining.'

'Jaga na Kala, apa paga na settlement ella,' Natlatan said coming to where Ruth was talking to John.

'Who else is coming here?' Ruth asked John

'Oh they will be my men I rode on they should make it here tomorrow.'

'Da meecha,' Ruth told Natlatan.

'Por.'

'Tak Ipojar porella hi meecha e mesh.'

'Da e Porellareela,' Natlatan asked.

'Da.'

Ruth turned towards John, 'I have sent Tall Mountain and Quick Deer with some food to them.'

'Thank you. They have food with them.'

'They will have more then.'

'I'm amazed; they are a day away and you know about them already. They are coming with a horse and cart I didn't know what else to bring I only have three horses.'

'You came with four last year.'

'Last year I had eight horses we had to eat them.'

Ruth did not like that answer, something had to be wrong if the settlers had to kill horses in order to feed themselves and a small band of Indians. 'We will feed you while you are here you know that, you say two are coming tomorrow.'

'Yes, Barns and Yates.'

'Oh right, Barns he was here last year.'

'Yates came the year before when we only stayed that one night.'

'You must have a good meal.'

'Will you come and talk to the other chief.'

'Yes. Stay by the fire I will go and talk to Big Bear and a couple of others.'

Ruth left John in the tribe lodge and went to find the others. She called them together in the cabin in order to discuss what they should do. Ruth was of the opinion that if there were Indians at the settlement that needed help then they should go and see what help they could offer. It was a very short discussion both Friend of Bear and Big Bear thought the same. They made plans and discussed what they would need in order to be prepared for any problem, which might crop up. Ruth mentioned her misgivings about the amount of food the settlement had and the possibility of the band joining the tribe came up. Friend of Bear was strongly in favour of offering them the chance to join and to do it correctly, as they had a chief even if they were a very small tribe. All agreed. Ruth mentioned the settlement did not have a lot of food again and suggested they should take some as there was a wagon coming. The other two thought Ruth should speak to John first and then decide. They did agree that they would take a lot of food with them so they could provide for the Eagle tribe.

Ruth returned to the Tribe lodge and took John back to the cabin. 'That is now organised; how is Rachel I didn't ask before.'

'Cold, isn't everyone, other than that she is all right.'

'Good, I have some food here to cook for you it will be a while before the evening meal and you look as if you need it now.'

'Pi pog.'

'Porpog. White Flower will get you something. Your lodge will be cold and it is full of oats at the moment you better stay with us here in the cabin.'

'I hope my men are alright.'

'The two I sent will find them; they will be fine.'

'It is nice and warm in this cabin.'

'You slept well,' Ruth said the following day when John stirred and woke up.

'Yes thank you, it's warm in here. Being a guest here is not quite the same as in the settlement. Guests are treated better here, nice warm bed for a start.'

'It is better to have the warmth of others in the winter.'

'Here is your family meal.'

'Thank you, I better get dressed.'

'Stay under the furs if you want.'

John stayed in the cabin that morning talking to Ruth. She explained they were going to talk to the eagle tribe and ask if they wanted to join with the wolf tribe. John again said the settlement could not afford to give them anymore, so Ruth explained they would put extra food on the wagon so the settlement could eat with the tribe in the evenings. John was pleased with the plans Ruth had made and somewhat relieved.

'Oh John come on,' Ruth said having glanced out of the cabin's window. 'There is a horse and cart outside the tribe lodge.

John and Ruth went round the cabin and across to the tribe lodge. Inside they found John's two men warming themselves by one of the fires. 'Barns are the two of you all right?' John asked as he reached them.

'They came and found us yesterday; brought more food with them we had a good meal last night, still cold isn't it.'

'They have a couple of nice large fires in here get yourselves warmed up.'

When Ruth next went into the tribe lodge, she found Barns and the other man who had come on the wagon trying to talk to White Mountain. 'Jaga na Kala,' Barns called out as soon as he saw her.

Ruth went across to him 'Problem trying to understand.'

'Yea, I think this one is trying to tell Yates that he is a guest, I think.'

'Meecha, Jaga na Kala tak meecha ella hi pi lodge, lodge por sor.'

'That is exactly what he is saying. He said friend, come to his lodge, it is nice warm there.'

'You go with him you will be ok. I am with Natlatan I was last time they are ok you sleep in the furs you will be ok. He has not been here before Jaga na Kala.'

'You will be looked after his name is White Mountain, Hishojar he will look after you and bring you here when it is the time to eat.'

'I was here the first time we just found somewhere over there to sleep.'

'Too cold to sleep out winter has not gone yet. Barns will tell you he has stayed here before.'

Ruth met John early the following day, 'Have them bring the wagon up to the large lodge there it's our store.'

'I'll go and find them the cart is over there, don't know where the horse is,' John responded.

Ruth went into the store, to find Big Bear there already sorting out what he thought they should take with them. Ruth went to count the sacks of beans; there were still a lot left. They could easily afford to give the settlers four sacks of them without causing a problem for the tribe. 'Natmegan, apa e apa, beans,'

'Da,' he responded

'E latan.'

'Da, apa latan, pi latan natumta.'

Ruth was about to agree when John spoke, 'Oh my God Ruth what the…How much have you got in here!' John said as he looked around the store.

'Enough, have you looked in your lodge?'

'No,'

'Well you can't move in there for oats. It's full; we have some over here as well. Just sorting out what we want on the wagon.'

'Can I buy some?'

'Not really this has to last us until the next harvest, though we have got one field of turnip we left until after winter to harvest. There may be some oats we could spare.'

'Name your price, what do you want knives, Bill spent all his money on knives.'

'They come in useful. I could let you have say, four sacks of oats and two turnip.'

'Yes please oh most definitely yes, thank you.'

'Ap,' Natmegan said pointing to a sack of oats.

'Nak, apa e apa e ap. Apa e apa na settlement.'

'Da, piapar apar e apar.'

'Ruth what…is that salt!'

'Yes, we get it out of a cave up in the mountains. Went somewhat mad last year had three trips there. Do you want one of them as well?'

'It is like a treasure chest in here, you have so much.'

'One salt then.'

'Yes please, you are going to get a lot of knives for all this.'

'You better cover it with a skin or two, they are over here. We will need a bearskin each; we need six of them that should do. You need a couple of deer…oh no look there is a moose one here that will do the job.'

'Ruth you have rack upon rack of skins! What is this for?'

'That is a sort of needle, Quick Fox makes them he is good at it. A squaw will come for say five of six deerskins, plus a couple of these, and a load of gut, and then she can make a new set of clothes. It goes down quite quickly.'

'I know that from our store but we never have this much in it.'

'Thinking of building another store, one for food the other for everything else,' Ruth explained.

The items, Big Bear had put aside, were then taken out and placed on the cart. Ruth checked it over. 'E ap latan, umta latan mesh,' Ruth told Big Bear

'Da Jaga na Kala.'

'Captain have you seen it all,' Barns said when John emerged from the store. 'They have loaded the wagon up there isn't going to be a lot of space to ride on it.'

'I've seen,' John responded, as he looked the cart over, 'I've seen in there too, they have food like you haven't seen before.'

'We need it John,' Ruth said. 'There's a lot of us here now. There's not a lot to spare.'

'What you have given us will be of great help. I will make sure you get good knives for it. How many are coming with you Ruth?' John asked as the last of the food in the shape of an additional moose carcass wrapped in a skin was put on top of the sacks already on the wagon.

'Big Bear, Friend of Bear and three others; I have to be seen as a strong chief, can't just arrive by myself. There is a bit of a ceremony to go through if it is going to be joining the two tribes, Friend of Bear will have to be there to talk to the Great Spirit, I will have to take Nan, others will come as well but they will look after themselves.'

'You are not going to bring wolves to the settlement are you?'

'I will have to show I am strong with Elena na kala, I will just get Nan to call them and then they will go and fetch me a rabbit of two, which should be more than enough for them.'

'I would think they would be most impressed.'

'And a little frightened of me, I will have shown I am strong with Elena na kala stronger than anyone they have seen before. They will know the Great Spirit is pleased with me and my tribe.'

'You put a lot in that don't you; you are always talking about pleasing the Great Spirit and doing what he says.

By the way I told them not to kill beaver in the settlement and do you know there is a group of them on a small stream, they dammed it up and now there is a large pond there and the water in it is good and fresh and it don't dry out in summer.'

'What did I tell you, the great spirit sent them there to help you now you have good water because you are doing the right thing and not killing them, they will look after the water for you as long as you leave them alone you don't even have to take them food they eat fish.'

'There is a lot more to this Barns.'

'Seems about right to me; we got lots of fresh water now better than the lake or trying to get it from the small stream that was there.'

'The only thing we are not sure of John is where we are going to sleep in the settlement.'

'In the outpost I would think, you can stay with Rachel and me.'

'That is not really suitable; I would like to set up a sort of camp with a circle. I need a circle.'

'I can let you have some tents, not very warm though.'

'We will have to make sure they are suitable. It's getting warmer every day. It will be better if we are separate from the settlers and make our own camp.'

With the cart loaded, it was almost time to leave. Ruth went to the cabin to get her things; she would need her full headdress along with a couple of spears. 'Is that you off now?' Bill asked.

'Almost,' Ruth responded, 'John was surprised how much food we have.'

'There is not that much spare, apart from oats maybe.'

'That is what I said, but what if we did have a lot of spare food. Like an extra field of turnip, or beans, or both if you have the seeds.'

'And would we be trading this extra food.'

'We do need things; think what we could do with nails.'

'We could have better fences round the enclosure for a start.'

'Grow me some nails then,' Ruth said as she gathered the last of the items she wanted to take with her.

Outside the store, she met John and his two men; those going with her were also there waiting for her to arrive. She placed her things on the back of the cart. 'Piapar ella?' she asked Meechamegan.

'Da,'

'We can take it in turns to ride on the wagon.' Ruth told John as they set off.

'Should make it in two days, may be not, should have brought the large wagon didn't think I needed it,' John told Ruth as they reached the plain.

They made good progress the first day; finding somewhere on the edge of the woods to camp that night.

'If you tread on me I will not be very happy,' Ruth said as she started to move the following morning.

'God all mighty; I never saw you there!' Barns responded.

'You stay warmer if you bury yourself in the undergrowth as well as wrap yourself up in furs.'

'Portag,' Big Bear said as he unwrapped himself from the furs.

Ruth and the Indians were far more organised than John and his men. They had a fire going and had a pot of oats cooking before Barns had his fire burning correctly.

'Meal will not be long John.'

'You start early in the morning, cold last night.'

They arrived in the settlement before mid-day on the third day. An area of land on the edge of the settlement looked about right for their camp. They unloaded the cart there then Ruth rode on the cart as Barns drove it to the outpost with John, on his horse, riding beside it. Ruth looked around as they went through two large gates into the centre of the outpost. Bill had said it was much like a stables with a couple of cabins. The stables were on Ruth's left as they came to a stop. On her right was the first of the two large cabins. They were built with smooth wood planks rather than logs. John helped her off the wagon and showed her into the cabin. The door opened onto a large room with a table and several chairs.

'Ruth you are here!' Rachel said as soon as Ruth entered the cabin.

'I am here, I have not seen somewhere like this in fifteen years, and even on the farm we didn't have a room as grand as this, with chairs to sit on and a table, it is so fine and smooth, and it shines.'

'I will leave you talking to Rachel and see to those tents.'

'You are not going to stay in a tent are you, you can stay with us.'

'No, I must stay with my braves it is important I do, Big Bear has gone to invite the others to our meal this evening.'

'You can if you want.'

'I can't, you can come and eat with us if you want to; you have a place in the circle and can sit there anytime you choose, no one can stop you. John is a brave of the tribe and you are his squaw, you don't even have to ask. Friend of Bear will lay out our circle here and he will have everyone's home marked with a stone including yours.'

Rachel showed Ruth the rest of their cabin; they had a separate room for sleeping in and a proper bed, which Ruth had not seen since leaving England. They returned to the main room; and were still talking when John returned. 'That is it they are on the cart.'

'We are going to eat with the tribe this evening.'

'Are we?'

'Yes, but I am not wearing my Indian clothes not here.'

Ruth returned to the area where they were to put their temporary camp. Big Bear was there he and Meechamegan had worked out what they wanted and even set up a circle. A sergeant with several men had accompanied Ruth back to where she wanted her camp. He now took charge of putting the tents up. Two of her braves worked with Barns who had a little knowledge of the Indian language the rest were trying to put the tent up with the sergeant telling them what to do in English. Everyone was laughing when the tent fell down with the sergeant on the inside.

'Barns what so funny,' the sergeant said as he emerged from under the tent.

'Nothing sergeant,'

'How come you lot managed to get it up.'

'Sergeant let me help, and explain to my braves in a language they will understand. Barns has spent some time with us,' Ruth said.

With all the tents up the sergeant strutted around checking them to make sure they were correct. Friend of Bear was still smiling.

'Meechamegan,' he said pointing to one of the tents, 'lodge na paga. Pe e Natmegan ap,' he added indicating other tents.

'Da,' Ruth said then wondered if that was wise here, everyone in the Indian village knew she and Big Bear were friends. She decided to carry on; the settlement would have to get to like it. Big Bear was her partner when Bill was not around or the two of them were hunting bear; even Bill knew that.

John arrived to find out if everything was all right. When Ruth said the tents were fine and they would soon have everything done John suggested they put the oats, turnip and salt on the wagon and take them to the store. This was done, and then Ruth set off with John towards the settlements store. John carried one of the sacks into the store 'Here you are Bruce, one sack of oats.'

'Where did you get that from?'

'Got two more of them as well and two sacks of turnips.'

'Where from; are the wagons here?'

'One is; this comes from the Indian's village.'

'Well wouldn't you know it. What are they like any...' he went to say as he looked in the sack. 'They're not crushed.'

'That's easy enough isn't it. The Indians use two large stones.'

'I guess.'

They brought the other two sacks of oats in along with the turnips then returned to the cart for the salt. Ruth took hold of one end of the skin wrapped round the block of salt with John on the other, 'Ready,' he asked.

'Yes,'

'Right up…hold it Bruce is here. Bruce get on the other end of this. It's salt.'

'Salt!'

'They have more salt than you have ever seen. Piles of it. We just have the one slab.'

Ruth followed them into the store. 'There you are Bruce; Ruth needs a good price for that lot.'

'Oats is a penny and a half for a pound when I buy it from the wagon, I tried to weigh that sack there but it's too heavy it's more than twenty-five pounds. I will have to weigh it out in two goes.'

'And the salt, what about the turnips,' John asked.

'Salt is a penny for four ounces. Can't weigh that, it's much more than the scales can do. Turnips should be two pence a pound.'

'Well Ruth here wants knives and the like. She will be here for a few days so you can let her know later.'

'There's a lot here.'

'Did I see supplies arrive?'

'Not the ones from the East Mrs Macadam we have oats, turnip and some salt.'

'Oats I will take some of them.'

'Need crushing, couple of stones and rub the oats between them.'

'We always used to buy them like that back in Culross.'

'Two pence a pound.'

'I'll take three pounds Bruce and four ounces of salt and I would like, say two pounds of turnip. That will make a grand porridge for my man.'

Ruth left the store with John the word there was food in the store was rapidly going round the settlement and many of them were coming to get some. 'What did I tell you?'

'We may grow extra food to send you.'

'Trade is what it is all about Ruth. What you have sent us is at least one pound ten shillings if not more. That will buy you quite a few knives.'

The work completed, the camp established and the meal almost ready the Wolf Tribe were ready to receive their guests. Ruth saw the other Indians approaching behind their chief. She sent Meechamegan to meet them and waited for him to bring the chief to her.

'Elena na Kala,' the chief said before Meechamegan could speak.

'Nak, Jaga na Kala Paga na Daga Kala. Portag Cafseeni Paga na Daga Glish ella meecha e umta.'

'Porpog, pi ella e umta.'

'E peapar,' Ruth said.

Those with Quick Water were invited to sit in the circle. Ruth was pleased when John also took one of the braves and his squaw as a guest. Barns and the sergeant sat with Big Bear more than pleased to be included in the meal. The meal was good, it filled and tasted pleasant moose meat was a good meat to eat and in a stew with beans and turnip, it made a fine meal. The Eagle Tribe left to return to their lodges the other side of the settlement.

John came up to Ruth, 'Is that it?' he asked.

'No, but I have asked him to talk when the sun is high and have placed a spear in the ground to measure the sun.'

'There is not a lot of sun.'

'That doesn't matter he will come around midday if they are interested in joining with the wolf tribe.'

'Thank you Ruth, thank you; you were certainly talking to him a lot. And thank you for that meal, that was very nice and there was a lot of it.'

'There's not going to be much of a variety we will be eating moose stew while we are here. I was telling him you are a man of strong words that I had tested them and you had proved yourself to be a man who is worthy of being a member of the wolf tribe. I said you had act as a friend would to those who need help but you had little and your food was almost gone. I suggested they should find a home for themselves where they could hunt and start to please the Great Spirit again.'

'Thank you, I knew you would be able to explain. I didn't just want to make them go away.'

The following day went well; the two tribes joined in exactly the same manner as Ruth had seen all those years ago when the Bear tribe joined her tribe. Ruth led the chief to one of the tents they had set aside for him holding the flap of the tent open so that the chief of the eagle tribe could enter. She let it fall then turned away; there was a lot to do before they sat in the circle again. Already she could see Natlatan starting the fire. 'Is that it Ruth, is that it; your braves seem to be busy,' John asked.

'They are preparing the feast. Your problems are over we are now all members of the wolf tribe.'

'I didn't know there were so many wolves with you that has got the people talking.'

'I can guess.'

'Please come and meet some.'

'Let me get out of all this first.'

'No please don't; I want them to meet a real Indian chief one who is strong and has a good tribe.

'I don't really look that good with my legs all done up in furs in order to keep warm.'

Ruth went with John to speak to some of the settlers who had come to watch the two tribes join. 'This is Tom Hutton Jaga na Kala.'

'Portag Tom Hutton meecha na Daga Kala.'

'I can translate that for you Tom, the chief said hello friend of the Wolf Tribe.'

'Portag Jaga na Kala, is that right?'

'Very correct I am pleased to meet you. You are all most welcome to come to the feast this evening; there will be plenty for all.'

'Most of the settlement are here,' John said as they moved towards another of the settlers.

'Tell them all they are welcome to come to the feast, but they must sit with a brave. They can't make a place for themselves; you know the importance of the circle.'

'Yes I will make sure they know.'

'The braves will accept them, so will those that were the Eagle tribe, and some can sit with you, you are also a brave of this tribe don't forget that.'

'I won't; at least it is not raining.'

'No and it should stay dry, might get a little cold but we have a large fire to keep us warm. Hello I am Jaga na Kala,' Ruth said as she approached one of the women settlers.

'I'm pleased to see you; you look different to what I thought. You are very young to be a chief.'

'I have been a chief for a long time as well, I was extremely young when I became chief.'

As the two of them moved to the next settler, Ruth suddenly remembered the settlers would need a plate. 'Oh, remember to tell them to bring a plate with them and a knife.'

'I will do.'

Ruth was glad to get back to the tent that was her lodge while she was in the settlement. For a while, she lay on the furs then thought she better not. There was bound to be something that needed doing.

The moose was being roasted over the fire the turnips and beans were ready, everything was ready when the first of the settlers arrived with a plate. Ruth welcomed them and a brave showed them where to sit.

Everyone had arrived they were all sitting around the circle, it had not been possible to maintain the circle position and in the end people just found a place and sat there. What Ruth would not have though was groups of settlers sitting by themselves she made quite sure that they were within talking distance of a brave. Some were trying to talk to the braves although there was a lot of arm waving and drawing in the dirt. She thought it about time to start the feast.

'Pi tak, settlers. I will stand up and go to the centre you can then all hear me. I welcome you, please excuse me if I speak a little different, I talk English to Bill and sometimes to Meechamegan but often it is a mixture of English and Indian. Those of you who came today saw the two tribes join and become one, this is our first meal we have roast moose and it smells good it looks as if it is cooked we also have you here as guests at our feast. The captain told you all to come with a plate I hope you have. The meat inside will not be cook properly yet; so cut only from the outside then the inside will cook and we can come and get more. There will be a bit of dancing and I ask you not to go for more food when the spirit man talks to the Great Spirit. The spirit man will thank the Great Spirit for the moose, much as you thank God for a meal. We are not a lot different; he will then ask the Great Spirit to look kindly on the tribe, as we have become larger. Again, I don't think that is a lot different to what a priest would say. I ask that when the spirit man is talking to the Great Spirit you remain quite so the Great Spirit can hear the spirit man's words. Thank you, I don't think there is anything else I want to tell you. Please eat with the wolf tribe. Paga, porpog pi tak meecha na settlers, settlers nak apar mesh Captain John hi apar mesh Daga Glish, porpog settlers nat meecha na Daga Glish, settlers meecha Daga Kala. Daga Glish, Daga Kala e settlers e kala piapar meecha umta latan.'

With the invitation for everyone to eat, Ruth returned to her place in the circle and picked up her bowl.

The feast went on into the night the clouds cleared and a large moon came out. After the meal, Ruth went to John's position in the circle.

'I think the feast was good.'

'This is just like your village.'

'Everyone is eating well, the settlers seem pleased.'

'I don't think they expected all this and to be eating this moose it has a lot of meat on it and there are lots of turnip and beans to have with it.'

'We feed the moose over the winter; this is one from the enclosure.'

'There is more than enough for everyone. I don't know where Rachel is.'

'Talking to Big Bear or trying to.'

During the feast, Ruth had agreed to visit various people the following day. Rachel said she would come and take Ruth round the settlement. Rachel arrived at the camp mid-morning. 'Hello Ruth.'

'Portag.'

'Sorry portag, everyone I have spoken to today thought last night was wonderful, I think they all ate more last night than they have for a while, they are all talking about it.'

'Good I am ready to visit those people now?'

Rachel took Ruth to visit several as they made their way down the settlement. They came to the store.'

'He was going to weigh out the oats we brought with us.'

'I heard there were oats in the store; let's go in and see then.'

As they entered the store, Bruce came up to them. 'Jaga na Kala come in, the oats and salt are selling well, seems like good oats as well.'

'Rachel is showing me the settlement. I wanted to know how much the food we brought you would fetch.'

'I have that all for you, detailed all of it so that you can see that it is correct.'

Ruth looked at the paper Bruce gave her. 'I can't understand it, I can't read.'

'Not all can, you want to know the total.'

'Yes just tell me that. I will take it and show Bill what we got.'

'Very well, it all comes to two pound one and seven pence.'

'As much as that.'

'Is that wolf all right?'

'He is a good wolf Mr Hampton; you don't have to worry about him,' Rachel told Bruce.

'If you say, it looks quite tame.'

Ruth looked round the store. It had many things in it but not a lot of food. Ruth picked up a small axe. 'This is a good axe, how much is this?' she asked.

'The price is on it. Oh, let me see. Two and three it is expensive but it has to come all the way here. Most bring tools with them.'

'This is a good one, we have what my father had and what Bill brought with him, they have new handles on them but the head is still usable.'

Ruth looked around again she saw a board and knew enough to know it had writing on it. 'I can't read, is that of importance.'

'Oh, it says no salt which is not right now you provided us with some.'

Ruth left the store having spent more than a pound on various items not sure, what she should buy with the rest. She let Rachel guide her to the next person they were to visit. She was pleased with the trade Bill could come and spend what was left; Bruce had said he would keep it safe for her. Pleased that trade could get them all the tools, she wanted the tribe to have; Ruth left the store.

As Ruth said good-bye to Miss Stanton, there was a loud bang and the wood of the door beside Ruth's head split open. Nan was off towards a youth standing between two buildings on the other side of the settlement, he was holding a smoking musket. Ruth reacted before Rachel. Nan had the youth on the ground, 'Off Nan off!' Ruth pulled the wolf away from the youth, he went to stand up Nan pulled free of Ruth and stopped him. 'Ruth! Ruth! Are you alright,' Rachel said as she arrived on the scene.

'I am fine; Nan has him on the ground.'

'Oh my God, what do you think you were doing?' Rachel screamed at the youth. The first person to arrive on the scene was Bruce the storekeeper. 'I heard a shot.'

'William Duncan tried to shoot Jaga na Kala.'

'I warned you! I knew; you have done it this time! This time the captain will have to deal with you!'

'Get this wolf off me.'

'I hope it bites you! You deserve it.'

'John is coming!' Miss Stanton said pointing towards where John was riding a horse at the gallop towards them. He arrived and quickly got off. 'What happened I heard a shot?'

'William Duncan tried to shoot Ruth he missed and Nan caught him,' Rachel explained.

'What! Oh my God no,' John exclaimed.

'I was saying good-bye to Jaga na Kala at the door to my shack and he shot at us. Hit the door.'

'Thank God he missed or we would all be running for our lives.'

'You have to do something this time Captain he is nothing but trouble,' Bruce interjected.

'I will Bruce; I will lock him in the outpost and have a word with his father.'

'I should go,' Ruth said concerned that word of this would get back to the tribe and she wanted to be there when it did; if there was any trouble she wanted to be there to deal with it.

'All right Ruth I will handle this, you go to your tribe.'

'Will you be coming for the meal?'

'No I will be busy with this; Rachel will though.'

That evening when they sat in the circle in order to have their meal there were calls from her braves for the youth to be brought in front of her. Ruth explained that John would deal with it that he had the youth in a place he could not leave. It seemed to satisfy them. Later in the tent, Big Bear and Ruth spoke at length about the incident.

The following morning John came to Ruth. 'Jaga na Kala I don't know what to say. You came to help us and he tries to shoot you.'

'Don't worry John, there is talk about him being brought in front of me, I explained that you would deal with it and say he is not good and make him work hard for a long time.'

'Rachel said you talked to them after the meal.'

'It will settle down no harm done, we are still friends with the settlers.'

'That is good to hear, I do not know what to do with him. I can't really do anything.'

'Make him work hard, that is what I do when someone has done something wrong, it is usually the young who get into trouble.'

'I can't see any of them shooting at me though.'

'They know the Great Spirit would be very angry with them and I would be as well. I might even be angry enough to send him away from the circle for a moon. That would be a very big punishment. I have never done that, I normally say they must work without rest for many days. When I think they have learnt I let them have days of rest again.'

'What if William was brought to you?' John asked.

'I would say many and many days of hard work, if one of my binpaga shot an arrow at you, nearly all summer.'

'I am only suggesting this but could you not do that.'

'You would make sure that he did do the work.'

'I was thinking that you would take him and make sure he worked.'

'I can't do that; what will the other settlers think. They will not like that; you have to deal with him.'

'I can't Ruth if I am honest, there is nothing I can do, I have no prison here and to send him back to where there is a stockade with a jail is not an option I have.'

'I can't take him away from here though can I? Not without all the settlers agreeing…anyway it looks as if Rachel wants you she is coming by the looks of it.'

'I wonder what has gone wrong now.'

'I feel like that sometimes.'

Ruth checked with Friend of Bear, everything in the camp was satisfactory; they had plenty of food and not a lot to occupy them until it was time to make the meal. Ruth found Big Bear and the chief of the Eagle Tribe and suggested they talk in her tent about when they should set off back home. 'Apa tag ella daqua na Daga Kala,' Ruth said believing that they should set off in two days.

'Da, por,' Quick Water said nodding as he did. 'Pi jad…' he stopped talking when someone pulled the flap of the tent back.

'Are you…' John said then saw the others. 'Sorry, I…'

'Come in John.'

'Rachel came to talk to Friend of Bear, nothing for me to get excited about.'

'I was just telling Big Bear and Quick Water that we would go home in two days' time. Sit down I can tell you what the discussion is about.'

'Cafseeni tak meecha na captain,' Quick Water said

'Portag Cafseeni meecha na Meechakala,' John replied, Ruth was pleased he had done so and got it correct.

'Por tak por,' Quick Water said with a smile on his face, 'Meechakala por tak.'

'Well done John that was correct.'

'I am leaning. Tell them I will learn more this summer when I visit.'

'Meechakala tak pi ella Daga Kala daqua ne ween pi pog apar tak.'

'Da.'

'Can I say something then I will leave you; I came to say I still think taking William and making him work for you is the best solution. If you are agreeable I was going to find out what the rest of those in the settlement thought of it.'

'Let me say then you will know what the others think. Meechakala tak William ella e pi e pi tak hi William ella Daga Kala daqua e apar pog.'

'Da,' Quick Water responded.

'Da por, pi William hi Jaga na Kala pi tak nak por,' Big Bear said.

'I didn't understand that last bit from Natmegan.'

'He said he will bring William to me and say what he has done wrong. Natmegan nak Meechakala, Meechakala tak William nak por.'

'Da, Da, Meechakala tak, Meechakala Paga na Settlement pe tak.'

'No he now is saying that you are the chief here and should say that William has done wrong. William would have to agree and take from the blanket to say he is wrong and will do as I say.'

'He has to agree.'

'Yes he must admit he is wrong and be prepared to work to show he knows.'

'I can't see that happening.'

'Tell him about the blanket.'

'I will, you will consider it as a course of action.'

'I will.'

'Thank you I will leave you to plan your return home. I will have the sergeant and Barns accompany you, that way you will have the wagon to ride on, and they can bring it back.'

'Thank you that will help a lot.'

With a large wagon to load with the Eagle tribe possessions planning the journey back did not take long. Ruth left the tent with the other two and generally wandered around. For a while, she spoke to the Sergeant and Barns who already knew they would be helping her get back to the village. 'We can get the tents on the wagon give you something to shelter in at night.

'They haven't got a great deal, that could be good and we only need have the food that we will use...'

'They're here!'

'Sorry.'

'There! The wagons have got through to us.'

'So I see; there's another one, and another. Seems like a lot is arriving.'

'There will be better food in the store now, about time we had a choice of food.'

The two of them left to go and find out what the wagons had brought. Ruth could see those in the settlement going towards the store. Rachel came out of the tent Friend of Bear was using. 'Your wagons have arrived.'

'That will be good.'

'How come you are talking to Friend of Bear?'

'Yes, he said I am with… well I am going to have a baby.'

'Oh wonderful, is that why you went to see him. He can say and he is usually right he is a good spirit man.'

'He didn't mind what I thought, it was off with the clothes ear on my tummy, and then he stroked me, felt between my legs and my breast and told me not to lie with a man after five moons.'

'So you are two moons. That will be the beginning of winter not a good time. You should lie at the right time of the moon in the summer not the late winter.'

'I will have to tell John.'

'He will be pleased, a little binpaja,' Rachel replied with a smile on her face.

'What is that baby?'

'No a boy.'

'I hope so.'

That evening before the meal, John brought William in front of Ruth. The Indians were sitting in the circle with others from the settlement looking on.

'Jaga na Kala, paga na Daga Kala, William nak por,' John said. Ruth was pleased that he had managed to say it correctly all those in the tribe would know that William was in front of her so she could judge him.

Ruth turned her attention towards William; he looked nervous. 'William, do you know why you have been brought in front of me?'

'Captain brought me here that is why,' he responded in an offhand way.

'He also told you why didn't he.'

'Because I shot at you; you've gone Indian.'

'And me living with the Indians is wrong is it?'

'Of course it is.'

'Who do you think would live longer alone in the wilderness, you or me?'

'You would you know how to get things with the wolves.'

'I said alone, I include the wolves.'

'You still would, you know how to, I don't.'

'So I have learnt to hunt, to grow food, to make a shelter, to light a fire without any tinder box; is that bad?'

'You live with Indians, that is.'

'Is it; who says that it is?'

'Everyone.'

'Does the captain say that?'

'No.'

'So not everyone.'

'Nearly everyone.'

'The rest of the settlement are watching this, can you find ten of them who would say it is wrong, you said everyone so ten should be easy to find.'

'They will not say it with you here will they?'

'So you can't find ten, how about five, surely five can be found.'

'They won't.'

'Would you like it if I threw a spear at you?'

'No.'

'Would you say that it is wrong?'

'Yes, no.'

'No; it would not be wrong to throw a spear at you, I would not miss you as you did me.'

'You confuse me.'

'I don't think so; you know it was wrong; you are not such a fool to not know that. What you don't know is what will happen to you and that frightens you; it would me. You are here to be punished for what you have done, but that punishment will not harm you. I have talked to the captain and others, they take this matter seriously; and have asked me to speak to you. It would appear you have not learnt the lessons of life yet. Some of the older boys in the tribe find themselves kneeling where you are now. They like you are frightened they don't know what I am going to say they don't know if the punishment will be hard or light. They fear that it will be too hard for what they have done. Too much work and that I will take many of their rest days away from them. They dread that I will say apar e apar e apar; three apars are a lot a great deal they want to hear just one. How many should you hear for what you have done, how many would you say if you were me?'

'I don't know.'

'Three,' Ruth suggested

'Maybe.'

'Two.'

'Probably.'

'That is still a lot; apar means many. Many, many days of hard work without a day's rest. It is a long time almost to the end of summer, all the rest days which summer brings would be lost, you would be working when everyone else was enjoying themselves, they would be swimming in the lake, or sitting round talking to friends in the sunshine while you were working. That is a hard punishment isn't it.'

'Yea.'

'It is the punishment you have been given for shooting at me. The Captain and those I spoke to, tell me I should take you to our village and make you work those days before I send you back here. I have told them you will not be harmed, you will not be beaten, or hurt in anyway but you will work. I am now going to tell the tribe what your punishment is going to be. William nakpor apar e apar tag pog e nak tag nakpog. Now that the tribe know you have done wrong you must take from the blanket to show you accept that you are wrong and accept the punishment.'

'I don't have to take anything, you can't make me.'

'That is true, but then the captain will tell you to leave the settlement you are not wanted here. That is a much harder punishment; I too can make that punishment by sending a person away from the circle. They then have to leave and are in the wilderness alone, is that what you want.'

'No.'

'Then take from the blanket to show you accept my punishment.'

'The captain told me to take the hide strips.'

'The choice is yours you know what taking each means.'

'The strips.'

'Take them then so others can see the strength of your words.'

'There I have taken them.'

'Good, that pleases me. We will leave in two days you should return here in two days early in the morning.'

'You mean I can go.'

'Yes you have given your word to return, you have said your word is strong by taking the strips. I now test your word, you may leave say good-bye to those you know, tell them you will be back, late summer or early autumn.'

'What if I don't come?'

'Then you will have nowhere to go. You can't stay in the settlement; where would you go, you can't hunt; what are you going to eat the day after tomorrow or the following day. The settlement will not provide food for you; you will be on your own in the wilderness. Now go back with the captain to his position in the circle and sit there.'

'Move William, this way.'

Ruth waited until John had sat down. 'Let me speak to the settlers first. What you have just seen is a trial, whatever name you want to give to it. I said William was not good and he will have to work for many, many days. I know the captain has spoken to a lot of you about this. I can tell you, and you have my word, William will not be harmed in my village but he will work if he wants to eat. I hope he learns from this. As I told William, the older boys in the tribe are brought in front of me for much the same reasons as William. They learn and become good braves. I hope that will also true for William. I will say no more about this. It is time we ate; I can see some of you have your plates with you. Please eat with the Wolf Tribe. Daga Kala mesh umta.'

After the meal, Ruth went across to Big Bear's stone and sat down with him. 'Portag Natmegan, hello sergeant, Barns.'

'You were right there Chief, seen a few on trial myself. You did well there.'

'We will see if good comes of it. Did you enjoy the meal?'

'Thank you, you lot eat well, better than here, mighty good of you to share it with us.'

'Food is the most important thing, you must have food.'

'You should see it in the village sergeant; they have lots in a big hut and a field full of moose. They cook it all in another big hut and then everyone just goes and gets some.'

'Paga tak?' Big Bear asked.

'Mesh, tak piapar apar mesh e settlement nak apar.'

'Da pe jad nakpor, bin mesh nakpor. Apar hish paga umta e Daga Kala, settlement nak por umta.'

'Da, pi tak Meechakala tak pog mesh e jadpog.'

'Da.'

'Did you understand any of that Barns?'

'A bit, you are talking about food not too sure exactly what you said.'

'Good, at least you know what Big Bear and I were talking about. He was saying much the same as the sergeant said, you have not got enough food here.'

'It's ok when the wagons get through; like today we have loads. Bruce will have it all sorted out by tomorrow.'

Ruth watched as the wagon was loaded with the Eagle tribe's possessions. Everything was ready for the journey back to her home. 'Are you ready to go?' John asked as he reached her.

'Tomorrow first thing we will leave, John I must talk to you.'

'What is wrong?'

'It is the settlement, you have not got enough fields you are more than we are but you have less than half the amount of crops. There are more moose around here than we have. Look over there, there are fifty or sixty in a herd there, why is no one going hunting. John you have to make people work properly.'

'I am only here to give protection; those in the settlement council say what will be done, we are building a church.'

'God is not here it is the Great Spirit here. Building a church will not feed you but the Great Spirit has sent you a lot of moose why do you not accept them?'

'I will tell them.'

'You have to; this is not England you can't build churches here they are not going to help you. You have to have more fields and accept the moose; the Great Spirit will send more if you do. You have to not be waiting for supplies that come on a wagon.'

'They came yesterday.'

'I know there are four of them and everyone is happy; I felt sad that you couldn't feed yourself. Did it bring you salt.'

'I don't know.'

'The French are not your greatest enemy, think what would happen if they stop the wagons getting here, they don't have to come here to beat you, you are not strong with the Great Spirit you don't take what he sends you. You will make him angry if you carry on like this and then how will you care for your son.'

'Is she...oh my God. Oh Ruth!'

'John calm down, I think I have said too much.'

'I have to go to her.'

'You do that.'

The following morning Ruth was standing beside the wagon with the sergeant. 'Jaga na Kala the captain is coming with his lady,' he pointed out.

'Thank you sergeant.'

'We are all ready to go when you say.'

Ruth waited for John and Rachel to reach her. John was all smiles. 'You look happy.'

'I am going to have a son.'

'It may not be, it could be a daughter.'

'If my daughter is a fraction of you I will be very happy.'

'Well we are all ready to leave, just a matter of saying good-bye and we are off.'

'You have three horses.'

'The sergeant will bring them back.'

'We will come and see you later before the journey is too much for Rachel.'

'Come early summer then.'

'We will.'

Ruth looked around they were ready to go but William had not returned. She felt disappointed. 'I didn't expect him to Ruth,' John said.

'You will have to deal with him John. Sorry I tried to help.'

'Thank you. Now what going on over there.'

'We will leave you to sort it out.'

'Thank you, have a good trip back, the sergeant and Barns will help you get back and bring back the wagon and horses.'

'Good-bye and thank you; I will see you early summer.'

'I will…' John stopped speaking the moment he saw who was coming towards them. 'It's William and his father!'

Ruth stood watching the man lead William through a small group of settlers towards where Ruth was standing with John and Rachel. 'Jaga na Kala he was frightened to come,' William's father explained when he reached her.

'I can understand that, he has no need to fear, but I can understand. Your son will return to the settlement late summer unharmed.'

'I know, I trust you, I wouldn't any other Indian but you I do. You have shown me that you are a good chief. You let us eat with you; you didn't have to do that.'

There was nothing stopping them from leaving. The good-byes had been said and there was nothing left to do other that start the journey. 'Don't go too fast sergeant some are walking.'

'You take the point Jaga na Kala I will bring up the rear with the stragglers.'

'We will take three days to do the journey.'

'I'm with you, nice and slow.'

'Now could you tell me what this point is?'

'Up the front.'

'Oh right, I lead do I.'

'You are the Chief that is your place.'

Ruth led the band away from the settlement. She walked beside Big Bear at the front of the group but after a couple of miles she let herself drop back to make sure everyone was all right. 'William, help the squaw she is old and needs help.'

'Why should I.'

'You want to eat that is why, she will be cooking your meal this evening so help her carry her possessions. Meecha William pog,'

'Porpog, porpog, hish paga por.'

'I can't understand what the hell she is on about.'

'Then learn, she said thank you, porpog means well done.'

Chapter 16

It took the full three day to reach the village. Those in the village knew they were coming and had a meal ready for them when they arrived. Ruth sat down in the circle pleased to be home. She saw William sitting with Big Bear and thought she had better sort that out, so after the meal she went to Big Bear's stone. 'Natmegan, porpog tak William ne pe lodge.'

'Da, e pi tak William pog.'

'Porpog Natmegan, William nak nakpor.'

'Da, nak pog ne settlement.'

'Da e nak Paga na settlement Meechakala pan paga nak Paga.'

'Nak por.'

'William, you will live with Natmegan while you are here and you will always do as he says. As far as you are concerned, he is your father while you are here. He will look after you, he will not let harm come to you and he will teach to the lessons of life.'

'I won't know what he is telling me.'

303

'Then you better learn fast or you will be very hungry. You knew enough to sit here with him this evening.'

Having left William with Big Bear, she went to see Barns who was sitting with Natlatan. 'Are you all right, you should know what to do.'

'I'm fine, Natlatan said come to his lodge.'

'Good, better check with your sergeant now.'

'I told him to be with him, he's Tall Mountain isn't he.'

'Yes.'

'He will be ok with the sergeant.'

Ruth went to Tall Mountain 'Porpog Ipojar. Are you all right with Tall Mountain sergeant?' Ruth asked.

'Yea, Barns told me what happens, I can manage.'

'Thank you for all the help you and Barns have given us.'

'You are safely back.'

'Please rest here a few days before returning. I am sure Barns will enjoy a few days here before returning.'

'He's been here before.'

Ruth had been back from the settlement for ten days. The building of the lodges for those from the Eagle tribe was well underway but the sun was not that strong, and it was felt the mud would not dry correctly. It had to dry hard; even with a good fire on the inside, it was not possible to finish the lodges quickly. Those from the eagle tribe were content to remain in the tribe lodge until the huts could be finished. Two braves, one look a little young to Ruth, and three squaws arrived and asked for food and shelter, which she provided.

Sitting with Friend of Bear Ruth discussed how the work was going round the village. Apart from the new lodges, everything seemed to be in hand. The one thing she did want to change a little were the clothes William wore. 'William, paga lementa, nakpor ne hish paga lementa ne daqua na Daga Kala.'

'Da, Pi tak Natmegan.'

'Natmegan tak William pog.'

'Da, pi tak pe.'

'Jaga na Kala porella!' Someone called out.

'Porella,' Ruth said as she quickly left Friend of Bear's lodge.

'Pi hi.'

'William nak por!'

Ruth ran to where the squaw was pointing then round the field to where William was lying on the ground. Natmegan was there kneeling beside him.

'Natmegan tak porella; William what happened? Natmegan tak,' Ruth said as soon as she saw the injury to Williams head. He had a nasty looking gash in it, which was bleeding a lot.

'Nak William, William porpog, Hishglish jad William e pog. Nak William, William nak pog.'

'William stay there, you need to see Bill, he will sort that out. Just stay there, you will be ok.'

'He attacked me.'

'So Big Bear said; you will be all right; Bill can sort that out for you. Ipojar! Ella Natkala, tak Natkala ella hi, porella.'

'Da.'

'Natmegan, Hishglish hi pe lodge e nakella.'

'Da.'

Bill arrived and immediately saw William on the ground, 'What's wrong? Oh I can see, how did this happen?'

'That new young brave attacked William.'

'Nasty, you will all right though William, let's get you to the cabin can you walk.'

'I think so, head is sore though.'

'Will be, I have a few roots you can have a chew on. They will make you a little dizzy but they will get rid of the pain for a while. Let's help you up.'

'I'm all right.'

That evening the spirit man brought the young brave before Ruth. 'Hishglish nakpor, pog William,' Friend of Bear said

'Hishglish tak Jaga na Kala.'

'Nak tak.'

Ruth did not think Hishglish was suitable to be a brave of the tribe. He was too young for a start. He did not have a blanket, but he did wear a feather on his head. Ruth thought that she should correct this. 'Hishglish nak paga,' Ruth said, looking directly at the feather, he was wearing.

'Da,' he responded his eyes cast down as he took the feather off and put in on the ground.

'Hishglish nakpor apar e apar tag pog e nak tag nakpog. Suta.'

'Da,' he said as he picked up the hid strips and held them up so that others could see. Ruth did not think this was the first time he had been in front of a chief.

'Natmegan tak Hishglish pog.'

'Da Jaga na Kala. Pi tak pi nakpor.'

'Ella pe daqua.'

'Da.'

The older of the braves who had asked for shelter came to the cabin the following day in order to speak with Ruth about his younger brother. He was ashamed and could not apologise enough. Ruth told him they were still welcome to remain if that was his wish, but if they did, then his brother must work and wearing a feather when not a brave was not permitted. 'Da Jaga na Kala da,' Ruth told him to go and speak with his brother. He left the cabin.

'As Grey Beaver said they had been attacked by white men, this is the only place where that sort of thing doesn't happen, the rest out there Ruth are not as happy as we are here,' Bill said once Grey Beaver had left the cabin.

'I know he has to work with William now; should be interesting to watch.'

'Or it will be trouble.'

Several days later Ruth was with Bill in the cabin. 'I'm getting more salt Natlatan and Hishglish are going to come. Best get it done before it gets too warm I don't want to do that in summer. All the work on the fields has been done.'

'Right see you when you get back,' Ruth said.

Two days after Bill set off to get salt, the man from the store in the settlement arrived on a small wagon drawn by a single horse.

'I am sorry I don't know your name. I am sorry.'

'Bruce everyone just calls me Bruce, Jaga na Kala.'

'Oh yes, I remember now, Portag Bruce.'

'I came to trade what I can, I know you want tools and the like and so I ordered some and they have come. I have knives, saws and that sort of thing on the wagon.'

Ruth looked at the items he had on the wagon, rather surprised he had come to them. She wondered why. He had two large cooking pots, metal ones that would serve them well. 'Can you get even larger ones than these?'

'It's not the biggest, there's a boiler on the list, they are over five shillings though. I can get one if you want me to but I can't afford to just get it if you are not going to buy it, that would be all our profit gone in one go.'

'I understand; I would like two larger than those. I will have those though.'

'By all means.'

'And nails.'

'I have those, four inches or small ones.'

'The big ones what do they look like.'

'I will show you.'

Ruth held the nail in her hand it was long enough to do what she wanted it to. 'I will need two hammers as well.'

'Got them.'

'You seem to have more than when I was in the store.'

'Ordered it special for you thought I would take a chance.'

'How much are the nails, how much have I spent of the nineteen and six.'

'I will recon it up.'

The trade with the store man was good, Ruth had more knives, lots of nails, two large cooking pots, a saws and a lot more. In return, he took more oats, another four sacks, two slabs of salt and two moose. They guessed the amount based on the previous sacks and Bruce said he would do it accurately when he returned to the store and let her know how much it was. Ruth was not too concerned; she was getting a good deal. Ruth told him they would have more to trade later that year after the harvest. Bruce said he would return then and possibly would have the two larger boiling pots.

Bill returned from his trip into the mountains with four large slabs of salt. Ruth wanted to tell him about the trade with Bruce. 'The one that looks after the store came here to buy from us.'

'What for, we don't want money.'

'Knives, nails, hammers, axes and the like, and I got another saw.'

'If that is right then let's have a look at them.'

Ruth took Bill to the tribe lodge and showed him the two new cooking pots, 'and he is going to bring two larger ones when he comes next I told him to leave it until after the harvest.'

'They look good.'

'We have ten knives to give out and another new saw.'

'Great.'

'And we will have some money left he was going to weight it when he got back to the store I only gave him four oats, two moose and some salt.'

'Looks like you have done all right.'

The additional knives were liked by the braves most of them now had a good metal knife and there were several in the tribe lodge.

Summer was showing every sign that it had arrived, Ruth was in the village when one of the squaws came to her pointing towards the entrance. 'Hish paga Meechakala e squaw ella, e paga.'

Ruth watched as John arrived in the village on the small wagon driven by Barns with four donkeys following the wagon on a long length of rope. 'John it is nice to see you. What have you got the donkeys for?'

'Portag Jaga na Kala,'

'Portag meecha.'

'I am here to speak to Bill officially.'

'Why Bill.'

'He owns this land.'

Ruth's heart sank, the mere thought that something was wrong with that frightened her. John must have noticed it. 'Sorry, there's nothing wrong. I sent a note back saying Bill was farming this land and it was some distance from the settlement and getting produce back to the settlement was a problem. I suggested a horse and cart, they sent us four donkeys.'

'Oh, so you brought them here.'

'You can't walk from here to the settlement with a sack of oats can you?'

'Well no.'

'You can get eight, on them, possibly more.'

'That's true or six and ride one.'

'That as well.'

'Meechakala mesh na Daga Kala,' Quick Water said coming to look at the donkeys.

'Nak! Nak mesh!'

While Ruth was laughing at Quick Waters statement Bill arrived, as did a lot more. 'I saw from the cabin, where did they come from John?'

'They are for you, so you can trade with us. Very interested in whatever you can supply.'

'We are growing extra; it will be a while before you can have it though.'

'Hello Rachel, how are you.'

'I'm fine,

'It's nice to see you both again.'

'It's good to be back here.'

'You are most welcome, your lodge is there and available for you.'

'I have our furs.'

'Where did you get this horse from it looks a good one.'

'They sent me a few more.'

'Put it the enclosure there is a lot of nice grass in there for it and the stream for it to drink from.'

'I will do, and thank you for all the oats and moose; people think Bruce got a good deal there.'

'We think the same, we have good tools.'

Ruth went with Rachel to their lodge while Bill and John looked after the horse and four donkeys. Bill was of the opinion the donkeys should not be in the same enclosure as the moose.

Ruth lit a fire in Rachel's lodge and had it burning nicely. 'It will just take the dampness out. It's not as warm as it could be today.'

Ruth and Rachel had been talking for a while before John came into the lodge. 'I have just seen William and an Indian about his age.'

'Those two, enough said about them, they are always getting into trouble.'

'Not here as well.'

'Not like that. William has worked hard, sit down I will explain what happened. Hishglish, that is White Eagle, came with his older brother his squaw, mother and another young woman. They had escaped from a bit of trouble with white men and when Hishglish saw William, he attacked him. I gave him the same punishment I had given William. They had to work together, now the two of them are almost one, they are always together. They both work hard, but they both get into trouble if you understand me.'

'I think so; high spirited.'

'Definitely but they will make good braves, both of them; they don't lack courage that is for sure.'

Ruth was still sitting with Meechamegan and John talking about how they could get salt and that it might even be possible for Bruce to send it back on the wagons that supplied them and in that way the settlement could even benefit from the trade, when the sound of a shot rang out.

That evening once again William and Hishglish were knelling in front of her to the amusement of the tribe. 'William I dream of a time when there will be a moon without you in front of me for some reason,'

'I was just showing Hishglish a musket and we went to shoot a deer so we could put it in the tribe lodge.'

'And did you hit it.'

'No,'

'You are not a very good shot are you? What happened to the deer?'

'It ran away.'

'And so did all the other deer and rabbits.'

'I didn't know that.'

'Hishglish, tak.'

'William tak por musket por jadpog e musket.'

'E reela.'

'Nak, porella.'

Ruth looked at the two of them; they had become inseparable friends after the initial attack on William by Hishglish. They were both good at heart. 'Peapa, apa tag nak pog.'

'Um, nak pog?' William questioned with a frown on his face.

'Yes William, see if that stops you from getting into trouble. Hishglish,'

'Da, apa tag nak pog da. Porpog Jaga na Kala.'

'Peapa ella daqua.'

'Da.' with that the two of them scrambled back to their place in the circle with the whole tribe laughing at them.'

'Daga Kala, apa tag nak pog.'

After the meal, Ruth went to John's place in the circle. 'Hello John, I thought that I would come and sit with you for a while.'

'You are very welcome to. That was quite amusing.'

'What.'

'William and his friend,' John said.

'Oh, the tribe has sat and seen them in front of me on many occasions.'

'I guessed that. Two days off this time though.'

'They have worked on making the enclosure better, and worked hard, it is about time they had a couple of days rest.'

Ruth along with others sat in the sun; it had turned out to be quite a nice day. John and Rachel came across and sat down with her. They sat and talked for a while. Ruth had started to explain she would be away for two days when Big Bear and William came across to where Ruth was sitting with John and Rachel. 'Big Bear said I have to ask you if I want to come on the Bear hunt,' William said

'I don't think your father will like it if I have to tell him that you were killed by a bear.'

'Just to see,' William said with a pleading tone to his voice.

'You will have to do as you are told William.'

'I will.'

'I really mean it though. This is not something where I can have you doing anything other than what you are told; it is dangerous.'

'I know; I will do as I am told Jaga na Kala.'

Ruth looked towards Big Bear. 'Pe tak William por, e jad jadpog megan.'

'Da pi tak.'

'Well Natmegan seems to think you will be all right. Very well make sure that you are ready first thing tomorrow morning we have to walk round to the other side of the lake.'

'Big Bear will be going so I will get ready with him.'

'See you tomorrow morning then.'

'You are going to hunt bear!' John exclaimed, after Big Bear and William left them.

'Yes, why, do you want to see what a bear hunt is like?'

'Yes I would. Um…' John hesitated looking towards Rachel.

'You go; I will be all right here. I can lie in the sun and sleep while you are out there hunting for bear.' Rachel said before John could finish.

The following morning the four of them set off for the Northern shore. The day was pleasant without being too hot. As they walked, Ruth explained to John and William they would go to a place, which had two platforms up in the trees. That the two of them would sleep on one of them and it would more than likely be first thing in the morning when a bear would come.

Ruth crouched on the edge of the platform a little after dawn; it was not the largest bear she had seen by a long way. She looked across to the other platform. John and William were watching the bear as it approached the tree Ruth was in. Big Bear indicted she should drop alone. Ruth nodded and watched as the bear below her reach the rabbit guts. She checked the point on her heavy spear then dropped onto its back, driving the point of her spear into the heart of the animal. It struggled pitching her first one way then the other as she worked the spear deeper into the body of the bear. It reared up, and Ruth had to hold on tightly to the spear her legs gripping the side of the bear. Then came down heavy on its front paws, the jar forced the spear deeper into its body. Ruth felt the bears legs start to buckle as it collapsed onto the ground. It groaned several times then lay still. Ruth pulled her spear out, lifted her leg over the back of the bear and slid off the dead body of the bear. 'Porpog,' Natmegan called down to her as he started to climb down the tree to where Ruth stood. She looked towards the sun and thanked the Great Spirit.

John came running towards her with William close behind him, 'Ruth! Are you all right, oh my god it's huge!'

'She got it! Did you see?'

'God Ruth I knew you were a woman who should not be tangled with but to kill a bear like that with a spear.'

'It is how the Great Spirit wants us to kill the bear, not all are asked to.'

'Ruth, oh my! Look at it!'

'It was a good bear; it will now be talking with the Great Spirit.'

'That William is not just a matter of killing a bear; I hope you have learnt a lot here.'

'I saw it, Jaga na Kala came out of the tree onto its back and stabbed it with a big spear.'

While Ruth went to wash in the lake, Big Bear skinned the bear. Then Big Bear led the group further down the shore to another place, which had several platforms in the same area. They sat and talked during the afternoon then prepared the meal. Big Bear took Ruth to one side after the meal. 'William e pi jadpog meecha.'

'Nak,' Ruth immediately replied.

'Da, William por paga.'

'William por paga da, e nak fron?'

'Da pi tak pe fron.'

Ruth though a lot about what Big Bear had said, William did not lack bravery, but it was asking a lot from him. 'Da,' she eventually said, 'William jadpog.'

'Por.'

Ruth woke John in the morning with her hand over his mouth. 'Be very quiet,' she whispered

'Da.'

She watched the bear approach the tree in which William and Big Bear were waiting. 'Will he be alright with Big Bear?' John whispered into Ruth's ear as the bear got nearer the tree.

'Watch, it looks a good bear,' Ruth said extremely quietly holding her finger to her lips.

William was only a few seconds behind Natmegan as he dropped onto the back of the bear. 'Ruth! It's...' even though the two of them had dropped onto the bear Ruth did not want John calling out. Her hand went over his mouth. 'Be quiet.' She took her hand away. She immediately looked back to where the two of them were still struggling with the bear. William was working his spear into the bear and was doing well; it would not be long now.

Ruth was down the tree faster than John was. She went across to where William was laying on the ground his whole body trembling. Big Bear nodded at her and she returned the nod.

'Is he hurt?' John asked as he approached Ruth.

'No, he is working out what turns a boy into a man. Let him be there.'

'Are you sure he is all right.'

'Quite sure, Big Bear will take him to the lake and wash him we will just wait.'

'He can't stand his whole body is shaking,' John said.

'He will be alright. Come away; let him and Big Bear skin the bear, they have to do it, and they don't want us there.' Ruth took John away from the bear to a place where they could watch without interfering. Ruth watched the two of them skin the bear. William could hardly use his knife as he tried to help Big Bear.

'Where are they going now?' John asked as Big Bear led William towards the lake.

'Big Bear is taking him to the lake. He will talk to the Great Spirit. I hope the Great Spirit will look kindly on William.'

'Did you know he was going to do that?'

'Big Bear asked last night, I had to think a lot about it but in the end I thought it right to at least test William. He dropped, that took a lot to do especially when it is your first bear.'

'I can see them what are they doing.'

'Come away John. It is between Big Bear, William and the Great Spirit; it is not for us to watch.'

'Did you go through a ceremony?'

'I killed my first bear with Big Bear he washed me and stood me in front of the Great Spirit, so I could thank the Great Spirit for sending me the bear. He will do the same for William.'

It was a while before William came back to where Ruth and John were sitting waiting for the two of them. 'Jaga na Kala I…'

'You don't have to tell me William, you feel different.'

'Yes.'

'You did well. Porpog William.'

'I talked to the Great Spirit as well. It's strange, I felt it.'

'Are you all right William?' John asked

'I am fine, I feel different though Captain. I saw a bear in the sun.'

'I guess that is imagination after having done that.' John said

'No,' Ruth said, 'Definitely not.' She turned towards William, 'What you saw William was Elena na Megan, it is the spirit that looks after you. Elena na Megan is strong and fears no one. That is a good spirit for you to have.'

'I know, I saw it, I know sort of inside me.'

'You did very well, porpog William, porpog.'

'It was good, not at the time though I was really frightened, even after it was dead.'

'Yea, I know. Well let's get that fur rolled up and head off back to the village.'

They packed up and started the long walk back to the village. William walked with Big Bear with Ruth some distance behind them talking to John. 'I never thought I would see William do something like that.'

'He is a megan paga now he has been asked to hunt bear.'

'Does Bill hunt bear...I suppose he does?'

'No, he has never come on a bear hunt not even to find out how a bear is killed. It is not that he is not brave enough it takes a special type of brave to hunt bear.'

'I can understand that, why was he shaking and trembling after it though.'

'Fear, it doesn't just leave you when the bear is dead, in fact it increases when you realise what you have done. You will only have to say to William – bear hunt – and he will remember this hunt and the feeling he had. I can remember my first bear as if it were yesterday, I too couldn't stand up. I couldn't even hold my hand up to see how much it was shaking.'

'He did seem different when he came back from the lake.'

'He was.'

'Did you see a spirit?'

'Elena na Kala.'

'I should have known that; what other spirit would you have seen, it had to be that one.'

The arrived back in the village after midday, they laid the furs out for inspection.

'Pe jadpog megan?' Hishglish asked William.

'Piapar jadpog megan. Jadpog apa megan.'

'He...'

'No John. We went bear hunting we all came back with two furs. That is all anyone needs to know.'

'Oh sorry.'

After the tribe had examined the skins, they were stretched out ready to be cleaned and prepared. 'I take it you don't talk about bear hunts,' John said.

'No you don't; as William said we went bear hunting and came back with two furs.'

'I was telling Rachel, I don't think she believes me. William isn't the person I know, you have completely changed him.'

'Half the trouble is that you haven't got the jobs for him to do in the settlement. You have to work people or they get fed up. Particularly the young, they complain a lot, but you have to give them lots of jobs to do.'

'Maybe.'

'Not maybe John,'

That evening after the meal, Big Bear brought William to her. Ruth stood up as they approached. 'William porpog, pe tak William paga Daga Kala,' Big Bear said.

'William do you know why Big Bear has brought you to me.'

'He said I was good,'

'Yes he did he said you are a good brave. William you have lived with us for a while, you have work well, your time of work has been completed, I am satisfied you have learnt the lessons of life.'

'I will not do wrong again.'

'I know, Big Bear has said you have done well and shown you are now a man. When a boy does that in this tribe, he becomes a brave, and has a place in the tribe. I ask you this question. As a brave of this tribe will you help anyone of the tribe should they need your help.'

'If I can, I don't know how to do everything. Big Bear said I have to learn to hunt first.'

'I would not expect you to, all I ask is that you help where you can.'

'I will, I like it here.'

'Then William I will give you the blanket of a brave, you know what goes in it.' Ruth passed William a blanket with a single feather on it. 'By what name would you like to be called.'

'Can it be Little Bear, some call me that anyway, Hishglish does, Binmegan is all he calls me.'

'Most certainly; portag Binmegan paga Daga Kala.'

'Portak Jaga na Kala.'

'Turn and greet the tribe, you have seen it done before.' William turned and faced the others. 'Portak Daga Kala.'

'Portak Binmegan,' the tribe responded.

'That's it go back to your home stone.'

Ruth remained standing waiting for the other boy to be brought to her. 'Hishglish, Elenapaga tak Hishglish por pog e por paga na Daga Kala.'

'Da Jaga na Kala. Da.'

Ruth gave him a blanket of a brave and a feather. 'Portag Hishglish, paga Daga Kala.'

'Portag Jaga na Kala.'

He turned and faced the tribe, 'Portag Daga Kala.'

'Portag Hishglish,' the tribe responded.

Ruth was in the tribe lodge when Rachel came in looking for her. 'I thought I should help do something. John has gone hunting with Big Bear and William. William is really pleased he has a feather on his head, eager to tell me it was right to have one now.'

'John should have one as well, he is a brave, he should have a feather.'

'No, he wouldn't look right with a feather, William does it suits him. Did he really kill a bear with a spear by jumping on its back?'

'You shouldn't ask, but yes he did.'

'That's what John said; he jumped out a tree onto the bear. Never thought he would do that. What can I do in here then?'

'Whatever you want; Clear Water is the main person in here; she will need to get the meal ready for this evening. If you ask her say pi pog pe, it means I help you, and then she will show you want to do.'

John stayed in the village for twenty days then thought it time he returned to the settlement. Ruth thought she would let William go back with John, as it would save him walking. She went to find him 'William it's time for you to go back to the settlement, you can go with John.'

'Do I have to?'

'I said you would and you must.'

'You said late summer early autumn it's not that yet.'

'You have learnt quickly and your time of work has finished.'

'I will not do anything wrong, can I come back next year? I want to I will work.'

'You may, you like the captain are braves of this tribe you can return whenever you wish to but I don't expect to be before the end of winter.'

'I will come after winter is over.'

'Show those in the settlement you are a different person show them you are a man, a brave of the Daga Kala. You will let the tribe down if you get into trouble.'

'I won't, I promise you, and the captain will tell you if I did.'

After John's return to the settlement the village settled down into the lazy days of summer, her tribe was strong they looked good to her as she sat with them in the evening. They would have to soon think about having and inner and outer circle. Their numbers had been increased considerable; not only by those who had come and asked to join the tribe, but they now had those from the eagle tribe who were all settling in well. The village was starting to look as if a tribe lived there rather than a few Indians.

Chapter 17

The harvest that year was exceptional. For a while it was everyone to the fields in order to gather it all in. Then Ruth and Friend of Bear, with Bill writing it all down in a book, started to take inventory of what they had and what they could safely take to the settlement. 'Bean's they will definitely have them and the turnip,' Bill said.

'That lot is more than one trip there.'

'If you take one lot, maybe John will let you have a wagon to collect the rest,' Ruth suggested.

'Maybe, yea ok I can do that, you have the rest to sort out, get plenty of moose then if we do get a wagon to come here we can let them have some of them.'

'I will sort that out while you are away with this lot.' Ruth had assumed that it would be Bill that went to the settlement, but he thought it would be best if she did.

The weather was fine; the sun was not as powerful as it was well past the height of summer. Three donkeys were loaded with three sacks each and then tethered so that the four of them formed a line. Ruth said her good-byes then rode out of the village on the first donkey with Nan walking beside it. She enjoyed the journey along the edge of the wood. It took her two days to reach the settlement arriving just after midday on the second day. She rode the lead donkey up to the front of the store. Bruce came out to meet her. 'Hello Bruce, I have some beans for you, nine sacks of them.'

'Yes, yes, oh yes that is good, I will get them inside and weigh them for you.'

'Jaga na Kala!' Ruth turned to see William coming towards her.

'Portak William.'

'Portak Jaga na Kala, pi jad pe ella.'

'Delivering some beans.'

'Is Hishglish all right, working hard is he?'

'He has been very busy with the harvest we all have.'

'Ruth.'

'Hello John.'

'It looks as if you have the harvest in.'

'I can let you have another five beans and then ten turnips. I don't know about moose yet but I would think you could have four.'

'Full carcases.'

'Yes, and there is salt if you want it.'

'You will need a big wagon for that lot. What do you think Bruce?'

'I can drive the wagon, there and back,' William volunteered. Ruth was not surprised he was keen to be considered for the job.

'If William came back then there is no need for one of us to come back with the wagon. William can sort it all out for me with Bruce.'

'If that is all right, you will stay for a couple of days will you,' John asked

'I would like to.'

'Be our guest, I will go and let Rachel know you are here.'

'All right John; I can sort this out with Bruce.'

Bruce weighed the beans out, on average there was thirty pounds of beans in each skin sack. Each sack of beans earned the tribe five shillings. Ruth looked round the store selecting several large knives and other tools she wanted. It would not be long now before all braves had a good knife. 'Get this Jaga na Kala, it's a good pistol,' William suggested.

'No, you should know that is not the way we do things.'

'It's still good.'

'It may be but not for us, however more of those nails would be useful.'

'The fence is ok I should know, I nailed most of it together.'

'It's fine but we could use these to make better racks in our store.'

'Oh yea, they are tied with vines, yea nails will be much better.'

Ruth selected several items, which Bruce put to one side for her. Then Ruth set off for the outpost. John was in the stable area he came out to meet her and took her into the cabin he used. Rachel was in the room sewing. 'Hello Rachel, I'm back here again.'

'It's nice to have you here and this time you are our guest,' Rachel responded putting her sewing down and coming to greet Ruth, 'I'm glad you came. We can talk; I'm getting a large tummy now.'

'So I see.'

Ruth enjoyed to two days in the settlement she went to see Bruce having agreed to meet William at the store that morning. 'With the items you took you have two pounds three and two left,' Bruce told her.

'That's good; we were talking about salt earlier this year. We could do a special trip just for you; with the donkeys, we could bring back at least eight slabs. That is more than you will need here.'

'Salt will definitely sell on to the wagons, so will any skins.'

'We will have to do that next year then plan it so we have the wagon to bring them down here.'

'Bill said he wanted another writing book I have that for him, it's only a penny so just take it.'

'Thank you, he will be pleased with that.'

'This is for him, it's all down there what you brought here what you took.'

'I will give it to him. He will keep it safe. Ah William is here by the sounds of it.'

'I will get your things on the wagon then.'

What Ruth had brought from the store did not take up a lot of room on the wagon. She said good-bye to Bruce then after tying the donkeys to the wagon she climbed onto it. 'Off you go William you know the way.'

'Be there tomorrow.'

Ruth arrived back in the village to find everything was coming along fine, and they had rounded up a lot more moose. William stayed in the village for two days. Ruth asked for four moose to be killed and the wagon loaded with the spare produce they had. 'Don't try to go too far in one day on the way back William, think of the horse, you have a large load there,' Ruth said as she saw William off.

'I won't Jaga na Kala I will take my time.'

'Make sure you do.'

'I will, Portag Hishglish.'

'Portag meecha.'

'Portag Jaga na Kala.'

Once William left, Ruth went back to the cabin to find Bill looking at the paper that Bruce had given her. 'Is it all correct?'

'As far as I can tell it is. We have a lot of money Ruth.'

'I know over two pounds.'

'That is before they get the rest of it. My guess is there is another three pounds at least that is five pounds! I don't know anyone who has ever had that sort of sum, and if we add salt to that say…well if we load a wagon up with salt, we could have as much as ten pounds. We are rich, really rich.'

'Enough to buy a horse and cart of our own?'

'Easily.'

'That is what I want. If we have horses and a wagon, we can do a lot more. A big horse like my father had could plough the fields.'

'And that will grow more and we will get more and more.'

'Enough, we have work to do, or we will not survive the winter.'

'Yea, but this is good Ruth really good, and to think you didn't want to be Chief; the tribe is going to be very rich if we carry on like this.'

The winter had been kind to them, and all the tribe were now working hard on the tasks of spring. John had a number of additional fields created and planted. It was late spring when John rode into the village. He was alone, and having seen Ruth, he turned the horse in her direction. 'Hello John how is Rachel.'

'Wonderful, I have a son.'

'Oh I am so pleased for you.'

'Have you seen William?'

'No.'

'The fool!'

'What's wrong?'

'We had some trouble the store was robbed, Bruce had all the money to pay for the supplies, and he is a sort of bank as well. Most of the money the settlement had has been taken by a couple of trappers.'

'What has that got to do with William; was he involved? I didn't think he would do anything like that.'

'No, no, he said he could track them and set off in this direction, why I don't know there is nothing this way they would have gone back towards the other settlements. Not come this way.'

'They have not been anywhere near here, I would have known.'

'William said they had come this way wouldn't be told. Put his Indian clothes on and set off with a couple of spears.'

'He is not here, not seen him.'

'He must be out on the plain then.'

'You have to go a long way to lose sight of the mountains, he will turn up.'

John only stayed the night then set off back to the settlement after asking Ruth if she would get a message to him if William turned up.

Four days after John returned to the settlement Ruth was making herself a new shirt from deerskin when she was disturbed by a brave. He was with a hunting party but had returned in a highly excited, they had heard wolves howling out on the plane and had gone to find out why and half a day's walk later they heard a bang, like the sound of a musket, coming from out over the plain.

Ruth couldn't understand who would be out on the plain, then thought about William, but if it was him where did he get the gun from? 'John said he had come this way,' Bill said.

'I know.'

'It could be them shooting at him.'

'I think I better go and find out.'

'Take Big Bear with you.'

That afternoon Ruth set off with Big Bear to find out what was going on. They had four wolves with them and sufficient food for three or four days. They had walked towards the south for half a day well out onto the vast plain without seeing anyone. They stopped for the night. It was the following morning while they were still eating when they heard a single shot. Quickly they prepared to move heading East, towards where they believed the report came from. Before the sun reached the horizon, they heard another single shot and adjusted their direction moving south again. Ruth and Big Bear were waiting the following morning for the sound of a single shot to reached them, it was some way off but they were getting nearer to whoever was firing.

Big Bear saw the distant figures first way off on the horizon. They approached with caution; the wolves had been walking with them they disappeared into the tall grass.

They were less than a mile away when Ruth saw someone standing while the others appeared to be on the ground. Ruth watched a distant figure hold his arm up; it was an Indian. She saw the smoke and shortly after the report reached the two of them. 'Binmegan,' she told Big Bear.

'Da.'

William had just fired another shot in the air and was cleaning the pistol ready for the next one. He would get one shot off before it became dark. As he prepared the weapon, he started to think of what he would do that night. He looked towards one of the men lying on the ground nursing a wounded leg. The man saw William look at him. 'You little bastard, you wait, I will get you sooner or later,' the dirty looking, roughly dressed trapper said spitting as he did.

William felt confident he had tracked them for six days and they had been completely unaware he was there. 'You not good enough,' he boasted, 'I would just disappear into the plain and put a spear in your other leg.' As William spoke a wolf appeared, its head down and its ears flat against its head.

'Shit, shoot the bloody thing!' The man said as he tried to back away from a wolf that had approach them.

'Portag, meecha na Binmegan.'

'Are you mad? Don't talk to it, shoot the bloody thing!'

'He's my friend, Portag Nan,' William said. The wolf turned and came towards him, William held out his hand towards the animal then after it had smelt it he stroking the wolf.

'I knew you would come and find me,' William said as he continued to stroke the wolf.

'What the hell do you think you're doing; shoot it.'

Another wolf appeared beside William. He smiled as he stood up. 'That's two wolves; I bet there are more, and someone who will frighten the shit out of you,' William said as he looked around. 'Can't see them,' William said as he continued to look around, 'they are better than I am at this, and I got you.' As William spoke, yet another wolf appeared. Then a voice said, 'Portag Binmegan.'

'Portag Jaga na Kala, pi nak jad pe ella hi pi,' as William spoke he saw Big Bear, 'Portag Natmegan paga na Binmegan.

'Portag Binmegan.'

'That's my Indian father and my chief, and another wolf, hello you. See you are just not good enough, teach you to steal the settlements money.'

'Cocky little bastard, the bloody Indians might just slit your throat ever thought of that, I hope they bloody scalp you, you little bastard.'

'See this feather!' William shouted at the trapper while he pointed at the feather that he had on his head. 'That says they won't!'

Ruth stood up and as she did so did Big Bear. 'Portag Jaga na Kala paga na Daga Kala,' William said as soon as he saw her.

'Portag Binmegan,' Ruth replied, 'Are these the two who robbed the store?'

'I caught them, Jaga na Kala. I've got all the money. I knew you would come if I kept on shooting this in the air,' William told her as he held the pistol up.

'What is wrong with them?'

'I threw spears into their legs to stop them running away. They can't walk much; I didn't know what to do so when I got this off them I shot it up into the air; I guessed you would hear it. I could see the mountain and knew it was not that far from the village.'

'Porpog Binmegan, pi tak porpog,' Big Bear said coming to where the two of them were standing.

'Hish paga nakmeecha, um...don't know how to say it, they stole the settlements money, they robbed the store.'

'We had John in the village looking for you.'

'Oh, he said they would go the other way but I could see they came this way,' William explained then looked at Big Bear, 'Pi jadpog hish paga.'

'Por jadpog, hish paga nakmeecha,' Natmegan said.

'Porpog Binmegan, porpog,' Ruth said believing they should use the Indian language so if the trappers could hear them talking they would not understand.'

'Get this bloody wolf off me!'

'Nan Poota hish paga. This wolf will not let you go anywhere, you can't escape now or it will attack you.'

Ruth prepared a meal then they sat there talking as they ate it. 'You sit there eating don't we get anything we can't even walk, you little bastard.'

'You are alive what more do you want. I'm not hunting for you, you stole the settlements money,' William immediately responded.

The following day William thought the two trappers were not walking fast enough. 'Come on you can walk, move or I stick this spear in your arse,' he said as he threatened to do just that.

'William!'

'I am just making them move faster.'

'They can't William you speared them in the leg.'

'I had to stop them from getting away.'

'I am not saying it was wrong, in fact you have done well.'

It took most of that day to reach the village. The tribe was about to eat when the three of them arrived back with the two trappers. Friend of Bear came up to Ruth. 'Hish paga nakmeecha, William jadpog nakpor hish paga. Poota e ap mesh tag.'

'Da,' Friend of Bear said and started to arrange for the two trappers to be bound and put in an unused lodge with two braves standing guard over them.

'Come on William they will make sure they don't get away your job is done.'

'I have all the money they took and I think there is more; it is more than fifty pounds I think, not good at counting.'

'You don't have to be William.'

'I will go to the settlement tomorrow.'

'It will take you more than a day to get there. I can send one of the braves. Bill can do some writing and he can go on one of the donkeys we have had a lot of fun learning to ride them.'

Ruth sent Natlatan the following day to the settlement to tell John to come to the village. Ruth thought John would understand ella daqua Daga Kala. Five days later Natlatan returned with John; Ruth went to meet him. 'You have William have you?' He asked.

'He's here, so are the two trappers, he caught them,' Ruth replied then seeing William she waved him over.

'What!' John exclaimed, 'you have them.'

'Hello Captain I got them,' William said as he reached the two of them.

'You caught them.'

'And I got all the money captain.'

'Is that right.'

'William caught them, and then he fired shots into the air until we heard them and went to find out what was going on.'

'How William, how did you overcome them.'

'Threw a spear into their legs so they couldn't walk that good, I threw it then hid when there were looking for me, then did it again until I got them both. They didn't find me and I was too quick for them.'

'Where are they now?'

'In a lodge they are guarded all the time they can't escape they are tied up now.'

John went over to the lodge in which the trappers were being held; he went in. 'I am captain Upton both of you are arrested for theft. You will be taken back to the stockade and put on trial.'

'That bastard crippled us both he should be the one that you should be after, little bastard nothing more than an Indian.'

'I would not speak like that here, or you are not likely to survive.'

Ruth walked away from the hut holding the two prisoners with John. 'Can someone take a note to my sergeant?' he asked.

'I would think so, if you can write it.'

'Natlatan has learnt to ride; he could take my horse it will be quicker than a donkey.'

John was writing the note when Natlatan reached the cabin. 'He's here now,' Ruth told John.

'I'm done.'

Ruth spoke to Natlatan, 'Ella na settlement tak sergeant.'

'Da Jaga na Kala pi jad sergeant, pi meecha na sergeant.'

'Por,'

Natlatan was delighted that he was going to ride John's horse to the settlement. He sat on the horse proud wanting everyone to see him setting off.

Four days later one of the braves called out as Barns drove a wagon into the village with a large group of settlers on it. John reached them first. 'We came captain, we are ready.'

'I said a wagon and two militiamen.'

'Ah, now, um we couldn't understand the Indian that good.'

'I wrote a note for you.'

'A note! That is what it was. I think he lost it; he kept on scribbling on a bit of paper and throwing his hands in the air. Your good wife told us that ella na daqua Daga Kala means come here, and the Indian kept on pointing at the wagon.'

'You are right that is what it means. There is no need for everyone though William got them and alerted those here, they went out and brought the thieves here, they are under guard now. I wanted a wagon and a couple of men to get them back to the settlement.'

'Captain is the money safe.'

'It is Bruce; William has given it all to me.'

'William caught them!'

'Yes,'

'Well I never, who would ever think that.'

'Why are they all here?' Ruth asked John when she reached the group that had arrived.

'Natlatan lost the note I wrote.'

'Oh no.'

'So instead of two I have ten of them all ready to hunt the outlaws down.'

'Hello to you all, welcome to our village, we have not had so many visitors before; you are all welcome. Go anywhere around the village, you are free to have a look at everything here. I think it would be best if you didn't go to the lodge over there where you see two standing with spears, they are guarding the thieves; it would be best if you didn't go in that area. We will eat early evening you are all welcome to join us.'

After the meal that day, Ruth went to speak to William. 'I have come to where you sit William to say porpog for tracking and catching the thieves. Several others will also come and say the same. I also bring you a feather you have earned another feather.'

'Natmegan said you would, you told the tribe that.'

'You did well and I should come and say this. You have knelt in front of me on more than one occasion.'

'I won't do that anymore.'

'Is that a promise?'

'Not for anything really bad.'

'I know and well done William I can see John is waiting for me to leave I am sure that he will come and speak to you.'

'Porpog Jaga na Kala.'

'Porpog Binmegan.'

Ruth left and went to her family stone. A little while later John came across to her. 'Is it correct to sit here?' he asked.

'Of course it is John.'

'We will set off tomorrow take those two away for you. Let you get back to your normal lives here.'

'This has not stopped us doing what we normally do.'

'You have a lot of crops here.'

'We need them; we don't get supplies sent us.'

'William got a couple of the moose early spring; they were a bit thin though.'

'They would be after winter; he should hunt them now for you.'

'He was saying he wants to remain here for a bit. I think he is going to ask you if he may.'

'He has a right to sit in the circle; he is a brave of this tribe he doesn't have to ask.'

'That's right isn't it, you gave him a blanket. I don't think he realises that.'

'He is more than welcome to stay, I am sure he will work as everyone else does.'

William remained in the village when John and the others left the following day. He went hunting with Natmegan and the others. It was not until mid-summer before John returned on a wagon with Rachel and his small son.

'I am glad to find you by yourself. Looks as if William did more than we thought. Sent those two back to the stockade, Barns went with them. They were a couple of real bad ones; apparently, they were wanted for murder, killed a couple back on the coast; they were real outlaws.'

'So what happened, you said they had murdered people.'

'Barns came back on the next wagon to tell us they were hung.'

'Oh,'

'Thought you would like to know. Barns said as soon as he got them to the administration there they knew all about the two of them.'

'How far away is this stockade?'

'Twenty-five days about five hundred miles it is on a huge lake.'

'I can remember that you can't see the other side.'

'That is the one, they are calling it a sea now, and have named it Hudson Bay, you came past it did you.'

'With my father, there was a big swamp there if I can remember right.'

'That is the one; the stockade is this side of the swamp there is quite a large settlement there, much larger than here.'

'Why are you here John I mean why is the settlement here?'

'Just a settlement, I would think we will in turn supply the next one further in land.'

'But you don't even have enough food to feed yourselves.'

'I know; they still don't hunt as you said or grow much.'

'You must do that John; you must make sure people work properly.'

'We have built the church now.'

'And have you a preacher?'

'No.'

'You have to do what the Great Spirit wants here John; he has sent you moose and good land where you are. You must accept this, make large fields.'

'They are going to send us cows and livestock, I don't know when.'

'I would like a horse and plough for here, get some fields out on the plain even. Given a year or two, I can supply you with food as long as you don't get too large. I would need to know how many there are in the settlement all the time.'

'That could be a possibility then we would only need supplies of other things.'

John spent twenty days in the village. When he left, William returned to the settlement with John and Rachel.

Late Summer William returned on the large wagon drawn by two good horses. 'It's for the crops; John said come ready for when you have them harvested. I have some things that Bruce said you wanted; two great big boilers, a load of knives and other tools.'

'That's great they want the boilers in the tribe lodge. Take the rest to the new store.'

'I see you have built it then.'

Ruth was pleased the tribe was starting to obtain items that were considerable better than they could make. With needles and thread, Ruth could make better shirts and with a few buttons down the side, she could undo it rather than pull it over her head.

They had a couple of rest days before they started the harvest. As in the previous year it was all those that could be spared from other work. They filled their store then started piling the sacks onto the wagon until they had it loaded. Then it was stacked in the cave.

Ruth went and found William. 'William I want a wagon of our own along with a horse. We have a lot of salt as well as the food that we have put on the wagon. I don't know what the cost of a wagon would be.'

'I don't know.'

'Could you ask when you take this load back then return for the salt?'

'I can do that for you Jaga na Kala.'

It took William five days to return to the village. He drove the empty wagon up to the front of the tribe lodge. Ruth went to meet him. 'Jaga na Kala, I have done it for you! Bruce said you can buy this wagon, he uses the small one and the outpost owns the other one. But he said he only ever uses this one to come here and it would be the same if you owned it!'

'How much?'

'I have it all down on a piece of paper for Bill to look at.'

Ruth took him to the cabin. Bill spent a while looking at the papers which Bruce had sent. 'It says here that we are owed eleven pounds fifteen and ten, added to that is another six pounds and two shillings. The wagon is eight pounds and each horse is four pounds. Plus when the tools cost and it leaves just one pound seventeen and six, before we sell them the salt.'

'We will have our own wagon and two horses.'

'Better get that plough you have at the back of the cave out and see what needs doing to it.'

'You think that we should.'

'It's what you want and we fetched extra salt this year there are six blocks to trade.'

'Bruce will make a lot of money on this, but it is what we could do with.'

'I would not think that way. We will make a lot more with two horses.'

Ruth went to look at the wagon it was sound and much better than the cart her father had. The two horses were also nice and strong and it was a stallion and a mare.

Bill slapped the horse on the rump. 'This is a good horse Ruth.'

'I know, yes we will do it.'

'I don't think you will regret that.'

'I will go back to the settlement with William, unless you want to do this trade.'

'No, you go.'

'I will not be long a few days that is all.'

With the harvest in Ruth had the hunters out rounding up the moose and herding them into the enclosure. Then she set off with William back to the settlement with six slabs of salt on the wagon along with six moose. By the time they reached the settlement, William had taught her how to drive the wagon. Ruth brought it to a stop outside the store; Bruce came out before she had got off from the wagon. 'Jaga na Kala, you have come.'

'To do the trade and I have six blocks of salt for you.'

'I can have that on the wagons that go back the last one for the year has not yet got here.'

Ruth agreed with Bruce the price of the wagon with two horses, what she had not known was that the wagon had a cover as well. William and Bruce got it out from the shed behind the store and then William started to fit it to the wagon. It consisted of a number of large hoops over which William pulled the canvas and tied it to the side of the wagon. Ruth liked what she saw, she was very pleased with the trade and if Bill got the plough working, they would be able to make large fields and grow a lot of food for the settlement.

The following day William turned up at the outpost dressed in his Indian clothes with two feathers in his hair. 'William,' John said as soon as he saw him.

'I'm going back with Jaga na Kala; I am going to my home there. My father said that is where I should be and I will be with my Indian father.'

'So I see.'

'I will come as see you on the wagon when we bring you food.'

'You do that William you will always be welcome here.'

Ruth returned to the tribe with William who went to Big Bear. With more in the tribe now, it was not so hard to prepare for winter by the time the first snows came; the tribe were well prepared for winter.

Chapter 18

To start with, the winter did not seem that harsh but then it turned very cold and it remained so for a long time. More snow fell and again the temperature dropped even further. It became almost impossible to remain outside of any prolonged period. Once again, snow piled up past the top of the cabin's door. The lake froze solid. It had partly frozen before but this year the whole lake froze over and then with snow on top of the ice it turned it into a vast uniformly flat expanse. During the day, most of the tribe huddled together in the tribe lodge, with the three large fires burning the tribe lodge was nice and warm. Some remained there during the night in order to keep the fires burning.

Bill put more wood on the fire in order to drive the cold out of the cabin. Ruth and White Flower cradled the children in the furs. 'Pi nakso.'

'I have never known it last this long,' Bill complained as the fire started to catch.

'It is a hard one, and long, we should be tending the fields by now.'

'It can't be much longer.'

Clear Water got up and started to prepare their family meal. Then Ruth chased the children out of the furs and got dressed herself. After eating and wrapping herself up well against the cold, Ruth went round to the tribe lodge. 'Portag Jaga na Kala apar nakso,' Big Bear said as he stood warming himself by one of the fires

'Portag Natmegan.'

'Kala!' Natmegan said pointing to a group of wolves.

'Pi jad apar kala,' Ruth responded as more came into sight. Ruth had just finished speaking when one of the tribe nearer the wolves called out 'Ella e pog e pi.' Ruth and Natmegan ran where they could, without slipping on the ice, towards a thin horse dragging a cart the wolves had guided to the village. She could see a man slumped down on the cart with blankets over him. 'Who are you?' she asked as she reached it. 'Come you need a fire.'

'Natmegan! Ella e pog pi! Ipglish!'

'Pi ella!'

'What is it Ruth?' Bill said as he arrived.

'Get them into the tribe lodge they are almost frozen, Careful with her she has a nasty looking leg.'

'Oh my it's broken,' Bill said, 'The cabin would be better. Ipglish tak Porliptan ella pi lodge.'

'Da.'

With Bill looking after the woman and Friend of Bear taking the man to the tribe lodge, Ruth and Big Bear took the horse away from the cart and threw furs over it tying them round its body then led it away to the corner of the village and into a large shelter where the donkeys lived. There was space for a small horse. Ruth put some additional hay where the horse could reach it. That done

Ruth went back to the tribe lodge. The man was sitting by a fire Ruth went up to him. 'Are you warmer now?'

'Jagan na kala, we are done for, no food,' the man said.

'Your wife is in my cabin Bill is caring for her.'

'Her leg, she broke it three days ago, slipped on some ice.'

'He and Porliptan that is Good Bird are trying to help her.'

'We are done for.'

'You are safe here, stay and get warm. Porjadseeni mesh hish paga umta.'

'Da.'

'You will get some food as soon as it is ready.' Ruth left the man and went to the cabin to inquire how the woman was. Bill was there with Porliptan and they were both trying to help the woman who looked as if she was not right. 'She is unaware she has eaten plenty of roots, she will not feel the pain.'

'Can you do anything it looks bad.'

'Da. I will straighten it then all being well it will mend but will never be strong.'

'He said the settlement has run out of food.'

'That was always going to happen with a winter such as this one; even with what we supplied them.'

'I will go and find out what I can.'

Ruth turned over in her mind what she should do. If the settlement did not have any food, what would the other settlers be doing? Would they be trying to make it to the village? She decided that despite the cold she would send some of the braves out to try to find any settlers who were in the area. They could take plenty of food with them. She left the cabin and went to the tribe lodge. 'Natmegan, jadpog hish paga, ella e apar paga e mesh e kala.'

'Da pi porella.'

Ruth went to where the settler was sitting, he had moved away from the fire a little. 'How are you now, a little warmer?'

'Thank you Jagan na kala.'

'It is Jaga not Jagan,' Ruth corrected him; it was the second time he had her name wrong.

'I am sorry,' he said.

'It's all right, have you had something to eat?'

'A big bowl of stew it was really good. Thank you, it warmed me up to.'

'Good, tell me about the settlement.'

'It's lost; some are trying to get back most I think will come here…' Ruth listened as the man explained what had happened in the settlement. He told her several had died, they were found dead in their cold cabins. Ruth's heart sank when he told her John and Rachel had lost their baby boy to the cold. They were interrupted by a cry from outside the lodge. Ruth went to find out what was going on. 'Jaga na Kala ella!' a squaw called Small Bird standing by the entrance to the tribe lodge called out. Ruth reached the entrance of the tribe lodge and looked out. The squaw was pointing to a small group of settlers. They looked a dishevelled bunch.

'Apar settlers pi jad.'

'Porjadseeni mesh apar mesh!' Ruth shouted back into the lodge as she set off towards the group of settlers. 'Jaga na Kala, we come to ask you for help,' a woman said when she reached them.

John Bacon

'Yes come to tribe lodge it is warm there and there is food,' as Ruth spoke she saw Natlatan about to set off with five other braves. There were well wrapped up in furs to keep the cold out. He waved at her as they started to leave in order to search for others that could very well be trying to make their way to the village.

'Porpog Natlatan!' she called out.

'Da Jaga na Kala,' came back the reply Ruth watched them leave not surprised that William was one of those going out to look for any settlers who were coming towards the village.

'Come on all of you come with me, you must get warm and eat something,' Ruth said turning her attention back to the group of six that had just arrived.

Later that day William returned with three settlers. 'William!' Ruth called out when she saw him with three other settlers.

'Natlatan told me to show them the way here. I am cold.'

'Take them to the tribe lodge.'

'Da, Jaga na Kala.'

Ruth looked around the tribe lodge; her tribe were looking after those who had arrived, so she went to the cabin to find out how Bill was getting on. The two of them had just finished binding small twigs round the woman's leg. She was still unconscious from the roots Bill had given her to eat. There was nothing she could do which would help in the cabin; Ruth made her way back to the tribe lodge.

'Mr Walters!' Ruth called out; most of the settlers were huddled up close to one of the fires eating a bowl of stew

'That is me,' Mr Walters responded from further down the tribe lodge. Ruth made her way towards him.

'Your wife will stay in the cabin for a while, Bill has straightened her leg and bound it with twigs to hold it there it is the best we can do.'

'Thank you.'

'He gave her some roots, they make you go to sleep she will wake up tomorrow and not feel very well but at least she didn't hurt when he put her leg back in place. She will be all right, but it does take a while for a leg to mend.'

'Thank you, thank you such a lot. Your people have been so kind. Can't understand what they are saying but you somehow get the meaning don't you.'

'I better tell you all what is happening.' Mr Walters followed Ruth over to the fire around which the others were huddled. 'There's a lot of you here, normally I would put you as a guest of a brave but there are a few too many of you this time. This tribe lodge is large and we have some furs. The furs and the blankets that you have I hope will be enough for you to find somewhere to sleep in here. There is plenty of wood there to keep the fire burning all night. Try to stay warm it will give you strength. In a short time we will all eat in here, we can't sit in the circle in the winter. It will get crowded but we will at least be warm.'

The following day Ruth quickly dressed. The cabin did not feel quite as cold this morning. 'I must go and find out how they are. Natlatan and the five with him didn't get back last night I hope they are alright out there.'

'He will be, he's good and strong.'

'It looked as if they took plenty of food.'

By the time, Ruth reached the tribe lodge Porjadseeni with another squaw were already there and had started to prepare family food in one of the larger pots Ruth had brought in the settlement. She went to where the settlers were sitting around another fire. 'Clear Water is making a meal for you; it is what we call family food. In the morning, we eat in families not all together, so it is only you in here for this meal. It is porridge, the sticky sort of thick syrup comes from a tree and is sweet it is nice with porridge.'

The cry was raised mid-morning when another who had set off with Natlatan returned with another five settlers. They were cold and hungry. No sooner than they had the five fed than another four arrived. Late in the day, Natlatan and those with him arrived with a horse and cart. Ruth went to find out believing he only had a horse and cart. When she saw the two bodies covered with a fur, she cried out. 'Natelena nak! Bill!'

'Porella pe daqua.'

'Da,' Ruth said climbing onto the cart. Her first fears were not founded, John and Rachel were not dead but there were not far from being so.

'What Oh my god.'

'They are only just alive.'

'Get them in the cabin. Porella Natlatan pi lodge.'

Ruth tried to do what she could as Bill and Natlatan led the horse to the cabin. Once there Bill and Natlatan carried the two unconscious bodies into the lodge. 'Por Alsor Hishpawa nat sor.

'They are so cold,' Bill said, 'Get them under the furs. Hold them; hold Rachel close to you warm her.'

Ruth wrapped a fir round herself and Rachel. Rachel's unconscious body was cold and almost lifeless. It took a while before Rachel started to move. 'Rachel can you hear me?' Ruth asked.

'I'm cold.'

'You are in my cabin under the furs, John is here as well, hold me and get warm.'

The anxiety was over; both John and Rachel were able to sit in front of the fire with a fur wrapped round them as their bodies recovered.

'That fire is hot,' John complained.

'Sit there, keep that fur round you and get warm. You frightened me; you were nearly frozen when Natlatan brought you here.'

'You warned me, they didn't listen, they wanted a church they said we had plenty of food and the food you supplied we didn't need more.'

'It's all right John don't get upset.'

'You were right, people killed for food Ruth; killed for a couple of rotting turnips. The store is full of things you don't need and we have a church and no one to go to it, because we had no food.'

'Don't be so sad,'

'How are you my dear?' John asked Rachel, who was huddled up in a fur next to him.

'Getting warmer. Are others here some were going to come here.'

'Quite a lot and few more have arrived today. They are being fed and cared for; you have stopped the way we normally live for the last few days everyone is helping the settlers. We will not leave you to the cold.'

'It was so bad in the end Ruth.'

'Try not to worry about it. When the warmer weather comes we can go and find out what the settlement is like.'

'There is no one there; I was the last to leave.'

'It is definitely warmer out there today,' Bill said as he came back into the cabin.

'That is good.'

'Rain just started.'

'That is a good sign, the Great Spirit is telling us it is over, and it will not be long now.'

'How are you two?'

'Feeling much better Bill.'

Ruth went to the tribe lodge and returned with enough food for all of them, believing that John and Rachel should not venture out into the cold rain. The fire was banked up well that night.

'I can't remember when I last woke up and was this warm,' John said when he woke.

Ruth turned round. 'You look a lot better; you have some colour back in your face.'

'I feel a lot better as well, thank you.'

Ruth left White Flower getting the family meal ready and went to the tribe lodge to find out how the others were. 'Phew, it's raining hard,' Ruth said as she ran into the tribe lodge. Most of the settlers were standing near the entrance looking out at the rain as it fell. 'How are you all today?'

'We are all right Jaga na Kala. Thank you so much, your Indians have been so good to us.'

'There is many of you. That's not the way you say it. You know what I mean. I have said that a moose should die so that a large stew with a lot of meat can be made. We all need a nice big meal today. It will get busy in here today all the fires will be needed to cook on. If you can give us as much space as possible, it will help. Braves will let you shelter in their lodge there is no need to be in the rain.'

'Let me in!' William called out as he dashed into the lodge. 'It's raining, has my father come yet?'

'Sorry William.'

Ruth sat in the cabin talking to John and Rachel; she was worried about William. He had looked every day for his father. Big Bear had just come and told her they had again not found any settlers out on the plain coming in this direction. 'We will go to the tribe lodge to eat today. It's a moose stew with lots of meat in it. I asked for the same again, it will give you all strength.'

'That was good yesterday.'

'You will be able to go to your own lodge tomorrow, spend another night here you will need to warm your lodge up anyway.'

John and Rachel went with Bill, Ruth and all her family to the tribe lodge. The settlers greeted John as soon as they saw him. 'You look much better than when I last saw you on the wagon.'

'Can't remember any of that Bruce, not a thing. I can remember I was on my way here then I was in the cabin here with Jaga na Kala warming the two of us.'

'Have you seen all the food they have? They have so much here, a store that has sack after sack of roots, beans, meat is hanging up. There is a cave full of oats. They have so much.'

'Jaga na Kala told John not to build the church that it should be fields and that we should hunt the moose. The settlement committee wanted the church.'

'Captain.'

'Hello Margaret, I was looking to see who was here.'

'Not many twenty-three of us and the two of you.'

'We are a sorry bunch.'

John Bacon

'Come on John spring will be here soon then you can start again.'

'No Ruth we can't, not without someone who knows what to do here.'

'You have to learn, we will help you; some can stay here and work to produce extra food we can then bring it to those rebuilding the settlement.'

'We will start with the fields this time.'

'That will be better but right now we should get ready for the meal today.'

The whole tribe was in the lodge that evening; everyone had plenty to eat the moose stew put strength back into the settlers.

'I have not eaten like that for many a day.'

'There is more if you want it.'

'Thank you Jaga na Kala, I have eaten all I can and it was very tasty. I am just happy the horror is over, and we are all safe here.'

'I hope so, it was a hard winter, the Great Spirit sends us them to test us. We were lucky though we had no unexpected deaths due to the cold.'

'Luck didn't have anything to do with it. Knowing what was needed, how to achieve it and good planning is what you had and we didn't.'

'I will need to talk to the settlers now that the trouble is over. You need to get back to your homes.'

When everyone finished eating Ruth stood up, 'Daga Kala,' she called out. The Indians became quiet followed by the settlers. 'Daga Kala pi tak hi settlers. I have just told the tribe I will talk to you. It looks as if those who are going to get here have done so. We have had no new arrivals in the last two days. We need to work out what to

354

do. Well more what you need to do, later…' Ruth stopped talking as a man unable to stand any longer collapsed in the entrance to the tribe lodge. William almost climbed over the others in order to reach him. Then others reacted and started to help him carry his father to the fire in order to warm and feed him. Ruth believed that what she was going to say could be said another day. William's father was now the important person who had to be cared for, and William was making sure his father was getting warm and had something to eat without Ruth needing to do anything. She turned away and sat down. 'I am so pleased,' she told John.

It was the following day before Ruth once again spoke to the settlers. 'Last time I was going to talk to you I was interrupted. I am glad to say that Mr Walters is now a lot better; William is looking after him. When it is much warmer, we will go and find out what is left of the settlement and then slowly you will be able to return to your life. After the battle with the Iroquois, we were much the same as you are now. I can remember thinking at the time we had won the battle yet we were a beaten tribe. I was not the chief then. I liked the old chief, he married Bill and me but he died in the battle. In our tribe, it is the spirit man, medicine man if you want to call him that, but Elenapaga means spirit man. Next to me, he is the most important person in this tribe he will never be a chief but he becomes one for the two days between each chief and if I am away, he takes my place. The next person you need to be aware of is Big Bear; I think you all know him. He is the son of a chief; he is also the hunting chief and as such is of importance. These two and myself look after the tribe. The other important people are Porjadseeni who looks after this tribe lodge and makes sure we have a meal, and Bill who looks after all the fields; his job is to make sure we have all the food we need. It is our job to ensure the tribe is strong, the braves expect us to have them doing tasks which will ensure they are strong. They expect the spirit man to say the right things to the Great Spirit. While you are here, you will learn this. I will treat you no differently, than I would one of my own braves, you have every reason to believe I will ask some to hunt, or to ensure the fields are planted and tended. After you have done a day's work there will be a meal waiting for you. We are not the same here in that we don't make our own meals apart from in the morning. The main meal is always taken as a tribe. If you hunt and manage to kill a deer, it is not yours to eat, it belongs to the tribe and this tribe lodge is where you bring it. You will be thanked and you will get a meal that evening, even if you don't manage to find anything, you will still get a meal. That can only be done if we all work together. When you are stronger, you will be able to rebuild your settlement, and we will grow extra food here for you, but that can't be done until the weather is much warmer. We don't have many spare lodges so you will; I am afraid, have to remain in the tribe lodge for a while. Later, in the summer, if you are still here we will build more lodges so that each man has a lodge. However, it will not be long before we have our first meal in the circle and if you are to sit in the circle to eat then each man will require a home stone. The women and children will then need to choose a man to sit with, you can't sit in the circle unless you do have a man and here I am not prepared to break that rule, so you will need to form families with a man as the head. If we get to the point, where we build lodges for you then the family will all live in the same lodge. I am sure you will learn more. I can't tell you everything in just one go, but I hope I have told you a bit.'

'Jaga na Kala may I say something.'

'Please do John.'

'Let me start by trying to talk to those of this tribe. Daga Kala, pi tak porpog, pi tak nat porpog. Apar settlers tak nat porpog.' Those of the tribe that heard all called out, 'Porpog, por tak,' or something similar and generally cheered what John had said.

'Well done John you got that right, they all understood that,' Ruth said.

John continued, 'I said thank you to the members of this tribe. I would like to thank Jaga na Kala here as well; she has helped us when we needed it without being asked. She helped us before I can see some here who were at the settlement not that long ago. They have become part of this tribe. I am honoured to be a brave of this tribe. William that we all knew as a troublemaker came here and became a different person in less than six months. He found himself here, don't ever question his bravery, I personally know he has a great deal of courage, he has done things I would find very difficult, and don't know if I would be able to do what I have seen him do. I guess what I am trying to say is you don't have to be worried here. You can trust anyone in this tribe with your life they will not let you down. I think while we are here we should show our appreciation by helping them where we can, help in the fields, help around the camp here. Trust Jaga na Kala's judgement she does know what should be done and when. I think that's all I have to say.'

The weather improved a bit, some work in the fields became possible. Ruth was pleased to see some of the settlers help without being asked to. She went and found John who was looking after the horses they now had along with the four donkeys. 'Portag John, I was thinking we should go and see what the settlement is like.'

'The horses are looking good they certainly have put on a bit of flesh. They will easily get us there and back.'

'Can you speak with Bruce about what it left in the store, I am sure some of it will be of use here, and you will need things when you start to rebuild the settlement. We should bring what we can back here for the time being.'

'I'll do that, that seems sensible or what's there will just rot.'

The food they would need for the trip plus a couple of furs where put in the waggon. The two of them left the village early the following day. Nan sat on the seat between Ruth and John looking around as they made their way towards the settlement. 'He likes riding on the wagon.'

'I don't think I have seen a wolf sitting on a wagon like this.'

John drove the wagon into the deserted settlement going directly to the outpost. John's cabin in the outpost was cold and damp. Ruth lit a fire in a fireplace and soon had a good one going heating the room. John put the horses in the stables for the night and returned with their food and furs. Ruth cooked the meal.

The following day they looked round the settlement. It felt strange going round with no one there. 'What was this one it was not here when I was?'

'That is or was the church.'

'Oh. Let's look in the store next; I would think that people took all they could.'

'Look moose,' John said pointing out onto the plain to a group of moose about half a mile away.

'This is a good place for your settlement but you have to use what is sent you here. It is not the same as we have you have moose and good land for growing things in. That what you have been sent, that is what the Great Spirit wants you to do. You only have to look around to see what has been sent to you. I can see the lake the beavers have made for you. You have everything you need here, it has all been sent to you.'

'I understand all that now. I only wish the others had listened to me.'

'You must take charge John, be the chief. You need others to help you.'

'Like you have Bill, Big Bear and Friend of Bear.'

'You need them to be the ones that say what is to be done in their bit. Then you have to make sure it all comes together. I thought it would be difficult to be the chief, but it's not, not really. I just make sure that everyone is working hard and they do and I then give them days of rest.'

'I have seen how you run your tribe, and the respect everyone there has for you. You have it right and we must learn from you.'

'Let's have a look in the store.'

The door to the store was not locked; it opened for John when he tried it. 'It is still full of things, look,' Ruth said as she walked into it, someone had obviously searched it items were scattered around the floor but there was a lot in the store still.

'No food though.'

'Look at all of it, clothes and other things.'

'You can't eat them. I can understand all you said before, you warned me; this would never have happened if we had listened to you. When we did, you said don't kill beaver we got all the fresh water we needed.'

Ruth ignored John she did not want him getting remorseful again. She bent down and picked up a large knife in a sheath. It was a good knife. 'Nice strong knife,' she said.

'Take it, take anything, you want I think the store owes you a fortune.'

'That's forgotten about, I don't need money John you know that.'

'But more tools axes, saws, knives; would help you a lot.'

'There is a lot here isn't there. If we take, all the store has and then what is in the various cabins you will have more than you need to start again. It may need a couple of trips to get it all back to the village but you will then know it is safe and there for you.'

'That would be best.'

'You have to make the people work properly, you have to do that. Forget the French unless they actually arrive here. If they do then talk nicely to them and send me a message, there were fifty Iroquois; a few French are not going to cause me a lot of trouble. They will not even know we have surrounded the settlement. I don't want to look for a battle but if there is no choice I will have the tribe fight to protect you as long as you start looking after yourselves.'

'Yea, we will, let's look out the back Bruce kept the larger things out there.'

The door to the outside the shack was locked. John broke the lock so they could look inside. It was neat and tidy. 'Another plough,' Ruth said as soon as she saw it.

'There is everything you need here; this is just as Bruce left it.'

By the time night fell, Ruth and John had packed the wagon with everything they thought would be useful. It would take at least two more trips to get everything back to the village. Early the following morning John hitched up the two horses and the two of them headed off back to the village. It took longer going back with the loaded wagon. 'Drive a little further there is a wider entrance which leads to the village further up,' Ruth said pointing to where the best entrance was to the village. The tribe and the settlers all came to see what they had brought back. Ruth checked with Friend of Bear to find out if everything had been all right while she was away. There had been no problem.

The weather was still not good enough to sit in the circle, so it was a meal in the tribe lodge again. After the meal, Ruth spoke to the settlers again. 'John and I have had a good look at the settlement, and we talked about what can be done. The first thing is that although there are some that have burnt down, there are plenty of cabins there for you all, so although you may not get back the one you had to start with you will have a cabin there to live in. We brought back everything we thought useful it will be at least summer before you can think of going to do anything in the settlement and you will need food. One of the things we brought back was a plough this will help a lot. I have told John we will help you build the settlement up again by growing more food here than we need. There are three wagons and two carts so we can move lots of food to you. It only takes two days to reach you a lot less than the other wagons take. John thinks there will still be a problem in winter, and it will be, though you should be able to store enough there to last the winter. Another question John asked was; is it possible to stay here. It is, but we didn't know how you would feel about that. Whatever you decide you will be here for a while. We have to be able to produce enough food for all of us; we will be in trouble this year if we have a winter such as the last one. I don't think we will run out but we haven't enough fields and moose to get through unless we work hard. I like having extra food going into winter. That is why we brought the plough from the settlement. I want you to make several more fields so they are ready to sow with, roots and beans. The roots will do us after the coming winter and the beans don't take long to grow. If you are good at ploughing, then please get one of the horses and plough us a nice big field. We found a small quantity of wheat seeds they will need to be increased for a year or two before we can take a crop and by then we need to be able to mill it, I don't know how maybe one of you do, you need to be able to in two years. That will produce different food that we can send to you or you can eat here. So you see whatever you want to do the first job is the same, and that is create more food. John will talk to you now.'

'I was on the council we should have one here to decide what is to be done.'

'No, I am the chief here I say what is to be done. If Friend of Bear, Big Bear, Bill or Porjadseeni asks you to do something, they are asking you for me. I decide on the way I wish the tribe to work, what large things will or will not be done.'

'Here is not the same Alistair, Jaga na Kaka knows what has to be done, she doesn't need a committee,' John said.

'You can always ask me for something, suggest or complain it is time we had a rest day, tell me whatever you want and you can do so from the circle so all can hear you. I will listen to you, but I am the chief I make the decision. We have a sort of council in that I will speak with Big Bear and the spirit man before I make the more important decisions. Here, as John said, is not the same as in the settlement. My overriding priority is food it always has been and always will be; nothing is more important. I think that is a lesson you have all learnt.'

John spoke to the settlers telling them that he wanted a couple of them to go back to the settlement and load the wagon up again until the store there was empty. He had a several volunteer for that task. Ruth was pleased to see that John was taking charge, he told some to work for Bill in the fields, he even told the women to help in the tribe lodge.

Once John had finished one of the settlers came up to Ruth, 'Jaga na Kala, you spoke of a mill for the flour. I know how.'

'That is good to know. Bill thought he could if he had to but would not get it completely right.'

'I can get it right, water or windmill; I can build one given the tools I need.'

'How long will it take?'

'One man at least two years.'

'That is good, but you can find help when you need it.'

'Should I look for a suitable place and the stone that I will need?'

'Look but that is all at the moment, I would think it would be best to build it in the settlement, but I leave that up to you to decide. How much would we need for a year do you know?'

'A lot, a hundred bushels at least.'

'I don't know how much that is, there were lots of sacks in the settlement round the back of the store.'

'You will need to get them before they rot.'

'Take a small wagon or a cart and get them then do things like that where you have to act now. Make sure you talk to Bill he is responsible for everything that is grown.'

'I will.'

It took three trips back to the settlement to empty the store, Bruce had taken over the second store and had organised a place for everything. 'You have it all in here now Bruce.'

'I have your things down that side and ours on this side. Plus there's a load down the middle.'

'We don't buy things when someone needs some...'

'I have that in hand Jaga na Kala. People work here and then get what they need; I know you don't use money.'

'I suggest you do the same for the settlers; let them take what they need.'

'I will do it your way,'

'Thank you, you should treat this store as your place of work I think. Look after it for me.'

'I will Jaga na Kala leave it to me.'

Three days later Ruth was looking at the fields with Bill, it was still on the cold side, but the work was under way. 'Go take a look out on the plain, the first bit you come to.'

'I will.'

Ruth left the village and walked the short distance to where the plain started. Three settlers were working there; they had one of the horses harnessed to the plough. 'Hello Tom.'

'We are ploughing this up for Bill, should have it ready in a couple of days, he wants to put turnip in here.'

'Work it out that we need one turnip per person per day and that way you will not go far wrong. Beans are not so easy to work out but one step per person per three days is about right.'

'I will work on that.'

'That will be good, you will have plenty of food if we can get the seed in within the next few days.'

'We will get there Jaga na…What's that, where did they come from?'

'Wagons!'

One of the settlers came running up to the four of them. He had been with a hunting party led by Big Bear, who had sent him back to the camp. 'Jaga na Kala! There are two wagons coming! Big Bear and the others are showing them the way into the camp.'

'I can see them.' Ruth replied. All of them set off back to the village to find out what the wagons had on them.

Those in the village started to gather as Big Bear led the two large wagons into the meadow. John went to meet them; he spoke to the man driving the lead wagon. 'Hello, how did you know to come up this end of the lake?'

'We met John Kemp in the settlement, he said come here with this.' The man on the wagon looked John up and down. 'Why you dressed like that; you not got any decent clothes.'

'These are fine for me, I'm Captain John Upton.'

'You don't look it.'

'We had to come here, no food.'

'Got plenty on the wagons, little else, should be enough to get you all back to the coast.'

'Why should we want to do that?' John asked.

'Haven't you heard the French have won we are leaving it to them, most are moving south better weather there anyway.'

'The French won!'

'You won't get any more supplies, you are lucky to get this lot. Are these Indians to be trusted?'

'They are fine, this is Jaga na Kala, she is the chief. Don't be worried about the wolf, it will not harm you.'

'Portag meecha na Daga Kala.'

'The chief said welcome friend, welcome to the home of the wolf tribe.'

'That's her! Is she this Jaga na Kala in person?'

'I am indeed, though I am sure the stories you have heard exaggerate my deeds. You are welcome to stay and eat with us today.'

'You speak English!'

'Of course, when do you plan to return?'

'Tomorrow, we aren't staying here long. Need to get everyone back.'

That evening after they had eaten the meal in the tribe lodge Ruth spoke to the settlers, telling them that they could remain, but those who wished to leave on the wagons should be ready first thing in the morning. One of the wagons was unloaded into the food store. It created the space for those who wished to leave.

'Good bye, thank you Jaga na Kala, I would stay but it is not a life for me,' Miss Blantar said as Ruth and the rest of the tribe saw the two wagons off.

'That is your choice,' Ruth replied 'Have a good journey back; I hope you all find a good place to settle down.'

'I'm sure we will thank you for everything you have done for us.'

Ruth watched with the rest of the tribe as the two wagons left. 'Civilisation is leaving you Ruth, leaving the wilderness to you and your people,' John said, as the wagons were lost to sight.

'You didn't want to go John.'

'No, like the others who want to stay, we just want to settle somewhere and here is the place for us. What do you say Bruce?'

'I guess you are right,

'Anyway I have that field to plough for Bill. Cost me a couple of days with wagons arriving,' Tom said.

'They will not be bothering you anymore.'

'You are all more than welcome to stay.'

That evening the tribe ate in the tribe lodge, it had started to rain mid-afternoon, Jaga na Kala spoke to the tribe, telling them that they were strong she ended with 'Apa e ap tag nak pog.' They had been left a lot of food, there is no reason why the tribe could not benefit and rest before another year started. The weather was improving soon it would be spring and then summer.

The tribe settled down those who had remained became members of the tribe, and learnt the ways of the Great Spirit. Within a few years, it was impossible to tell a settler from an Indian. In their ones and twos, others came and joined the tribe; all that came were made welcome. The tribe grew larger additional areas were cleared, fields were made on the edge of the plain and as the tribe numbers grew the meadow was extended, trees were cut down, the land cleared and addition lodges were built. The tribe became stronger and stronger; it passed the point where it had a hundred braves. It learnt how to make bricks from those who joined them after the "Bad Winter"; they also learnt how to make better pots, again from those who had joined them. Wolves always had free range to come and go as they pleased. If they needed food, they were fed. In the thirtieth summer of Jaga na Kala's time as chief, the tribe held a big feast. Two other tribes gathered for the feast. Wolves found their way to the village in huge numbers. Fifty moose were eaten during the ten-day feast, eaten by over a five hundred Indians, from three tribes, and a hundred wolves. The spirit man, now a lot older than he had been when he had first seen Zak, thanked the Great Spirit for sending them not only Jaga na Kala but also her protector Zak, the Spirit of Wolves.

Ruth, a girl of fourteen, the youngest daughter of an estate worker when she left England, lived a full six-four years, forty-four of them as Jaga na Kala Paga na Daga Kala. She left her tribe to meet and speak with Natelena knowing her people were strong.

Seventy years after the abandonment of the settlement civilisation again pushed west. It found the Wolf Tribe living in peace with its fields, moose and horses. This time civilisation did not retreat; it tore the heart out of the tribe, and shot any wolf that came into the area looking for a friend. Within ten years there was no trace of the Daga Kala or the place where Jaga na Kala Paga na Daga Kala lay in her grave close to Zak, surrounded by her friends and the remains of forty-four spears, one for each summer she had led them.

* * *

The Indian language

The Indian language is not difficult to understand. It was devised for this story and although it may contain some actual Indians words, it does not attempt to represent any real language. The small dictionary provides a list of all words used with their English equivalent. Some of the more important compound words are also listed.

In keeping with several native languages, numbers are not evaluated above two; one, two and many is a common feature. In the language used in the book this is ap apa and apar. Six can be made by apa e apa e apa (two and two and two) but only when accuracy is vital; normally six would, like seven, be apar.

There is no, thank you or please. Por is the word for good and is used extensively with the word for do (pog) to form Porpog good work, well done and is a common response and often used for thank you. Likewise if used prior to the event porpog could be used as please.

Pog is a general action verb for play work do. It is left to the context as to what is being done; jadpog the word for hunt literal means looking work or Pogtod, do dead, kill. Porpog jadpog e pogtod latan, please hunt and kill a moose.

The word for and is e and denotes a joining or the and as in English it can be use where English uses with. Daqua ella e Natlatan, go home with tall mountain (note the ella follows daqua in this case). Pi ella daqua e Natlatan, I am coming home with Tall Mountain. Ella e pog e pi, becomes come and help me, literally come and work with me.

The position of ella the verb to go is important ella daqua is come home where as daqua ella is go home, However pi ella daqua is I am going home. With the negative prefix nak - pi nakella daqua, I am not coming home, or I am not leaving my home. It will depend if you are already at home. Ella daqua e nakella. Go home and stay there.

The negative nak can be used in front of any adjective to create the opposite. Por is good therefore nakpor is bad, note that bin is small or little and bin is always used to make a small item such as bin latan small moose never nak nat latan; however tall is ip short is nakip. Mist or fog can be created by using bad nakpor and look jad to create nakporjad - mist fog.

Nak can also precede certain verbs if it makes sense to do so Nakella is stand still or do not go from ella the verb to go. Nakpog is do not work and so on. Nakella e nakpog means standstill and don't do anything.

John Bacon

Pi is I or me, and Pe is you. We is constructed with the word for two or many. Piapa the two of us; piapar all of us. The same would apply to, peapa you (two), peapar you (many).

Na; of, is not always used; it gives importance. Meechamegan is friend of bear where na is not used but Jaga na Kala has the na to show importance.

Paga is a multi-meaning word used generally it means man or brave, when used with na it takes on a different meaning paga na Daga Kala is chief of wolf tribe; paga Daga Kala demotes it to brave of the wolf tribe or father of the wolf family it is left to context as to which. Ruth's full title is therefore Jaga na Kala Paga na Daga Kala; Mother of Wolves Chief of the Wolf Tribe.

There is no past or future tense if for the sake of clarity it is necessary or the speaker wants to emphasise that it was in the past or will be in the future then ya is used to denote the future and yar the past. I came home before you, would be pi yarella daqua pe. It would not make sense to have daqua yarella you can't be told to go somewhere in the past.

As in the examples above words in the language can be constructed from two or more other words such that clear is 'good' and 'look' porjad clear water is therefore porjad seeni and big moose is nat latan however where it forms the name of a person it is a single word. Natlatan is the name of the brave Big Moose.

Indian to English

Alsor	Fire
Ap	One
Apa	Two
Apar	Many
Aparpaja	People
Bin	Little / Small
Binaparpaja	Children
Binjaga	Girl
Binkala	Wolf Cub
Binpaja	Boy
Caf	Quick / Fast
Cala	Moon
Canada	Land
Cash	Salt
Da	Yes
Daga	Tribe / Family
Daqua	Home / Place
Di	From
Du	Here
E	And / With
Elean	Spirit
Ella	Come/Go/Move
Ema	Yellow
Flata	Arrow/Spear
Fron	Strong
Gash	Broken

Gegenta	Rabbit
Glish	Eagle
Hi	To
Hish	White
Ip	Tall
Jad	Look
Jadpog	Hunt
Jaga	Mother
Jehi	There
Kala	Wolf
Kalema	Beaver
Krath	Circle
Latan	Moose
Lementa	Clothes
Liptan	Bird
Looa	Red
Meecha	Friend
Megan	Bear
Mela	Make
Mesh	Food
Na	Of
Nak	No
Nakcaf	Slow
Nakhish	Black
Nakmeecha	Enemy
Nakpor	Bad
Naksor	Cold
Nat	Big / Large
Natumta	Feast
Ne	In
Neta	Flame
Ojar	Mountain

Paga	Chief / Father / Man
Pal	Sky
Pallar	Blue
Pap	Baby
Pawa	Flower
Pe	You singular
Peapa	You (two)
Peapar	You (many)
Pi	Me / I
Piapa	We (two)
Piapar	Us (Many)
Pland	Green
Pog	Work; play; do
Pogtod	Kill
Poola	Wash
Poota	Guard
Por	Good
Portag	Hello / Good-bye / Good day
Reela	Deer
Seeni	Water
Sham	Paint
Skish	Fruit
Sor	Hot
Squaw	Woman
Suma	Take in love
Suta	Take
Tag	Day
Tak	Talk
Tala	Sun
Tashka	Sleep
Tencha	Turkey
Tod	Dead

John Bacon

Umta	Eat
Ween	Summer
Ya	Future prefix
Yar	Past prefix
Yartag	Yesterday

Printed in the United States
By Bookmasters